AMERICAN CINCINNATUS

A Novel

By Stephen M. Krason

American Cincinnatus, by Stephen M. Krason. ISBN 978-1-62137-984-3 (softcover).

Published 2017 by Virtualbookworm.com Publishing Inc., P.O. Box 9949, College Station, TX 77842, US. ©2017, Stephen M. Krason.

Table of Contents

CHAPTER 1

A New President Takes Office

T he temperature was surprisingly warm for January. It was 52 degrees, only a few degrees away from the all-time high at Ronald Reagan's first inauguration in 1981. There was a slight chill in the air, but it was remarkably sunny for that time of January in the Nation's Capital. There were no reviewing stands along the one-and-a-half mile parade route from the Capitol Building to the White House, since the new president, Stephen Gregory Bernard, was emphatic that that day in all respects be simple. The inaugural parade would be very short, with him near the front behind a military honor guard and extending only another block or so behind him. Against the wishes of the Secret Service and various police agencies, he insisted on going against recent practice and walking the full distance. This was to exemplify "republican simplicity." He wanted to connect as directly as possible with the people, the way he had done during his campaign.

As the sun shone brightly but not blindingly in a nearly cloudless sky it made one feel like it was dawn. It seemed to herald the "New Day" that the new president kept invoking during his many campaign speeches, so often to crowds of average citizens, for several months the year before.

The crowds both in front of the sprawling East Entrance of the Capitol Building and along Pennsylvania Avenue kept gradually growing as the morning went on. Since the night before had been unseasonably warm as well, many younger people had started to assemble hours before and had virtually camped out. Now whole families were taking their places. That might have surprised some people, since most of the capital area's schools went against what had become their usual practice and announced that they would be in session that day. In fact, the District of Columbia's public schools took the unusual step of canceling the Inauguration Day holiday on their

1

calendar only the month before. Many of the families with young children were homeschoolers and from various religious schools in the metropolitan area. Several class groups of students, wearing one version of uniform or another, were visible along the route by mid-morning. Some among these clusters of people held homemade signs with terse sayings like "A NEW PRO-LIFE ERA" and "FOR THE FAMILY—FINALLY." Also along Pennsylvania Avenue, there were several larger groups a few of whose members carried placards identifying themselves as TEA Party or Patriot groups from one or another location. Many of their members carried mass-produced signs with phrases like "NOW THE FIGHT FOR THE CONSTITUTION BEGINS" or "WE STAND WITH YOU TO DEFEND THE CONSTITUTION." A few held such signs with a more tentative message such as, "DON'T FORGET: DEFEND THE CONSTITUTION."

Reagan had set the new precedent of having the inaugural ceremonies at the West Entrance of the Capitol Building so he could face his home state of California. The new president returned to the practice of facing east. It was generally thought that this was because he wanted to honor his home state of Pennsylvania, which was viewed as the most conservative state in the Northeast. However, a story that seemed to come from within his small transition staff said that it was for other symbolic reasons: the Far West, especially California, had increasingly been the place where trends that he had strongly criticized during the campaign first took hold and because east also pointed to Philadelphia, where the constitutional principles had been laid down which he said he meant to restore.

There would be other changes in usual practice. The outgoing president would not be attending the inauguration. This would be the first time this had happened since 1921. It was widely believed that the reason was the deep polarization between the parties and the success the new president had had during the campaign in claiming that his predecessor had undermined and weakened the Constitution and American traditions. Even a number of the organs of the media that consistently had supported the president and his party criticized him for that. That as much reflected their ongoing fascination with the new president as well as the view that such an action was vindictive and downright impolite. Even in a time of cultural upheaval, old-time manners could still be important. There were scattered protesters, with signs displaying an assortment of slogans. They were not anywhere near as numerous as would ordinarily have been expected, considering the strong positions the new president had taken against the ruling

2

dogmas of the left during the campaign and his resolute pledges to reverse, wherever possible, their achievements during twelve years in power. They were possibly still shell-shocked after their unexpected defeat at the hands of an opponent who was so dedicated to opposing their agenda. Various activist groups had threatened some weeks before to disrupt the inauguration, but the U.S. Park Police had made clear that laws would be vigorously enforced and there was no sign of unruly activity. There was not even chanting by the protestors present; they just stood silently with their signs. In fact, the relative calmness of the day contrasted sharply with the rancor that had characterized the country's politics for the previous several years as the two deeply polarized parties representing two different worldviews faced off against each other. This had even begun to spill into the streets with a noticeable rise of demonstrations and counter-demonstrations, "agents-provocateurs" from certain labor unions and other leftist groups that routinely showed up to shout down speakers, and even some physical clashes.

For two-and-a-half months, even the "talking heads" on television political talk shows had been expressing uncertainty and disagreement about what the immediate effects and the ultimate meaning of the unusual November election would be. True, there had been a buzz in early December about a few possible defections in the electoral college in three key states that in the divided election had gone for the new president. Two had electoral registration majorities by the other party, and there had been deep divisions in the other within the new president's party. Then there was the matter of his modest popular vote advantage, the lowest percentage for a winning presidential candidate since 1860. The defections did not occur, however, and he won a razor-thin electoral-vote majority. After this, the talking heads, and not a few editorial pages of the remaining mass-circulation metropolitan dailies around the country, speculated that his ever-so-close win meant that he would not have enough popular support to pursue his initiatives. This was so despite the fact that his party had secured control of both houses of Congress. Even more likely, he would just decide not to proceed as he had promised; he would quickly "moderate." Still, a surprisingly small number of them evinced a deep-seated antipathy for him. They had been caught off-guard by his whole campaign approach and persona, and still were not fully sure what to make of it or of him. Even his transition efforts did not provide a clear answer. He did not have the oversized transition team that had become the norm for recent presidents-elect. It was known that the small group of highly competent and dedicated people, who were philosophically aligned with him (but

3

independent-minded), who he had assembled carefully examined the activities of almost the entire executive branch and a full range of areas of federal policy, but they had been strikingly quiet about it and there were few statements to the media and, amazingly, hardly any leaks. The talking heads and opinion columnists were saying that his inaugural address could be key to revealing the direction the new administration would actually take.

Since the outgoing president declined to take part, the new president decided to dispense with the usual initial stop at the White House, and proceeded directly to the Capitol Building. He declined to stay at Blair House, as was customary for incoming presidents in the days right before the inauguration, because of the sitting president's coolness. He and his wife instead had arrived in Washington only the day before and spent the previous night with a long-time family friend who lived about fifteen minutes outside of the city. He declined to be driven to the inauguration in an official limousine—again, republican simplicity—but instead insisted that his own personal car be used. His driver was the family friend who, as might be expected, was thrilled to be part of the nation's great quadrennial event. He was insistent about having only a minimal Secret Service detail, both outside the friend's house and then to accompany them to the ceremony. He had emphatically made the point during the campaign that security had gotten out of control in the country—regarding government buildings, official events, sports venues, and airports and other public transportation venues—and had the effect of isolating the president, other executive officials, and members of Congress from the public, without really making anyone safer. People usually invoked 9/11, but he kept driving home how bureaucratic bungling—by security agencies—had helped cause that and events like the Boston Marathon bombing and how it had been average air passengers who had thwarted the would-be shoe and underwear bombers.

They were joined at the friend's house by the new vice president and his wife and children, who were driven in a car owned by one of the top party officials in northern Virginia whose residence they had similarly been guests at for the previous few days. They, too, had only a minimal Secret Service detail. The new vice president had the same view about republican simplicity and the need to connect with the people as his boss.

At eleven forty-five, the new president's car followed by the car carrying the vice president and his family and accompanied only by the Secret Service detail's car behind them and two District of Columbia motorcycle officers in front and singular ones on each side—they had

4

relieved a comparable-sized Virginia State Police unit at the Potomac River—approached the inauguration site after following a circuitous route through the city that he had agreed to and that avoided the crowds at the West Entrance. Still, many people had spotted them along the route and the new president and his wife were almost constantly waving and smiling at them from inside the car. When they arrived, it was so sudden that it seemed to catch the crowd by surprise, but when he opened the car door and began to step out a loud, approving roar went up. It sustained itself for about two minutes, and then a series of chants followed as he walked up the stairs to the platform on which the inauguration activities would take place. The crowd shouted, "New Era!" and then "The Constitution Lives!" and then "Bernard for the People!"

He politely motioned the new vice president and his family to precede him and his wife up the stairs to the platform, even though this went against the usual protocol. When reaching the platform, he first shook hands and embraced his old friend, Bishop George LaGrange, the Catholic bishop of Greenburg, Pennsylvania, who he asked to deliver the invocation. As a courtesy, Stephen also asked the elderly Archbishop of Washington, Robert Scanlon, to be present. Stephen and his old friend had similar agendas for reform and renewal—perhaps the better word would be restoration—in their respective spheres of church and state. After the day's events, some commentators speculated that he shook hands with his bishop friend first to underscore his frequent campaign theme about restoring the religious underpinnings of the country and the Constitution. No one then knew that the bishop from the small diocese of Greenburg would soon be appointed the new Archbishop of Washington. Next, the new president and new vice president shook hands with Robert M. Johnston, the Chief Justice of the United States, who would administer the Oaths of Office to both of them and then with the various political dignitaries who were there. Their number was smaller than usual at inaugurations since he had insisted that this should be a people's event. Most of the leadership of the other party in Congress was present, but their facial expressions betrayed a noticeable coolness and displeasure.

As usual for inaugurations, the U.S. Marine Band was present to play between the administering of the vice presidential and presidential oaths. Not all of the Band's members played at the various ceremonial events at which they took part. They alternated. The Band included a few female Marines. The new president insisted that only the male members of the Band be assigned to perform for the inauguration. He did this because of his intentions for the Marine Corps overall. Some of the media caught wind of this a few days before the inauguration and a few commentators excoriated him for it, but he didn't flinch. Nor did he issue a statement about it. With everything else going on, the news reports failed to generate much attention.

The crowd raised a renewed roar when the new president and vice president reached the platform. It continued through all the handshaking. Then the bishop came to the podium, and the crowd noise gradually diminished. On the massive loudspeaker system he was announced: "Now to lead the invocation is Bishop George LaGrange of the Catholic Diocese of Greensburg, Pennsylvania." Men's hats went off in the crowd. This was mostly an audience of people who understood and respected such traditional propriety. It was certainly different from the major political party convention of several years before that booed after a narrow vote to retain a singular reference to God in its platform.

Bishop LaGrange began to read the prayer on the paper in front of him. "As we gather here for this historic occasion"—while any presidential inauguration fit that description, many in the audience wondered if he did not also refer to the ascendency to office of this particular president—"we ask the abundant blessings of Almighty God on our country and on our new national leaders. Be with them and their families as they undertake perhaps the most challenging tasks they will ever undertake on this earth. God, in this difficult time we ask you to enlighten our new leaders to always know the correct path and give them strength and courage. Help them to always stay faithful to Your Law and to be able to discern Your will at all points along the way. We were a country founded by God-fearing men for whom belief in You was the cornerstone of their lives." One of the opposition party leaders on the podium noticeably winced at that last sentence. "Help us to remember that and to constantly realize that without You we can do nothing as individuals or as a people and that all of our efforts must be for Your greater glory." The last phrase also brought a glare from a couple of the opposition leaders. "Please continue to shine Your grace on our nation, its people, its leaders, and its efforts. Please protect all of our freedoms, especially our First Freedom of religious liberty." He was obviously thinking of the controversies that had raged in recent years in the U.S. Then, he adapted a famous phrase from the inaugural address of a past president of the opposition party, in very different times. "Let us always keep in mind that Your work must truly be our own." Then he closed: "Please do not judge harshly our transgressions either as individuals or as a nation, but always be there to right our course and to renew us. Help us solve our problems and heal our divisions"—this was obviously referring to the deep conflicts that had raged in the country—"which, despite our own brave efforts, we always need your assistance to do. Amen." The Bishop left no doubt from his invocation that, contrary to a prevailing mindset by a substantial element in the country—actually, it was an attitude that had begun to take hold centuries before with the Enlightenment—that man could not hope to thrive if he disconnected himself from God.

Unlike most inaugurations, there would be only one clergyman giving both the invocation and the benediction at the end. The new president, a Catholic, had offered to have a clergyman from the new vice president's denomination give the benediction, but as a conservative Episcopalian who was known for sometimes attending services at Evangelical churches he was happy to have Bishop LaGrange do both.

After the bishop finished, the Chief Justice rose along with the new vice president. He was going to be administering the Oath of Office to both the new president and vice president, even though that was not customary. The new vice president put his right hand on the Bible (the family's King James Version) and repeated his Oath of Office after him: "I, Michael James Clarke do solemnly swear..." At the end of the Oath, he emphasized very strongly, "So help me God." As the Chief extended his hand to him, the crowd—which now carpeted the area for as far as the eye could see— erupted in thunderous applause. A couple of minutes later, the new president rose and also shook his vice president's hand and two warmly embraced. The crowd's applause seemed to intensify, partly because the spotlight was about to shift to the new president but also, one had the sense, because it perceived that these two men would operate as a team and a formidable one at that.

As Vice President Clarke turned to go back to his seat, the new president took a few steps toward the center of the platform where the Chief Justice picked up another Bible on one of the shelves of the large podium near the front. It was a Catholic Revised Standard Version, which looked just a bit shopworn. The new president and his wife had each used it for Bible studies that they had taken part in during the early years of their marriage. He put his right hand on it and repeated after the Chief: "I, Stephen Gregory Bernard, do solemnly swear..." In the same manner as Vice President Clarke, but even more clearly and distinctly, he stressed the "So help me God" at the end. The roar from the crowd began almost as spontaneously as if a large applause sign had lighted up when he finished and began to shake the Chief's hand. As he turned slowly right behind the podium to face the crowd the crescendo seemed to escalate. The slight but gentle smile that had become his much-commented on trademark during the campaign became a broad grin as he waved with both hands to the multitude of cheering spectators. His wife, Mary-Elizabeth (Marybeth), joined him at the podium to wave to the crowd. Although she was approaching fifty, it had often been commented during the campaign that she was one of the most physically attractive and photogenic presidential candidate wives in recent memory. Both Stephen's mother and Marybeth's parents, all of whom were in their eighties, had also been on the platform for the inaugural. The new president motioned to Vice President Clarke and his wife Alicia (Ali) to join them at the podium, and very quickly all four were waving at the loud supportive crowd. It was not like campaign style waving, however. There was an air of restraint, decorum, and respectability in it, and the crowd, while loud, seemed aware of it. Its response was surprisingly devoid of the hooting and yelps that had become so typical of approving audiences in recent decades.

After three or four minutes, President Bernard moved a step forward to the podium and Marybeth and the vice presidential couple turned back to their seats. His reaching down to the podium shelves to pick up the written text of his inaugural address—Bernard would have nothing to do with teleprompters—seemed to signal to the crowd to quiet down. While the people's support meant everything to him and he viewed the inauguration as a celebration of the average citizen, he did not want to seem to be inviting excessive adulation focused on him.

"My Fellow Americans: I stand before you at a time when any thoughtful person would say that our beloved country stands at a crossroads. The stakes for the United States are nothing less than whether we can breathe new life into the kind of government our revered Founding Fathers established, whether we can restore and commit ourselves anew to the principles that they embraced. We cannot pretend otherwise that their great project has not been weakened and that many have been impervious to their principles if they have not sought to outright discard some of them. Maybe on this occasion we need to reconsider what those principles are and remind ourselves about how crucial ones of them have been in peril, and to firmly recommit ourselves as political leaders and as a people to the Republic as the Founders established it and to those principles." He then paused for a long moment, and then stated firmly, distinctly, and a decibel above the level he had been speaking at: "I, as your President, intend to do precisely that."

This sparked a loud round of applause from the crowd. No one seemed to doubt what this meant after his campaign: Not only was he determined to work to restore weakened constitutional principles, but there was going to be some kind of extraordinary assertion of presidential power to do it. Even though he had never said this directly during the campaign, the fervor and insistence that accompanied his message led many to speculate about his intentions. It had even been the occasional topic of political commentators. This had caused uncertainty in some who had supported him, since many pro-Bernard groups believed that the political conflict and polarization of recent years had been due partly to excesses and abuses of executive power by the two successive presidents of the opposing party. The first of the Founding principles that President Bernard talked about showed, however, that he was aware of this.

"Perhaps the most important principles about government that our Founders stressed were separation of powers and checks and balances. As the Father of our Constitution, James Madison, said about separation of powers, 'No political truth is certainly of greater intrinsic value.' The principle of checks and balances is partnered with it. To sustain our Republic—our democratic republic—power must not be allowed to concentrate itself in any one place or person. This is the very stuff of tyranny. We have experienced a disturbing movement in this direction recently in our government. We must correct the imbalance that has occurred, even if it requires a strong medicine to accomplish it. We must always be aware, however, that power—even if undertaken for a good cause, although some of the causes for too long have been troubling and damaging—can be a strong temptation and seduction even for the best of men. If cracks in the armor of the institutional processes of our Republic have appeared, we must move quickly to repair them.

"Another key, indispensable principle of our Founders was a strong and healthy federal system. They feared the evils of centralized power. For nearly a century, we have advanced bit by bit toward a centralized administrative state. It has mostly happened with the best of intentions—to address various problems, at times to even deal with crises—but it has now advanced to the point where it has stifled both our freedom and our prosperity. We have reached the point where states are financially dependent on the central government, just like a massive number of individuals—even businesses—have become dependent on it. This has not only stifled incentive, creativity, and inventiveness, but has turned us into a regimented people. Our states seem like puppets on a string pulled by bureaucrats and politicians in Washington. Our people, especially our most responsible and productive ones, are increasingly controlled by centralized decision-makers and regulators down to small things that they do. Even parents are not permitted to make decisions about the welfare of their children. This completely offends the spirit of our Founding. You have heard it before, too many times by too many politicians, that this must stop— this time, *it will*. Many have been deceived into thinking that this kind of control actually makes them free, when in truth it despises liberty and treats our citizens as if they are permanently infants. It has become a 'freedom' that is really a kind of servitude—sometimes literally, as we see with such shameful practices as businesses and even private homes raided by SWAT teams and the like—backed up with the butt of a gun. As Abraham Lincoln said, it's time for a 'new birth of freedom.' It is time to return to a correct notion of freedom—freedom that is intrinsically tied to responsibility, in all areas of life, as was the freedom championed by our Founders. It will be a proper freedom for our lower levels of government, for our private sector, for families, and for individuals—a freedom to be responsible for themselves and not to be controlled by an overbearing centralized government.

"Moreover, we have witnessed in the United States an increasing and sustained attack on private property rights. Indeed, there are very strong forces—right in the mainstream of our politics—whose suspicion of private property is evident. They have sought to infringe on that right not only by regulating to an extreme degree— "regimenting" is the proper word—the private sector's and individual citizens' use of their property, but by runaway taxation. The oppression that many of our citizens experience from it reminds one of the words of our Declaration of Independence: it has begun to 'eat out their substance.' Although hardly anyone mentions it, excessive taxation not only has bad economic effects but is also immoral because it is a form of thievery and violates the natural right to private property—one of the central rights embraced by our Founding. While it's true that private ownership of property has never been absolute—our whole Western tradition has emphasized that responsibilities go along with it, which sometimes must be enshrined into law—the heavy regulation of it has been without merit and has often been justified by spurious or nonexistent reasons. Claims of environmental concerns have been a typical one, even though the evidence is often not present to validate the claims and instead ideology is behind it. So, we see ideology masquerading as science to supposedly legitimate the trampling on property rights. At other times, we have seen environmental claims used as a pretext to carry a wholly different agenda of reckless redistribution of income, wealth, and resources. The aim is supposedly to make people more equal, but in fact—as the experience of communism and socialism invariably shows—it will just impoverish everyone, make everyone miserable. The exception will be those who push or support such schemes, who will somehow find a way to carve out privileges for themselves."

Then he paused and looked up from the text of his speech on the podium and resolutely looked out to the crowd and said firmly: "This wanton violation of property rights comes to an end *now*. In fact, regarding this and other areas where liberty and the prerogatives of the people have been unduly restricted you can expect, as much as possible, to see *rollback*." He said the last word with strong emphasis. The crowd responded with wild cheering and a chant of "Restore the Constitution," which began somewhere in the mass of people and was picked up by more and more until the President motioned for silence.

"Speaking of the rights of our citizens, we have witnessed an assault on the most basic rights stressed by our Founders. Religious liberty—the "first freedom," it has been called—has particularly been under attack. Religious institutions, churches, clergy, and religious believers have increasingly been in the sights of government. Leading politicians, bureaucrats, and opinion-makers now hold that the First Amendment's guarantee of free exercise of religion means nothing more than being able to worship, and religious expression in other contexts is to be suppressed and Christian religious beliefs, especially, can have no role in shaping public decisions. The alarming refusal of various local governments, backed up by Washington, to permit churches to build new buildings—reminiscent of the old Communist bloc—and to allow public religious processions shows that even freedom of worship in in jeopardy. We even have an increasing consensus developing among some prominent opinion-makers that all that freedom of religion means is the freedom to have religious beliefs, the freedom to think about religion, so long as they are not expressed. That illustrates what I believe has been at the core of the push of "freedom from religion" groups who claim they are working to uphold church-state separation: they believe, in the manner of the French Revolution, that a republic—they have a distorted notion of what that is—should be devoid of religion, that somehow religion threatens republican principles. How different that is from the Founders' thinking—in fact, it is just the opposite of it. George Washington said, 'Of all the dispositions and habits which lead to political prosperity, religion and morality are indispensable supports.' Thomas Jefferson said, 'No nation has ever yet existed or been governed without religion. Nor can be.' James Madison, who again was called the 'Father of the Constitution,' said about America, 'We have staked the future of all of

11

our political institutions upon the capacity of mankind for self-government; upon the capacity of each and all of us to govern ourselves, to control ourselves, to sustain ourselves according to the Ten Commandments of God.' Fifty years after our Founding, Alexis de Tocqueville, perhaps the greatest commentator on our democratic republic, said that America was where 'the Christian religion has kept the greatest real power over men's souls' and 'the ideas of Christianity and liberty' were 'completely intermingled.'

"We have also seen such other crucial rights as freedom of speech and assembly violated with increasing impunity by agents of government. Not long ago we witnessed a spectacle never seen in the United States before, but which is familiar in authoritarian, despotic states: mass arrests of entirely peaceful, lawful demonstrators against a new public policy that they found potentially harmful to them. Regarding free speech, we have seen the notion of 'hate crimes' used aggressively and illegitimately to suppress speech that is viewed unacceptable by ruling authorities, opinion-makers, and groups politically aligned with them. We are even now seeing writers to 'Letters to the Editor' pages prosecuted for 'hate speech' because they have opposed initiatives of certain groups who have garnered special protection under federal law. We have seen the use of laws to regulate political campaigns to stop candidates who merely want to tell the truth about entrenched incumbent officials. Someone once said that after suppressing every other right, free speech would be the last right to go. This is now happening before our very eyes.

"These traditional rights—grounded in a sound conception of man and imbedded in the long history of Anglo-American law—are undermined to make way for a whole slew of ersatz rights, some of which are promoted by and identified with certain politically activist groups and would have historically been understood to undermine human dignity and welfare. Too often, it has been the courts that have given legitimacy to these ersatz rights and enshrined them into law and have permitted traditional—real—rights to be neglected or outright pushed aside. We have recently seen state courts impose unconscionable demands on citizens in the name of protecting the 'rights' of a favored group."

Most of the crowd knew immediately what he was referring to as it literally erupted in approval at his clear statement of condemnation. A judge in one northeastern state had upheld the state human rights commission's finding of discrimination and the fining of a woman who refused to accept a date with a lesbian through a dating service. The judge had even suggested that a refusal to accept a marriage proposal from someone of the same sex could, under some circumstances, be illegal discrimination. In another case in the Midwest, a judge resurrected the archaic tort of breach of promise to permit a massive lawsuit to proceed against a man who broke off an engagement when he learned that the "woman" he planned to marry was actually a man who had undergone a "sex-change" operation. The decisions had gained widespread media attention and generated much controversy. Even some of the usual defenders of the homosexualist movement had criticized them.

Bernard continued: "Sometimes, courts have opened the door for the aggressive, and tragic, destruction of traditional rights of entire classes of people. Nowhere is this seen as vividly as with abortion, where the Supreme Court's *Roe v. Wade* and *Doe v. Bolton* decisions of 1973 said that human persons, by virtue of their age and state of development, may be summarily deprived of their right to life—the first right, the foundational right—and that government—whose first task, after all, is to protect its citizens—is supposedly forbidden to do anything about it. This, despite the fact that one of our organic documents, the Declaration of Independence, speaks about the rights to life, liberty, and the pursuit of happiness and the English common law, which stands behind our law and constitutional principles, protected unborn life from the moment it understood it to exist. Not only have countless millions—the most vulnerable and innocent among us—been destroyed in a brutal and ugly fashion—no one who takes the time to learn about what happens in abortion can describe it any other way—but we have become increasingly desensitized to violence and perhaps even brutality and the value of human life in other ways has been diminished."

The overwhelmingly sympathetic crowd responded with its loudest applause yet. The glares from the opposition leaders on the platform were striking. For a moment, it looked as if one were going to get up and depart. Many probably did not notice the possible significance of his use of the word "supposedly," but his next terse statement perhaps gave a glimpse of a future constitutional confrontation.

"The courts, for the great esteem in which they must be held and the absolutely crucial role they play in our system of checks and balances, must not and *will not* go unchallenged when they sanction a sustained attack on a whole, broad group of persons or clearly act unconstitutionally."

Again, the crowd roared, although President Bernard did not make clear what he meant by "challenge."

"Another one of the cherished rights that has been compromised for many years has been the right of trial by jury. Americans have long believed that a person can be found guilty of a crime only upon the unanimous decision of a jury of his peers after full legal process. This right, which descended to us from our English forebears, has been a major way that arbitrary government has been restrained. Today, over 90% of criminal cases around the country are concluded by plea bargains and never go to trial. Plea-bargaining is one of many aspects of our dysfunctional criminal justice system. To be sure, this situation emerged because of the genuine need to deal with the problems of a system inundated with cases because of the disgraceful national crime explosion. This, in turn, has happened because we have thought that we can be oblivious to sound morality; we have long since downplayed, if not dismissed entirely, the need for proper moral and religious formation of the individual person. This results, of course, in more criminal behavior. We can see here what our Founders meant about how crucial religion and morality were to a healthy nation. One of the consequences of the near disappearance, in practical terms, of the right of trial by jury is that too often innocent people are convicted, even in capital cases. Recently, we have even seen the use of this increasingly arbitrary criminal justice system to suppress those who oppose people in power. It is time to sweepingly reform our criminal justice system. While much of it is not controlled by the national government, national officials must take an active role in urging its reform—from top to bottom. *They can also never permit the criminal law to be used to suppress unpopular political views.*"

After the last sentence, the crowd erupted again. They remembered the raids of several TEA Party offices on trumped-up—completely false, it turned out—fraud and tax evasion charges under federal campaign finance and income tax laws.

"This is all on top of a tendency to criminalize everything, even things that any average person would never think of as being against the law. So many of our laws and pursuant regulations have become so vague and even contradictory that our citizens no longer know what's expected of them. This is the very 'stuff' of arbitrariness. To this, we add the prevailing viewpoint of our political and opinion-making classes and the bulk of those in the legal community that law has no higher standard to govern it. The natural law tradition that was at the very core of the American Founding—the 'higher law' that was appealed to as the basis for our struggle for independence—stands rejected today. The result of all of this is that yet another central principle of our Founding is taking a beating today: the rule of law. I am committed to making sure that we are once more a government of laws and not of men. Regardless of viewpoints and what group one belongs to, the laws will be applied equally. Abraham Lincoln insisted that not only must our citizens respect and follow the law in order to remain free; they must also *love* it. However, we cannot expect them to follow it, much less love it, if it is arbitrary, discriminatory, and disconnected from the justice that the higher law provides." There had been much controversy over the past several years about how certain demographic groups had been unfairly and discriminatorily singled out for federal civil rights prosecutions on very shaky grounds, when egregious cases involving other groups—sometimes concerning violent acts and election fraud—were consistently ignored. "If any of the U.S. attorneys or other Department of Justice officials who I appoint act arbitrarily or try to 'manufacture' cases by stretching provisions of federal laws or try to conjure up criminal cases against people, businesses, organizations, churches, or other entities—if they try to undertake prosecutions when they *clearly* have no grounds to—they will be summarily dismissed."

His firmness and clarity of intention resonated through the crowd, and a roar came forth from it. President Bernard did not sound at all like a run-of-the-mill politician, just as he had not during the campaign. This was why citizens so concerned about restoring what they saw as an eroded constitutional tradition had readily rallied around him, and also why those who seemed to want a new constitutional order had so bitterly opposed him. Yet, as his next statement indicated, *one* of the ways he was different from the usual politician was that he didn't just offer slogans, but explained things in a way that even ordinary people could understand.

"It is because men no longer believe that there is a law above human making that we have seen the subversion of the rights that I mentioned were a central part of our Founding. Our nation was built on the foundation of an inalienable natural rights philosophy—rights that could not be taken away from men, and that they could not give away even if they wanted to. If rights originate just in the will of men, however, they can easily be wiped out. It is not too far from there to the destruction of the liberty our Founding Fathers cherished—and for which they were ready to lose everything—to repressive, authoritarian government.

"Our democratic republic"—during the campaign he always used this term, never "democracy"—"is democratic, a representative form of government, and involves majority rule where the people's voice must shape public decisions and policy. It is also republican, meaning not

15

only that it must respect minority rights but also be restrained and responsible. Law and not raw human will or the passions of a moment—whether they are of a majority or just determined minorities—must be the foundation of a democratic republic. We have lately seen many 'determined minorities' and political figures who have risen up around them in a demagogic manner to threaten our liberties in the name of advancing a destructive vision. They have confused many of our people. To be sure, we have somewhat invited them. This is because sustaining a democratic republic requires virtue—both by our leaders and our citizenry—and also a way of life that we have long since allowed ourselves to move away from. We have to restore our character, not just as a nation but also as a people and as individuals.

"The culture that spawned our Founding as a nation was made up of people who were frugal, industrious, temperate, self-controlled, honest, courageous, and always ready to sacrifice and oriented to the welfare of others beside themselves. We have often forgotten about these as we have focused on an inordinate, and often illegitimate, pursuit of pleasure, luxury, and a satisfaction of ourselves for the moment. This was the very thing that so many in our Founding Era feared could cause the dissolution of our democratic republic. In some cases, it has been a pursuit of base pleasures and fleeting passions that have badly wounded individuals and damaged family life—the foundation, as our Founding culture recognized, of sound political and social life—and in others it has been a desire for quick material gratification. There is nothing wrong with living well, but we must be financially responsible. The crisis of debt that has engulfed America—and portends not material satisfaction, but material decline—exists at different levels: personal, household, businesses, government. It can lead to deep strain for marriages and families; it can imperil liberty for a nation. As Thomas Jefferson said, 'We must make our election between economy and liberty or profusion and servitude.' He understood that taxation follows debt and, he said, 'in its train wretchedness and oppression.' Our national fiscal crisis has come from our ignoring this warning and the wisdom of our Founders and the republican culture of their time." He paused, then said in a way that so resonated with hopeful resoluteness that it electrified the crowd, "My fellow Americans, it is time for renewal of the self, and renewal of the nation. These things are possible, these things are essential, these things can be done, these things *will be done*!"

The crowd's reaction was the loudest and most enthusiastic that it had been at any time during the inaugural speech. This time he allowed the applause to go on longer and then the crowd broke out into a chant:

"Renewal! Renewal!" The chant seemed to proceed in a wave, as it started with people closest to the platform, then was picked up successively by those not far behind them, then those farther back. Then he waved for silence again.

"We are insistent that our traditional rights as Americans—these rights grounded in the very nature of man—be respected anew. We understand, however, that rights are always coupled with responsibilities. This means first that we must carry out our obligations as citizens. We have to be informed, we have to vote, we have to actively work for the right causes, work to further the *truth*. Part of what is needed to make this possible is to restore knowledge about our Constitution and our sacred national traditions, which have been a casualty of either thoughtless neglect or willful, ideologically generated distortion and even assault in so much of our formal education. We must always understand that to preserve our liberty requires repeated effort. As it has often been said: 'Eternal vigilance is the price of liberty.' This time, perhaps more than at any time in our history as a nation, we need such vigilance. In fact, we need more, much more. We need to recoup what we have lost because many have not been so vigilant." A kind of hum went through the crowd, and some slightly nodded. They knew what President Bernard meant: the state of American constitutional principles had become precarious. Many in the country, and probably most of the political class, didn't seem to believe in them anymore. Then he changed to an instructive kind of tone, reflective of the university professor he had once been.

"We have obligations of another kind as well, however. It is one thing to talk about the reasonable pursuit of self-interest. A family does that; it has to be concerned first about the good of its members. Obviously, it is the same with a business: Its owners have to pursue their self-interest and turn a reasonable profit, or they can't stay in business. There are virtues involved in either case: the virtues needed to be a good husband or wife and a good parent in the case of a family; the virtues—such as hard work and risk-taking—of entrepreneurship needed for success in business. The reasonable pursuit of self-interest can be reconciled with the good of a community or a nation. It is another thing to talk about excessive self-interest, which focuses narrowly on oneself or one's entity almost to the exclusion of others. Our Founders understood that with the great right of private property comes the obligation to use it rightly, to help and respect others. At a certain time in our history we deviated from that spirit of our Founders—reasonable self-interest became greed—and the result was that it spawned a reaction the full flowering of which we are now

17

witnessing with unprecedented levels of governmental intrusion into property rights. This happened, ironically, while greed by some has continued, especially those who have been well-connected with top governmental officials and have poured large funds into political campaigns to buy influence." This last phrase evoked a loud set of "boos" from some in the audience. They remembered Bernard's criticism of this during the campaign, and how he backed this up by refusing to accept campaign contributions of larger than $500 from anyone. "The result," he continued, "has been crony capitalism—a government-corporate 'collaboration' of the worst kind. We do not suggest that there is no room for *some* measure of government regulation—not the runaway type that now prevails—but mostly we think there has to be a recovery of this spirit of the Founding of using property and wealth rightly. There also has to be an expansion of the 'civil society' idea into the business sector: a building up of structures of self-regulation—with government able to take a step back—pursuant to standards of proper conduct decided upon by companies and participants in different areas of the economy. Franklin Roosevelt all too briefly attempted some version of this early in his administration, which he unfortunately later abandoned and followed the course of what decades later became increasing oppressive governmental micromanagement. Those who have also owe an obligation to those who do not. We must take care of the truly poor, if they are unable to adequately provide for themselves through no fault of their own. Indeed, the Bible talks about assisting the widow and the orphan. To be sure, this obligation sometimes, to some degree, falls on government. The problem now, however, which has both crippled government fiscally and created injustice, is that government has not known the limits of this, has extended the hand of assistance to more and more people who can hardly be called poor or needy, and expects nothing from those it gives to even when they are capable of it. Also, when government provides such aid the imperatives of bureaucracy often take the place of the imperatives of people. A concerted effort must be made to build up civil society institutions (the non-profit sector), which is the proper place for most of this aid to come from. Those in the business community at all levels must understand that their highest ethical calling beyond basic honesty in their operations is to provide a truly just wage to those who work for them. That would go a long way toward eliminating the need for government programs at all."

The "crony capitalism" remark received an almost spontaneous response from the crowd. The rest received a respectful attention and brief, scattered applause. This was an advance from much of the campaign when the people normally in his camp were unsure what to make of his early attempts to get them to thinking about these ideas. The conservative radio talk show hosts and commentators criticized him, even as they realized that on what they viewed as the real crunching issues he—unlike the other candidates they liked—meant what he said. There was now more receptivity, even if it was still tentative. His professorial attempts at instruction during the campaign had begun to have an effect.

"There is no question that government has an obligation to insure that such common goods of the community as the physical environment are protected. Again, however, we must not rely on government alone or even primarily for this. In the Founding spirit, we must recover a sense of ethical obligation. As individuals, as businesses, as government, we must practice good stewardship of the bounty of physical nature." He paused and then said emphatically, "We do not need to trample on private property rights to correct environmental problems. We do not need to retard sensible economic development in the name of environmental well-being. *We certainly will not allow ideology posing as concern for the environment to dictate our public policies.*" The crowd roared its approval at that last sentence. Then he shifted back to his instructive, reflective tone: "Still, we must not be profligate, and we must always think about posterity. We must think, in line with the thinking of our Founding Era, about a greater spirit of moderation and self-restraint. While there is nothing wrong with pursuing our legitimate enjoyments and luxuries, we must be cautious as they were about giving ourselves over to a life of luxury and excess."

President Bernard's next statement addressed directly the deep divisions—some commentators said they were the most serious since the Civil War—that had riven the country in recent years. "The virtue of civility was evident during our Founding Era in America. It was an individual virtue, but also a social one. To be sure, America then was a nation deeply committed to justice—not perfectly, as we know, because of such realities as the national sin of slavery—but it was also committed to and lived a life of civility. Civility meant nothing more than different groups of people respecting each other and trying to live out, as best they could, Christian charity. Civility, or simply civic friendship as Aristotle called it in the ancient world, is necessary for a good or even a tolerable political community. Justice is needed, but by itself is not enough. That is even apart from whether the views about what is just on a particular matter are correct or not. As some feel disadvantaged even by legitimate claims of justice they can become angered and resentful. We can disagree, to be sure, but we must recover a spirit of civility—a charitable intercourse with each other—so that our disagreements no longer become a basis for division. A course of action that I am committed to above any other—this will define my administration—is that while we will not pretend that the true and the good is something other than what it is, truth and justice will always be pursued in charity."

The crowd cheered loudly again. Many were thinking that they had never heard such words from an American president. Many in the crowd believed that people who thought like them—that is, who believed that government had gotten out of control and sought to drastically change its course—were routinely put down as "mean-spirited." Many had experienced visceral, almost irrational, hatred from those who politically disagreed with them. So many had been political neophytes—really, they were just average citizens—and had been bewildered by such reactions. When President Bernard spoke about civility, it touched a welcome chord with them.

Bernard then turned to the last few points of his inaugural address. "Although our traditional principles are no longer believed in by some—in fact, are all too often simply rejected or attacked—they are the greatest principles of governance that have been embraced by any human society. They were—as our national seal states—"a new order for the ages." With this the crowd erupted in sustained, loud applause that he allowed to go on for over two minutes. Then, waving the crowd to silence again, he continued: "Like our Founding Fathers, we must understand that we cannot aggressively promote these principles around the world, however; we cannot impose them upon others. Others will look to us and see how well we carry out those principles— principles that are the very definition of a democratic republic—and, if we are once again true to the legacy of our Founders, we will influence them by our example. That means that we will not—indeed, wise thinking makes us realize that we *should not*—go to war to make other countries and peoples like we are." This was something that both major political parties had done in the not-so-distant past. Many people rallied around him during the campaign because he spoke against it, although certain elements in his party were cool to him because of it. "We will assist peoples in need, as America has long done, in times of, say, natural disasters, humanitarian need, and to promote economic development and self-help. We will speak for *true* human rights"—the strong stress he gave to the word "true" was picked up by some in the crowd and by commentators afterwards: he was not going to go along with the promotion of abortion and sexual freedoms that had lately

20

been aggressively promoted as fundamental international human rights at the UN and some other international bodies—"so we can further that cause throughout the world. What's more, we shall not, say, stand by and refuse to act when slaughters and genocide are occurring." During the campaign, he had lamented that the U.S. could not see its way to a military intervention to stop the obvious case of genocide that was occurring in Rwanda back in 1994. "Our foreign policy will be one of principled realism—the furthering of true principles, true morality, the promotion of—to use Lincoln's term—the 'better angels' of our human nature. We will do these things because we understand that even while we are proudly American citizens—not supposed citizens of the world, as some would have it—all men are our brothers." He did not say all "people" but all "men," and did not say "our brothers and sisters," but "brothers." "We will always understand, however, our limitations as a nation, we will not allow ourselves to become haughty and overbearing. Even while we will not shrink one minute from protecting our nation and upholding and furthering national interests—as well as safeguarding every aspect of our sovereignty—we will give our strong stress to diplomacy and negotiation, to furthering our interests peacefully and seeking peaceful resolution to problems and conflicts." He paused for a long moment, then made the firmest-expressed statement of his entire inaugural address: *"Our present and potential adversaries, however, should not doubt that if needed we will respond with the full military might of the United States."*

That brought what could only be called thunderous applause. What he said touched a deep chord not only with the largely philosophically supportive crowd, but also millions watching on television around the country. Many average citizens had come to believe that the other party's successive administrations—and, in fact, the political class in Washington that had encompassed a significant part of his own party, as well—had allowed the U.S. to be pushed around internationally and the nation's prestige to sink to a low point.

He came to his conclusion. He paused and first looked over the crowd from side to side and then seemed to stare for a few seconds right in the direction of where many of the television cameras were before saying with a crescendo of almost trembling emotion, "America as a nation, as a people, can be morally great—and an exemplar for the world—once again. It can once again be the fountainhead of liberty and constant striver for justice. As leaders of the past have said, America's greatness derives from its goodness. Whether it is restoring our nation morally, reviving our foundational political principles, or achieving economic renewal, *America can still do what it puts its mind to!*" In the final instant before the crowd reaction, he added two final appeals, to men and to the Divine. "I ask all of your prayers constantly for me at this utterly critical moment. May God—who is Father, Son, and Holy Spirit—bless all of us and bless our troubled but beloved country." It was the first time in recent memory that a president had invoked the Trinity, in spite of the country's distant strongly Christian background that he had alluded to in his earlier Tocqueville quote.

The explosion of applause was almost spontaneous. It went on and on as he first embraced his wife and then walked around the platform shaking hands with the kind of personal warmth that had been so evident during the campaign and had often disarmed his critics. He began the handshaking excursion with Vice President Clarke and his wife and then Bishop LaGrange and then made his way to the rest of the dignitaries on the platform. The opposition leaders struggled to put on a brief smile. He spent a little extra time with them, and by the time he moved on for one or two the smile seemed less forced. Bishop LaGrange delivered the benediction and the new First and Second Families left the podium with continued waving and in the midst of incessant applause from the crowd.

Additional traditions were going to be broken. Due to the unwillingness of most leading opposition members of Congress to attend the inauguration, President Bernard had asked the new leaders of his party, which was now slightly in the majority of both houses of Congress, to cancel the customary luncheon in Statuary Hall. He did not want the luncheon to seem like a rump gathering of the majority to "rub in" their newly attained dominance and to strategize about their first steps. Instead, he asked them and their families to walk with him in the presidential procession from the Capitol to the White House, and then to join him, the Vice President, and their families in a small buffet luncheon there that would include no speeches or fanfare. He also had requested that the inaugural parade down Pennsylvania Avenue past the White House, which traditionally was reviewed by the new president and vice president and their families, be cancelled. Not only had he wanted to avoid what had become an excessive expense and maintain the spirit of republican simplicity, but many had a lingering bad taste from recent inaugural parades staged by the other party. Among what they had featured were the well-publicized leadership of the parade by two lesbians in the Army who had "married" the day before at Fort Belvoir and treated the crowd to an occasional kiss, a male homosexual marching band from New York City, and a float sponsored by a Washington, D.C. abortion clinic dominated by a giant "Proudly Pro-Choice" banner. Wanting to promote patriotism, however, he arranged

22

for the procession to the White House to be larger than usual with the Marine Band marching, a well-known marching band of Revolutionary War enactors from Williamsburg, Virginia, and cars carrying military personnel who had been disabled in recent conflicts and their families bearing the flags of their units. Both Bernard and the Washington National Cathedral jointly agreed that it would have no national prayer service the day after the Inauguration, a tradition revived by Reagan in 1985. Bernard was too out of sinc with the theological and moral latitudinarianism of the Cathedral clergy and he would not give credence to a church that was routinely performing same-sex "weddings." Instead, he arranged for Bishop LaGrange to say a special private Mass before dinner that evening at the Catholic Cathedral of St. Matthew the Apostle. FDR had refused to attend his own inaugural ball in order to immediately get down to the work of battling the Great Depression. President Bernard insisted that he not have an inaugural ball at all, both because of the costs and his need to meet with a few close advisors to take the first steps in addressing the constitutional and social turmoil of the current time. There had been the New Deal, now could there be a New Day?

CHAPTER 2

The Molding Of A Man And A Leader

H unnicutt, Pennsylvania is a small town almost equidistant to the urban centers—none of them huge—stretched out along the northeastern part of the state. It bloomed in the 1960s into a desirable residence for the young and middle-aged executives of steel, textile, and other manufacturing companies that were then still going strong in that part of the state. It afforded the advantages of a small-town atmosphere for their families, an almost exurban existence that enabled them to easily commute to their offices in one of the small cities. Stephen Gregory Bernard was born there in 1970 to one of those middle-management executives, then in his late thirties and his wife who was nearly the same age and had struggled during the course of the ten years of their marriage to have children. The physicians they had consulted had told them that, due to premature ovarian insufficiency, she was very unlikely to have children. They had started to think of adoption, although wondered if their approaching of age forty might be against them. So, when they received notice that Mrs. Bernard was expecting it was a joyous time for them. As Mrs. Bernard's age and fertility problems would have presaged, Stephen Gregory—he was named after his paternal and maternal grandfathers—was to be their only child. Catherine (Cassie) Bernard was an enthusiastic homemaker, but as her expectations of motherhood had diminished she had taken a job as a part-time teacher in a Catholic grammar school. She had graduated from a small Catholic women's college with an education degree. Now, she savored the opportunity finally to be the mother that was her almost life-long ambition.

The Bernards were devout Catholics. Their life, outside of work and their household, focused around the Church. Cassie was a daily Mass-goer and her husband Jim was there, besides Sundays, on virtually every day he was off of work. They were prodigious volunteers for activities at their parish church and also regularly helped with Catholic charitable activities. Their fervent Catholicism had been instilled in them by their families. Jim's ancestors had emigrated from Poland early in the twentieth century and initially were coal miners. Cassie's had come from Ireland (the O'Donoghues) a generation before that. As had been the case with so many Catholic immigrants of that era, family, job, and the Church were the three prongs of their existence.

When he was yet a young boy, Jim Bernard had developed an insatiable desire for learning. He routinely brought home one or another of the Harvard Classics from the local public library from the time he was twelve years old. Although literature captivated him, he had a special ardor for politics. He not only dived into the classical thinkers, but also savored reading Lincoln and the writings and biographies of the Founding Fathers. Both he and Cassie had worked their way through nearby colleges while living at home. He had gone to a Catholic men's college. Their evenings at home were often spent cuddled up on the living room couch each reading their current choice of a tome. When Stephen came along, Cassie began reading to him very early and began to teach him how to read at age four. Both she and her husband were careful about pushing too hard. They both knew that learning was something that one had to want to do and come to love, and that it could not be forced. She did not send Stephen to kindergarten, but preferred to "ease him into" learning at home. Her experience as a teacher had convinced her of the problems of putting children into structured learning situations too early. By the time Stephen started school, he quickly became one of the best pupils in his class. For several years, school was supplemented by family reading time aloud for a half an hour after dinner most nights. The result was that by the time he took freshman English in high school, Stephen found that he already had read or heard read most of the assigned books.

Academic formation was accompanied by religious and moral formation. The Bernards were well aware of the serious troubles that had befallen Catholic schools starting in the late 1960s. Religious education downplayed—at times even distorted—doctrinal content significantly, with the result some students were scarcely practicing Catholics by the time they were halfway through high school. When it came time to enroll Stephen in first grade, they found a parish elementary school about forty-five minutes away where the pastor had kept tight rein over things and maintained its Catholic character. When it came to high school, some years later, the Bernards joined with a number of other families to establish one of the early "independent" Catholic schools—not run by dioceses or religious orders, as most were, but by laymen—which later became an accelerating movement around the country.

Stephen's formation had begun almost from the beginning, when his parents took their baby boy to church each Sunday. As became apparent by the time he began school, however, he was a naturally "good" boy. Temptations seem to confront a child almost from the time he begins to associate with peers, but Stephen seemed always to decisively recoil from them. The only times he got into "trouble" were when he naïvely did something that he honestly didn't think was wrong. When he was in fifth grade, the teacher had periodic class-wide spelling bees to help the pupils learn their spelling lessons better and to create an incentive by giving small trinket awards to the top spellers. In one bee there were a few words in the speller that he knew he was unsure of. Stephen was in the last half dozen pupils still standing; those who had misspelled their word had to sit down. One pupil seated in the row next to him pulled out his speller to go over words for the next test once he was out. Stephen inadvertently looked at the pupil's desk and saw one of the words that he was not sure of. When the teacher came to him the word she posed to him was the very one he had seen. He deliberately misspelled it because he was not certain he would have known it if he had not seen it. As he left school one spring day in the seventh grade he came upon two boys in his class who were unobtrusively sitting under one of the large evergreen trees that formed the back border of the playground twenty-five yards from the school building. As he stopped to say hello, one of the boys suddenly held up a picture in the girlie magazine they were apparently indulging in thinking that he might also enjoy it. Instead, he gave them a stern, disapproving stare and quickly went on his way. In his sophomore year in high school, a group of the male students got together on a Saturday afternoon to go to a small theater in their town that showed old family movies from the 1950s and early 1960s. When they arrived at the theater a few of the his compatriots pealed off to quietly go instead to the theater at a small shopping plaza a couple blocks away that routinely showed "R" rated films. They were coaxing the others to join them. Even though the school was set up to be a strong Catholic high school, all the students were not in line with their parents' objectives. This was a way that some rebelled. Even though one of the boys had become a good friend of his, he steadfastly refused. Inside, he was shocked and deeply disappointed in the boy, and their friendship cooled after that. Such things were the mark of young Stephen's character.

27

Stephen got his first direct taste of injustice as a ten-year-old. A boy down the street who was a couple of years older made a habit of antagonizing the younger children, including Stephen, on the block. Finally, Cassie resolved to talk to the boy's parents. They listened to her with a none-too-friendly demeanor at their front door. A couple of days later they received a letter from the boy's uncle in the next block claiming that the boy had only been responding to Stephen's trying to let air out of the tires of his car. It was all a complete fabrication, but Stephen got his first taste of how some people were all too ready to disregard truth to achieve their ends and cover up for those they wanted to protect. It was an early exposure to the kinds practices he would see all too often in politics many years later. It would also foreshadow a false allegation he would face one day in politics.

Stephen was in no way bombastic—a "life of the party" type—nor was he a budding young athlete (a non-life threatening heart valve problem that he apparently had been born with precluded intense participation in sports), but he was popular with his classmates, both in elementary and high school. He was personable, and people were attracted to his quiet sincerity and kindness and his inveterate helpfulness. So, when he first ran for class president—the first time there was such an election—when he was in sixth grade he was an obvious choice. Typically, such school elections at that level were little more than honorific, but he viewed his office as a genuine call to service. He did such things as routinely staying after school to offer to help his teachers with whatever they needed. They came to respect him and admire his maturity.

He was elected class president again in seventh grade, but by eighth grade—the last year of elementary school before students would peel off to different high schools—what he sometimes called the "star-athlete syndrome" became operational. A tall, chatty classmate who was the leading back on the school's football team and a prodigious scorer on the basketball team was elected. Sometimes Stephen wished he could have taken part in sports, but he was never one to indulge in self-pity. Whenever such a thought entered his mind, he said a quick prayer thanking God for all that He had given him. Even though he couldn't be involved in sports, he occupied his time with many other school activities along with his fervent commitment to his studies. Moreover, some of his eighth-grade classmates turned against him when he reported that he had seen a couple of his male classmates in the cafeteria after school collaborating on a take-home exam that each was supposed to do on his own. The word was that several other students had done the same and the undercurrent was that Stephen was

28

acting in a "holier than thou" manner in reporting the boys. Some also had the attitude that you simply shouldn't do anything to get your classmates into trouble—even if they richly deserved it.

It was different at the very small high school he went to. There were no sports teams until his senior year when they cobbled together boys' and girls' soccer teams that played a very short schedule. Many of the activities were religiously oriented, although a debate team started in his sophomore year. The teachers and many of the parents thought that to learn how to witness to their faith better the students needed to engage the culture, and that meant learning more how to address public issues. Stephen quickly became the debate team's leader. He had a mind that could readily dissect a question and get to the heart of a problem. He also possessed the gift of eloquence, but even more impressively of being able to explain even complicated subjects in a readily understandable—and not "long-winded"—way. He did not aim to "thump" the other side, as seemed to be the normal *modus operandi* in school debate competitions. The school was able to become part of a regional high school debate league and featured a weekly competition over a four-month period. Over time, Stephen's efforts became almost legendary in the league and he won several trophies over his three years. More, opposing coaches often commented on his spirit of sportsmanship and obvious respect for the other debaters he went up against.

One of the students who was among the discontented about being sent by his parents to the school was one Jacob Rogers, known mostly as "Big Skipper" because of his large frame and often intimidating manner with his classmates. He got into the practice of challenging other boys to a fistfight, carefully arranged to be after school and off school property so he would not get into trouble, if they crossed him in some way. He usually made quick work of them because of his superior body-build, but almost without exception they acceded to his challenge for fear of being thought cowardly. One time, Stephen came upon him in the small school cafeteria speaking mockingly to one of the girls whose homeliness, social ineptness, and lack of fashion sense—even though the girls wore modest school uniforms, she made hers look retrograde—had made her something of an outcast. Stephen told him to leave her alone, that his antagonizing her was wrong. Big Skipper told him to "butt out, or else." Stephen held his ground and Big Skipper said that he would see him after school "over the hill" (that is, the place where he staged his fistfight conquests). As a group of other students began to gather around, Stephen told him that he had to start realizing that fistfights don't solve problems and rebuked him for his behavior not just toward the girl but his fellow students generally. After heaping a slew of curse words on Stephen, he challenged him to the fight again, almost in a goading manner. Stephen knew that the real cowardly one was Big Skipper, whose scheme of having his fistfights "over the hill" was manipulative so the school authorities wouldn't learn about it. The "buzz" around the school was that his father was a tough disciplinarian who would make Big Skipper pay if he got in trouble at school. Out of the corner of his eye Stephen saw Mr. Shaughnessy, the hard-nosed school principal, changing some signs in the hallway outside the cafeteria. Stephen said to Big Skipper, "If you insist on resolving this with fisticuffs, let's go and do it right out in the hallway." He pointed in the direction of Mr. Shaughnessy, and when Big Skipper looked in that direction his face seemed to noticeably whiten. He began to stammer and started to back off. Stephen had calculated perfectly; he had struck him in his Achilles tendon. Still, as in his debates, Stephen was not out to thump his adversary. "I'd be happy to forget about all this, but just don't talk like this to Mary again." He quickly agreed, and even mumbled an almost-apology to her and then quickly slipped out of the cafeteria. Big Skipper never again picked a fistfight with anyone in the school. The Big Skipper episode was a taste of how Stephen later would handle the bullies of politics: outthink them, stand your ground against them but not on their terms, expose them as phonies, whenever possible let them back away without being hopelessly embarrassed and so fueling lingering resentment. He always remembered the Biblical quote about being "as gentle as a dove and wise as a serpent."

Stephen was a top student in his high school. He poured himself into his studies, and ultimately graduated as salutatorian. He especially excelled in history and civics, but also won awards at graduation for his proficiency in classical and modern languages. In spite of his academic commitment, this was not all he did. While he couldn't compete in sports, he had consistent summer jobs as a lifeguard at the local municipal pool. He was an Eagle Scout—at the time no one envisioned that the Scouts would one day extend membership to open homosexuals and even allow openly homosexual leaders—and even accumulated one of each color of Eagle palm. He had no disagreement with his parents' rule that he could not date until he was sixteen; too many other things occupied his time. Still, he struggled with a basic shyness around the opposite sex that sometimes frustrated him. He dated only a few times in his last two years of high school, and found the strong stress of the school's parents on dating in small groups to be helpful. With the group-dating norm, classmates often helped someone "break the ice" and introduce him or her to members of the opposite sex and so the dates themselves seemed more relaxed.

The Big Skipper episode by itself did not forge Stephen's reputation as a precocious young man as far as wisdom, courage, and good judgment were concerned. His teachers and peers came to recognize this just from their normal interactions with him. These qualities and his kindness and gentleness in dealing with his fellow students made him someone they came to admire and even want to emulate. When a classmate was having some difficulties with course material, he frequently offered to help the person with homework or a difficult assignment. He was also universally known as a hard worker who stayed with a project to its completion. All these things made him an obvious choice for class president when he finally chose to get into school politics early in his junior year. In office, his continued hard work and geniality made him popular, but his demands on the other class officers and committee chairmen—who weren't always so industrious—aroused opposition among some of the other prominent juniors. At the end of the year, at the urging of some classmates and the not-so-veiled suggestion of Mr. Shaughnessy and a couple other teachers, he decided to run for student body president. While Stephen always completely respected his elders, they had such a regard for his maturity that they sometimes sought out his opinion about certain things and they could accept his readiness to speak up about certain issues. His discontented fellow student class officials put together a competing ticket to run against him and his vice-presidential candidate. The candidates always ran campaigns of a sort, but the election was largely decided by the presentation they made to an assembly of the small student body. A strain had developed between Mr. Shaughnessy and the parent-dominated board of the school that semester because of their unwillingness to permit an end-of-year formal. While Stephen had faithfully presented the views of the students petitioning for the formal and even arranged a special meeting with them and the board, he held back from advocating their position since he could see the legitimate concerns raised by the people in charge. The opposing presidential candidate—whose ticket won a coin toss and chose to speak last, so there was no opportunity for response—misrepresented to the assembly what had happened and suggested that Stephen was controlled by them and had been their mouthpiece. Youthful rebellion was a bit at work, and Stephen lost a close election. He learned a lesson to carry into his future in regular politics, which at that point he had no anticipation of having: always be prepared for adversaries to misrepresent or twist the truth about you and make sure you have taken the right steps to get out the facts at the start.

Although disappointed by the defeat, he did not become discouraged or angry with his fellow students because of it. He went on being what he had been at the school and at the beginning of the next year was elected senior class president without opposition. His former adversaries avoided further clashes with him and one, who was in charge of the student government treasury, got the student body irritated by excessive spending on a few events.

Despite his consistent high academic accomplishment, Stephen's scores on the SATs were only good, not stellar. He had trouble understanding how a few-hour test should be accorded more weight by many colleges than consistent outstanding four-year performance. It was only years later that elite universities began to deemphasize standardized tests, since they found no clear correlation between their students' test scores and their classroom performance once enrolled; the lesser schools didn't seem ready to follow suit. Still, his credentials were enough to win him a couple of partial scholarships to a Catholic university in a distant state that was known for its generally wholesome campus life and commitment to its traditional solid liberal arts program at a time when most schools had long since turned away from that. His parents had gently steered him in the direction of that university, but the early background they had given him had already made him enthusiastic about the liberal arts.

Stephen's scholarships from the university and from the Knights of Columbus—which his father had long been a member of—along with his accumulated summer earnings from high school and the summer after graduation and his holding down two part-time jobs at the university when put together enabled him to meet all of his first-year expenses. In the late 1980s and early 1990s college tuition was not yet so high that that was possible. He was insistent that he would cover his own costs and not depend on his parents, who had paid so much for his elementary and high school tuition. They insisted, however, that they be permitted to cover his travel and other sundry expenses.

Stephen plunged into his college studies, and quickly became a top student. At a university where many students, so contrary to the mentality of the typical American college student, were "on fire" for the liberal arts, he became known for his extraordinary enthusiasm. Many classes were seminars, where students were expected to come to class having read the books—usually "great books" or other original works—in advance and be prepared to discuss them. There was hardly a class meeting where he was not heavily involved in the conversation.

Despite the prevailing interest in the liberal arts, the norm for students for these seminars became a minimalist one: Don't bother reading the book, but just go through it enough so you can take part in the discussion and seem to be doing your work. By contrast, Stephen read every book from cover to cover, took the time to jot down notes or thoughts about them, and determined to get everything out of them that he could. He seemed to be transformed by the great authors he read. He was deepened not only intellectually, but philosophically, ethically, attitudinally, and spiritually. His remarks in the class discussions betrayed not just knowledge and understanding of the readings, but wisdom as well. By the end of his sophomore year, some of his fellow students were jokingly—but also seriously—calling him a "sage."

Perhaps it was Stephen's awareness of his classmates' frequent lack of preparedness or the comments he frequently heard in conversation denigrating the education other college students were getting compared to *their* superior liberal arts program, or the frequent references of some of the professors in class to their "elite" university, that caused him to develop a feeling of distaste for the university community. Despite his consistent academic and other achievements, his parents had always stressed the need for humility. Superciliousness and condescending attitudes were something he had little patience for—even more so when people truly were not all they made themselves out to be. Besides, he knew students at other colleges that did not have the same kind of institutional commitment or structured curriculum, but with careful course selection and good advice were getting a solid liberal arts education. Still, he recognized the value of the education he was receiving and never thought of transferring. Such campus attitudes discouraged him from getting involved in student politics, but he excelled on the debate team as he had in high school and took an active part in the Philosophy Club's gatherings where discussion of the great issues of Western thought that were introduced in class continued. He would have joined ROTC, but his defective heart valve precluded it. He always got along with people at the university, but made few close friends there and developed a closeness only to a couple of professors who he saw as both true scholars and gentlemen, and who embodied the humility that he associated with both of those categories.

Just after the end of his sophomore year, tragedy struck the family when Stephen's father died suddenly of a heart attack. The solicitude of their parish church community and people from the further Catholic circles that they had been so involved in was overwhelming. People came forth not just with expressions of condolence, but also with heartfelt offers of help for Cassie and Stephen. Stephen offered not to return to the university in the fall and instead to get a full-time job to help his mother in whatever way possible. Cassie would hear nothing of it. He needed to proceed with his education. Jim and Cassie had been provident people. Their house was paid off and they had respectable savings and no debt. They were always people who only bought what they had the money to buy. Cassie would also have the proceeds of a half-million dollar life insurance policy that Jim had the good sense to purchase years before. Moreover, Cassie was confident that she could get back into teaching. Stephen hadn't known the ins-and-outs of the family's finances, except that his parents were responsible people. When he learned all this, his already-high admiration for his father abounded that much more. Jim's death, as might have been expected, left a void for him and made him painfully grasp what he had sometimes been told in his religious instruction about the utter transitoriness of this life.

While Stephen was not one to allow himself to remain dispirited for long periods of time, his summer was understandably difficult. His summer job and the summer reading program that he had set up, and which he determined to stay with, enabled him to brush away his sadness. The only real silver lining was that he forged a closer bond than ever with his loving mother. They helped each other out in ten thousand different ways during those difficult months. Before he prepared to return to the university, he was elated by the news that she was offered a teaching position at a Catholic elementary school in a town not too far from theirs.

When Stephen returned to the university, he made a pledge to himself not to allow his father's untimely death to weaken his commitment in any way to his studies or his other campus activities. He told himself that he would drive himself that much harder. It would be his tribute to Jim and all that he had given him. His academic success continued unabated and the debate team set school records. Still, throughout the year he exhibited a slight dispiritedness and detachment that was noticeable to his few close friends. At he end of the school year, he secured a ride home from one of them, Mike Halloran, a newcomer to both his dormitory floor and the debate team with whom he had worked closely during the past season. Mike was from a northern New Jersey town away from the urban and suburban sprawl of the extended New York metropolitan area. Like the Bernards, Mike's family was fervent in their Catholicism. He had talked to his parents on the phone the day before to tell them how final exams had gone and to let them know about when he would be arriving back home. During the conversation, they told him about how downcast his younger sister, a senior at a local diocesan Catholic high school, was because no one had asked her to the senior prom to be held a week later.

"She was not asked last year either. She really had hoped it would be different this year. This is something she has long looked forward to," Mike's mother said. She, and the rest of her family, all knew the reason. It wasn't that she was unattractive, or unintelligent, or even very unpopular. It was just the opposite: By the reckoning of many of her classmates of both sexes, she was genuinely beautiful—easily the prettiest girl in the class. She was also a top student, probably in line to be class salutatorian. Even though she was a down-to-earth, sociable, and very considerate person, her beauty alone was intimidating to the boys. Her top-flight academic standing compounded that.

Mike thought for a moment, and then said, "Mom, maybe I can help. Let me talk to you as soon as I get home." She didn't ask for any explanation. Mike was one who was known for hatching schemes, and it was best to wait until he came forth about them.

After Mike and Stephen had been on the road for a while the next day, Mike brought the subject up. "Stephen, I know she's three years younger than you, still a high school kid, but she's really hurting about this. Even though I'm her brother, I can tell you honestly that she's a very nice girl. I'm sure it would be a very nice evening for you. You shouldn't feel that as a college guy you'd be out of your element. Usually, each year at the senior prom a few of the girls are escorted by college guys. We can still get tickets. I know that money's a little tight for you, but my parents have planned to buy the tickets as an early graduation gift for her and you don't have to rent a tux. As many or more of the guys wear regular suits now as wear a tux, and I know you have a couple suits. I'll buy the bouquet for you to bring her and a boutonnière for you to wear. I know it would be a bit of a drive for you, so you could just stay over at our house as our guest that night after the prom." He paused for a moment and then said, "I think it could be good for you, too." He was well aware of how difficult of a year it had been for Stephen since his father's death and how he had done almost no socializing during that time.

Stephen thought for a while and then broke into a slight smile and said, "Don't worry about costs. I'll buy the bouquet and boutonnière. Just don't forget to tell me the color of her gown. I'll make sure that the color of my tie coordinates with it."

"You can be sure that I'll do that," Mike replied and then thanked Stephen profusely.

A week later Stephen arrived at the Halloran home decked out in a becoming medium blue suit—his favorite suit color, it was a color that was appropriate for almost any occasion—with a yellow-gold tie. Mike had called him to say that his sister's gown would basically be that color, along with a blue sash. Stephen had bought a bouquet/boutonnière combination so their colors would further complement. He drove his mother's car from their house in Pennsylvania a little over an hour away. He would get his suitcase from the trunk at the end of the evening since he would be the Hallorans' houseguest. The next day was Saturday, but he figured he would leave shortly after breakfast so as not to be an imposition.

Mike answered his knock, with a big welcoming smile. Mike introduced Stephen to Mr. and Mrs. Halloran, whose beaming faces showed how much they appreciated what he was doing for their daughter. Both also told him so with obvious sincerity.

"Marybeth will be down in just a few minutes," Mrs. Halloran said. "Come on into the living room." She introduced him to the three youngest Halloran children, a fifteen-year-old boy and two other girls who were ten and eight, who were already sitting in there. They all wanted to see their sister make her appearance in her special apparel on this special night. From where everyone was seated they could see the staircase that Marybeth would soon descend.

After a little small talk about Stephen's drive in and the past semester at the university, everyone looked up as they heard quiet steps on the stairs. It was an unobtrusive entrance for someone who was meeting a waiting entourage, but that was in character for the quiet and humble Marybeth. When she finally turned toward the living room and began to walk toward them, everyone stood up and Stephen got his first good look at her. Immediately, his heart pounded. She was *stunning*. She was slim and well proportioned but not skinny, with blond hair and an almost perfect complexion with just a touch of red in her cheeks. Momentarily, he saw that she wore no make-up except for a touch of eye shadow. Her beautiful complexion was natural. Her hair was shoulder-blade length, richly textured and full. As might be expected when a young woman was preparing for what for her was a big, glamorous evening like a prom, she had gotten her hair styled—but only very slightly. It had a natural slight wave, and she chose not to have it put up as girls often do for a prom. Stephen was fairly tall at 6'1", but so was she for a woman at about 5'10". Her height initially surprised him, but then he recalled that Mike had said that she had played on the school's girls volleyball team in her senior year. Still, she did not in the least bit appear lanky. Her gown accentuated her beauty, although it was entirely tasteful and modest. Its squared neckline arching up from her collarbones exposed no cleavage at all. It had just slight sleeves, from which her well sculptured long, but not dangling, arms descended. When she entered the room, her eyes immediately found his and for a long moment they gazed at each other. For a split second their gazes were exploring to discern what the other thought, then they turned to joyfulness. Marybeth had bubbled in happiness during the past week that someone was going to escort her to the prom, but she had more than a slight trepidation that it would be a college guy. The joy of her gaze showed that her nervousness had quickly almost melted away. Each of them had an inner feeling of reassurance.

She walked slowly but resolutely right to Stephen. Their eye contact continued as both stretched out their arms to clasp each other's hands in a gentle handshake. Marybeth was very restrained about wearing jewelry, and studiously avoided anything gaudy. Tonight, she had on only the small gold-silver 14-karat birthstone ring that her parents had bought her for her sixteenth birthday, the pearl necklace they had just bought her for her eighteenth birthday earlier that month, and small gold attachable earrings with pearls in them that coordinated well with the necklace. Stephen remembered thinking that her jewelry altogether added just the right touch to her attractive gown.

Mike had offered to drive Stephen and his sister to the prom, but Stephen said he would do it. Marybeth would be able to direct him; it was held at a nice banquet hall not far from her school. As they left the house, both beaming, Mrs. Halloran remembered thinking how they seemed to match very well as a couple.

Stephen had been concerned that he might not have much to say to Marybeth at the prom. After all, she was in high school and he in college and he wasn't sure what they would have in common. As it turned out, whenever they weren't dancing they were talking, and the two of them shared many topics that interested them—from Great Books to public affairs to history to Catholic subjects. Even though he knew that she was a top student, he was surprised at how knowledgeable she was for a high-schooler and was struck by the maturity of her thought and judgment. They enjoyed each other's company immensely and this was noticed by not a few of the other couples there. Marybeth kept thinking throughout the night how kind and considerate Stephen seemed to be and how much of a gentleman he was. There were moments as they danced when they looked longingly into each other's eyes. A few times, as they sat down from a dance before picking up with their discussion, they shared the same deep mutual glance—almost as if they were looking into each other's hearts and souls.

They were among the last couples to leave the prom. It was already late, and they returned directly to the Hallorans' house. There, after talking with Mike and her parents for a short while, they continued talking alone in the living room for another half hour. Even though Stephen had planned to leave right after breakfast the next morning, plans changed. The two decided to take a walk, and then Stephen asked Mr. and Mrs. Halloran if he could take Marybeth to lunch. He called his mother to say it would be later in the afternoon when he would be home, and the two seemed almost inseparable that whole time. Her parents and Mike couldn't help noticing the glow that seemed to be evident in both their faces.

During the following summer, they called each other weekly. If email and texting had yet existed the communication might have been even more frequent. Stephen visited on a half dozen occasions, and usually they repeated their lunch engagement and sometimes also extended their date to an amusement park or a matinee movie. That fall Stephen was returning for his senior year at the university and Marybeth was starting at a fairly new Catholic college there in the East, which had been set up as a reaction to the secular trends that had enveloped most of the established Catholic institutions of higher learning.

During the course of the next year, while both were away at school, they wrote to each other almost weekly. During the Christmas break between semesters, they visited back-and-forth at their parents' homes. Their bond grew closer, and they deepened their relationship romantically, socially, and intellectually. They also got along very well together, and genuinely enjoyed each other's company. When visiting each other on weekends, they attended Mass together—not just on Sundays, but often on Saturday mornings as well—and took time for brief prayer together. Marybeth also flew with Stephen's mother to his college graduation in May. Their parents all happily saw an engagement looming, but there were practical complications. Marybeth had three more years of college, and Stephen had decided that he wanted to pursue both graduate studies in political science and law school (a joint J.D.-Ph.D. program). With his outstanding academic record, he was accepted into at a major Catholic university in the Midwest and received a scholarship and assistantship package that held out the prospect of paying for almost the entire program. Moreover, completing such a program would all but insure long-range economic security. So, finances would not pose a serious obstacle to marriage.

38

Still, he knew that graduate-student married life would not be easy and he had more than a little hesitation about subjecting Marybeth to that. Marybeth, for her part, was not deterred, but as a young woman with mature judgment well beyond her years knew that it would be a challenging time. They talked many long hours about it. It was clear that neither wanted to abandon the possibility of marriage; probably from the moment they set eyes on each other they knew that they were intended for each other. The logjam was resolved when Stephen learned that by intensive summer study he could finish law school, complete the bar exam, and be ABD in his graduate studies in four years' time and Marybeth resolved that she would similarly double up on a campus job and taking courses during the next two summers so she could compact her remaining projected three years of college into two. They decided, with the help of much active mutual prayer, that they would keep their relationship at a medium flame until Marybeth's graduation and, unless God had other plans, that would be the time to consider an engagement. The next two years were a time of much perspiration and prayer for each of them and a routine of frequent letter-writing, phone calls, and visits across half the country whenever possible. They knew that it is said that God opens doors if He wants something of people, and closes them if He doesn't or if He wants something different. From all that either of them could tell, the doors remained open. Stephen rented a car and drove from the Midwest for her graduation. She rode home to New Jersey with him, while the rest of her family went on ahead. On the way home, they planned to stop for dinner at a well-known restaurant on a hillside overlooking a beautiful valley in a state park just off the highway. There, he took out the ring and they were engaged. He returned a week later to his summer studies, but was in frequent communication with Marybeth as she and her mother planned the wedding. They met with her pastor, Fr. Patrick Reilly, who also did personalized marriage preparation sessions with them. He also officiated at their wedding late the following October.

As it turned out, life in Stephen's final two years of studies went surprisingly fast. Marybeth worked as a junior administrative assistant and was their primary breadwinner during that time. Still, his assistantships brought in money as well and at the end they were in good shape financially. Their plan was for Stephen to then look for a job, either in law or in what he had decided was his deepest ambition as a university professor. He had two final obstacles to overcome late that spring and then late in July: his Ph.D. qualifying exams and the bar exam. He decided to see where his best job possibilities would be before making a decision about where to take the bar exam. He and

Marybeth were flexible about where to settle down; anywhere in New England, the Mid-Atlantic Region, the Midwest to the Mississippi River, and the near South down to North Carolina were acceptable. In the mid-1990s legal jobs were quite abundant, full-time University teaching positions less so. They decided to delay starting a family until those final two years of his studies were over; they often joked that they had become masters of what a couple noted authorities on the subject called "the art of natural family planning."

Also as it turned out, Stephen heard about an unusual joint professorship in law and political science that had just been established between a law school near Pittsburgh, Pennsylvania and a Catholic university not far away in Ohio. He applied, was quickly called for an interview, and somewhat to his surprise was quickly hired. Although he would be a professor at both, his primary affiliation was with the political science department at the university. He thought it was almost a dream job for him, and was amazed that something like this happened at the beginning of his professional life. A further unexpected bonus came when one of the adjunct faculty members at the law school, a well-respected local Catholic lawyer who handled a lot of constitutional law cases—one of Stephen's special areas of interest—invited him to become of-counsel with his firm, which would enable him to get needed practice experience. So, he decided to sit for the bar exam in his native state of Pennsylvania that summer. He was successful in the two most important exams he had ever taken over his long academic career, his Ph.D. qualifying exams—he garnered a rare "high pass"—and his bar exam. He also graduated *summa cum laude* in his law school class, as he had from his undergraduate university. He had no doubt that that, his associate editorship of the law review and his outstanding graduate school record made possible his hiring.

Marybeth also looked forward to a new career, as a mother. After Stephen's law school graduation, they tried—and prayed—hard to have a baby. A number of months passed by, and nothing happened. She was normally one of the most vibrant and upbeat persons Stephen had ever known, but she gradually became discouraged and—something Stephen had never noticed before—moody. One evening when he came home, she came up to Stephen and embraced and affectionately kissed him and said how sorry she was for her behavior. He smiled and joked, "Yes, remember that moodiness is my weakness. Don't tread on my monopoly on it." They laughed and she said that she decided during the day that she was not going to go down that path any longer. They talked and decided that each would have fertility testing, and resolved that they would be prepared for the worst.

It turned out that the problem was Marybeth's. She had a condition similar to Stephen's mother. It was at least very unlikely that she could conceive. After she told Stephen the news, she said calmly, "We have to accept God's will in life, whatever it might be." They agreed that it would be good for her to go back to work and she planned to do some religious charitable work as well. She also wanted to support and help Stephen in his efforts in the best way she could. "You have to work on a Ph.D. dissertation. You could use a research assistant. You know how good I am with research." It turned out that she got a position as associate director of a small Catholic non-profit. She worked daylight hours and spent many evenings in either the college or law school library. They talked about adoption, but decided to wait and in any event in the abortion culture there were not too many babies out there to adopt. Foreign adoptions were also getting increasingly difficult and expensive, as different governments began to see this as a way to bring more American dollars into their economies. They also knew a number of couples who had had bad experiences with foreign adoptions. They wound up being childless, but as Marybeth's siblings married and had children they grew especially close to their nephews and nieces. This was a heavy burden for both of them, but Stephen knew it was especially difficult for Marybeth who had literally bubbled whenever she talked during the first two years of their marriage about the children they would soon have. He was always attuned to providing Marybeth the emotional support that she needed.

As Stephen settled down into his teaching positions, he quickly developed a reputation as a highly competent and demanding professor but one who was always readily accessible to his students. All this was so even though he pushed hard to finish his doctoral dissertation about constitutional issues concerning presidential power—which he did despite all the demands of his new academic career in just eighteen months. Even more importantly, he developed a reputation at both of his schools for fairness and a strong sense of ethics, respect for his faculty colleagues, and charity and consideration in his dealings with them. Although he always was ready to take part in the myriad internal academic policy discussions that characterize university faculties—not a typical thing for a junior professor—he did it in a remarkably kind manner. He had a way of intelligently but gently explaining his positions, so that his senior colleagues who disagreed with him and also might normally have had little patience with "upstart" younger faculty were willing to listen. They also appreciated his consistent willingness to take on extra tasks and committee work and to give them help whenever they needed it. He often enunciated ideas that, when one thought about them, made a great deal of sense even though they went against the grain. They were against what had become standard ways of doing things in the academic world, like having students evaluate their professors (which he always sharply criticized as promoting popularity contests, encouraging lowered academic standards, and damaging the professor-student relationship). In a certain sense, his ideas were often markedly innovative, even while they were strikingly traditional. A few of his colleagues started to call him a visionary. His hard work and prodigious scholarly production became almost legendary, but he never evinced a hint of haughtiness. He might have been in line to become the academic dean at the university, but in spite of the respect and admiration he received from most of his colleagues the vocal sustained opposition to some of his ideas from a small number of them eliminated that possibility. He learned that academic politics could be notorious for its nastiness. It prepared him well for the political world, and he learned how it had to be dealt with.

For all his active involvement in faculty affairs and his noteworthy charitable efforts to help his colleagues, Stephen was by nature a kind of introvert. He worked alone a lot—a scholar had to do that—and he was never a big social mixer and was impatient with "life of the party" types. When he left the campuses he preferred to spend his time with the love of his life, Marybeth. The two had friends, but they were biggest friends with each other. He was fond of telling Marybeth that she was his "wife, lover, and friend."

Stephen poured himself into his professorial role. For him it was not a job or even a career, but a calling. The years flew by, and pretty soon he had been in his two university positions for a decade. There were the usual aggravations and inanities of the academy, but he became considerably accomplished and despite frequent philosophical disagreements with some of his colleagues was much respected by them. He secured tenure—no mean feat—at both universities and figured that he would stay in his position for the rest of his career. Moreover, when Stephen took his position Marybeth had gone with another Catholic non-profit organization—this one was a national organization—and had since become deputy head of the regional branch and they had become heavily involved in community activities. In the midst of all this, Stephen became increasingly troubled by the drift of politics both in the country and in Pennsylvania. An ongoing series of financial scandals involving various state officials of both parties, the push to enact an increasingly culturally leftist agenda in the traditionally socially conservative state—someone once said that between Philadelphia and Pittsburgh, Pennsylvania is Alabama—as the

Philadelphia and Pittsburgh areas came more and more to dominate the state's politics, the ongoing efforts in Washington to make the U.S. more like a European social democracy, its transformation into a kind of centralized administrative state, and his observing that so many politicians were playing fast and loose with traditional constitutional principles made him wonder if he should do much more. Teaching and scholarship were critical, to be sure, but he increasingly perceived that the immediate situation had to be addressed or the old American Republic might not still be around to benefit from the long-term payoff of his academic efforts.

Even his additionally fulfilling work with the law firm—he had the opportunity to be involved in several cases that dealt with important constitutional questions and concerned some of the critical cultural issues that so troubled him, and even once had had the opportunity to argue before the U.S. Supreme Court—did not seem enough. The conviction became stronger and stronger in him that he should do more, that he should embroil himself more directly in politics. This conviction was fueled by his reading of different major historical writers on the subject of the decline of regimes. He unmistakably saw so many of the same conditions in present-day America that had brought down great nations and cultures of the past. He knew, though, that social and political collapse or even transformation—the greatest threat to America now was not a collapse, but a change to a different kind of political order than had been fashioned by its Founding Fathers—was not inevitable. Spurred on initially by his Ph.D. dissertation work on the Constitution and executive power, he read extensively about great leaders who had saved their nations from overwhelming threat and peril.

He had gotten mildly involved in a couple of losing Congressional campaigns and had become active in a citizen group interested in fiscal responsibility and upholding constitutional principles, but was giving much thought to a more significant involvement—perhaps even running for office. A number of the people in the group and even some party people who he had gotten to know in the Congressional campaigns were much impressed by him: his easygoing manner with people, obvious integrity, attachment to principle without being ready to beat people up over it, capability of explaining things in an understandable manner, and his obvious smarts. They encouraged him to seek office. Still, a jump from the academy into politics was a major change and not one he was sure he was prepared for. He and Marybeth talked a lot about it and, when he loosely mentioned electoral politics to her, she even encouraged him. She followed public affairs closely and,

43

as might be expected, shared his concerns about the country's politics and culture. Developments in an indirect, and not really intended, way opened the door for him.

One of the high administrative officials of the law school headed up a small consulting firm on the side and was deeply immersed in discussions within the law school about plans for the building of a new classroom wing for the building. Rumors circulated about a conflict of interest and a questionable opportunity for financial gain. It was a topic of frequent discussion in faculty offices, but no one wanted to say anything openly. They were all fearful of retaliation, especially since it was well known that the official in question was close to both the law school dean and the university president. Initially, Stephen did not pay too much attention to the matter. Even though he and Marybeth lived a short distance from the law school in Pennsylvania, he spent most of his workweek at his other university in Ohio. Also, he was aware how there was always a lot of chatter and speculation about things and the realities were usually quite different. However, one day one of the secretaries came by his office at the law school and asked if she could talk to him. She said she came to see him because she knew how honest and ethical he was, that he was the best person for her to talk to. She recounted a conversation she had accidentally overheard when she was in the dean's office suite. She was waiting to see the dean because she had an official document that he had to sign. When she arrived at the suite the dean's secretary, whose desk was in an open area outside his office, was not there—apparently she was somewhere else in the building—and his administrative assistant was not in that day. The door to the dean's office was closed, but through the mostly drawn blinds covering the small window on the door she could slightly see that two people were there and she could hear some voices softly talking. She decided to wait a few minutes to see if the dean might quickly be finished with his business and then she could get his signature. She thought the voices were coming from the office itself. Then, she suddenly realized that they were coming from the intercom on the dean's secretary's desk. Apparently, the button had gotten stuck in the "on" position; perhaps his secretary had had to summon the dean about something just before having to go elsewhere. For a moment she tried to ignore the voices, then she realized that she should leave the suite because she did not want to be hearing what was probably a confidential conversation. As she turned toward the door, she heard the dean say—she remembered the words distinctly—"I'll be sure to put the paperwork through for your outfit to be paid and don't worry, I'll take care of the conflict of interest thing." The other person softly said,

"Thanks much." She recognized the voice as that of the other administrative official. She was very well aware of the university's strict conflict of interest policy, and it seemed unmistakable to her that the dean was helping the other official to violate it. She had hurried out of the dean's office suite badly shaken.

For a moment Stephen was stunned when he heard what she said. He faltered a little as he tried to think of what to say. "Marie, I am deeply disturbed about what you have told me. I have to think about what to do." She replied: "Professor Bernard, I didn't know whom to speak to about this. Please understand that I don't mean in the least to put you in a difficult position. I really don't expect you to do anything." After she left, he sank down in his desk chair and said to himself, "But I *have* to do something." There was a faculty meeting two days from then, and there was always a small amount of time at the end of the agenda for people to bring up additional items. After completing the specific items on the agenda—which were mundane, as usual—he raised his hand and, without giving the slightest indication that Marie had talked to him, he asked pointedly about the issue. The dean, who was presiding and who Stephen directed his questions at, literally stammered for a moment as he started to respond. He was obviously flustered by Stephen's questioning. He hesitated for a moment and looked quickly over the faculty who were all looking intently at him. He saw unmistakable looks of impatience and insistence that he answer Stephen. If his colleagues had lacked Stephen's courage to bring the subject up, the dean knew that they were now ready to back him up. Suddenly, he said, "Ladies and gentlemen, the meeting is over," and he began to step away from the podium. From the back of the room, one of Stephen's colleagues said in a firm, loud voice, "He's entitled to an answer. What do you have to say about this?" Other objections were voiced, and the room seemed to descend into near pandemonium. The dean scurried out, and instead of returning to his office headed for the parking lot. His action betrayed his dirty hands, almost as much as if he had admitted everything.

The next day, the buzz was circulating around the law school that the official connected with the consulting firm had resigned and that plans to move ahead with the new wing were going to be delayed. The day after that, when Stephen was at his other university in Ohio, the Pennsylvania university's student newspaper ran a front-page story about the episode in the law school. It reported that the university president had stepped in and ordered the planning stopped. The story also discussed how "Professor Stephen G. Bernard, of the law faculty, had investigated the suspicious situation in the law school and led the charge against the law school administration to make it come forth to admit their violations of the university's conflict of interest policy." One of Stephen's law school colleagues phoned him at his Ohio office that day to tell him about the story and the developments, including the further striking information that was going around the law school that the dean was also stepping down. He told Stephen, "It was your guts that did this. Everyone else was seething with anger over what was happening, but we were all afraid to say anything. We complain about a lot of things here, but we were unwilling to take on the dean." The colleague called Stephen back a short while later to tell him that a notice had just been placed on the faculty bulletin board officially announcing the dean's resignation, and saying that he would go on leave for the rest of the semester and then return to teaching. The expectation was that the senior member of the law faculty would be replacing him on an interim basis through the following academic year, and a search for a new dean would take place that following year. Stephen asked his colleague to read the whole university newspaper story to him. After he finished, Stephen was silent for a few moments. Then he said, "That story puffs me up in a way that is not true. It makes me look like a hero." The colleague said, "That's because you are. Don't worry about such things. The important thing is that the scheming is over with and these people are out."

Still, Stephen was troubled about the story and tried to call the editor of the university student newspaper, who had written it, to make clear to him that his role was more modest than suggested. He couldn't reach him and the young man did not call him back the next day, Friday. He resolved to go to see him when he returned to the law school campus on Monday. When Stephen got home that night, Marybeth rushed out the door as soon as she heard him get out of his car. "Did you see the Pittsburgh paper this afternoon?" He shook his head and looked at her with puzzlement. She was gripping it in her hand and pointed to one of the secondary stories on the first page. It was about the episode at the law school, and spoke about Stephen prominently. It actually seemed more objective about his role, although he figured that the city paper had picked up the story from the university paper. It made reference to sources on the law school faculty. Maybe they had made clear precisely what he had done, but still Stephen shined in the article.

As Stephen and Marybeth talked about the articles in the university and Pittsburgh newspapers over dinner that night, the phone rang. Stephen answered it and Jim O'Grady, the senior partner at the law firm with whom he had done much constitutional work, was on the

46

line. Jim was calling from Philadelphia, where he had been for a few days on legal business. They had not talked since the developments at the law school had started to unfold.

"I just thought I'd let you know that one of the main Philly evening news shows made a very brief mention of the affair at the law school and your name was included. There were things there I was wondering about, but not being a regular I didn't think it was my place to say anything. Congratulations on doing the right thing."

CHAPTER 3

First Foray Into Politics: A Different Kind Of Politician

O ne evening the next week, Stephen received a call from John Frost, who had been a major advisor to one of the Congressional candidates he had supported. The candidate lost, but Frost had continued his political work as a member of the state party committee and also as president of a new "good government" group with loose ties to the party. He told Stephen that the group was trying to recruit candidates for different offices for the party primaries the following year. "A lot of us on the state committee are fed up with the stuff that's been going on in Harrisburg and around the state. They are welcoming what our group is trying to do to recruit some different people to be candidates. It's really time for us to find people who haven't been in politics, people who are accomplished and who, of course, would do a good job—but also people of integrity. Your name was brought up by some of the people who know you from the campaigns in the western part of the state. With these news stories about what you did at your university, a couple of people on the state committee also asked me about you. People are wondering if you'd be interested in running for lieutenant governor next year."

Stephen was astounded that they would consider a political neophyte for a statewide office like that. After he recovered from the momentary shock, he stammered a slight bit as he said, "John, I know that the lieutenant governor candidate is nominated separately in the primary from the gubernatorial candidate, but won't the leading gubernatorial candidate still have a lot to say about it?"

"The state party often gets behind a slate, but next year's governor race seems like it's going to be wide open. I'm doubtful that the party will even endorse anyone in the primary," John replied.

"I am certainly honored that a number of you would think of me. I really don't know what to say. I'll have to think about it and talk to my wife." `

"Yes, talk about it. Can you get back to me by next week at this time?"

Stephen promised that he would. Stephen and his main adviser, Marybeth, talked and talked about it that entire evening. The next day, they exchanged several calls from their respective offices and then talked more at home in the evening. They also prayed together intently about it, and they devoted much of their individual prayer to it for the next couple of days. There was no disagreement between them about whether Stephen should put his hat into the ring. What they discussed was what his ground rules for campaigning and dealing with the party, the organizations that might back him, and the media would be. When Stephen called John Frost back, he set out for him what the conditions for his entering the race would be.

"John, I'm willing to enter the race and I would appreciate the support of your group and the other people who are interested in me. I welcome the support of other organizations. I would have to do this, however, in the way I want to do it. I have to be in charge of my own campaign. A lot of candidates say they want to talk about the issues, but I want to do more than that. I want people to *think* about the issues, and to do that I want to educate people about the realities behind the issues. I want to be independent. I want to be a candidate who comes forth from the people, to understand what is important to them, to be one of them. A big part of our problem is the elite, whose self-centeredness and convoluted way of thinking is wrecking havoc. 'The people' have their shortcomings, to be sure, but I have the conviction that the greater reservoir of strength is there even though on many things the elite has led them astray. I said I have to be independent. The only way I can do that is not to be financially beholden to anyone or any groups. If the price of having an office is to be indebted, then the office is not worth having. It needs to be a broad-based campaign, with the funding coming from the mass of people in small amounts. So, I would have to insist on a self-imposed campaign contribution limit of fifty dollars a person. We have to get a lot of small contributions from a lot of people. We can use the Internet and social media to do that; that has been the way other candidates have been able to do similar things. I also want to be out among the people, and I want to be able to shape the debate and not let others do it for me. If I am going to try to educate the public I have to have the time to speak at length to them. I would have no use for the typical sound-bite campaign. I want to do what Lawton

Chiles did in when he ran for the U.S. Senate in Florida around the time I was born: I want to walk across the state both from east to west and from north to south. I know Pennsylvania's a big state, but so was Florida. When I do that, I want to find places where I can literally set up a podium in public and talk to people the way I talk to my classes. The rest of the time I want to talk to the people right from my front porch. They might say it can't be done in the Media Age, but I think what's needed is a revival of the old front-porch campaign. Instead of my going to the media—who might not be too sympathetic with a lot of what I have to say—they can come to me. The people can come also, and they can hear it directly. That way, I don't have to speak substantially through the filter of the media, and they might be more faithful in reporting what I say. I know this sounds much outside the norm, but I assure you these are not the ravings of some idealistic academic—I actually don't have much use for the lack of realism of most academics—but it is really how I think it would be best to proceed. This is the kind of thing that is needed in our politics today."

John had been listening intently. He was impressed by the thoughtfulness of Stephen's comments, even though the thought of how realistic such an approach might be distinctly went through his mind. Still, in a way he was captivated by what Stephen said. He shared Stephen's belief that "politics as usual" had become the problem, and although he didn't possess the depth of Stephen's understanding about how current politics reflected an American civilizational crisis the reason he had gotten involved with politics himself was to try to do something about some of the social and moral problems he saw. "Stephen, our outfit is a 'good government' group and one concerned about traditional governmental principles, so I certainly understand what you're saying. However, I don't think it would be possible to run a statewide campaign in a big state like this on contributions of $50 and less."

"John," Stephen said resolutely, "I know it seems that way, but this is the way I would have to do it."

"Okay. We have a couple of people connected with the group who are real computer whizzes. They could be of some help in putting together the online contribution thing. They have helped a couple of Congressional candidates with that. I think that the meaning of what you say is that you don't want either well-heeled individuals or groups pouring money into your campaign." Stephen said emphatically that that was precisely what he meant. "You wouldn't need to shy away from getting endorsements—at least by small citizen groups like ours— or even getting some volunteer help from them. It also wouldn't hurt to meet with different groups and even with the state party committee, and different county committees for that matter, to let them know what you're about. It would also be a way to attract interested individuals to your campaign—to knock on doors and lick envelopes for you."

Stephen agreed. Then they discussed how he might launch his campaign. Stephen had already researched the procedures for filing for the office. The number of signatures to get on the ballot was not overwhelming: 1,000, with at least 100 from five different counties. They agreed that the first thing that should be done is to have a small meeting of the people who were pushing his candidacy and others they would bring who may also be interested and plans would be made to line up volunteers for the gathering of signatures. Stephen thought the way to actually kick off his campaign would be to send press releases to media outlets and a variegated assortment of organizations to invite them to his front porch, where he would make the announcement, set out his walking schedule for the state, and deliver his first campaign speech to set the tone for his candidacy. This would also begin the front-porch thrust for much of the rest of the campaign.

There was one other thing that Stephen said he would have to do if he were going to undertake this. Pennsylvania had passed a law a year before, which was motivated by the nastiness of recent campaigns in the state, which made it a misdemeanor to "misrepresent or distort the record of a political opponent during a campaign." Stephen had written a highly critical article about it when it was passed, saying it violated the First Amendment free speech clause and would easily be abused. He told John that he would file suit in federal court to get the law declared unconstitutional. He had to be strongly on the offensive in the campaign and there was no doubt in his mind that as a strong "anti-establishment" candidate he would evoke ugly opposition, which would claim he was violating the law in order to knock him out of the race.

"You know," John said, "that the media will say you're pushing a legal action like that just so you can be free to unfairly attack your opponent and lie about him."

"I'll be prepared for that. This is the way it has to be," Stephen replied.

"I knew you weren't going to be a typical political candidate."

This all was precisely how Stephen proceeded. Stephen secured the blank petitions and scheduled the meeting of supporters the one evening and the press conference on his front porch the next day. As with John Frost, the others interested in pushing Stephen's candidacy were indeed interested in a "good government" type of candidate. Arrangements were readily made with their groups and others they

brought to the meeting and additional people that Stephen invited—
who were connected with government integrity, pro-life, religious, pro-
family, and public morality groups—to strategically circulate the
petitions. It turned out, as Stephen expected, that securing the needed
signatures was not a problem, and the campaign was careful to get
many more than were required. Stephen did not want to have a
campaign manager; he was going to be in charge and it was going to be
a low-budget operation. John and another friend of his from one of the
Congressional campaigns agreed to be his ongoing, "close-in" advisers,
who he would be in contact with almost daily. Marybeth contacted the
media about the press conference and she would serve as his "press
attaché." She fit the bill for this well. She had extensive experience
dealing with media from her non-profit work and, in fact, for a period
of time had served as Communications Director for one of the
organizations. John's computer people quickly went to work on a
"user-friendly" fund-raising website and very quickly different groups
linked to it.

The number of media representatives at the press conference
surprised even Stephen and Marybeth. Stephen's name was familiar to
them because of the news stories about the law school. Stephen's
announcements of the front-porch campaign and walking the state
astounded them and obviously captivated their interest. They were
tiring of the monotony of so many run-of-the-mill candidates and
campaigns; they might find this one interesting to cover. That was
enhanced by the fact that they already had him etched in their minds as
a gutsy crusader. He emphasized that the recent corruption in state
politics was a significant reason for his entering the race, and that
people concerned about it both inside and outside the party had
encouraged him. He said that perhaps the most important issue
concerning government was the integrity of those in it. People were
easily compromised by the need for campaign contributions and the big
money that floated around in politics. That was why he would accept
only contributions up to a maximum of $50 from any one person. He
observed the looks of disbelief on their faces when he said that and they
noticeably scratched more intensely on their notebooks. That, he said,
was one reason for walking the state. He would not have to depend on
media and further people—average citizens—could contribute to his
campaign after he talked to them if they liked what he had to say. He
added that—with their absorption in his campaign financing statement
they missed the full implications of this—while political reform was
necessary, the real imperative was moral men—he said "men," not the
fashionable "people" of the post-feminist era—and one could not

53

expect high standards of public morality if there were not high standards of private morality or if it was believed that in certain matters there was not certain morality.

He said that in addition to walking the state, he would issue written analyses and position papers on numerous issues as time went on. He mentioned only a couple of the public issues he would be addressing, such as the excessive state tax burden and getting control over "runaway" state spending—caused by such things as excessive public education costs at all levels and the high state personnel costs. In the last part of his announcement Stephen turned to some political positions that he figured the media people would be none too sympathetic with, including "what's still the most crucial moral issue of our time in the U.S., abortion." They were unprepared for the professorial-like educative approach about them that he already was starting to take. Before stating his opposition to abortion, he provided a mini-biology lesson to the assembled journalists. He also, in a surprisingly terse but informative manner, discussed a range of adverse health consequences to women from abortion. That got their ear, especially in light of recent major news stories about two women dying and several others suffering serious side effects after abortions at three clinics in different parts of the state. Reports subsequently brought out how state regulators had paid little attention to the abortion clinics despite persistent complaints about grossly unsanitary conditions, personnel who had no medical credentials, careless procedures, and the pressuring of uncertain women into having abortions. After the Gosnell case, the state had gotten tougher for a while on monitoring the abortion clinics, then they seemed to back off and these latest episodes came to light. He next emphatically said that the "so-called" child-protective system in the state and nationally was "long-since out of control, spending most of its time chasing reports of child abuse and neglect that were without foundation and were intruding left and right into innocent families." There was a "widespread belief that the system and child welfare policies generally needed drastic reform, but no one wants to lift a finger to do anything about it." He provided another nutshell teaching lesson about this, which the media people listened closely to since they knew nothing about it. Also, he said he would be making a defense of traditional marriage—he emphatically called it "true marriage"—and also be attacking gender theory throughout the campaign. The Supreme Court's decision on same-sex "marriage" was unconstitutional, he said, and in no way could anyone say this was a closed issue and "we should just move on." The Court's abuse of power would have to be addressed by the other branches, but leading state officials should put up the drumbeat to do something about it. Gender theory was destructive, and it was "maniacal" that people thought that one's sex was something that one could just choose "like the flavor of an ice cream cone that he wanted." He attacked some courts in the state for ordering school districts and private companies and stores to permit people use whatever public restroom they want, and thus put women and girls in jeopardy from potential sexual predators and voyeurists. He said it was "pathetic" that the other party went along with whatever the homosexualist movement forked up, the latest thing of which was transgenderism. He also pointed out that a few of their elected officials in Pennsylvania and elsewhere were "astonishingly" beginning to call for the decriminalization of pedophilia "if somehow there was consent." He also faulted his own party for seeming to be increasingly mum and on the defensive about all this, some of their members in the state legislature even counseling not to appeal the state court restroom decisions. The media people initially seemed ready to pull out their figurative knives after he started talking about marriage, homosexualism, and transgenderism, but his pedophilia point caused them to pull back. Even they were embarrassed that the political left, which they normally identified with, had begun to advocate this. Stephen deftly had juxtaposed these different issues, to make people face how they were related. When a reporter asked Stephen about the gender identity issue during the short question period after he finished speaking, he said that "government—whether it be legislatures or courts—could not change the nature of marriage or the reality of someone's sex any more than it could decree that two plus two equals five." Then he proceeded to provide another brief educational lesson about the folly of this and what it would likely lead to. He also told him to keep following the campaign for his ongoing discourse about how trying to transform marriage and embrace homosexualism would hurt the entire culture, with the full consequences manifesting themselves only after years. Along with these "hot-button issues," Stephen talked very perceptively and intelligently in his remarks about fiscal and tax questions in the state. This, plus Stephen's heavy-duty academic credentials and his way of raising hot-button issues, made it difficult for the media to just dismiss him as a "right-wing crank" and even made them want to hear him out.

Another reporter asked him what his schedule to walk the state would be. It was then past mid-May, and he said it would start within the next two weeks. His academic schedule would permit him to do this full-time through the summer. During the fall, when he was back teaching, he would focus on the front-porch campaign. During his walk, in addition to seeking the small citizen monetary contributions, he would try to get campaign volunteers wherever he went. He would work to build up his campaign organization during the entire time. He said that volunteers knocking on doors and making phone calls locally—not the increasingly used (and, he thought, annoying) robocalls from some central location—would be as important to his success as his walk of the state and front-porch efforts. He said, "Ladies and gentlemen, as you can see, this is definitely going to be a grass-roots campaign—a campaign close to the people of the Commonwealth and communicating directly with them and listening to them."

Then, at the end of the press conference, he provided the *coup de grâce* (it would turn out that his instinctive sense of timing would be illustrated repeatedly in the years of campaigning and political life ahead). He informed his listeners that he was preparing papers to file in federal court against the state's law on distorting a political opponent's record and he explained why he thought this would readily be abused. That caused a real buzz among the media representatives. Some editorialists around the state had criticized the law when it was passed as threatening free speech, and a few newspapers claimed it was another "incumbent protection" law—like campaign finance laws—that would be used by incumbent officeholders to insure that their records would not be closely scrutinized. The state ACLU had criticized the law on free speech grounds. Until now, however, no politician had challenged it in court.

Stephen got the sense at the end of the press conference that the media representatives' heads were almost spinning as they got their first exposure to this utterly unconventional candidate.

That evening and the next day the media around the state, and even elements of the national media, ran stories that mostly talked about the type of campaign that this "political unknown" or "political neophyte" was running statewide. It was something, many of them said, that Pennsylvania was not used to. Several editorialists commended him for not taking money from organized interests or wealthy movers-and-shakers. This particularly struck a chord in light of the financial scandals that had rocked the state's politics. They wondered, though, if this would work in a big, usually media-driven state like Pennsylvania. Many talked of his planned lawsuit, which attracted such comments as "new political crusader in a corrupt state" and "Bernard has moved from cleaning up his law school to trying to clean up the state." A few stories talked about him as "an anti-abortion candidate," and one said he was "apparently a new crusader for traditional values from the

56

unlikeliest of places, the academy." These latter assessments were meant to be critical, but they mostly had the effect of coalescing early support for him from people in the pro-life and pro-family movements who were not previously familiar with him. The state's leading homosexualist newspaper called him "a threat," but basically dismissed the "political upstart" as having little chance to win.

Stephen filed his case just before Memorial Day weekend, although it was unlikely that the court would take it up until early in the fall. His walk of the state began on that weekend. His routine was to walk two weeks and then take a week off throughout the summer, when he would rent a car and drive back to the Pittsburgh area and then reverse this and after the off-week drive back to where he left off with the walk. He was in daily phone contact with Marybeth, and on Fridays of on-weeks she drove to his current location to join him in the campaign walk on the weekends. He started right in his backyard of western Pennsylvania. He started walking in Mount Morris near the West Virginia border. He progressed up U.S. Route 19, which ran parallel to Interstate 79, visiting communities of all sizes all the way north to the City of Erie on Lake Erie. Marybeth and his incipient all-volunteer campaign committee headed by John Frost sent advance notices to the media in the different locales announcing his projected arrival, based upon his regular mobile phone contact with them. When he was within twenty minutes or so of actually setting foot in a particular locale, he sent a text message on his smartphone to the local or nearby media outlets that they had previously contacted to let them know of his arrival time and point of entry. He had bookmarked detailed road and street maps of each town on the smartphone—which seemed virtually necessary for him to carry on this statewide walk effectively and efficiently. If Route 19 was the main street through a particular town, he just followed it. If not, he quickly got onto the main business street. He had two changes of clothes that he carried in a small backpack, along with a few thousand business cards that he would have available to leave with people he met as he saw fit. His three shirts were all golf shirts on which he had had "Stephen Bernard for Lt. Governor" monogrammed near the pocket. His trousers were thin long summer pants. He also packed a small collapsible umbrella. The backpack had the same thing monogramed across it in large, clear letters whose color contrasted with that of the backpack so it could readily be read. He also wore a name badge under the monogram on the shirts that said "I'm Stephen Bernard." When he drove back on off-weeks or connected up with Marybeth he got more of the business cards and usually fresh sets of clothes with the same monogramming. He spent his nights either in the homes of prospective supporters that John had lined up for him or else in budget motels. Almost nightly, he washed his clothes. He avoided campaigning on Sundays when it was an on-the-road week and Marybeth was with him. They drove to the nearest Sunday Mass and spent the rest of the day enjoying each other's company and took time for prayer together. He persistently prayed for strength to face this challenging undertaking. In addition to his clothes, personal items, business cards, and a notebook, he carried in his backpack a small New Testament and a different small book of spiritual reading, which he switched every other week when he returned home. He had a rosary in his pocket, which he prayed frequently when between towns. Whenever he could, he went to daily Mass before beginning the day's trek.

He walked through one community after another. He walked up to whoever he saw on the sidewalks and said, "Hi, I'm Stephen Bernard. I'm running for Lieutenant Governor of Pennsylvania." Whenever people seemed particularly interested, he would ask them about what they thought about the politics of the state and what they thought were the major problems confronting the state and their communities and their biggest concerns. He often spent much more time listening than he did talking, although frequently people asked him about his views on various issues or what he would propose to do about different problems. He sometimes got into extended conversations that attracted a small group, right in the middle of a sidewalk. While he stressed listening, and used his notebook to jot down both people's thoughts (as well as the names and contact information of prospective volunteers), he always kept in mind the educative function of politics—those seeking to lead were not supposed to be blindly whipped along by the opinions encountered in the public. They were also supposed to help shape thinking. At a deeper level, he knew that the true statesman is one who has a moral vision and, while aware of the difficulties that often presented themselves in navigating the ship of state toward it, he must make the effort to try to help people see that vision and the ways it can be attained. He learned about this from his extensive studies, but now for the first time he was in the position to try to apply it.

One topic that frequently came up, especially in the bigger communities like Washington, Erie, and certainly Pittsburgh was crime. People often didn't know about the crucial role the Pennsylvania lieutenant governor played in the state's criminal justice system as Chairman of the Board of Pardons. Many of his natural supporters tended to be "tough-on-crime" people. He tried to give people a broader picture of the subject, raising the problems of the criminal justice system and—especially when people said that "the problem was the government coddling criminals"—explaining the importance of constitutional protections and how there was a significant problem of people falsely accused and convicted of crimes, even serious ones. He also invoked St. Augustine of Hippo about how it is perhaps better to err of the side of mercy with criminals—instead of simply "throwing the book" at them—to try to encourage them to correct themselves and put their lives on the right path (and ultimately to get themselves right before they face God at judgment). This was especially important for those who were younger and had not committed serious crimes. He knew that prison would often harden men—and women—and make it even more likely that they would become habitual criminals afterwards. He cautioned about making deterrence the major concern of the criminal justice system. Justice, he said, always had to be kept foremost in mind, and inordinate punishments—supposedly for the sake of deterrence—could not be just. Nor did he think they conformed to the Constitution's proscription of "cruel and unusual" punishment. He reminded people that the U.S. Supreme Court had to finally overcome its reluctance and declare in some cases that the punishments imposed were disproportionate to the offense committed. "Three strikes you're out" laws, which some people touted to him, were good examples of this. In the end, it also wasn't so clear—with massive rates of recidivism in the state—that harsh punishments even had such a clear deterrent effect. He kept stressing that the problem was that "people's souls were out of order," and the aim had to be to put *them* in order. This didn't necessarily mean that current schemes of "rehabilitation" were to be embraced, which typically featured flawed conceptions of human nature. He said that something like the Alcoholics Anonymous approach, which recognized that a spiritual commitment was needed for change to occur, would be much more reliable. He also stressed that the protections of the Bill of Rights applied to criminals as well as the innocent and that police had to be properly trained so they would know them. He even went a step farther than almost any politician by what he said about the police. The typical politician, afraid of being tagged as "soft-on-crime" and incurring the wrath of the police unions, went out of his way to express a "rah-rah" attitude about the police. Stephen, on the other hand, said they had to be carefully selected from the ranks of "morally-straight," self-restrained individuals. They should arrest only as a last resort and should return to the nineteenth-century practice of being something like social workers as well as law enforcers. Service and connecting well with their communities should be stressed, and with that would come the rebuilding of respect for the police that many had lost. He made clear, however, that none of this in the least justified the frequent, random violent attacks on police in recent years. He condemned these in the strongest terms.

When the media following his campaign—who, both because of the simple advance work and the initial attention given to this unconventional candidate, did so with surprising frequency—beheld such dialogues with average citizens, they were further engrossed. Unlike the politicians they were used to, who slapped hands, said a few words about how great they were, pandered to people, and then moved on, he took time for discussions. He spoke like the professor he was, but seemed to have a way of engaging people, keeping them in the conversation, and always respecting them. They also were taken aback at how his thinking on issues like this one didn't fit so easily into predetermined political categories. The reports initially scoffed at his talking about things like the soul, but then he began to make gentle sidebar explanations—directed mostly to the media people—about why there is a soul. It seemed to be Aristotle for everyone, spoken at a very basic, understandable level. Some of the media people took a few minutes to listen, even after they had gotten their taped segments for the evening news. This was something they had never heard during their college educations—which, of course, illustrated how the liberal arts had almost evaporated.

Related to crime was the gun question. Gun control had never been a popular position in Pennsylvania, but in the cities people sometimes thought that gun availability helped contribute to the crime problem. He emphasized the Second Amendment and what he specifically called people's "natural right" to self-defense. He tried to reintroduce into the public discussion natural law and natural rights whenever he could, and followed up with an understandable explanation of them: natural law was a higher law, that governed man by his very nature, and there were rights that were part of it so man could do the things he needed to do, and it was a central part of what our Founding Fathers believed and placed at the foundation of the Constitution and our country's political life. The police often could not get someplace quickly enough, so it had to be acknowledged that people should have a right to protect themselves. He stressed two other points, however: the gun-owner had to be well-trained, responsible, and restrained and guns were not the ultimate solution to crime. Moral formation, right ordering of the soul, was. This meant restoring strong family life, within sound and lasting marriages. The father was particularly important in that, since so many people—especially young men, who get in trouble with the law come from a background where a father was absent. This meant, of course, that marriage had to be between a man and a woman. The media that picked up on this mostly scoffed at him, of course, but sometimes thought for an extra moment because a connection between crime and what he called "natural" marriage hadn't occurred to them. He also said that the restoration of traditional religion in people's lives was critical, since most people get their moral formation—the absence of which was profoundly evident in so many criminals—from religion. This gave him the further opportunity to talk about how important religion was in the political thinking of the Founders and to explain how Alexis de Tocqueville—who he often introduced people to for the first time—had said that while there was complete religious freedom in America, many sects, and no state church nevertheless religion was the "first" of the country's institutions. While the media similarly was inclined to scoff about this, they again took a moment to listen. They hadn't before heard a politician giving a civics lesson like this.

Especially in the western half of Pennsylvania, environmental and energy-development questions often came up. That part of the state was in the thick of oil and natural gas exploration by means of hydraulic fracturing ("fracking"). He impressed people with his ready command of facts about it and reasonable assessment of the ecological implications. He always stressed the need to be knowledgeable about this or any activity involving the environment, avoiding knee-jerk kinds of reactions and slippage into an ideologically driven perspective, respect for property-owners' rights both with respect to energy companies and governmental actions, and that making sweeping judgments about all companies on the basis of the actions of some was not appropriate. Some individual companies and managers may be more trustworthy and reliable in taking account of environmental concerns than others. Government certainly had to act to protect the common bounty of physical nature that concerned all citizens—he always used the term "good stewardship"—but it could often work with the private sector instead of automatically casting itself as its adversary.

He often encountered questions about education. Some said that more money had to be given to public education. He brought up the fact that research had consistently shown that there was no necessary connection between the money poured into school systems—per pupil expenditures and the like—and good academic performance. He also criticized the educational spokesmen and even the courts in some places in the country for saying that parents had no control over their children's education once they decided to put them into the public schools. Education, he said, was fundamentally a parental right and when parents chose to delegate it to a school—public or otherwise—it still was a partnership. That, and not a "schools know better" attitude,

61

was the proper spirit to bring to education. He used the opportunity in discussions with people about education to introduce to them the principle of subsidiarity: how in the nature of things, it's best to do them at the level closest to the people. That generally insured that an activity would be done more efficiently and effectively, and would insure better morale by those most involved in carrying it out (in the case of education, teachers). So, he opposed more control of education from the state capital, superseding the wishes of the school district. Even the individual school should have much freedom to carry on its educational efforts as possible. As he talked about a partnership with parents, however, he made clear how important parental *responsibility* was. It was another thing that got him to talking about the need to strengthen and indeed rebuild the family. When someone complained that the schools were not preparing young people adequately for the job world, he responded that he sympathized since often they came out weak on basic intellectual skills, but began to engage people about the question of the purpose of education. He did it, as in his discussions about other issues, in a way that the man in the street could follow and be motivated to think about. Was there a higher purpose? Was it especially important for those who would be leaders in different realms? He made a connection between education and morality that was all but lost for most people. He also suggested to them that what might be appropriate in terms of job preparation was another kind of partnership. Companies and businesses of different kinds should not just look to the public schools—even vo-tech schools—to prepare their future employees. This was partly, most fundamentally, their responsibility. It was another question of responsibility: they had to step up to once again assume that responsibility. The schools could arrange for their students in the later grades to get strictly on-the-job training that could count for their graduation credit, or something along those lines.

While some of the editorialists were clamoring for new ethics laws and tighter campaign spending rules as a response to the recent corruption in Harrisburg, Stephen told people who brought it up that we had plenty of laws and they didn't solve the problem and just made campaigning and public service more difficult for good people. He used the law he was challenging in court as a good example of that. What was needed was that morally upright, strong, courageous, and self-limiting people would go into politics, but leave after a reasonable time. We needed a "new era of citizen politicians," he said. Occasionally, he met someone who blurted out that all politics was dirty and no politicians could be trusted. As a result, they were uninterested in politics. He told them he could understand how they would think that, but he went on to try to engage them about the importance of citizen involvement and the assumption of citizen responsibilities to make "dirty politics" less likely. He also talked about the fundamental obligations of the public official, starting with integrity. Once more, he underscored the theme of responsibility.

Whenever Stephen's walk brought him to county seats, he was sure to stop in at the county headquarters to meet the local party officials and regular workers. Almost always they wanted to converse with him, sometimes over lunch or a snack. He exchanged business cards with them and tried to learn as much as he could from them about the party and the politics of the county. After he left their offices, he always pulled out his notebook to jot down from his sharp memory the major points they had made.

Occasionally, John Frost's friends who were his hosts arranged to have small groups of people, usually local party activists, over to their houses to have them meet the candidate, converse, and listen to a short impromptu talk by him. His ability to gently engage people in a topic, often involving dimensions of it that they had hardly thought of, resulted in many of them leaving the meetings at party offices and these other get-togethers with a smile on their faces and thinking that this was a pretty interesting candidate.

In Pittsburgh, Stephen received a lot of media attention since the law school episode was fresh in people's minds. The media reported two encounters he had there with hostile individuals that could have hurt him, but he thought in advance how he could use them to his advantage in getting across a needed message. He wanted to talk about the abortion issue and was making clear that abortion was gravely immoral and could be permitted in no cases. The expected pro-abortion response would be to gloss over the fact that only about 2% of abortions in the U.S. are for the "hard cases" of life or health of the mother, rape, incest, or fetal deformity. They often like to fixate on these to characterize abortion opponents as "callous and unfeeling" or something like that and to gain a rhetorical advantage. He decided to go right to the "belly of the beast" and arranged a small rally and press conference right next to the campus of the arch-secular University of Pittsburgh there. He even made sure that the rally was publicized on the campus, which set the tone for his political life of engaging not just the uncertain common man who hadn't thought about certain issues, but encouraging dialogues with avowed opponents. He got up at the rally and stated his position and began to mention facts such as the small number of abortions for hard cases, the biological realities of

63

embryonic and fetal life, and the logical arguments. He also arranged two pro-life activist women whom he had gotten to know well in Pittsburgh, one who was informed during her pregnancy that her child had Down's syndrome and despite being aggressively urged by her physician to abort refused to do so. The other became pregnant after being viciously raped by a serial rapist, who was being sought by the police. They both gave passionate and deeply moving testimonies that left even some of the ardent pro-abortion feminist students in the crowd overwhelmed and uncertain about what to say when they tried to object.

The media may not have wanted to report on something that cast such a negative picture on the abortion liberty, but they weren't in a position to refuse. It turned out that one of the local television stations ran a short segment of one of the women's talks and the main Pittsburgh newspaper did a short feature article on the other one. While the women's experiences were their focus, they didn't fail to mention that the context was Stephen's campaign rally and he appeared momentarily in the television report.

The other Pittsburgh episode concerned a confrontation he had with a black woman, a community activist who was tied in closely with the other party. She showed up as he walked through one of the black neighborhoods in the city with two black ministers whom he had gotten to know from pro-life efforts. She said that he was too concerned about abortion and not enough about people who were born, and that he wanted to cut state and federal government programs that would "hurt poor and black people." He responded by providing her much information about how poor people kept getting government aid, but still remained poor. He also mentioned the notorious inefficiency of governmental programs, with their high overhead to pay the ever-increasing salaries and benefits of public employees. He kept pressing her, politely—with the almost infectious smile that he was becoming known for—but insistently, to say if she thought that government dependency was a good thing and if she truly believed that government was the only way to help people. Finally, she pulled back and said, "What other way is there?" He proceeded to tell her about building up the private non-profit sector—civil society organizations—so that government could gradually withdraw from social welfare programs, except when no one else would be available to assist. When government definitely had to do something, it should be at the level closest to the people because it would better know localized situations and problems and the variety of nuances that would be present. What government's role should be would be to encourage and help build up the civil society sector and coordinate the efforts in various ways and insure that true needs be identified. He also said that the ultimate aim always had to be to make people responsible for themselves—unless they were, say, chronically ill and unable to work or take care of themselves—and that involved perhaps changing attitudes. The alternative was ongoing dependency, being bound to government, and the loss of freedom. Further, he said, there is a connection between the compromising of freedom by government dependency, the imperviousness to the humanity of the unborn in abortion, and the increasing readiness to let the elderly and infirm die instead of providing them proper medical treatment or even in some cases food and water—they all debased human dignity and the things that gave value to a person. He asked her why she would oppose this and invited her to instead give up the political positions she espoused and join him in supporting human dignity across the board. He repeated this again, then a third time. She began to stammer a response, but obviously was taken aback. The ministers then expressed support for what he said. Stephen made sure he interjected his points enough into the discussion so local news programs could not just make it sound like he was put on the defensive by her initial accusation. They actually wound up running part of his repeated gentle challenges to her.

After Stephen spent time in Erie, he followed state Route 8 through the communities in the northwestern part of the state, such as Titusville and Oil City, where the Pennsylvania Oil Rush of the 1800s had taken place. He turned onto U.S. 322 a short distance south of Oil City. The most sizable community he was heading for was State College, the home of Penn State University. While mostly rural, this part of the state had been the home to light industry that had mostly left since the 1990s. It had experienced the same manufacturing downturn that the rest of western Pennsylvania had, but was hit harder because of its smaller population and lesser economic diversification. When he met people there who asked about what he would do about their economic problems unlike many politicians he admitted that he did not have a program, but mentioned two things: lower taxes—lowering the percentage of the state's flat income tax—usually tended to stimulate economic activity, and every area needed to look to its particular strengths and try to build from them. It had long troubled him that as the decades went on in America, people had more and more lost control over their economic destiny.

In one of the old, small industrial communities in that part of the state, a retired small businessman told him during the course of a conversation about the troubled local economic situation about a young family who lived down the street from him and his wife. The husband had been working with a local forestry company, but had become incapacitated by an unusual early-in-life heart problem. The family was struggling with mounting medical bills—once he had to leave his job he lost company health insurance benefits, and they couldn't afford a non-employer policy—and had been unable to keep up payments on their modest house and were about to lose it. The wife had gotten a part-time job, but it didn't pay much and working was difficult for her because they had young children. "It's a sad case, " he said. "I know that a lot of the young people these days aren't go-getters, but they were the hardest-working young people I've ever known. I've gotten to know them well. They are trying to help them out some at their church, but people here don't have a lot of extra money." Before they ended their conversation, Stephen got contact information from the retired businessman. Afterwards, he called Marybeth. She arranged for an intermediary to get in touch with the man to say that a husband and wife who wished to remain anonymous wanted to provide the family with financial help, and asked him to arrange it. He agreed that he would do that. Again, the condition of the husband and wife giving the help was that they had to remain anonymous. That husband and wife, of course, were Stephen and Marybeth.

As Stephen approached State College, he saw a large billboard along the side of U.S. Route 322 that said "God Is Imaginary—Don't Pretend." He later learned that in north-central Pennsylvania, which was a most unlikely place to see such sentiments, there were a number of billboards with that identical message. He later learned that a small businessman from one of the towns, who had long been know for lambasting religion (including regular letters to different newspapers in that part of the state), was responsible. It was thought that he had received financial assistance from an avowed secularist organization in another part of the country that went around threatening cash-strapped local governments with lawsuits whenever they in the least bit made an expression favorable to religion, or even when they allowed citizens to engage in religious expression on public property. They were currently engaged in a couple of well-publicized lawsuits to stop local governments from renting municipal auditoriums to congregations to have religious services and even other meetings in them—they were arguing that even if other organizations could meet in them, churches and religious organizations could not.

When he arrived in State College, a small crowd that he quickly discerned to be hostile met him. It looked like most were college students, but there were a few middle-aged types among them. He sensed that one or two were college professors. He knew the type well: leftist, activist professors who became a magnet for similarly inclined students. One middle-aged man began to verbally challenge Stephen as soon as he got close. "So you think the country is religious." He obviously had read something in the press about one of the position papers that Stephen had released, in which he had talked about the Christian religious culture of earlier America and both the contemporary Supreme Court's flawed understanding of the First Amendment establishment clause and the heightening threats to religious liberty. "The country isn't religious and never was. We're a pluralist country. If religious ideas are allowed into our politics we'll lose our freedom. Religion has been the cause of war. And what about all those people who claimed to be religious but oppressed people and even had slaves? Besides nobody can prove there's a God, or angels or devils or anything like that! That's why I put up all those billboards." It was the unbelieving businessman that Stephen had heard about.

Stephen answered him gently, but clearly and directly. He began to mention the religious characteristics of early American culture and mentioned about what Tocqueville had said about religion and America. He also began to refer to what several of the Founding Fathers had said about the essentiality of religious belief for a political society, but especially one that wanted to remain free. The man kept interrupting Stephen, but Stephen responded in an even tone (he was remarkable for "keeping his cool" in such situations and not allowing his voice to rise). "I'm sure that in the interest of free discussion you'll let me finish my point." The man continued to interrupt, but Stephen, in an insistent but even-keeled manner kept repeating that. Then, as he picked up on another of the objections to religion that the man raised, the man began to relent. Stephen's combination of strength—he had an uncanny ability to take control of a situation—and kindness and considerateness began to make itself felt.

"You are right that sometimes people have gone to war about religion, and that sometimes religious people—including Christians—have oppressed people. Maybe that's because the people weren't as good Christians as they should have been. As far as wars are concerned—even what are called wars of religion—I'm sure you know that historically many different causes have actually often been behind them. The twentieth century was history's bloodiest, and the forces that were mostly behind that were anything but traditionally religious. They were proponents of modern ideologies—which became substitute, man-generated and man-centered religions—and disdained what we usually call religion. You mentioned slavery. It was pervasive in the ancient

67

world, which was primarily pagan. The Roman Stoics began to challenge the morality of slavery; in some respects they took us to the threshold of Christianity. If you look back on it historically, slavery started to disappear as Christianity began to take root in European culture. It only reasserted itself later in modern times after the religious turmoil that tore Europe apart and caused much confusion in men's thinking. It cannot be called something that was simply supported by Christianity. Let's not forget that it was Christians, both in Europe and in America, who led the opposition to slavery once it had reappeared. You are concerned about pluralism, but America has made religious pluralism work better than probably any country in the world. A country that stresses the need for religion, even in the public arena, is not necessarily headed for some kind of renewed intolerance. It is possible to believe in truth, even religious truth, and still practice civility, which has its root in the greatest of the Christian virtues, charity. You say that there is no God and no spiritual world. If, on the other hand, it's *moral* pluralism that you are calling for, that is a recipe for disaster—and you better understand the implications of that, which would mean that no one truly could then judge such things as racism and genocide to be evil." He knew that such practices were not the kinds of things that even the proponents of moral relativism were ready to defend. "Please don't say that condemning such things comes about just because this is the general agreement of people or civilization. That general view could easily change, and has throughout history about many things—including, again, slavery. The general view of people is not a very solid basis to ground beliefs on, and if you take this view what truly can you say to affirm the certainty and correctness of a moral position even on these things? About the existence of God and spiritual things, keep in mind that Aristotle proved this by natural reasoning—he had no benefit of Revelation—including even the existence of the realm that we call the angelic. When you reject religion and claim it isn't based on reality, you have a lot of things you have to explain away." Then he made an appeal, as he often did to people such as this, on a personal level to try to get them to look critically at the problematic positions they embraced and to consider how the views they spurn and even sometimes hate might help them. "Why don't you give religion a chance? It might just have many good things for you that you are missing out on."

The man scoffed. Stephen was not surprised. He was a very tough nut to crack. As he quickly looked at the faces of the others in the small crowd, he slightly detected that one or two—the students—had fallen silent and they betrayed just a slight look of uncertainty about what they were doing. It was almost as if they had never heard the things he was saying. As today's typical college students, Stephen thought, they probably actually hadn't. Then he turned his attention to one of the other individuals in the group.

This young man stood out readily. His clothing had an outrageous quality to it, his hair was combed in an obviously feminine manner, and he wore lipstick. It was almost as if he was fixed up to march in a "gay rights" parade. Stephen had no doubt that this was deliberate. He wanted to confront Stephen when he came into State College in an "in your face" manner. He also carried a sign that said, "Why do you hate gays?" Stephen remembered reading that the homosexualist movement had started to employ a strategy of trying to confront and embarrass candidates on the stump who were not in agreement with their agenda, even those who deviated just a bit. Their aim was to create whatever bad press they could for them to hurt their campaigns. He figured this was one of those schemes, especially since he had emphasized his opposition to same-sex "marriage," transgenderism, and the like from the start. He had also mentioned on different occasions that even before its outrageous decision on same-sex "marriage" the U.S. Supreme Court had "invented" what was essentially a constitutional right to sodomy—"that no such thing truly existed." The way Stephen decided to address him showed his embracing of the Christian notion that one had to speak the truth in charity, but also that in his campaign and in the broader context of the "culture wars" there was no substitute for being on the offensive. Most politicians shied away from that, but Stephen saw that the issues were much larger than just winning an election.

"You speak about hate, but are you sure that you members of the homosexualist movement are not the ones who are hating? Why do you try to just shut down everyone who disagrees with you in the least way? Why have you moved to harass people who contributed a few dollars to state referenda and organizations opposing your view of marriage? Why have you brought legal actions against elderly couples running beds and breakfasts because they won't rent a room to couples, same and opposite-sex, who want to have sex outside the context of what everyone knows is real marriage? Why won't you even stand up and debate, and try to seriously defend your position? Why do you shy away from that, and just use strong-arm tactics of different kinds to force people not just to tolerate you, but to positively endorse everything that you do? Why are you being a totalitarian?"

The young man could come back with only, "You hate gays." Stephen persisted with what he had left off with. "Why are you being a totalitarian? Why are you suppressing others? Why will you not let them freely speak and think?" He reasoned that if he kept pounding away at the basic points, they could not avoid being noticed—especially by the media and thus the broader public. He was also emphatic that he would not allow others, especially cultural and political adversaries, to set the terms of the discussion. Again, the young man said, "Why do you hate us?" Stephen countered, "Your movement wants to suppress people who oppose what you stand for, and you do it viciously. Are you sure you are not the ones hating? Why are you being a totalitarian? Why are you being a totalitarian?" The young man had become emotional and his voice had elevated almost to a shout, but Stephen was nonplussed and his voice stayed at a conversational level even while he made sure what he said was pointed and distinct. A young woman reporter who was standing to the side, who Stephen had noticed as he was walking up to the group had been interviewing some of them, showed a confused look. She wasn't sure what to do with this. Some other media people from a local television station had since arrived, and Stephen continued. He tried to mix his "being on the offensive" stance with his firm conviction of having to carry out an educative function of politics and incorporating a personal approach. He thought that this was particularly important here because he knew that deep down most people with same-sex attraction problems were hurting badly. The anger exhibited by the homosexualist political movement was, in fact, in part a displaced anger about themselves and their situation. Stephen asked him pointedly but gently, "Why do you want to persist in behavior and living in a way where you are almost certain to hurt yourself physically? It is not inevitable that you have to do that. Do you think this is the proper way to treat your body? You are capable of better. You are obviously not happy. Why don't you take your life in a different direction?" He responded, "How can you say that I'm not happy? Besides, I am what I am." "You don't seem at all happy, even if a political movement tries to tell you otherwise. A movement does not control you. Don't be hesitant to think for yourself, to make yourself truly a free person. You're not stuck being what you say you are. There may be a way out. At least, you can be in control and responsible for your actions." The young man protested more, and others from the crowd started to ridicule Stephen's remarks. Stephen thought it was time to move along. He said to the group, "I'll be happy to publicly debate any of you at any time, but the debate has to be civil and focused on the issues and the arguments." They kept making noise, but Stephen turned one final time to the young man who he sensed despite his clamor was really anguished. "Contact me if you think I can help you."

It was Friday when Stephen arrived in State College and Marybeth drove there and the two returned to the Pittsburgh area. The people he confronted didn't represent everyone in State College. He received a number of campaign contributions from other people he met in the area. All told, he returned with nearly a thousand dollars in contributions from the preceding week. He also garnered about two-dozen campaign volunteers from the north-central part of the state. When he was back home, he called John Frost who gave him a gleaming progress report. His computer guys had succeeded in raising nearly $40,000 in contributions of $50 and less. It was their biggest fund-raising week yet.

"Your walking effort is beginning to attract attention around the state. Just yesterday there was a story about it in the Philadelphia *Inquirer*, complete with a picture of you walking—I think when you were in Erie." Stephen remembered some media people snapping pictures of him in Erie. "We think this will generate even more contributions. Your natural conservative supporters are stepping up, but we're also hearing from people—just grassroots people—who aren't necessarily conservative or religious activists who are contributing because they think you're an interesting and different kind of candidate. The fifty-dollar thing has impressed some, and they are stepping up to help you because they figure you aren't a candidate of the big-money types." When Stephen told him about his own fund-raising along the walk he was even more enthusiastic. "As far as the activists are concerned, they are increasingly getting involved. They know where you stand and they want to support you. It's a surprise that even some of the party people are saying that you might just be a strong candidate. Your making a point to stop to talk to the party leaders when you go through the county seats is a plus." They talked about plans to disseminate several more of Stephen's position papers over the next two weeks. The people in charge of getting them to the media were John and Marybeth, and John's computer people disseminated them through their email and social media networks.

"By the way, speaking about the media, I hear that the Pittsburgh *Tribune-Review* wants to interview you. That could be helpful. Their editorial line is a bit more receptive to candidates who stand for the things that you do. I hope it goes well." Stephen asked him to say a prayer about it, since one can never be sure what will happen with the media. Marybeth had arranged for a phone interview on Saturday morning. The reporter asked a lot about a couple of his position papers, but when the article ran in Sunday's edition—a choice edition for a feature story—the storyline went mostly like this: "Bernard cleaned up the law school and now aims to clean up state government." Its stress was on the fact that here was finally a citizen politician whose strict fund-raising regimen showed that he would be beholden only to the public and to principles of clean, ethical government.

Further, the *Centre Daily Times* from State College, whose reporters were present when Stephen had his exchange with the atheist and the homosexual activist, ran a short story that went much better than he might have expected. While they might have been inclined to give him a rough time because of his opposition to the homosexualist movement, they could not help but pick up on his confronting the young activist about its suppression of the opposition. They particularly mentioned his use of the term "totalitarian." It's possible that they thought that they could make him look extreme by that. As it turned out, the whole report touched a nerve. Newspapers and even some of the electronic media around the state and even beyond picked it up. Stephen immediately received a flood of messages from people who applauded him for his comments and said they were happy to see a politician who finally was willing to face down the "gay rights" movement. They said that they were tired of the movement trampling on people, and had seen enough of it. It also resulted in a further uptick, almost immediately, of people from different parts of the state who wanted to volunteer for his campaign. He also heard from various Christian and orthodox Jewish clergy who had increasingly perceived themselves to be on the defensive. There was even some informal political pressure on them to perform same-sex "weddings," in spite of the fact that such a thing would have been an outrageous assault on religious liberty.

As Stephen resumed his "Walk of the Commonwealth," as some in the media were calling it, the following week, he next headed northeast along Pennsylvania Route 64 through such small communities as Lemont, Zion, Lamar, Cedar Springs, Mill Hall, and Flemington, and then to Lock Haven, site of another, much smaller state university. For much of this stretch, Route 64 ran parallel to Interstate 80, the major coast-to-coast highway that was referred to as the "Keystone Shortway" as it traversed the mostly mountainous region of northern Pennsylvania. From Lock Haven, he followed U.S. 220 through Avis, Jersey Shore, Williamsport (the largest community on this part of the walking route), Loyalsock, and Montoursville, before turning south onto U.S. 15 toward the state capital of Harrisburg.

U.S. 15, and later U.S. 11/15, ran along the western side of the Susquehanna River. The Susquehanna Valley was a more populous area than the northern part of the state, and there were many small cities and towns along it that Stephen went through on the way to Harrisburg. John Frost got to know many party people in the region because of his close ties to Harrisburg, and smoothed the way in advance for Stephen's meetings with them when he was on this leg of his walk. In fact, John joined him for some of the meetings and even agreed to walk with him one of the days. "It would be my exercise for the year," he joked. Many of these party people had been following Stephen's walk from the media and with the low state that politics had fallen into in the Commonwealth were enthusiastic about his campaign. These were not the high-roller people in the party leadership, just the ones who interfaced with the rank-and-file in a region that had mostly traditionally supported the party. Stephen's citizen-politician standing, insistence on taking only small contributions, and generally populist approach resonated with them. John and Marybeth had done exceptional advance work in making the connections with media and other contacts. He was against having staged groups of people to meet him or mini-rallies in communities that he walked through, but did not object to John's urging people to show up if they wished at the times he projected arriving. In some towns, thanks to the media attention to the "Walk of the Commonwealth," people showed up spontaneously. They often had signs that simply welcomed him to whatever town it was. Occasionally, he saw a sign from the more politically charged-up among them that said such things as, "Welcome, Citizen-Politician" or "Let's Clean Up State Government." He pushed ahead to visit communities on both sides of the river, crossing bridges wherever they were available that sometimes linked sister towns across the waterway. He walked through such towns as Montgomery, Watsontown, Milton, Lewisburg (where the noted federal penitentiary is that people such as Alger Hiss and Jimmy Hoffa had served time in), Sunbury, Selinsgrove, Duncannon, Marysville, and Enola. This brought him to what was called the West Shore, the western suburbs of Harrisburg. He arranged his walking schedule so he could be in Selinsgrove on a Friday so he could stand outside Selinsgrove Speedway in the evening to meet and greet people as they went inside. The speedway was known as one of the leading spring car racetracks in Pennsylvania and the northeast.

He found another good response to fundraising on this leg of the walk, as well. The contributions were small—most of the region was not affluent—but they added up to $5,000. He also had the chance to be interviewed by several print and electronic media outlets along the way, whose coverage—even while brief—was more welcome exposure. The twin themes they seemed to pick up on were "good government" and "traditional values." That was fine with him. He resolved to link these up more and more, which was a combination that unfortunately didn't often get made in politics. It seemed as if the leftists, who were leading the way at trying to transform traditional—morally solid—culture were the ones who mostly embraced the "good government" mantle.

In Harrisburg, Frost arranged meetings between Stephen and state party leaders and some state legislators from the party who shared his views on major issues. He also contacted a friend who was a political reporter in Harrisburg to set up a press conference. The state party leaders were noncommittal about his candidacy, which he expected. They were known for not normally endorsing candidates in primaries and he was, after all, challenging the establishment. They initially seemed cool as he sat down with them in a big conference room in state party headquarters, but Stephen's natural warmth caused them to loosen up some as the discussion went on. He made it very clear, however, that issues such as those concerning life, marriage, and the family were basic moral questions of civilization-wide importance and that the party had been seriously mistaken to ignore them and be nebulous about where it stood. There could be different approaches to public policy and most things in politics could be the subjects of legitimate disagreement, but certain things were not subject to compromise. He respected and supported the party, he said, but it could not be viewed as an end in itself. It was a means to the end of bringing forth solid public officials who sought to further the common good. He made it very clear that, even while supporting the party, he was a citizen-politician whose first allegiance was to "the people" and his beliefs and actions "always had to be governed by moral truth." He also made it clear that the party had to get out from under the excessive influence of big-money interests of all kinds and avoid the favoritism and corruption that had recently afflicted state politics. Further, he said that the party not only had to appeal to the grassroots, but also had to be part of it. His walk around the state so far had made it clear to him that state political decision-makers and both parties seemed to many people to be detached from them and aloof.

While Stephen's kind manner, his evident humility and effort to not talk down to them, and his eloquence captured the party officials' attention, they were plainly uncomfortable with some of the things he said. As the meeting was breaking up, one of them took Stephen aside and said earnestly that he appreciated Stephen's letting them "know where he was coming from."

Stephen's meeting with like-minded legislators went well. A number of them said that it would be good to have a person on the statewide ticket who was so firm in his convictions about the social and moral issues, and a few outright offered their support.

During the press conference, Stephen surprised the correspondents by his knowledge of state issues and they were particularly taken by his stress on the state working to build up civil society as an alternative to many of its social welfare programs. A couple of them wanted to hone in on the marriage, homosexual, and abortion issues. Stephen was prepared for thoughtful, incisive explanations that had the virtue of not being excessively long. He succeeded in keeping the discussion focused in the way he wanted, which was something he thought critical in dealing with the press on these topics. Numerous questions focused on his walk and his "good government" theme, as had been typical of the media in the course of his incipient campaign.

Harrisburg was the largest city Stephen had gone through on the walk since Erie, and with the extra time he spent there because of the meetings he made a special effort to visit several of its neighborhoods. Marybeth joined him and together they walked through them, shaking hands, passing out his cards, and talking to people on the sidewalks and in shops and eateries.

He went east from Harrisburg along U.S. Route 30, the Lincoln Highway. Small groups of people enthusiastically met him in such places as Elizabethtown, Mount Joy, and Landisville. He had an enjoyable lunch and discussion with a couple of long-time conservative professors at one of the colleges in the area who had contacted him when they learned he would be coming through. He met many people in the city of Lancaster and even stopped to say hello to Amish families he met in the nearby environs of Lancaster County. He chuckled as one Amish man said to him that he had heard about his walk and thought he was one of the "most interesting English" he had ever met.

From Lancaster, he walked northeast on state Route 272, which essentially paralleled the limited-access U.S. Route 222. He often took time to visit historical sites along his route. As he passed near Ephrata, he stopped at the Ephrata Cloister. It had been an uncommon Protestant monastic-type community, which also had some married members, started in the eighteenth century. They had the additional unusual features of recognizing Saturday as the Sabbath and practicing a regimen of vegetarianism and daily fasting. He got out of the campaign mode at historical sites. He thought that campaigning at such places

75

would be a bit tacky and disrespectful. He had made advance arrangements when he reached Reading, an old small industrial and railroad city that was said to have more people below the poverty line than any other city in the country, to visit one of the Catholic parishes that had a predominantly Puerto Rican congregation. The city had the highest percentage of Puerto Ricans of any community in the state. Many were not financially well off, and often almost reflexively voted—when they turned out—for the other party, which they somehow believed was for the "little guy." He wanted to worship with them, and also meet them and show them that he was interested in them as much as other groups of people. The pastor invited a number of the active members of the parish to lunch with Stephen at the rectory. He had a good conversation with them, which featured his typical stress on personal responsibility and self-help. It resonated well with the people at the lunch, and they acknowledged that it had become a problem that many in their community had developed government dependency.

From Reading, Stephen turned southeast toward Philadelphia on state Route 724. All these routes that he followed tended to be main commercial arteries where he could meet the maximum number of people. He went through or into many towns and smaller urban centers as he entered the Philadelphia metropolitan area. In Norristown, he got a taste of the tightly concentrated geography and compact neighborhoods that loomed ahead massively in Philadelphia with the many streets of row homes (in Philadelphia, they were sometimes called "blockhouses"). Then he got back onto U.S. 30, called Lancaster Avenue in the western Philadelphia suburbs, and progressed through one old town after another on the famous "Main Line."

All told, Stephen spent a week walking through Philadelphia, during which time Marybeth joined him again. Besides the walk, John Frost had arranged numerous meetings with party activists and officials and Marybeth had arranged for the two of them to visit many nonprofit organizations where he could talk about his stress on civil society. They visited the various sections and neighborhoods of the city. They first walked into West Philadelphia, down Chestnut Street that leads past University City, site of the University of Pennsylvania, and ultimately to the historical district in Center City. Arrangements were made for a small pro-life rally at the site of the former clinic of the now notorious abortionist Kermit Gosnell, with Stephen as the featured speaker. He explained why all abortion was morally wrong, an assault against an utterly vulnerable part of the population, and could never be permitted by the state. Permitting abortion sent the message that it was moral and acceptable. The state had an obligation to protect all its citizens, and particularly had to protect and help the weakest and most vulnerable.

After West Philadelphia, Stephen and Marybeth went south into Southwest Philadelphia. It had traditionally been Irish but recently had become a center for refugees, especially from West Africa. Some of the people he encountered there had seemed surprised that he took the time to visit their area, especially since he wasn't from the other party. Like the Puerto Ricans in Reading, they had been led to think of it as the party that was sympathetic to the immigrant, the newcomer, and the "little guy." He explained to them why that wasn't so, and in fact how its leadership had become a political elite in alliance with an elite of "interest group" leaders who gained votes and sustained themselves in power by giving government largess to people. The result was that people became dependent on them, instead of learning to stand on their own feet. Again, he preached the gospel of personal responsibility. He also pointed out that the centerpieces of its political agenda were such issues as abortion, same-sex "marriage," and transgenderism, which are deeply opposed to the traditions they came from. They listened with interest; it didn't seem to be something they had thought of before.

From Southwest Philadelphia, the couple turned east until they reached Broad Street, the main traditional north-south thoroughfare in the city. They then went north into the heart of South Philadelphia, which was renowned as the place where many entertainers over the years had hailed from. They walked past many blocks of row houses. South Philadelphia had become ethnically and racially diverse, but still had a large concentration of Italians. As he went up to people in the Italian neighborhoods, he was surprised at the number of them who were familiar with his "Walk of the Commonwealth," and said they were happy to meet him and wished him well. This part of the city was one where his party had shown some strength in recent decades, even while they were perpetually submerged in a sea dominated by the other party. They had a pre-arranged meeting with his party's leaders from that part of the city.

At the famous Italian Market, they mixed for an hour with patrons and workers, who in recent decades were not just Italians but also increasingly Hispanics (especially Mexicans) and East Asians. Then they visited Little Saigon, perhaps the largest Vietnamese émigré community in the U.S. They walked through many of the Italian neighborhoods and through the Irish working class neighborhood of Pennsport, known as the focal point of the Mummer's clubs that make up the city's annual Mummer's Parade on New Year's Day.

77

They worked their way up Broad Street to Center City. City Hall stood at the middle of it, where Broad intersected with Market Street. Atop it was the famed statue of the city's and the Pennsylvania Colony's founder William Penn, which for nearly a hundred years was the highest point in the city. A few people from the city's media met them there and asked Stephen a few questions about how the walk was going and how he was being received in the city. Then, Stephen and Marybeth turned east and walked down Market Street to visit, again without campaigning, the various historical sites at the Independence National Historical Park. For each of them, it was the umpteenth time they had visited there but they couldn't pass up yet another opportunity. They were taken aback and dismayed to see a display at Independence Hall celebrating the homosexualist movement, proclaiming "Gay Rights: One of the Greatest Civil Rights Achievements in American History." They understood that the homosexualists had hijacked the notion of civil rights to justify blatantly immoral behavior and, as he had pounded away about in his encounter with the homosexualist activist in State College, they were now using "rights" to suppress anyone who opposed them. The longer Stephen stared at the display, the more incensed he became. He asked one of the Park Rangers standing on duty if he might speak to the person in charge of the exhibits. The Ranger told him that she didn't know who that was, but he could talk to her supervisor. She escorted him to a small office where a short, cordial middle-aged man in a Ranger uniform sat. Stephen introduced himself and gave his background as a scholar of the American constitutional tradition. He stated some basics about the background of civil rights and explained why homosexualism shouldn't be included in it. The gentleman knew who Stephen was. He seemed to be familiar with his "Walk of the Commonwealth." He listened to what he said and they had a brief discussion. At the end he said, "This isn't something I decided about. It came from Washington." They shook hands and Stephen left the office and rejoined Marybeth.

A little while later, as they gazed at the Liberty Bell, Stephen said something that Marybeth in some form had heard many times before from him, "They stood for great principles, perhaps the best that any nation in history represented. It was truly a 'new order for the ages.' Sometimes Catholics have been hesitant about saying this, believing that it seems to immortalize a nation—something made by men. The great Catholic thinker Orestes Brownson had no problem recognizing the uniqueness of America, however." Then, he went on as he glanced in the direction of the Constitution Center across Independence Park, "those principles were enshrined in the Constitution. Now, people don't

78

appreciate or even seem to be aware of them. Some have actively worked to twist them or have corrupted them." He paused for a moment, then added, "I think you know, Marybeth, that to do something about this is why I took the opportunity to do what I'm doing."

She looked down momentarily, and then gently gazed into his eyes and said softly, with a slight smile, "I know."

It was late afternoon and time for them to walk several blocks back toward Center City for a get-acquainted meeting with a few of the Philadelphia party leaders. He sensed a distinct attitude of respect from them at the meeting. Despite his consistent frankness about the "social issues" that he figured some of them were uncomfortable with, his "Walk of the Commonwealth" was garnering increasing attention and touching a chord with the rank-and-file voter—even some who weren't in the party.

John Frost had arranged for Stephen and Marybeth to spend that night with one of those leaders, who was a state party committeeman from Far Northeast Philadelphia known as being a very active Catholic both in his parish and the archdiocese generally. When he met them, he knew that Stephen and Marybeth had wanted to visit the national shrine of St. John Neumann, which they had never been to. It was north of Center City, not far from the route to his home, and he gave them a kind of personal tour of it. The next day, he dropped them off in the Lower Northeast where they resumed their walk through such areas as Kensington, Bridesburg, Port Richmond, Fishtown, Frankford, and Mayfair. They had been traditional Irish and Eastern European enclaves but more recently had seen newer immigrants, especially Hispanics. Fishtown was one of the communities profiled in noted social scientist Charles Murray's book, *Coming Apart: The State of White America, 1960-2010*. The farther-up parts of Northeast Philadelphia had a newer, almost suburban look, but still featured the characteristic Philadelphia row houses.

At Frankford, as he introduced himself to shoppers in a predominantly black neighborhood, a young black man came up and accused him of being a "racist."

"What do you mean by 'racist?'" Stephen responded firmly, but not angrily, looking him directly in the eyes.

"You're against black people," he shot back.

"What do you mean by 'racist?'" Stephen continued to press him, but refrained from raising his voice. "What do you mean, 'against black people?'"

"Your party's against black people."

79

"What do you mean, 'my party's against black people?' Tell me what you mean by that. What do you mean and where is your proof?" Stephen refused to back down.

"You're against the government helping black people. You want to cut programs."

"Do you think all government programs, by their very nature, help people? Don't you think that some government programs fail to do that no matter what their intent? Don't you think that when programs don't work they should be changed or even eliminated? Is it possible that government programs might, in some cases, actually turn out to be bad for people? If so, should we still continue them? Are you sure that government necessarily knows what's best for people? Aren't you putting quite a bit of confidence in the people in government?"

"Those programs help people. You're a racist if you want to cut them because they especially help black people," the young man responded.

"Well," said Stephen, "You haven't answered almost any of my questions. To say that one is a racist if he doesn't down the line support government programs that some people think—whether it's true or not—help a certain group of people is not very different from the responses of some people when Mr. Obama was president that anyone who does not support whatever he wants to do is a racist. Do you really think that is a very thoughtful argument? Let me ask you this: Would you not agree that everyone should be treated with respect and dignity, and that there should be justice? Is this not something that we should strive for?"

The young man simmered down. He didn't respond immediately, almost as if he wasn't sure what Stephen's point was. Then he said, "Yes."

"I presume that you're talking about government social welfare programs of different kinds. If these programs encourage people to be dependent on government and discourage them from being responsible for their lives, so that they lose some of their freedom or are not encouraged to use it wisely, is that truly giving them more dignity? Don't you think that people should be able to rely more on themselves, and when they need help seek it especially from their families and others who are right around them—instead of some distant and impersonal government agency? When government bureaucracies are more concerned about their own ways of doing things and they treat people like numbers or cogs in a wheel, is that showing respect? Do you know that justice involves not only the community giving to people what it owes them, but also people contributing to their communities? It works both ways; the first is called distributive justice and the second social justice. You talk about people having a right to something, but you don't want to talk about duties or responsibilities. This creates an imbalance, which hurts not only the community—which you seem to be expecting just to provide for people no matter what—but also hurts those people themselves. God intends people to be better, to be more like his Son, Jesus Christ, was. I don't hear this from you. You seem to be focusing just on people taking."

At that point a late middle-aged black woman who was in a small group of people whom Stephen had been introducing himself to before the young man started his verbal attack broke into the conversation. "How can you call him a racist? He saying just what Our Lawd says. We can't jes be gettin' things from people, we got things we have to do for other people too." The young man just slipped away. Stephen chatted for awhile with the woman. "These younger people don't understand what's goin' on," she said. "I spent my whole life workin', even when my kids was little. When I had some hard times, the church helped me out, so now I try to help it out as much as I can. I'm not interested in takin' from the government."

After they left Philadelphia, Marybeth returned to their home across the state. Stephen embarked on the final stage of the "Walk of the Commonwealth" through Bucks County along State Route 313, to the Allentown-Bethlehem area, then north along State Route 309 to Hazleton, Wilkes-Barre, and then State Route 315 to Scranton. He then turned back south and the walk would terminate in his hometown, Hunnicutt.

Marybeth had made arrangements to meet him when he arrived in Hunnicutt, and they coordinated a time because she planned a get-together with Stephen's mother, her family, and his old friends there to mark the conclusion of the "Walk of the Commonwealth." Actually, without Stephen's knowing it, she was arranging something much bigger. She didn't have to do much of the arranging, however. She learned from Stephen's mother that several of the townspeople wanted to have a rally for Stephen when he arrived in Hunnicutt and had already begun the planning. Marybeth just helped with coordinating times. When Stephen entered the town on its main road, within half an hour of his planned time, he was met by a group of people waving welcoming signs and the community band. Marybeth and his mother were right up in front. The mayor of the town, a man in his late sixties named Jim Duncan who had been a friend of Stephen's father and an active member of their parish, congratulated him and said, "We're with you, Stephen." After many handshakes and hugs, Stephen made some impromptu, but as usual eloquent, remarks to the crowd. Stephen's campaign committee and Marybeth made sure the state's media were informed in advance about the end of the walk, and an unusually large number of them were present. Stephen spoke to them for about fifteen minutes after his remarks. Their questions reflected that they were still in a state of awe about the entire effort. Stephen didn't hesitate to refer them to his position papers, about a dozen of which Marybeth had released for him to the media during the time of his trek. Sometimes he had worked on them in the evening after his day's walk. Afterwards, the family members proceeded to Stephen's mother's house, where he had grown up, to have dinner together.

The next day, several of the state's newspapers ran stories about the end of the walk. A few picked up on both his willingness to engage critical people in discussion and take the offensive, even if gently, as with the young black man in Philadelphia.

The new semester was set to begin two weeks after Stephen and Marybeth returned home from Hunnicutt. The court case challenging the state law on misrepresenting one's political opponent was scheduled for argument right after Labor Day. The Pittsburgh *Tribune-Review* did a story about his return to the classroom after the summer of walking the state. He argued the case in court himself, with Jim O'Grady's assistance, and it made front-page headlines in several newspapers across the state and in *USA Today*. The day after the oral argument, he was interviewed about the case on NPR. While things were quiet during the fall—the primary for statewide offices was not until the following May (elections for the main Pennsylvania state offices were held at the same time as the national mid-term elections)—Stephen, with the notoriety he had gained from the walk, was asked to speak at numerous party, pro-life, pro-family, and grassroots citizen organization dinners and events around the state. He also continued releasing position papers, one virtually every two weeks. He certainly didn't start to duck the social issues as he gained strength—after all, that's a major reason why he decided to enter the political fray—but he thought it incumbent to provide an increasing number of position papers on questions that concerned the duties of the lieutenant governor, such as crime, emergency management (the lieutenant governor was on the state Emergency Management Council), and local-state relations (since the lieutenant governor was chairman of the Local Government Advisory Commission). His grasp of these kinds of issues and ideas were frequently favorably commented on in the state's media. A few editorials said such things as how it was good to finally have a candidate for lieutenant governor who talked about what the lieutenant governor actually did. At least one news outlet called him for a short interview almost every week on one issue or another. Just along the walk itself, Stephen raised donations of over a quarter-million dollars. His small volunteer campaign committee nearly matched that with donations within the same $50 per person limit.

Shortly before Christmas the court issued its decision declaring the misrepresentation law unconstitutional as a violation of the First Amendment. This led to a new flood of media attention to Stephen and, in fact, for a couple of days—during final exam period, it turned out— it seemed as if he was having media interviews in rapid succession. The state announced it would appeal to the U.S. Court of Appeals for the Third Circuit. Stephen and Jim O'Grady busied themselves over the holidays preparing and then filing a response to the appeal. Before the primary campaign season got underway the following year, however, the Third Circuit in a split decision declined to take up the case and upheld the lower court. The result was additional media attention to Stephen as the campaign unfolded.

Actually, Stephen had no primary opposition. Using some of the money previously raised, his campaign was able to undertake a direct-mail effort. The mailing made it clear that $50 was the limit; in cases where people went ahead and sent more or got a duplicate mailing and sent amounts twice that exceeded $50, the amount above that was returned. Stephen also instructed that money was to be raised only from within Pennsylvania. Direct mail netted another quarter million dollars. They would have the funds to enable them to do some limited electronic and print media advertising for the general election campaign. Stephen was adamant about not descending to the level of sound bites, however, and he intended to do a lot of front-porch campaigning. Still, he understood that the way Pennsylvania elections were set up was that once the candidates for governor and lieutenant governor secured their separate nominations they ran together as a team. The focus, of course, was on the gubernatorial race. People essentially cast their votes according to whom they wanted for governor and his running mate just came along for the ride. Nevertheless, there had been elections when some voters were more attracted to a party's lieutenant governor candidate. Stephen resolved that he would be a "team-player" to only a certain extent. He would act prudently and not embarrass the gubernatorial candidate in any way, but he would address crucial issues even if the person at the top of the ticket and the party leaders didn't want to stress them. He would also do it in an educating kind of way—again, the educative function of politics.

The leading candidate for the party's gubernatorial nomination was the state attorney general, Sheila Klinger. She had been a successful attorney with a Philadelphia law firm and lived in Delaware County, one of the populous suburban counties around the city that had once been solid bastions for the party but in the last couple of decades had gone more for the other party. Her husband was a Philadelphia attorney with a different firm. Both had been long active in the party in Delaware County, and he had even been county party chairman for a couple of years. She was a fiscal conservative, but not very interested in the social issues. She said she thought abortion should be permitted for all the "hard cases": life and both physical and mental health of the mother, rape, incest, fetal deformity, and once said that even "social reasons" could fall into "mental health." That seemed to be virtually endorsing abortion on demand. She gave no indication that she saw a problem with same-sex "marriage," and seemed happy with the U.S. Supreme Court's decision about it since it wouldn't be a political issue anymore. All she would say about it was that it was now the law. She commented how she had had many open homosexual clients in her law practice, and went out of her way to say that she would not "judge" people.

When Stephen accepted John Frost's overture to enter the race, he thought that a stronger pro-life, pro-family, pro-true marriage candidate would lead the ticket. The state's auditor general, who had for several years been a popular and respected state senator from north of Harrisburg and fit that bill pretty well, looked like he was going to make the race and he initially looked like the favorite, but health reasons forced him to forego it.

Although Stephen had no primary opponent, John Frost learned that Mrs. Klinger had tried to convince two state senators from opposite ends of the state to enter the primary to oppose Stephen. One, from one of the other suburban Philadelphia counties, had been rumored to be interested in running before Stephen entered the race. When both of them saw Stephen's stock rise as the result of the "Walk of the Commonwealth," they decided against it. Now, she would have to team up with someone who wasn't exactly an ideological soul mate. The state party committee had decided a year before to make no endorsements for the primary.

Even though he was unopposed, Stephen's small campaign committee made a strong effort to bring out a respectable primary turnout. Working from connections around the state that John Frost and Stephen's other leading supporters had, as well as people whose names he had gotten as prospective volunteers during his walk, the committee had lined up coordinators for all sixty-seven counties. They led the way in getting out the vote. The result was a surprising turnout for a primary, especially for one in which the people running for the top offices were unopposed.

It turned out, as the general election campaign developed, that Mrs. Klinger made a notable effort to keep Stephen at a distance. She scheduled few joint campaign appearances and there was limited communication between the campaigns. The word had gotten out that Stephen was not going to take direction from her staff. He would work with her, but he also intended to conduct an independent campaign and talk about certain issues. She did not try to put any pressure on his campaign—it seemed clear to her that that wouldn't work anyhow—and appeared at times almost as if she wanted to ignore him. Stephen's appeal to the voters during the general election campaign always was to support the party's candidates and the ticket, but he would also routinely launch into a discussion of various issues that Mrs. Klinger avoided. His front porch campaign seemed to captivate both the public and the media, and he started to be known for colloquies with members of the media on issues after he made his "educative" talks about them—often linking up current questions with broader culture-wide ones—which went surprisingly deep but were completely coherent and understandable by the average person. He was very good at providing readily quotable phrases. He also didn't hesitate to directly and firmly, but always with evident charity, confront members of the media if they showed bias or tried to ask "gotcha" type questions. Some in the media said they appreciated his approach, even if they didn't agree with his views. It was very unusual, even refreshing for a politician. A few began to talk about his "professorial approach." He maintained his twin approach with the media and in his speeches generally, which would have been unmanageable and contradictory for a lesser rhetorician, of educating but also maintaining an "offensive" posture. Some in the media and different interest groups would have liked to have "sandbagged" him on such questions as same-sex "marriage," but his powers of analysis and explanation, care in choosing words, and uncanny ability to turn the question around and put the interrogator on the spot didn't give them the chance. Also, they were only willing to spend a limited amount of time going after him. After all, the gubernatorial race was the central feature. If he were a lesser candidate, they might have tried to go after him in order to damage Mrs. Klinger. They realized that wasn't going to work, so he wound up getting more of a pass than he and his campaign expected. Besides, the good will and support built up by his "Walk of the Commonwealth" kept buttressing him.

When he was not campaigning from—literally—the front porch and at set-up campaign events, his committee, which had been made up entirely of volunteers the whole time, often arranged meetings with pro-life, pro-family, good government, and other citizen groups. He also made arrangements, with John Frost's help, to get to any party functions anywhere in the state that he could. On alternating weekends he made sure he was in different parts of the state shaking people's hands at major shopping malls and plazas. He did all this, by the way, while he continued his regular teaching schedule at both schools.

As the race headed to its final two weeks, the Klinger-Bernard ticket opened a lead of half a dozen points in the polls. There was no question—even if she wasn't willing to admit it—that Stephen was helping Mrs. Klinger. Polls showed that in a head-to-head race with her opponent, she led by only three points. Stephen led his opponent in head-to-head polls by eight. Polling questions asking which ticket voters favored—showing the names of the candidate for both governor and lieutenant governor together—doubled her lead as opposed to when the gubernatorial candidates were just listed by themselves. In the final month, two televised statewide debates between the gubernatorial candidates had helped Mrs. Klinger. The two parties had made the decision not to have any face-to-face debates between the lieutenant governor candidates. Stephen's opponent said in an interview that he lamented this. It might have given him more exposure. He made a similar rueful observation to that of Lawton Chiles' opponent in Florida in 1970: "I've tried to run hard, but the problem was that Bernard already walked."

On the Sunday before the election one of the Pittsburgh newspapers ran a feature story about Stephen that looked back over his unlikely and unplanned emergence as a political figure in Pennsylvania and the campaign. The article was said by some to be a final boost for the Klinger-Bernard ticket as it got currency throughout western Pennsylvania and the election-day turnout of Stephen's natural constituency was strong in that part of the state.

The Klinger-Bernard ticket ended up winning by 8%. Stephen and Marybeth had gone to Harrisburg the day before the election since both the Klinger campaign and the state party leadership planned on a joint appearance and speeches by the two candidates at a party gala on election night. Even there, Mrs. Klinger and a number of the top party leaders—the regulars who all along had been put off by John Frost and his "reformers"—kept Stephen at arms length.

Their attitude was inconsequential now, however. Stephen was the incoming lieutenant governor of Pennsylvania.

CHAPTER 4

An Unexpected State Governor And A
Sudden National Figure

E ven though as the Pennsylvania lieutenant governor, Stephen was considered part of the Klinger administration the governor distanced herself from him when in office the same way as she had done during the campaign. After eight months in office and despite the fact that they had offices not too far apart in the Capitol Building in Harrisburg, they had met only twice—and both times were on questions related to the lieutenant governor's statutory role as Chairman of the Local Government Advisory Committee. The meetings were cordial, but the governor's coolness was evident to Stephen and the meetings clearly went on only as long as necessary to discuss the topics at hand.

The arms-length relationship was discussed some in the cloakrooms of the Capitol, but the media people covering the Hill had not shown any awareness of it or at least had not commented on it if they did. The general thinking was that philosophical disagreements— especially on social issues such as abortion and the homosexual agenda—were at the core of it. However, there was speculation that the governor may also have resented the favorable publicity that Stephen received in the few weeks right after taking office for trimming the perks of the lieutenant governor's office to the bone, which pushed her out of the limelight just when she wanted to build up momentum to launch her early initiatives.

The lieutenant governorship in Pennsylvania had come under increasing scrutiny for some years, both as to the costs associated with it and its actual value to the Commonwealth. Its budget had been voluntarily slashed by one of its recent occupants and there was even an effort in the General Assembly to abolish the office. Its constitutional duties were limited; the most important were to preside over the State Senate and be Chairman of the Board of Pardons. Lieutenant governors also took on whatever additional tasks governors requested of them. It wasn't likely that Governor Sheila Klinger would be doing this much with Stephen. Perhaps the most important fact about the lieutenant governor in the state constitution was that he succeeded to the governorship if the office became vacant, until the next scheduled election. The lieutenant governorship in Pennsylvania had not been a stepping-stone office to the governorship, as the U.S. Vice Presidency had become in the twentieth century to the Presidency. Relatively few Pennsylvania lieutenant governors had gone on to be elected governor since the office had been established in 1873.

When Stephen became lieutenant governor, he announced that he would not accept a sizable portion of the statutory salary of nearly $150,000. He would accept nothing more than his previous professor's salary—when he took office, he went on an extended, unpaid leave from both of his universities—which was below six figures. He also turned down the personal expense account. There was little official travel associated with the position, so he said he didn't need it. He also slashed the lieutenant governor's professional staff from eight to only two. He was sensitive to the fact that the people occupying those positions would be losing jobs, but they had all been partisan appointments by the outgoing lieutenant governor of the other party and it was understood that they would depart with him. As it turned out, they all had lined up other positions before he took over. Stephen and John Frost agreed that it would not be wise for John to take one of these positions because it would look too much like a political payoff and thus the cronyism that had too often been seen in the Commonwealth. Instead, Stephen hired two highly accomplished, reformist-type lawyers who were very knowledgeable about state government who John suggested. There were also two secretaries in the office, both of whom had been there for many years and had served lieutenant governors of both parties. He only needed one, but he informed the other that he would keep her on for the remaining nine months until she became eligible for retirement. Apart from his salary, he was able to bring the office's budget down to almost what it had been about a decade before when it had been slashed by the earlier occupant. He also declined to live at the small state-owned mansion over twenty miles away from Harrisburg that lieutenant governors and their families had occupied for nearly a half-century, and instead he and Marybeth rented a modest apartment not far from the Capitol. Just as with his barebones campaign that operated only on small contributions, he drew raves from the state's media—and even a few national outlets—for his efforts, even though they tended to disagree with many of his political positions.

Stephen faithfully carried out his official duties, of which presiding over the State Senate took the most time. The legislature was in session much of the year, but business was not conducted on the Senate floor throughout that time. The Board of Pardons usually had public meetings monthly and some months had a working meeting (they were called merit review sessions) of the members. At most, this involved two days a month. There were substantial gaps of time and he resolved to use them to advance as best he could the positions on crucial public questions that motivated his plunging into politics in the first place. With John Frost's help, who continued as his kind of informal, unofficial public organizer, he lined up speaking engagements with as many citizens organizations as he could. Through a few conservative contacts John had at university campuses in the state he also arranged to go into 'the belly of the beast" and speak about such social issues as abortion, the dangers of homosexualism and the defense of true marriage, and even the contraceptive culture. He also spoke, especially on the campuses, on such topics as the true and false nature of liberty and the American constitutional tradition and the current threats to it. The word circulated around the Capitol that these efforts further strained the relationship between Stephen and Governor Klinger.

After a particularly long and trying day of presiding in the State Senate, Stephen came home feeling discouraged. Marybeth had left her job in Pittsburgh, but had gotten similar part-time position with a nonprofit organization in Harrisburg and spent the rest of a typical day doing volunteer work for the Catholic diocese there. She met him at the door as usual with her gentle smile and affectionate hug. She immediately noticed the look of self-doubt that occasionally came over him.

"Tell me what happened today," she inquired, as they sat down on the couch.

"Oh, it's nothing particular. It was just the monotonous work of presiding over another day of long, droning talks about small points in legislation involving nothing very important. Today, it was about the conditions of reimbursements to local governments about sewer repairs. Marybeth, I agreed to run for this office because I thought I could make some difference about the really crucial questions that go to the heart of civilized life, and that seems far away from what I'm actually doing. It's nice that I can give these talks, but they haven't even been as abundant or as often as I had hoped. As I sat there in the Senate chamber today, I kept thinking that I've been lieutenant governor almost a year and I was doing more good as a professor. I knew that politics, like any job, has a lot of routine, tedious work associated with it, but that seems to be almost all there is to this position. I'm wondering what I thought I could reasonably accomplish by doing this."

Marybeth tried to encourage him, as she always did, but she also always spoke frankly. "Stephen, you're right that all jobs no matter how important they seem will be somewhat tedious and even downright boring. We both know that what we do may often seem to be unrewarding and not very useful, not something we think we are making much of a contribution in doing. The good we are doing is not something that we can see right away. Remember that we talked at length about this, and about entering politics as opposed to staying permanently in the academy when this opportunity presented itself. We prayed a lot about it. You went through a lot to win this office, and you wouldn't have done so if God didn't want you here. Remember that God opens doors for us, and He wouldn't open them if he didn't want us to go through them. He has a reason, you know that, even if that's not yet fully clear."

Stephen looked up and within a few moments the gloom disappeared from his face. "Of course you're right, Marybeth, as you always are. I need just to accept what the demands of this position entail and to think more about making use of the visibility it gives me to further the causes and principles that we know are true—after all, it's the second-highest office in the state."

He held her hands lovingly between his and they kissed longingly. Then she said, "Let me double my efforts to work with John and also some other solid people I've gotten to know in the local non-profit community to line up more talks for you. John is working on having you speak to the county party groups in the region and at the convention of the party young people's organization. In the meantime, go right at them at your college lecture tomorrow night. You know that I'll be in the audience rooting you on. I'll have to drive out myself from the place where I'm doing volunteer work. Some people from the diocese will be there, too. They also tell me that a group of students from the Newman Center—the Newman Centers are pretty good in this diocese—and some people from the local parish pro-life group will be, too. We'll all be your cheering squad. It won't just be an audience of adversaries when you try to defend true marriage."

The college at which Stephen was to speak was one of the oldest in Pennsylvania, and in its long history had produced some famous people in politics, science, and business. It was only a half hour or so drive from Harrisburg, and was one of a large number of old liberal arts colleges in the state. Like a number of them, it had originally been connected with a religious denomination but before the middle of the twentieth century had simply become a free-standing private college.

Stephen thought it was strange that even though he was the lieutenant governor of the state, there was no one from the college's administration or even the faculty to formally welcome him to the campus. He drove there with his administrative assistant, Jim Downey, one of his two professional staff people. Jim came along on his own time out of a desire to support Stephen. It was not official business. They had been instructed to pull into a visitors' parking lot, which was near the building where Stephen would speak. A couple of campus conservative groups were sponsoring his talk and representatives from each of them met Stephen and his assistant at the entrance to the building. They were warm in their welcome, and obviously were looking forward to Stephen's appearance. A taste of what Stephen was to encounter in the lecture hall was seen just outside the building, where two young men and a young woman were holding a big banner proclaiming, "No Equality Means Hate." Stephen would have liked to engage them in discussion as he did the young man in State College during the campaign, but he figured that he had to defer to the student group leaders who were managing the evening's schedule. Inside, they walked down a long corridor to a large looming room at the end from which the din of an assembled crowd filled the air. When he was about five yards from the lecture hall, Stephen spotted Marybeth waiting for him outside its large open double doors. She kissed him on the cheek when he approached and introduced him to two of her associates from the diocese standing there with her. A few representatives from the Harrisburg area media were also standing there and introduced themselves, and Stephen agreed to their request for comments after the talk. Marybeth seemed to have already struck up an acquaintance with a friendly young woman from the student newspaper who was also standing nearby, who Stephen promised an interview to afterwards.

When they entered the lecture hall, Stephen quickly scoured the crowd. It was made up mostly of college students, to be sure, but he saw a respectable number of people who looked to range from their thirties to retirement age. The lecture was free and open to the public. Some of the students were waving an assortment of similar signs to what he saw outside. There was a particularly large concentration of the student crowd on one side of the room, and it was from there that a chorus of "boos" erupted when he came in. His student hosts escorted him to the large dais in the front of the room and one of them went to the podium to introduce him. The boos continued until some of the people started turning to the impolite protesters and told them to be quiet, while others from various parts of the room repeatedly "shushed" them. After the introducer said, "we welcome Pennsylvania Lieutenant Governor—and Professor—Stephen Bernard," and Stephen began walking to the podium, the same sequence of boos—although noticeably more subdued this time—and then verbal rebukes of the protesters followed. It flashed very quickly through Stephen's mind that maybe the student protesters were taken aback to learn that he was a professor, and so some instinctively felt reluctant to continue the rough treatment. The audience noise diminished to the point that when Stephen stepped up to the podium to start to speak, there was a surprising moment of almost complete quiet in the room.

Stephen had made a brief outline of points for the talk, but he did not take them out of his suit coat pocket. He had developed a reputation from the campaign and his other appearances as a very capable extemporaneous speaker. He looked up from the podium and over the audience and a smile that radiated genuine sincerity came over his face and he said, "It is my pleasure and honor to be able to speak to you and *with* you this evening." His opening seemed to disarm the audience. Besides coming across to them instantaneously as a very kind and appealing person, his stress on the word "with" made the audience, unruly students and all, believe that instead of just a straight-up talk this was also going to be a dialogue.

He proceeded to talk to them about what marriage is and its good for the people connected with it (men, women, and children) and for the social order. He told them about the complementarity of men and women and some basic information about the purpose of parts of the human body that often seemed to elude college students in an age in which any kind of sexual activity goes. He went into a short discourse about the real nature of love, and how some vague notion grounded solely in the perceptions or passing feelings of the moment cannot be the basis for the commitment demanded in marriage. He informed them that no people or culture in human history has ever tried to redefine marriage, and challenged them to consider why the current time was any more prescient in its thinking than the ones before it. He also gave them a litany of various cultures that had gone into deep decline after embracing an ethic of sexual libertinism. Knowing that many of them believed themselves to be concerned about "social justice," he asserted why a self-gratification ethic in sexual matters was really no different from one in economic life. He explained why marriage was not just a private matter and so society and the state had, at least in some basic

94

ways, to regulate it. He explained that the law's treatment of marriage, sex, or any behavior was a great teacher to people about what was morally good and right, and why law is never truly neutral and always embodies a position even when silent about something. He argued that the "homosexualist movement"—that's what he preferred to call it—was not seeking to protect people's rights, but was seeking acceptance for its behavior. That led him to a brief sojourn into what the true nature of rights was—he spoke about the great classical philosophers and the thinking of rights in the American Founding and constitutional background—and the great dangers to social order if we carried out to its fullest extent a notion of rights based on desire. He paraphrased some of the leaders of the homosexualist movement and their leading allies that showed that they were just using the same-sex "marriage" issue to promote an agenda of radically changing the institutions of marriage and family. He told them that the term "gay" had long been used as a propaganda tool, which was why he did not use it, and questioned whether in light of the disproportionate amount of physical, psychological, addiction, and other personal problems found among active homosexuals they could in any way be called "gay" as the term had traditionally been used. He mentioned how even same-sex couples in "committed" relationships tended to a much greater degree than male-female married couples to engage in sexual activity outside of their "marriages." He provided an impressive array of statistics from memory. He also discussed the growing number of ways in which the homosexualist movement was trying to suppress those who would not legitimize their behavior, including using the coercive power of government. He said that this was why some called them the "gay mafia." He mentioned the serious public policy consequences of weak families and the further undermining of marriage and family life.

Although there were some groans at different points that he related and a continuation of scattered boos, the audience became increasingly transfixed as he talked so eloquently, providing just enough information to back up his points but not inundating it so the people couldn't absorb what he was saying. He additionally captivated them because he said all this from memory. He was a politician like they hadn't seen before, with a professor's knowledge and insight, the eloquence of an outstanding orator but whose rhetoric had substance, the courage to address a controversial issue in its many different dimensions, and an ability to challenge those who opposed him with evident charity. There wasn't a hint of nastiness or even anger in his presentation, and many of the students who had been used to hearing how "mean-spirited" conservatives were suddenly thought that maybe that wasn't so. One of the local newspaper reports noted his "composure" throughout the evening.

He opened up the floor for questions afterwards, and this went on for almost an hour. This, again, was not what people typically identified with politicians. The most noteworthy exchange occurred between him and one of the students, who tried to argue that there was no basis for morality other than the individual's preferences.

Stephen responded, "I presume, then, that you don't see a problem with stealing, or murder, or even genocide."

"I didn't say that," the student insisted.

"But if you say that morality is just formulated by each individual, why can't someone say that he can legitimately steal or kill or wipe out whole groups of people? After all, if the individual rightfully makes up his own morality, then every person's morality is as good as every other person's."

"Some people might say that something's stealing, but somebody else might not say that it is. It's a matter of opinion."

Stephen made a brief pause, then looked at the student straight in the eye, "If someone came and stole your stereo set, I'll bet you wouldn't be so ready to assert that what is stealing is a matter of opinion." That brought a laugh from the audience.

"Maybe someone needs it more than me."

Stephen replied, "Maybe then you should start a charitable effort of raising money to buy stereos for people who can't afford them." There was more laughter. The momentary levity was almost welcomed in the serious discussion. Stephen continued, "Of course, if you want to give your stereo to someone that's your free choice. That's a different thing than saying that a person has a right to take it when you don't want him to." Then Stephen turned the exchange back in a somber direction, "You didn't address murder and genocide. Are they okay because some people think they are? Is killing an individual or a group of people alright because someone judges that for some reason—even if they are no immediate threat to them—they deserve it?"

The student countered, "That's not the same thing. Somebody is hurt there. When people agree to have sex, no one is hurt. They both want to do it."

"Are you sure that no one might get hurt, even if sex is consensual? Can't—don't—people in fact get hurt in a variety of ways, immediately or later on, even if they have mutually agreed on the course of action? Isn't it true that people often can't see the consequences of something they have done that might appear much later on? That's what happens with many things in life. Why wouldn't it happen with sex?" He took the chance and went a step farther, even though he knew it would cause sudden feelings of guilt in a number of the young people in the audience—and probably a strong immediate negative reaction because of it. He decided in a split second, however, that it was worth saying because it might cause some of them to reflect a bit and perhaps think about changing the way they act. "The solid social science data shows that people who have even one sexual encounter before marriage reduce their chance of a successful marriage later on by 40%."

There was indeed a dismissive reaction from some in the audience, but more of an almost stunned silent reaction overall than he had expected. The statistic was obviously surprising, even jolting, for some. After the reaction, he added a reassuring note, "Always remember that this is the *tendency* with people who have had sex before marriage. It is not inevitable that a person's marriage will not then succeed. One can turn one's life around, and firmly resolve to change and then keep it on the right path."

When the event came to an end, Stephen was surprised by the cordial applause he received. There were other supporters in the audience besides Marybeth and her associates, to be sure—it was public lecture that attracted a certain number of people from an area that away from the college was fairly conservative—but he also left thinking that what he said had had an impact on some of the students as well.

The next week progressed slowly for Stephen, as the legislature had a short recess and he had no meetings scheduled. Some well-wishers dropped in on him and he even walked around the Capitol building for awhile greeting visitors. Once, he even volunteered to spell one of the Capitol tour guides and took a group of high school students who were on a class trip around the building. He capped it off by answering their and their teachers' questions about state government for half an hour. There were other times during the week that he just sat in his office reading newspapers and a book. Again, his doubts about whether he should have sought this job clouded his day.

The legislature came back into session at the beginning of the following week. It was another long day of dry proceedings: a series of minor procedural motions and speeches, mostly not very eloquent, on mundane matters pertaining to the benefits the Commonwealth provided to its employees. What mostly went through his mind as he half-listened was that the benefits were far out of line with those in the private sector, both for-profit and non-profit, and how despite much comment about that in the press and much private talk among state politicians of both parties no governor had acted to try to rein them in.

That had been done to varying degrees in some other states (including next door in Ohio), but they shied away from a confrontation with the powerful public employee unions in Pennsylvania. For the rest of the time, he thought about his scheduled talk that night to a citizens group in Cumberland County, across the Susquehanna River from Harrisburg. His communications with the gubernatorial administration continued to be very infrequent and, since the governor had distanced herself from him the leading figures in the state party stayed away from him too. A good relationship with a governor from their party was much more important than cozying up to the man who occupied what some were now calling the Commonwealth's "dead-end office."

As Stephen was getting ready to leave his office to meet Marybeth to go to dinner and then drive to the talk, the phone rang. It was Governor Klinger's Chief-of-Staff, Jim Mansfield. Stephen was surprised, since he had never called before. His voice was hesitating and he sounded obviously troubled. "Sir, I'm sorry to have to tell you that the Governor collapsed and was rushed to Harrisburg Hospital about forty-five minutes ago." Stephen was stunned and seemed for a moment to have trouble catching his breath. For several seconds he did not respond as he tried to absorb what Mansfield said.

Finally he managed to recover his composure enough to respond. "What happened? How is she?"

"We're not quite sure yet. I'm on my way out the door to the hospital now. The governor's husband and her son should have arrived there by now. The Capitol physician accompanied the ambulance. We'll let you know as soon as we get the word. Could you please come up to the Governor's Office as soon as possible? We need to have you stand by in case some serious situation were to develop in the state and you would have to act in the governor's stead."

Stephen almost began to stammer, but finally said, "I'll be right there."

He quickly called Marybeth on her mobile phone before heading to the Governor's Office. She was as stunned as he had been by the news. There had as yet been no news reports about Governor Klinger's hospitalization, although about ten minutes later the first news flash came over the media. She promised to call to cancel Stephen's talk that evening and to join him at the Governor's Office as soon as possible.

It turned out that the governor had had a serious stroke. It was certainly atypical for a person of fifty-two. It was only three hours later that that news was released by the hospital, which also said that she was in a coma. After the announcement, Stephen and Marybeth got ready to leave the Governor's Office and told Mansfield to call him if he was needed at any time during the night and he would come forthwith. Otherwise, he would plan to return there at 8:00 in the morning. It was arranged that the President Pro Tempore of the State Senate, who was also from the governor and lieutenant governor's party since it controlled the Senate, would preside in the coming days as long as the governor was incapacitated.

As Stephen walked Marybeth out to her car a couple blocks from the Capitol—his was in the Senate parking lot, but he had given up the special reserved spot for the lieutenant governor—she started telling him about her conversation with Governor Klinger's personal secretary. The secretary had been in touch with the governor's son, a college student who was their only child, who had told her earlier in the evening before the announcement that the governor had had a stroke. She said there had been some family history of high blood pressure and blood clots, and that the governor had been on blood pressure medication for some time and had had increased problems with her blood pressure during the campaign and since assuming office. She had resisted going on the medication for some time and when she did wasn't always faithful in taking it. Later on, the word circulated that she had been a long-time user of oral contraceptives beginning when she and her husband married just out of college. She was concerned that she not be burdened with a child while trying to build her legal career. When she was thirty-three, they decided they were ready to have a child and her son was born. The story was that they tried to have another child for a couple years after that, but nothing happened and she went back on the pill until menopause. A couple of her doctors had cautioned her about the risks of blood clots from the use of the pill, especially in light of her family history, but she brushed it off. Stephen remembered that she had pushed hard for the easy availability of contraceptives for women and girls regardless of age, and even was a promoter of providing contraceptive services at school-based health centers. She even hedged when asked if parental permission should be required.

Over the next few days, Stephen and Marybeth both spoke to the governor's husband and son and assured them that they were constantly thinking about the governor and them and were praying for her recovery. They offered their Masses during those days—Stephen normally could not go every weekday, but made a special effort to do so during these difficult days—for the governor's full recovery.

As it turned out, the governor never regained consciousness. Despite aggressive medical efforts, she died five days after the stroke.

Governor Klinger's death seemed to hit Stephen harder than when he learned of her stroke. It was just before dinner at their apartment when he got the call. Right afterwards, he told Marybeth and then just slumped onto the couch. She came over and they embraced for several minutes and he collected himself. Marybeth was his pillar and source of strength and encouragement with his entry into political life, as he had been for her during the difficult times when she kept failing to conceive and finally learned that she wouldn't be able to.

"They said I should come over to the Capitol building. The Chief Justice of the State Supreme Court will be there at about 8:00 this evening to administer the Oath of Office to me. Sheila Klinger's body will lie in state in the Capitol Rotunda tomorrow and the next day and the public can come to show their respects. There will be a special memorial service in the Capitol on that second day and after that her body will be flown back to Delaware County for burial."

He barely finished saying this when the phone rang again. It was the Speaker of the State House of Representatives, Rob Erlanger, who was also a member of their party. In addition to the executive branch, it had the majority in both houses of the legislature. Erlanger asked Stephen if he would come to a caucus room not far from his office at 6:30 that evening before going up for the swearing in. He vaguely said that it was something pertaining to the governorship, and asked him to come alone. Stephen said he would be there, but after he hung up a partly perplexed, partly skeptical look came over his face as he reported Erlanger's request to Marybeth.

"That seems a bit odd that he would seem to want to talk about politics or something like that right after the governor has died. And why in some caucus room instead of in his office?" Stephen said. He recalled that Erlanger, who hailed from Delaware County, had been close to the governor.

"Oh, maybe it's just some point of immediate state business that he needs to talk to you about, some decision you'll have to make quickly as governor," she replied.

"Why, though, did he make a point of asking me to come alone to talk about that? Governors always bring aides to meetings like that since they rely on them to write down details that are discussed and then carry things out for them."

Marybeth nodded, "You have a point."

He thought for a moment. "I'm going to make a few calls—to Jim and Dave and to Bill O'Grady. I'm going to ask you and them to do something when I go to that meeting." Dave Hardesty was his other professional staff aide in the Lieutenant's Governor's Office and

Senator O'Grady was the leader of pro-life and pro-family forces in the legislature who had long since become estranged from the party's leadership who seemed embarrassed with his uncompromising positions on such cultural issues. During the months that Stephen had served as lieutenant governor the two had worked together closely and become friends. "Just before I go into the meeting, I'll link up with the three of you on my smart phone, which will be in my pocket. A few minutes before 6:30, turn on your smart phone. I want the three of you to also hear the conversation. Tape recording a private conversation without notifying all parties is illegal in Pennsylvania, but it's not illegal to privately cut other people into a conversation. Erlanger was very close to the governor and was tied in with the element of the party that has had no use for the principles we have been working for. I've heard from some people that he doesn't care much for me. If there's anything untoward that's said, whoever all's at this meeting won't be able to deny it or say it's just my word against theirs." Stephen called Dave and Jim, and explained the matter to them. They readily agreed to "link into" the conversation. Stephen didn't have to make the call to O'Grady, as he called first to offer his support in whatever way he could. He too readily agreed to the plan. It was arranged that at exactly 6:27, before going into the meeting, Stephen would call all four and they would be on their phones and linked up with him to listen in on the conversation. After this, Stephen tried to eat some dinner, but with the tension of the evening's developments had virtually no appetite.

At almost precisely 6:30, with the phone connections made, Stephen knocked lightly at the caucus room door and Erlanger immediately opened it and welcomed him. There were three other men with him. One of them was Senator Mike Andrekanic, Chairman of the Senate Finance Committee. He was one of the most powerful senators, leading one of the most important committees. He was also known to be very close to Jim Peterson, the President Pro Tempore. Stephen recognized one of the other men as the State Chairman of the party, Andy Grosvenor. Six months ago he had been installed as chairman after Governor Klinger made a strong push for him. He was from Montgomery County, one of the other big Philadelphia suburban counties. John Frost had been skeptical of him. He said that he was ideologically close to the governor—much like Erlanger—and cool to Frost and Stephen's other strong supporters on the State Committee. Stephen did not know the other man. He was introduced to him as Representative Lou Gagliardi, the Chairman of the House Judiciary Committee.

"Mr. Lieutenant Governor," Erlanger said as soon as they sat down, "Let me get to the point of asking you to this meeting right away. We are concerned that you may not have either the necessary governmental experience or close enough connections to our party to become governor. Our majority is not large in either house, as you know. We need someone who can command support from the party's caucuses, who is a skilled legislative tactician, and who also can work not just with our party but the leadership of the other party. You have taken some strong, uncompromising positions. Up here, you have to play ball with both sides, you have to observe the rules of the game. I know you're a professor, but this is actual politics and not a textbook."

Stephen was taken aback by that comment, but of course he had smelled a rat. Before he could respond, Gagliardi intervened. "Like Rob said, you're a professor. We know you're a legal scholar of considerable accomplishment. Here is what we'd like to propose to you: We'd like to ask you to decline to take the governorship. We got a legal opinion from both the Legal Counsel for the House and the Deputy Attorney General that the lieutenant governor, even though he's constitutionally next in line to fill the governorship, can decline to do so. The Senate President Pro Tem then would be in line to become governor. You would still be lieutenant governor, but as a legal scholar maybe your talents could be put to better use for the state in the judicial branch. The party would get completely behind you for the open seat next year on the Superior Court. It's a very secure position, a ten-year term and then retention elections that hardly anybody loses. The pay is very good; in fact, it's higher than the governor's salary. You can maintain your main office in Pittsburgh, where your home is. You can spend part of your time back doing your teaching, which other Superior Court judges do."

Stephen was having trouble absorbing all of this. He saw clearly what they were trying to do. They wanted him to step aside not really because he was inexperienced as a "legislative tactician," but because he wasn't ideologically the kind of governor they wanted. They were sweetening the pot to entice him. For a few moments he thought that the alternative deal they were proposing sounded very appealing. Not only would he be back in a domain that was more natural to him, since the Superior Court was an appellate court that dealt with the kinds of big legal questions that he did as a law professor and he could also resume that work, but he would not have the intense pressures and aggravations of the highest office in the state. Then he remembered that he had entered politics to promote the high principles that were under unremitting attack and that a decreasing number of public officials wanted to be identified with. Also, it occurred to him why Erlanger asked him to come alone: so they could deny this scheme if he refused to go along and brought out what they had done. By the phone arrangement, however, Stephen had been one step ahead of them.

Stephen was not saying anything, and he made sure in the midst of this that his facial expression was neutral. This was probably what motivated Gagliardi to speak up again. He rashly and injudiciously said, "I'm in charge of the Judiciary Committee. I can easily push a bill through to raise the salaries of Superior Court judges."

With that, Stephen abruptly stood up. "Gentleman, there is no use continuing this conversation. I am not interested in what you propose." Then he looked Gagliardi squarely in the eye. "Mr. Gagliardi, what you are essentially trying to do is to bribe me." Amidst protestations that he didn't understand, he strode toward the door and left.

Andrekanic and Grosvenor started having second thoughts about the conversation. They told Erlanger that they were concerned about the fallout if information would get out about the meeting. Erlanger, who was known as a kind of operator in the House who could make things happen, waved his arm and reassured them. "None of us will say anything about the meeting, and if he tries to say anything about what was said we'll just say we asked for a meeting with him to talk to him to make him feel at ease before taking office and to talk over some business." He had no inkling that four other people had heard the conversation. "He's going to become governor, but we'll deal with him in other ways. He won't be able to accomplish anything. We'll cut him off at the pass, and the other party will right away join us to stop a lot of the things that he might want to do."

Stephen proceeded to the Governor's Office to prepare for the swearing in. He met Marybeth and his other three "listeners" there, and they huddled before others began to trickle in. Stephen was still fuming, but unsure what should be done. He did believe that he had an obligation to go to the U.S. Attorney who had been investigating Commonwealth politicians in the corruption probe that had been going on for four years to inform him about Gagliardi's seeming bribe.

"Stephen, I know you're a decent guy and don't want to descend into political gamesmanship, but these people will become a thorn in your side. They are not such nice characters. I've seen that for a long time. What they were trying to do is outrageous. You need to expose them to get them out of there," O'Grady advised. Stephen looked at Marybeth, and could tell immediately that she agreed with O'Grady. From the night they met, she communicated with him by her eyes. She was the gentlest of wives, but in her dealings with the outside world, especially those she perceived to be opportunists, manipulators, or just dishonorable adversaries, she was hard-nosed.

Stephen didn't need any more coaxing. He had long since decided that the *modus operandi* that was needed in the big stakes era of current politics—which he had demonstrated in a limited way in the campaign—was a combination of directness, confrontation, education, repetition, a constant emphasis on a clear moral vision, and a readiness to appeal to the people over the almost inevitable opposition of entrenched institutions, interests, and powerful individuals. Prudence, especially in times like these, meant that often people had to be "called out" and denounced openly.

Stephen was sworn in and made only a short statement to the small group of people and media who were there. He made it clear that he did not think a long statement would be appropriate in light of the circumstances of Governor Klinger's sudden illness and death. He promised the people of the Commonwealth that he would only do his best on their behalf. He told the media, however, that he would have a press conference at 3:00 p.m. the following day.

In the morning, he contacted the U.S. Attorney's Office in Harrisburg, and told him about Gagliardi's statement, and that there were four others who heard it on the phone and would back him up. The U.S. Attorney promised to investigate.

Stephen appeared at the press conference with Marybeth, Jim, Dave, and Senator O'Grady. John Frost was also there with a few others from the State Committee. In a terse statement, Stephen told them about the meeting and the phone hook-up and how the others would affirm what had been said. He mentioned how he had spoken to the U.S. Attorney about Gagliardi, and said he believed he had an obligation to let him know about a possible bribe. He emphasized how he thought it was inappropriate for the speaker, the state party chairman, and two other prominent legislators to try to entice the elected lieutenant governor, who constitutionally had the right to succeed to the governorship upon its vacancy, to take a judgeship so that the Senate president pro tem—who they were close political allies with—could take over instead. From the looks on their faces, the media people present seemed genuinely stunned. He answered the few questions they had after his statement: No, he had no idea what Erlanger had wanted to talk about when he contacted him about the meeting, and the request to come alone under the circumstances had made him suspicious. He did not know any of the people at the meeting well, and had never even met Gagliardi before. The phone hook-up was the only way to handle this because of the state law forbidding taping conversations when the other parties to the conversation were unaware. Maybe this was typical of politics as usual in the Commonwealth: behind the scenes maneuvering, trying to corner the state's highest offices for a party faction, a small group of insiders trying to run the show, an increasing detachment of the state's political leaders from the voting public. As he had said during the campaign, it was partly because he was tired of hearing about this that he accepted the invitation of John Frost and others to enter the lieutenant governor race. What would happen next was up to the people of the Commonwealth.

The meeting was front-page and first-story news around the state for the next several days. It was obvious that Erlanger and the others were caught completely off-guard. They could hardly defend themselves. When an anonymous Hill staffer went to the Harrisburg media to report that when he was in Erlanger's office waiting for one of his staffers a few hours before the meeting he overheard part of his phone conversation discussing the plan, that fueled the fire even more. Editorialists began to call for the four to resign. Even though many news outlets did not agree with Stephen philosophically, they responded to this as they did his "good government" appeal during the campaign. For them, this was just more of the "smelly" politics that the state had seen enough of recently. Some even said that state judgeships had become political bargaining chips. John Frost led a group calling publicly for Grosvenor's ouster and demanded an immediate meeting of the state party committee. The crescendo reached a high point and Grosvenor resigned before the week's end. President Pro Tem Peterson also came under increasing criticism. He denied any involvement, but Andrekanic's role and Peterson's being the obvious beneficiary made him highly suspect. Some of the media even said that the "Gang of Four"—a few media people called it the "Gang of Five," putting Peterson into it, as well—despite being aligned with Sheila Klinger actually dishonored her with their actions right on the heels of her untimely death. There were even some in the party's legislative caucus who were simply unwilling to cross a new governor of their party, and pulled away from its legislative leadership.

In the end, the public and party pressure became too great. Erlanger, Andrekanic, Gagliardi, and Peterson all resigned their leadership and committee posts. The U.S. Attorney decided not to prosecute Gagliardi because he thought that under prevailing legal precedents what he said might not constitute bribery, but the party turned against him on the Hill and in his home county. His popularity also dropped precipitously with his constituents, and he resigned his seat. The entire episode had been a clumsy miscalculation by them, and instead of pushing Stephen aside created the situation where he would now deal with a new legislative leadership that would be more favorable to him and his principles.

What Stephen proceeded to do next was to make a careful assessment of the holdover Klinger appointees he thought could help the new administration and which should be let go. He made it clear that he would not retain Klinger's personal aides. Virtually all were lawyers or previously lower-level eastern Pennsylvania politicos, and could easily go back to their former or similar jobs. Like when he became lieutenant governor, Stephen made clear that he wanted only a very small staff in the Governor's Office. He had no use for the kinds of palace guards that surrounded the typical political executives and even members of Congress. He was going to resurrect the old practice of viewing the cabinet as his main advisors. He would have a professional staff of only three: Dave, Jim, and another person he would shortly be adding. He decided that most of the cabinet and sub-cabinet appointees would have to change, as well. Their views paralleled Klinger's and they were mostly from her wing of the party. He was not about to let them quietly undercut or refuse to implement his initiatives. Although a few people suggested to him that he should do this gradually so as not to arouse unnecessary political opposition, he said that that was not his way. Immediately after he notified the cabinet members whose services he no longer desired, he called a press conference to announce this. He emphasized in his statement and further drove home when answering the reporters' questions—in fact he persistently brought the topic back to this—that any governor must have his own people at the helm and that he has a basic perspective and will have a program and he needs people who fully agree with them and will enthusiastically carry them out. "Any executive," he added, "needs to listen carefully to competing views about a broad array of things so as to avoid miscues, but everyone must be 'on board' with regard to the basics." In the days ahead, Stephen fashioned opportunities to reiterate his explanation in various public forums. He understood that he must start now with the educative function of politics, and the public—and even some of the opinion-makers—could be educated about things by repeatedly making and explaining the case. He also realized that some in the State Senate might seek to oppose his nominees on ideological grounds, so consistently making the argument of the governor being able to appoint his own people might be a necessary rhetorical tool to secure Senate approval.

As far as the state party chairman was concerned, he announced that he was not going to insist upon anyone and so passed on the customary practice of the governor naming him. Senator O'Grady and some in the state committee started to push John Frost. Stephen encouraged him to run for it, but asked John to respect his belief that the committee should strictly be the determiner about who its chairman would be. John understood. It was a matter of integrity for Stephen, and John knew how important integrity was to him. As it turned out, John ran and was narrowly elected over a candidate of the Klinger, left-of-center or "moderate" wing of the party.

The Klinger people, including a number of the dismissed high administration officials, argued strongly in party circles—some even took to the op-ed columns around the state to make the case—that Stephen should not substantially depart from the deceased governor's agenda. After all, she was the one nominated by the party and then elected governor and had a mandate of sorts. Stephen's response was that this was a new gubernatorial administration and he had the full authority as governor to proceed in the direction he thought best. They weren't pleased, to be sure, but they were now on the sidelines. They had lost control even in the legislative branch by their foolish gambit to try to get Stephen to decline to accept the governorship.

Stephen had a very good idea about his broad objectives and the things he aimed to accomplish. He was intent upon not just insuring that the state budget be balanced—that was a state constitutional requirement, but some various innovative efforts were usually undertaken to get around it—but on reducing it. In fact, the standard that he enunciated for approaching the role that state government was to play—which would be a major guide for his whole political future—was gradual disengagement. Government had some basic roles and when it had stretched over a long period of time into other areas people had increasingly come to depend on it, so it had to pull back slowly, over an extended period of time, so no one would be harmed. He was emphatic that budget balancing would not be achieved by raising taxes of any kind or by establishing new fees. In fact, a central part of his program was to begin the effort of reducing all state taxes to the lowest levels possible and to outright eliminate the imposing of taxes by either state or local governments on elements of the population where they would be particularly burdensome, such as inheritance taxes on the middle class for receiving a close relative's small estate or even small bank account. A key part of gradual disengagement was to reduce the size of the state workforce—substantially over time. He delivered an address to the citizens of the Commonwealth—he requested and was given free air time by a number of media outlets in the state to do this—explaining his gradual disengagement vision and how it involved

107

working to help stimulate the non-profit and charitable sectors—not by state funding, but by encouraging and promoting their work and clearing out any governmental obstacles to their efforts—to play a larger, and eventually the major, role in addressing human needs. He recognized that the state could only do so much to clear the way for this because federal obstacles would also stand in the way. Still, it would do all it could. He emphasized that such an undertaking was a long-term effort and that one gubernatorial administration could only begin it. He made clear that government always had the responsibility of maintaining a "safety net" when the private sector could not completely address human needs. He mentioned that he would be convening a series of meetings in Harrisburg with representatives of all kinds of non-profit, civil society groups to listen to their ideas and concerns and motivate them to begin to forge plans for such an expanded role that the state would coordinate.

One of his first acts as governor was to freeze all state hiring and make new arrangements for external contractors to do jobs in lieu of state employees. He would reduce the state workforce by attrition. Since he viewed a promise as something not to be broken, he said that current state employees and retirees would in no way have their benefits cut back. He proposed a substantially less generous benefit package for future employees, however, so that it would be more in line with private sector benefit schemes. He announced, however, that no abortions of any kind, including abortifacient drugs—which included most oral contraceptives—would be covered under any state employee health insurance plan. As expected, the state employee unions rushed to criticize these moves and to initiate legal action to stop the tightening of abortion access. Stephen, however, had worked out arrangements for the governor's legal adviser to work with certain pro-life legal advocacy groups to oppose their suit. As he had expected, the rabidly pro-abortion state attorney general, who was from the other party, would not defend his position.

He announced that he had directed the Health Department to immediately put into place a plan to vigorously enforce all state regulations of the abortion industry. Finally, the state was going to be committed to insuring there would be no more Gosnell cases. He announced also that he would veto any attempt to reinstitute state funding for Planned Parenthood or any other abortion provider that had been ended some years before.

He also announced that the state funding of embryonic stem cell research would be eliminated from the budget he was preparing for the next fiscal year. He said resolutely that if such were slipped into it, he would veto the entire budget. The state was now going to be out of the business of paying for human embryos to be experimented on and then destroyed. In fact, he was going a significant step further to enact legislation—a challenge to which, once enacted, he vowed to fight all the way to the U.S. Supreme Court—to ban such research within the Commonwealth. With these initiatives, the state's pro-life community, which was strong, vocally rallied to his side.

In the meantime, however, with the changes in the state legislature accompanying his becoming governor, it had become even more pro-life than it had been before. Stephen didn't have to worry about vetoing such research funding in the future. A major effort started in the legislature to eliminate even the funding that had been enacted in the current budget year by the Klinger administration. Stephen encouraged this. He knew that he didn't have the power to impound already-enacted funds, but if the legislature would agree it could be immediately ended. It was another educational opportunity for Stephen. He kept explaining in a series of public addresses how, in effect, embryonic stem cell research was a fraud. Not only did it result in dead unborn children—and he took the opportunity to discuss why biologically and logically the destroyed embryos could be nothing but that—but further the research was a dead-end that had achieved none of the medical treatment successes that its promoters kept promising.

Both houses of the legislature narrowly voted to repeal the funding provided for in the current budget year. Stephen, of course, signed the repeal measure. This set the stage for one of several episodes that would define his governorship—and open the door to his and the nation's political destiny.

As this began to unfold, he was also moving quickly on numerous other initiatives. They came so quickly that they left likely opponents off-balance and were underway before they could even react to them. His alacrity also stymied quick efforts of different organizations and legislators to coordinate their disparate efforts to oppose him.

He appointed a Secretary of Education who was a strong supporter of private and religious schools and of homeschooling. They had a lengthy meeting and then convened a press conference to announce, first, that they wanted Pennsylvania to go from being a state that heavily regulates homeschoolers to the one that would become perhaps the easiest to do homeschooling in. The Secretary was using all his discretionary authority to minimize state imposed requirements on homeschooling families. Any change in law that was necessary would be proposed immediately to the legislature. The governor said he would not tolerate attempts by local school districts or prosecutors to use truancy laws to harass homeschooling families in any way. In fact, he said it was time for a review of truancy laws generally. The secretary would also be using his authority to minimize state regulation of private schools, religiously affiliated or not. He was also taking all steps his discretionary authority would allow to insure that local public school districts controlled their own schools and affairs. State regulation would not exceed points that were specifically legally mandated, and any benefit of the doubt under the law would be given to local authorities. He also began his repeated criticism of how the public schools had too often substituted ideology for solid evidence in their natural science programs, citing their treatment of such subjects as "the grand theory of evolution" and global warming as unchallengeable laws when they were hardly scientifically proven. He said they probably didn't actually even rise to the level of "theories" on the hierarchy of scientific certitude, but evolution was at best a hypothesis and global warming not even that. Despite criticism in the press, he came back to these topics repeatedly during his governorship, especially at talks he gave frequently about education, and pounded away at them. He gave deeper explanations, chalk full of evidence and citations, of why these positions were flawed—it was more of his emphasis on the educative function of politics. He also referred to many great political thinkers, starting with Aristotle, who argued why education should forge solid citizenship and patriotism. Schools trying to do that had become controversial. He also repeatedly made the case in his talks about why American exceptionalism was true, and that especially justified a strong stress on proper citizenship formation in schools.

Stephen had long been a critic of what he referred to as the "so-called child protective system," the sweeping system of county agencies around the country, under the control of a central agency in each state, and funded partly by the federal government. He had talked about it during his campaign for lieutenant governor, mostly to educate since in that office he would have had no power to do anything about it. The CPS came into existence with the Mondale Act in the 1970s, which supposedly was enacted to address the national "epidemic" of child abuse and neglect. It was only years later that it had become apparent that there never was such an epidemic and that the CPS mostly investigated entirely innocent parents and intruded into a vast number of families for no good reason, as Stephen had said during the campaign. The CPS operatives spent much of their time trying to clamp down on innocent child-rearing practices that they, or the "experts" they took their cue from, didn't like. Their effect was to actually harm children and solid families and, as they chased such trivialities, often the real abusers slipped through the cracks. Stephen knew the realities of the CPS inside out and had done considerable scholarly writing about it and worked on cases to defend falsely accused parents. He intended to clamp down on what he saw as a systemically abusive bureaucracy. The State Senate had not yet approved Stephen's Secretary of Public Welfare designee, Dr. Anne Lipinski from the Philadelphia suburbs, but he wanted change to begin immediately in the state CPS agencies. Lipinski had had been a leader in the Pennsylvania branch of the socially conservative Eagle Forum organization. Stephen had gotten to know her from his contacts in the Catholic Social Workers National Association. Like him, she advocated sweeping changes in child welfare in the Commonwealth and across the country. Stephen knew there would be much opposition in the agency, and by the DPW employees union, to her appointment. He short-circuited that opposition by calling a meeting at the Public Welfare Building auditorium of all the professional-level civil servants in the agency where he introduced her and gave a talk with his usual opportunity for give-and-take where he made clear what he sought from the agency, but also what gubernatorial prerogatives were and how he expected career employees to go along with the political executive. He also made clear that open or surreptitious opposition to the administration's decisions would bring a vigorous response and sanctions.

He also generated support for his designees for this and the other cabinet positions by arranging meetings with different groups and just showing up with them at places like shopping malls where the public gathered to briefly speak and let the designees speak also. This attracted the media and what he and the designees aimed to do became better known—and so it became more difficult for opponents at the Capitol to defeat their nominations.

He convened a meeting in a large caucus room in the Capitol Building with Secretary-designate Lipinski, the acting secretary of the department (who was its highest civil servant), and the acting head of the department's Office of Children, Youth and Families, which was in charge of overseeing the state CPS agencies (she was also a civil servant, but Stephen would shortly be making his own appointment to that office), and the heads of all the county CPS agencies. At the meeting, he made clear that amendments to the Mondale Act of some years before to screen all reports of supposed child maltreatment, which had still not been adopted in many counties, would have to be immediately put in place. Any county agencies that delayed any longer in implementing this would immediately have their funding suspended. What's more, some showing of the reliability of a person making a

111

report would have to be made; anonymous reports could no longer be taken. Also, the standard that would have to be used in considering whether some parental behavior was maltreatment would now be what a "reasonable man"—a traditional standard in the common law—would consider such. While he did not threaten funding suspension if these latter policies were not immediately implemented, the context of his comments didn't leave anyone in the room doubting it.

Afterwards the acting head of OCYF came up to him to object. "Mrs. Gordy," he responded with unmistakable firmness and a cold stare right into her eyes. "This is what I expect. Previous administrations may have not exercised the oversight of OCYF that they rightfully should have. *I intend to*, and I expect that your agency on the state level and all the county agencies you oversee will faithfully carry out these directives."

She said nothing more, but Stephen didn't trust her. He knew that additional pressure had to be exerted, and had already made plans to expose in an ongoing way the abusive CPS. His aides and Anne Lipinski had worked with the Home School Legal Defense Association and a few smaller state groups to arrange a public rally for the next day outside the Capitol Building. The rally featured testimonies of numerous parents from around the state who had been falsely accused of abuse or neglect and badly mistreated by county CPS agencies. Many of the stories were outrageous. Stephen spoke last at the rally and showed his considerable understanding of the CPS and explained how these episodes were the rule, not the exception, and how the nature of the system was the cause. What followed over the next several months were similar smaller rallies around the state that Stephen also spoke at. Media attention was generated on an issue it too often ignored and after all this, he had definitely put the CPS on the defensive. The effort also helped secure Anne Lipinski's confirmation and she closely monitored the system around the state to insure compliance with Stephen's new policies.

An ongoing police scandal in Philadelphia gave Stephen the opportunity to address police abuses and other issues, which he had researched and written about as a law professor. The police department was using civil forfeiture with an abandon to get possession of businesses, houses, vehicles, and other private property if it had even a slight unwitting connection to a crime to fill its coffers, pursuant to the provisions of a federal program. There were cases where teenagers had a small amount of marijuana at home, unbeknownst to their parents, and after the juvenile court prosecutions the police moved to seize the family's home by civil forfeiture. There were other cases where drug transactions took place on someone's front lawn or porch when they were not home and were completely unaware of it and their property was seized. A few cases involved cars stolen and used in criminal activity that were never returned after the culprits were caught, but instead forfeited to the department. Civil forfeiture had been happening around the country, but the actions of the Philadelphia department were especially egregious and had been the subject of much media coverage and criticism. The legislature had been unwilling to act to put limits on police department's profiting from civil forfeiture and the recent state attorneys general, who had been members of the party that long controlled the city's politics, had stayed clear so as not to offend the city administrations.

Stephen made clear to the city administration and police department that, irrespective of what the attorney general would do, his administration was going to challenge in court every case of civil forfeiture that looked unreasonable. He also was going to use his full power under the law to withhold state funding and other support for the department if it didn't change its forfeiture policies. He knew that he needed to generate public support for his stance in light of the expected onslaught of criticism by the city's politicos and police department and union leaders that he was "anti-police." He began to hit hard on this in public speeches and arranged small public appearances with innocent people who had been victimized by the unjust application of the forfeiture laws. He also met with some members of the state's Congressional delegation to try to motivate them to push for change in the federal forfeiture program.

His legal and scholarly work had made him knowledgeable more broadly about police abuses and overreaching of their authority. On this topic, he forged an odd political coalition across the spectrum. He repeatedly made clear that he sought to properly control police departments, not weaken or unduly hamstring them. He insisted that the two things were not mutually exclusive. He pushed legislation to require enhanced training on constitutional questions and emphasized the vision of police work he had mentioned during the campaign as involving service, being part law enforcer and part social worker, and being better integrated into the neighborhoods they worked in. He set up regular meetings with members of police departments to help them to see that such an approach would actually have the effect of aiding them in their jobs by enhancing community respect and support for them. He also appointed a high-level task force to examine the role of police and establish statewide standards for police officers and departments along these lines. He believed that this would both help develop well thought out changes and generate popular support for their enactment. He also arranged for forums where open discussion between police, community leaders, organization representatives, and the general public took place to discuss the proper role of the police and their relationship to the community.

Criminal justice reform more broadly was a major point of the agenda that Stephen pursued. As he wanted to act against police abuse, he also wanted to address the rising tide of prosecutorial abuse. He gave talks around the Commonwealth, to legal and general citizen groups, making it clear that prosecutors were to be held to the stated standard of legal ethics codes of securing justice. Running up a record of successful prosecutions, getting notches on one's belt, and looking to further one's political career were unacceptable as motivations. He also said that he would personally campaign against the reelection of any district attorney in the state of either party who acted in this manner. His campaign against what he called "unmerited prosecutions" or "excessive prosecution" generated much attention in the media. As with his campaign for the lieutenant governorship, they had never seen anything quite like it and it was further evidence that he didn't easily fit into the usual political categories. He also wanted to have a dialogue with prosecutors as he did with police, so he arranged a series of meetings with prosecutors in different parts of the state. He was combining the carrot and the stick: dialogue but with the threat to politically oppose them if they pursued questionable prosecutions instead of justice. It was in the manner of his simultaneous stress on education, confrontation, and trying to "bring people along"—and also trying to change institutions and deep-seated practices where necessary by working with those in them but also by appealing to the public over their heads. He knew the realities of going up against entrenched attitudes and interests and in dealing with a public that was ignorant or uninterested in many crucial civic matters. He realized, as most politicians didn't, that the pay-offs would usually take a long time. While prudence should always be kept in mind, political obstacles or the remoteness of success should not be a deterrent. He didn't push just any initiative, but didn't hesitate when he thought the stakes were high for the common good, American constitutional principles, and genuine human rights and dignity. That was why he also proposed and pushed legislation to narrow the possibilities for plea-bargaining. He thought the innocent were too often trampled on and their Sixth Amendment rights denied when over 90% of criminal cases never went to trial.

Stephen understood that the problem of the criminal justice system and of American law generally could not just be laid at the feet of prosecutors. There was simply an inordinate amount of law. The famed Harvard Law professor Alan Dershowitz said frequently that the average American daily committed three federal felonies and wasn't even aware that he was violating the law. It was not just that there was a plethora of laws that people were not aware of, and could not reasonably be aware of, but legal provisions were often vague and in conflict with each other. So even if they knew what a law was and sincerely tried to abide by it, they might be going against another law. This was especially the case of regulatory law, and it wasn't just a problem at the federal level. The effect was that the cherished American principle of the rule of law was taking a beating. Stephen responded by arranging to speak to bar associations, judicial organizations, and citizen groups about these serious issues. He also appointed a "blue-ribbon" state commission made up of legal scholars, practicing lawyers, social scientists who were philosophically well formed (which as one of them he knew perilously few were), retired jurists, a former state attorney general, a few business leaders who had faced the burden of state regulatory law, an ethician, and also average citizens—he never left average citizens out of anything—who were attuned to the problem and charged them to undertake a major study about what kinds of state laws could be trimmed back or outright repealed and how the state's legal codes could be cut down. They had to make a formal report to him in a year.

Right after the immediate repeal of the embryonic stem cell research funding, two scientists and a research facility they were associated with in Philadelphia sued the Commonwealth. They claimed that the state had a legal obligation to continue funding what it had committed itself to. The Commonwealth Court, which has original jurisdiction to hear appeals from final orders of state agencies (in this case, after the funding repeal the state Health Department ordered the funding cut), decided for the plaintiffs. The leftist state attorney general refused to handle the case, so the governor's office took responsibility for the defense. The state's Supreme Court refused to take the case up on appeal. The state media proclaimed that Stephen had suffered a serious setback, one that had the potential of grinding his wide-ranging initiatives to a halt. It turned out that they were too hasty in their judgment.

Stephen responded to the courts' action quickly and decisively. He called a press conference and said that under the state's constitution and the entire constitutional history of the Commonwealth the courts had no authority "at all" to order the allocation of state funds. Only the legislature, in conjunction with the governor, could do that. "So,"

Stephen said with the unmistakable firmness in his tone that he was becoming known for, "the court's order will not be carried out. It will be *ignored*." The press conference was held on the sidewalk right outside the Pennsylvania Judicial Center in Harrisburg to have maximum effect. He didn't stop there, however. He laid out the argument against funding of embryonic stem cell research, which ranged from a clear, but detailed discussion about the nature of unborn human life to a point-by-point refutation of the claims of the promoters and practitioners of such research. He showed how, contrary to adult stem cell research, it had produced no results and helped no one with medical needs. Its claims, as he had said before, were "patently untrue, even fraudulent." Its promoters couldn't any longer get private funding because of this, so now they were "trying to take the measure of the Commonwealth's taxpayers—they were trying to exploit them."

Stephen didn't cease making his case with that. There had been no tradition of Pennsylvania governors getting free airtime to speak to the state's citizenry, but Stephen made the effort anyway. A number of media outlets around the state agreed as they had for his gradual disengagement speech, since they saw it as a way to focus more attention on state news. It seemed to some, especially the ones that had a limited cadre of reporters in Harrisburg, to be an easy way to do it. In his talk, he went into even further detail about the courts' lack of authority constitutionally to do what they did and the absence of historical precedents and about the case for unborn human life and against embryonic stem cell research. He pledged to lead a major effort, from his position as governor, to stimulate more private funding for adult stem cell research in the Commonwealth. For a governor to do something like that, as opposed to just pledging more public funds (usually a grossly inadequate amount) for something, was almost novel.

Again, Stephen's approach had caught the state's media and editorialists off-guard. His action was the main topic of media discussion about Commonwealth issues for the next few days. Despite its general leftist tilt, however, the criticism was far from unanimous against him. First of all, some were simply impressed with his decisiveness. It was almost refreshing for them to see that in an age of politicians who routinely went out of their way to avoid taking a stand, he took one so resolutely and forcefully and seemed so unconcerned about the political reaction. Second, some commented that his position was sound, that there had been no precedent for the courts to order monies to be either appropriated or expended. Third, he had made a strong effort to appeal to the public over their heads before they could even get their bearings and so he set the terms of the discussion. He continued to do that in his usual manner of speaking to citizen groups and just informal citizen gatherings about what he had done. Thus, his opponents had to address the issue on *his* terms, and faced the even greater burden of answering his substantial arguments, which were heavily supported by evidence.

While there was some grumbling by various opposition legislators, they didn't push the matter too far because they were themselves concerned about the legislature losing control over the state budget. They also figured that it wasn't worth the fight since the embryonic stem cell research funding was already out of the budget for the following fiscal year anyway.

This episode had hardly passed when another situation developed that Stephen saw the need to vigorously intervene into. It involved, again, the courts and the CPS. In spite of the restraints Stephen had imposed on the agencies, they were trying to carry out their practices as of old. A couple in the Philadelphia area refused any longer to take their young son who had childhood cancer for chemotherapy at a hospital there. The child was suffering, in an ongoing way, serious side effects from the treatment. Tests had revealed for some months that the boy was now cancer-free, but the hospital insisted on continuing the chemotherapy. The family's private physician and an oncologist he referred them to jointly arranged an alternative treatment regimen. The authorities at the hospital rejected this and reported the parents to the CPS, who came to their house with police back-up and removed the child. They quickly placed him in foster care and ordered the reinstitution of the chemotherapy and the boy became gravely ill. The parents' attorney could make no headway with the county juvenile court, which almost perfunctorily upheld the CPS (as usually happens). The case had begun to generate local and even national publicity, as the Justina Pelletier case in Massachusetts had done. Stephen openly and vigorously criticized the county CPS agency and the juvenile court and accused them of violating the law. He and Secretary Lipinski gave the agency twenty-four hours to drop the case and return the boy to his parents or "state funds for the agency would immediately be cut off." The agency complied. Then, after consultation with Stephen, Secretary Lipinski ordered the agency to expunge any record about the family and to cease and desist any further monitoring of them. The episode gave Stephen the opening to consolidate his reform efforts of the state CPS. He made sure that he seized the rhetorical high ground and began a new round of "exposure" of routine CPS abuses. He kept pounding away at it and it helped move public opinion to stronger support for his effort to sweepingly change the CPS in the state.

Stephen's governmental efforts to strengthen the family were seen also with his unprecedented push to end no-fault divorce in the Commonwealth. Stephen knew that all divorce was objectionable, since by its nature it permitted the weakening of marital commitment, gave an official imprimatur to the breaking apart of families, and had a deleterious impact on children. He knew that America had become a "divorce culture," however, and he could not hope to bring it to an end in Pennsylvania. After extensive consultation with the new group of his party's legislative leaders, who shared his sentiments about family and life issues, legislation was pushed to move away from no-fault divorce and to begin to restore fault-based standards for divorce. While some criticized the legislation as meaningless in practice, since the "fault" categories it established were so broad as to almost insure no-fault divorce, Stephen and his legislative supporters hailed it as an important symbolic step. It made Pennsylvania one of the few states to pull back on the outright no-fault standard. The bill passed very narrowly in each house, but the effort showcased Stephen's capabilities as a legislative tactician. He coupled his vintage educative approach with the broader public, not just with sound arguments but also with the personal dimension that he had used on the campaign trail. He kept hammering at the consequences of divorce for families and children, and spotlighted a steady stream of children and especially wives who had suffered in many ways because of it. They told their stories in a long series of public forums his staff arranged and before legislative committees. His staff and Marybeth also worked with pro-family and divorce reform groups to arrange letters to the editor and op-eds around the state on the topic. They were often written by victims of the state's no-fault divorce regimen. Marybeth used her podium as the state's first lady to speak frequently for pro-life and pro-family objectives, issues that one seldom saw any American first ladies address. They were viewed as "too controversial" in the political climate of recent times; talking about such things as education and the arts seemed safer for them. This was a big effort and when it came to pushing legislation Stephen knew there were few initiatives he could go all-out for. This and ending the embryonic stem cell research were his main efforts. The state and Stephen gained much national attention by the successful legislative struggle to end no-fault divorce.

Stephen was not too popular from the start with the leftist state employees unions because of his views. The main state employees union, an affiliate of one of the largest national unions, bristled at his hiring freeze. His putting the constraints on the CPS and trying to stop the police abuses in Philadelphia irritated their respective unions. It was said that some of them scoffed at him and certain legislative leaders of his party as "moralists" or "religious fanatics" during the debate on the divorce bill, even though the union officials didn't get involved in it. Furthermore, his attempt to reach out to state employees, to have "listening sessions" with them about the workplace problems they saw, to take into account ideas that even the lowest level employees had, to tell those in policy-making roles how they were expected to uphold the political leadership's agenda (instead of one fashioned by the career employees of an agency who had no accountability to the public), and his frequent exhortations in the sessions to personal morality angered the union leadership. He was going around them and as far as they were concerned this was meddling with civil servants. They couldn't fathom the notion of a governor being in charge of the state's employees other than his political appointees. The union leaders were probably his most vocal critics. Unlike previous governors, he went toe-to-toe with them persistently, focusing the public on how well state employees were paid and treated compared to the private sector and making it difficult for the unions to make a case that he was being unfair. He didn't just persistently make the public case against their position, however. He did not attack them personally or use polemics against "the public employee union leadership." He invited them to the Governor's Office for discussions with him. He listened to them and found areas where they could agree, but also strongly but respectfully and charitably made his arguments to them on other issues. The personal rapport they developed from these meetings made it more difficult for them to made vigorous public attacks on his. It was part of his approach of educate, confront temperately and charitably, and dialogue.

The back-and-forth with the unions came to a head with a pay-raise controversy that developed near the end of the following fiscal year. Even though the national economy was in recession and private sector employment and wages were contracting, the state unions were demanding a salary increase larger than they had three years before when their contracts with the state last came up for renewal. They also demanded an expansion of benefits, which were acknowledged as being a major cause of the fiscal strains that had beset the government of the Commonwealth in the last several years. In Pennsylvania, public employees had the statutory right to strike though there had been only one relatively brief strike decades before. Now, the unions were rattling sabers. This was one more of many battles Stephen had to fight, but he nevertheless rose to the occasion. He consistently went to the public to answer the claims being made by the union leadership. He had shown a knack for defining the terms of the debate and this was no different. He pointed out the advantageous position of state employees in difficult economic times. Not only were their salaries considerably above the average of comparable positions in the private sector and benefit packages far outstripped them, but they also had utterly secure employment. This was at a time when the state's unemployment rate was at a ten-year high. When he imposed the hiring freeze, a few people advised him to institute some state employee layoffs to get better control over the state's fiscal problems. He refused to do that, however, because it would put many strains on people and their families. As governor, he was the employer of the Commonwealth's workers and said that employers should be concerned about the well-being of their workers. As he talked about the need of the Commonwealth's employees to make sacrifices as those in the private sector were having to do and pointedly and repeatedly challenged the false and self-serving assertions of union leaders, he also stressed that all workers—including public ones—had to be treated with dignity and have their rights upheld. Pennsylvania was an open shop state for state employees, so the state labor leaders had only a limited constituency. Despite Stephen's deft efforts to blunt their public criticisms, the tension and public exchanges now reached their peak. Still, the public was squarely on Stephen's side on this. It helped that his party also controlled the legislature, but with the public sentiment as it was even the other party—that was usually so close to the unions—wasn't eager to come to their defense. Stephen's position on the salary and benefit issue prevailed and the talk about a strike came to nothing. Stephen didn't want to lord his outright win over the unions, however. He reached out to the leadership afterwards in a spirit of kindness and respect, and sat down with them for further discussions on matters of common concern.

The mid-term elections intervened. In the midst of all these challenges he faced as governor, he worked with John Frost to have the party focus a great deal of attention on grassroots organizing, something on which it found itself strikingly outstripped by the other party and its interest groups. This involved working through county and local party committees, some of which had become almost moribund and had to be rejuvenated. He especially encouraged them to reach out to members of citizen organizations and to 501 (c) (4) organizations that were philosophically sympathetic to the direction he had taken the state administration. They coordinated efforts with these organizations within the limits permitted by state and federal law. He and Frost were very careful about party organizers knowing the law and staying within it, and exercised close oversight of their activities to insure this.

Although it was a work in progress, it bore some early fruit as their party—surprisingly, in the minds of the commentators—held control of both legislative houses and even captured a few additional seats.

Stephen's public outreach and educational efforts were not just, or primarily, geared to short-term political success or to current voters. They were ultimately geared to restoring public morality and to cultural renewal. So, they had to involve the upcoming generation as well. He invited different organizations and high school and college students to come to the Capitol for what were called "Time with the Governor" discussions with him. These were opportunities for him to make the case and explain the rationale for traditional American political and constitutional principles, for sound cultural practices, and simply for moral truth. The talks he gave—almost always extemporaneous—were a small part of the meetings. Mostly, they involved questions, give-and-take, and dialogue. He wanted to bring up and explain things to people that they didn't give much thought to or that they routinely accepted a superficial understanding about simply because it was "in the air." He also wanted to stimulate them to think and ponder about these different subjects.

About a month after the mid-term elections, a couple of weeks before Christmas Day, the greatest challenge of his governorship was developing. Some days after it was first reported in the media, Stephen realized that he had to address a controversy that had developed at a nursing home in the Philadelphia area. (So many problems seemed to confront him from that part of the state!) Lisa Allen was a woman in her late forties who had been in the facility for three years after suffering a brain aneurysm. She had never been married, but had had a daughter out of wedlock who had drifted in and out of her life for years before her illness and institutionalization. Allen had been a small businesswoman and had done very well financially before her illness. Apparently, she had cut off all financial assistance to the daughter, who was then in her late twenties, a year or so before after her patience ran out with the young woman's irresponsible way of life. She had dropped out of college—which Allen was paying for—moved from dead-end job to dead-end job, and had had a series of sexual affairs. Allen had no real prospect of significant improvement and had begun to develop other health problems. The nursing home had no next of kin on record and had made no effort to search for anyone. It got the county court to name one of the nursing home's administrators as Allen's guardian. The facility then quickly put in place a DNR order. After being out of Allen's life for almost five years, the daughter reappeared. She told the nursing home staff that her mother never would have wanted to live in her current condition, and claimed that she had told her so on different occasions. She had never drawn up a written directive, but the daughter said that she had talked about a living will. The mother's funds had gone down because of her care and the story was going around that the daughter wanted to "cash in" while she could. There was no will, but she would be the one to receive any remaining assets. As Allen physically declined—although there was no evidence that she was terminal—the nursing home, at the daughter's urging, gradually began to withdraw nutrition and hydration. What that meant, of course, was that they were starving her to death. Their effort was sidetracked when Allen's cousin's daughter, who lived in another part of the country but was temporarily in the Philadelphia area on a work assignment, decided to visit her after hearing that she was in the facility. She saw that something was amiss, and when she asked some questions at the facility got evasive answers. She had had some limited medical training since she was an EMT in her home state and then talked to some people after her visit, and then pieced together that Allen was being starved. She consulted with her mother and some Philadelphia area pro-life and disability rights people who she had been referred to and, with the help of a local pro-life volunteer attorney, tried to intervene in the case to stop what the nursing home was doing and have her switched to a different facility. The judge summarily turned down her petition. The volunteer attorney quickly tried to appeal, but the Superior Court rebuffed him. The leftist state attorney general, who had suggested that the state should consider enacting "aid in dying" and assisted suicide legislation, did nothing, so Stephen intervened to ask the Superior Court—which, of course, he had locked horns with before—to reconsider. The Court refused, and that set the stage for a tense confrontation.

By this time, the matter was generating much public attention around the Commonwealth and even nationally. There were protests outside the nursing home. Allen's cousin flew in and joined her daughter at a rally pro-life and disability rights leaders organized at a small park a few blocks away. A small number of "right to die" activists had a counter-rally, and some angry words were exchanged but there were no clashes. A twenty-four-hour candle-light prayer vigil started in the parking lot of a church just down the road from the facility, but no picketing was taking place. It was almost Terri Schiavo *redivivus*. The judge, buoyed by the Superior Court's action, dug in his heels. He seemed to think that someone might come into the facility and snatch Allen and remove her, and he ordered the county sheriff to send a detachment of deputies to back up the enhanced private security already deployed there.

Meanwhile, information leaked by a sympathetic staffer at the nursing home indicated that Allen was weakening. Stephen ordered his General Counsel, who had taken the matter to the Superior Court, to now prepare an emergency appeal to the state's Supreme Court. It seemed unlikely that the Supreme Court would get involved and, in any event, time was running out. Stephen decided that it was time for a showdown. He was resolved that the outcome would be different than with Terri Schiavo.

He convened an urgent meeting of Dr. Lipinski, the General Counsel, the state Physician General, the State Police Commissioner, and members of his personal staff. Almost as if he could foresee an eventuality of having to decisively project executive power in some crucial situation, he was careful to choose a State Police Commissioner of high integrity and solid moral principles who shared his constitutional vision and knew how to command loyalty and discipline in the ranks of his force.

Jim Davidson was the State Police Commissioner. He had not been elevated from the ranks of troopers, as was usually the case, though he had been a trooper for a number of years before going to law school, becoming an FBI agent, and then being in private law practice in Pittsburgh. Stephen assigned him a sometimes difficult dual role as both a liaison with county and local law enforcement agencies throughout the Commonwealth to assist them as needed, but also to put pressure on them to adopt the standards of professionalism and proper conduct, covering everything from their relations with the community, to excessive force, to abusing civil forfeiture like with the Philadelphia Police Department. He was to be the front-line man in carrying out Stephen's plan to rescue Lisa Allen.

While they had little time, they made sure that the "rescue attempt" was carefully planned. Davidson received information from the pro-life groups that had been active in the protests that while there were usually four deputies and a couple private security personnel at the nursing home during the day, only one or two deputies and no private security were there at night until about 8:00 a.m. They had also told him that with the changing of the shift just before 7:30 a.m. the facility seemed to leave its main entrance, which the staff entered and exited from, unlocked. Davidson arrived at the nursing home at a few minutes before 7:30 with ten uniformed State Police, an ambulance team and a physician under contract with the State Department of Health. He wanted the action to be taken when it was light enough out so everyone could see everyone else and there would be no uncertainty about what was happening that could lead to an ugly confrontation. The State Police were part of an elite group that handled internal investigations and investigations of local police charged with criminal activity and worked closely with him. It turned out that there was only one deputy there that morning. He was sitting in a squad car in front of the main entrance. He exited the car in a confused manner and stood in front of the short walkway to the facility's entrance as Davidson and the troopers approached. Davidson politely introduced himself and then read a statement from Stephen to the effect that the action, or inaction, taking place within the facility with respect to Lisa Allen was a violation of state law and, as governor and in light of his duty under the state constitution, he had ordered the State Police led by Davidson to take custody of Allen. His statement cited pertinent provisions of the Pennsylvania Crimes Code. Davidson directed half of the troopers to follow him into the facility with the medical people, who were carrying a transport stretcher, and the other half to stay outside with the deputy. He had instructed them to engage the deputy in polite conversation, but to not permit him to go to the squad car to use the radio. As it happened, the deputy showed no signs of wanting any kind of confrontation or of departing. He was noticeably shaken by the whole episode.

Staffers coming and going stood aside as they entered, a few with a perplexed look but others whose expressions seemed to indicate that they just figured this was all part of the ongoing police security arrangements at the facility. The entering cohort had the information about Allen's location in the facility, which was modest-sized and only two stories high, from the cousin's daughter who had been barred by Allen's daughter from further visits but who had befriended certain staffers who she kept in phone contact with. At that early hour, there was no one at the reception desk or in the first-floor administrative offices, and with a pieced together map of the facility they proceeded to the staircase to the second floor, where Allen's room was located. Davidson stopped at the nursing station with two of the troopers, where he again read Stephen's statement, and the rest of the entourage went to Allen's room. Within three minutes, they had her in the stretcher and had begun intravenous hydration and feeding and were heading back downstairs. They went down the same stairs, carrying her. This was part of the plan, so nothing could delay them in the elevator. Within another three minutes after putting her in the stretcher, the entire rescue group was on the road with Allen to a different well-chosen nursing home that would take proper care of her.

Stephen followed up very quickly, asking for airtime on television and radio around the state. Again, many outlets agreed as they did before. He got on the air almost as quickly as the news outlets reported what had taken place. Unlike the previous time, he fashioned this also as a press conference so that he would be sure to reach a broader part of the public since if particular media outlets would not give him time to deliver his whole address they would at least run small portions of his comments on the evening news.

He began by explaining exactly what was going on in the nursing home: that Lisa Allen was being denied water and starved to death—like the Nazis did in some of their concentration camps. He quickly mentioned St. Maximilian Kolbe and the men starved with him. He knew many of the audience had not heard of him, but knew they could relate to what Stephen was saying about his brutal martyrdom. He briefly stated the physical anguish Allen was facing, what a person experienced who was dying of thirst and starving. He mentioned how utterly contrary to the purpose of a medical facility such action was. He went for the jugular against Allen's daughter, telling the full story with all the details about her relationship with her mother and the circumstances of her reentering her life. He said that he had an obligation in light of his oath of office and under the laws and constitution of the Commonwealth—and under "the moral law that directs the actions of all men"—to intervene to stop this. He strongly criticized the judge's decision, and the statements he made in issuing it. He said—repeatedly—that the decision was unlawful and called it "an assault on Lisa Allen's basic rights." He said that when courts acted in such a manner, trying to "arrogate to themselves the absolute power to permit the destruction of an innocent, infirm, helpless person's life, and in such a cruel way to boot," they had to be stopped. That's exactly what the principle of separation of powers sought to insure. The court's interpretation of the state constitution to justify what was happening was "unrecognizable," and he insisted that when the courts "make interpretations of constitutions—state or federal—that have no basis in the text or history of the documents, it is the right and solemn duty of the other branches to correct those misinterpretations. This is especially so when the decisions made outrageously depart from what all the evidence makes clear is the true meaning of a constitutional provision." As the legal scholar, he invoked Andrew Jackson and Abraham Lincoln on this point. It was a reassertion of what was once called "the departmental notion of constitutional construction." He also quoted Federalist 78, which said that the courts possess neither the purse nor the sword. "I could and would not support the Superior Court's decision when they tried to assume the legislature's prerogative of appropriating funds on the matter of embryonic stem cell research funding, and now I will not uphold this county's judge's authorization—more, facilitation—of starving and not even giving water to this poor, ill woman. Those with the appropriate governmental authority must act to stop such blatant—the correct word indeed is *blatant*—disregard of the law and of human decency." He added with that look of his jaw squarely set, "That is what I have done."

In the days that followed, he kept battering away. He also carefully explained both the reality of Lisa Allen's situation and what was being done to her, the distinction between providing food and hydration to someone not dying and extraordinary or any medical intervention, the law of the Commonwealth about assisted suicide and the obligations of nursing facilities, and the rightful and excessive powers of the judiciary. It was the signature Bernard combination of taking the offensive, education, and clarifying and stressing the facts and what was at stake. Stephen made it clear that in no way would he permit any further harm to be done to Allen. The nursing home they moved her to was in a different county—that was all part of the plan— and Secretary Lipinski declared her an adult person in need of DPW protection. The daughter tried to contest that in the new county's court. Stephen's General Counsel made clear that the state would in no way relinquish control of Allen's care, and the court upheld the state. Stephen's challenge to the judge in the other county had left a loud and clear message.

Stephen's action in the Lisa Allen case by far gained more attention outside of Pennsylvania than anything else that he had done. He was being hailed as a hero by pro-life and many disability rights groups. A vocal pro-assisted suicide element in the state and the opposing party and all the usual leftist interest groups attacked him as abusing power and mainstream media commentators initially went after him, but their voices subsided in short course in the face of his repeated, vigorous defenses of what he had done. The public didn't seem to know what to make of it, but as the days went by public opinion tilted more in his direction. After initial hesitancy, the general public seemed both to agree that he had stopped outrageous behavior by her daughter and the nursing home and to recognize the courageous character of what he had done. Then the episode quickly slipped out of public discussion. Stephen gained fervent supporters and also bitter, uncompromising enemies from the episode. The reactions mirrored the deep cultural and moral divisions in America.

Three months later, Stephen received a call at home that a potential contributor to his party wanted to meet with him. Stephen went against the grain as in so many things by not dealing with big money contributors. To the extent that future campaign funds had to be raised he planned on doing it from the grassroots, in small amounts with a limit of how much would be taken, as with his upstart lieutenant governor's campaign. Still, he was willing to meet with some of them because it would be of benefit to the state party that, with the help of John Frost and others, he was working to transform into a vehicle for organizing the public in support of the new, moral politics he was trying to promote. He wanted John, who was the state party chairman, to be with him when the man and an aide came to meet him. Neither John nor others on the state committee who he consulted knew the man, Lewis Tyler from suburban Philadelphia. He thought it was odd that no one seemed to know this man of supposedly considerable means and that all of a sudden after having had no prior record of supporting the party he wanted to become a major benefactor. Stephen was made further suspicious by Tyler's insistence that John not be present. His suspicions were further intensified when a search of published phone listings in the five-county Philadelphia area showed no Lewis Tyler, though there were several "L. Tylers." Stephen talked this over with John, who was similarly vexed, and they decided to have John's secretary call the different L. Tylers and ask for Lewis Tyler. None of them was a Lewis Tyler. Stephen and John then worked out a plan. Since this involved politics and not official business, Stephen made clear to Tyler that he would not meet with him in his office or anywhere in the Capitol Building. Tyler seemed a bit displeased with that, but agreed to meet in a private meeting room at the state party headquarters after hours. John would be sitting hidden in an anteroom off the meeting room where he would be able to hear everything.

Only one staffer was still working when Tyler and his aide, a Fred Dayton, arrived. Stephen and the staffer greeted them and then he showed them into the nicely paneled, well-furnished meeting room a considerable distance away from the reception area where the staffer was working. The various offices were empty at that hour. John was in place in the anteroom. They sat down and instead of the usual small talk that initiated such meetings, Tyler got right to the point.

"Governor, I know from my different contacts in the state government that every few years you have to upgrade computer equipment in the different departments. I have background in the IT field and I recently started a company, Efficiency Computers, in Philadelphia. Here's my card." He took it out of his wallet and handed it to Stephen. "We act as a kind of middle-man. We purchase the best computer equipment that is on the market and sell it to our customers. We can arrange to get it in bulk and we deal with large-scale buyers. So, we can easily equip whole agencies with equipment that interfaces supremely well and can address well different aspects of an operation. With our connections, we can get all kinds of equipment inexpensively, so we are in the position to provide a substantial discount to the state and save the taxpayers a lot of money. The problem is that we'd have to have some way to get around the competitive bidding process."

Stephen responded quickly. "I had thought that you wanted to talk about support for the party, not something concerning state government. As far as the state is concerned, we're bound by law to follow competitive bidding procedures for virtually all state contracts. I'm not able to waive those requirements."

"Governor," Tyler continued, "I know that you would like to be elected governor in your own right. I know that you need money for your next election campaign. I can easily tap a few million dollars to help you out."

"What are you saying?" Stephen replied.

"What I'm saying is that if you can help us with the competitive bidding problem, we can help you with your campaign needs."

Stephen's face showed his customary resolute look coupled with a blaze of anger in his eyes. "Mr. Tyler—or whatever your name is— besides the fact that I don't take campaign contributions from high rollers but only small donations from the public, what you are asking of me is probably illegal. This is the end of this meeting. It's time for you both to leave."

Tyler looked very disturbed by Stephen's quick reaction, and the "or whatever your name is" seemed especially to evoke a momentary look of shock and consternation. As Stephen looked him squarely in the eye he seemed to betray that he had unexpectedly been found out.

Tyler and Dayton left quickly. John Frost came out from the anteroom and stood in stunned silence. Stephen said, "I'm going to call the FBI office."

From there, things unraveled. Even though the office was closed, Stephen insisted on being put through to the mobile phone of the agent in charge of the Harrisburg field office to report what had happened. When Stephen reported what had happened, the agent seemed surprisingly reluctant and defensive. The next morning, Stephen called the U.S. Attorney, who was from the other party, and also got a runaround. He and John Frost talked this over and they realized what had happened. He called the head FBI agent again at his office and directly confronted him on the phone: "This was a sting operation, wasn't it. These were your agents trying to talk me into taking a bribe." The long silence at the other end was definitive confirmation. Stephen decided to go on the offensive, as he was so adept at doing. He called a press conference for the next day to speak about "a matter of the gravest importance for the conduct of the government of the Commonwealth." He made a particularly strong effort to reach as many media outlets in the state as possible, asked again additionally for airtime, and even contacted national media.

At the press conference, with John Frost standing behind him, he bore down to speak right into the microphones with an even more serious look on his face than usual. "Yesterday, the FBI and the U.S. Attorney for the Middle District on Pennsylvania targeted me in a sting operation to try to get me to take a bribe." He recounted all that bad happened, and mentioned that because of their suspicions John Frost had listened to the conversation while hidden in the next room. John came before the microphones and confirmed all that Stephen had said and added that they were "shocked by the whole matter." Stephen continued, "I believe that Mr. Reddick"—he was the U.S. Attorney— "needs to answer a number of questions. Was this part of a larger probe? Were others targeted with a sting operation, as well? It had been my understanding that Mr. Reddick's investigations of political corruption in the Commonwealth ended three months ago. Usually, the U.S. Attorney's Office has spearheaded these investigations and, for all practical purposes, set out the plan for the FBI to follow. It has gone along with the U.S. Attorney's investigative plans, here in Harrisburg and elsewhere around the country. Why did Mr. Riddick—who's a member of the opposing political party—decide to target me? Was this politically motivated? Did he make the decision to do this or did someone else? Was the FBI, which is supposed to be outside of politics—and has to be lest it become a tool of oppression—drawn into a politically motivated action? While sting operations seem to have become par for the course for the FBI, when one sees episodes such as this one he can understand why the legendary, long-time FBI Director J. Edgar Hoover would have nothing to do with them. This is a brazen assault on the *Office* of Governor of Pennsylvania. It *looks like* the federal government, which is run by the other party, is misusing the law and its law enforcement personnel to change the politics of the Commonwealth. The ball is in Mr. Riddick's and the Harrisburg FBI Office's court to come clean about this."

Stephen's press conference had its desired effect. The media reaction, even among the elements of it that were not supportive of

Stephen, was critical. As judged by comments on call-in radio programs around the state, it looked like the public saw it the same way. Then came the *coup de grâce*. A news report appeared, citing an unnamed state legislative staff member as its source, that a few well-connected supporters of former Speaker Erlanger had teamed up with a few leading figures of the opposing party to urge Riddick to undertake the sting against Stephen.

The story became a national issue. Stephen was already in the national limelight because of the Lisa Allen case. Various commentators were saying that it illustrated what had become a new norm in politics that criminal investigations, sting operations, and indictments—even without any basis—were the way to deal with political opponents. The administration in Washington—controlled by the other party—took a hit in public opinion, and they promised to review the grounds for deciding to undertake sting operations. The episode led to Erlanger's abandoning an attempted political comeback and a state senator and the staff director of the other party in the House who were involved resigned. Pressure also build up on the U.S. Attorney Riddick to step down and after a few months' delay, he did so claiming that he had been contemplating returning to private law practice for some time. Stephen did not hesitate to follow up with further strong public rhetorical attacks, saying that it was to end behavior like this that motivated him to enter the public arena. His popularity in the state increased. Even if people didn't always agree with him, they admired his courage, toughness, and integrity. Even while he was looking ahead to the gubernatorial election a year and a half down the road, some commentators thought he should enter the presidential race instead. He had begun to receive a steady stream of mail from party people around the country, leaders of pro-life and other organizations, and just average citizens urging him to do so, and it increased after the sting operation.

Prominent people from within the party, especially in its conservative wing, also started to approach Stephen. He only knew most of them by reputation, and he felt humbled that they would think of him as a presidential candidate. Still, he thought of himself primarily as an academic and not a politician—much less a national leader. He was essentially an accidental governor, and the only thing he had been elected to was the Pennsylvania lieutenant governorship. He wasn't even sure he was going to run in the coming gubernatorial election, much less for the presidency. He had never planned for something like that and did not think himself anywhere near qualified for it. He didn't think he was in any way made of the "stuff" to be the president of the most important and powerful country in the world. That was when Bishop George LaGrange came to see him.

Bishop LaGrange had been named Bishop of Greensburg, in western Pennsylvania, just two years before. The diocese abutted the Pittsburgh Diocese to its west. He had been a priest of the Toledo Diocese, and had spent the previous six years as one of the youngest pastors in the diocese. Then, he had been an auxiliary bishop there for two years. He had developed a reputation as a pastor completely devoted to his flock and to Catholic orthodoxy. More, he insisted on appropriate discipline and on "resacralizing" Catholic practice and liturgy. His parish had quickly become a mecca for Catholics seeking Masses that seemed to elevate the congregation to the gates of heaven. He was also vigorous as a pro-life advocate and worked assiduously for the cause of sound family life. His efforts had attracted the attention of some important figures in the Vatican and he had been invited to speak at a few important conferences there. The thinking was that that opened the door to his bishop appointments. He and Stephen had met in his graduate and law school days, when George was a young priest who was at the university a couple of summers for graduate studies. They had become good friends and had maintained a steady correspondence over the years. Stephen had sought his advice on different things and he was sometimes a spiritual adviser to him.

Bishop LaGrange visited Stephen and Marybeth at the apartment that they continued to live at not far from the Capitol Building in Harrisburg. Both the Pennsylvania governor and lieutenant governor have official residences, but Stephen refused to live at either of them. He said that he and Marybeth would pay their own rent, instead of the taxpayers footing the bill for them.

"Stephen, " said the Bishop, "The reason I wanted to come to talk with you concerns what you have been communicating with me about. You're telling me that people are urging you to run for president. I'm hearing the same thing from some people I'm in contact with. They know I'm a friend of yours, and they're—pro-life people, people worried that the country's falling apart—telling me that you can offer the leadership that's needed now. They see what you've been doing as governor. They see the courage and exercise of authority for the good in a way they haven't seen before. Religious people—decent people in general—are on the defensive in an unprecedented way. They say that a strong leader is what's needed now to protect them. You've shown that you'll act to get government under control and face down those who want to use it for outright wicked and destructive purposes. You don't just say things are wrong, but you actually try to change them and to

131

reverse the direction things have gone in. They see that unlike almost all politicians they have ever observed, you say what you mean and, more, you act upon it. Frankly, I think they are right. You could certainly do much more as governor—even though you haven't even been sure about running for a full term for that—but it seems to me that the whole country needs you. What's more, maybe God is calling you to this."

"Fr. George," Stephen said, "Running for president is almost an unimaginable undertaking. The responsibilities of that position, especially today, are staggering—beyond staggering. I never thought of myself doing anything like that." He stared at the floor and the look of uncertainty and unease, even fear, that Marybeth was familiar with when he doubted his ability to do something came over his face. "I honestly don't think that I'm made of the stuff to be President of the United States."

"Stephen," the Bishop responded, "That, of course, is something you would have to resolve in your mind. No one can know about that for sure before undertaking it. It's the same with being pope, or maybe even a bishop. I can tell you, though, from all the years I've known you, from our discussions, from my observing—more than most people have, you know, because we've been friends—that I have no doubt that you are made of the stuff to be able to do it, and do it well. What's more, you'll have a lot of people pulling for you, ready to help you, and praying for you."

After the bishop left and in the days following, Stephen and Marybeth had some of the deepest and most profound talks they had ever had in their marriage. They also shared intimacies more intensely, which was something that gave Stephen comfort in very trying and difficult times. They had probably never drawn closer in their marriage than they did in those days. Marybeth made clear to him that she would support him, do her part, and be happy and at peace with whatever decision he made. He found it difficult to concentrate on his routine, daily tasks as governor and the thought of his choice weighed on him almost every minute. Marybeth would not try to influence his decision. She knew that for a man such a momentous decision was ultimately a personal one that only he could make. In the final analysis, it had to be his choice, one that would have to come from deep within his mind and soul.

A little over two weeks after the Bishop's visit Stephen told Marybeth one day after coming home to a late dinner and a deep welcoming embrace after a long day at the Governor's Office, "I'm going to do it."

CHAPTER 5

The Nomination Battle

W hen Stephen made his announcement that he was running for his party's presidential nomination the country was descending into deepening turmoil and political repression.

Racial tensions deepened, and ugly demonstrations and rioting that had started with incidents akin to the Rodney King and Michael Brown cases—almost always involving young lawbreakers in serious clashes with the police—spread to more and more communities around the country. The other party, claiming to be the champion of the cause of minorities, seemed to be fanning the flames of racial conflict with the administration in Washington and some of its leading members of Congress making not so veiled attacks on the police. Interestingly, Pennsylvania had not been afflicted by the racial turmoil. Some said it was because of Stephen's tough stand against the abuses in the Philadelphia Police Department and his efforts to forge better police-community relations.

A steep crime wave had hit a number of large and medium-sized U.S. cities. A significant cause of it was youth gang activity that was traced to a near suspension of immigration laws along the southern border by the previous leftist administration. Vicious, well-organized gangs from Mexico and Central America, some of which had connections with drug cartels, had gotten a foothold in the Southwest and spread from there. Besides drugs, they were involved in a range of criminal activities and were known for brutal reprisals against anyone who crossed them. They were making the streets of some inner-city neighborhoods more violent even than they had been in the past. The current administration, which some accused of "faking to the right but running to the left" as columnist George F. Will had said about President Jimmy Carter, had tightened up border security a bit. This only caused disaffection among its leftist base.

The homosexualist movement was advancing its agenda virtually unimpeded in institution after institution, with the assistance of the leftist federal government. They brooked no opposition and with their success in toppling executives who expressed hesitation about any piece of their agenda, there was hardly a significant business corporation that didn't bend over backwards for them. Their latest public objectives were heavy criminal penalties for anyone who in any way "discriminated" against them—such as in not offering services for their "weddings"—working aggressively to strip the Catholic Church of its tax exemption because it would not perform same-sex "marriages," and making a big push for affirmative action programs for homosexuals in hiring and promotion in all levels of government. Some military units were said to have become homosexual havens and those resisting were facing court martials.

As the homosexualist agenda made apparent, religious liberty had become a contentious public issue. The other party, during twelve consecutive years in power, had become increasingly repressive as they moved toward the hard-left. Some prosecutors were arranging to have informants present at Sunday services of clergymen known to be traditional to see if they could nail them for "hate crimes" violations for statements against homosexuality or seemingly supportive of traditional roles for women. Religious colleges and universities had come under increasing oversight and control by the federal government, which had begun to mandate secular-oriented curricula. And these were only a few examples of the assault on religious liberty.

The situation of running for the party's presidential nomination was much different from his run for the lieutenant governor's nomination in Pennsylvania. For one thing, there were his duties as governor and he could be away campaigning for only so long. For another, there was virtually a new election that one had to compete in almost every week during the primary season and considerable organization was needed for party caucuses from the beginning, since things started with Iowa. The numbers of primaries had been reduced and spread out more, but the electoral season was still an overwhelming strain on candidates. Stephen had an advantage in Iowa because there were many conservative and Christian political activists in the state and his efforts in Pennsylvania had become fairly well known there. There were many people ready to support him, but they had to be mobilized and that would take a formidable organizing effort. More, Stephen was insistent that fund-raising, as in his lieutenant governor run in Pennsylvania, would be limited to small donations. For a national campaign, he would go as high as $500 per person, but no more. He refused to take any federal matching campaign funds. That meant that he was not going to be buying many, if any, national media spots. He would focus his efforts on local media markets, taking out thoughtful ads (not sound bites), seeking out interviews on news shows and talk radio in local markets, and having the local media—and whatever national correspondents were interested—come to his appearances and rallies in the different states. Then there would be the candidate debates in a few different states. There would be many fewer than there had been in past primary seasons. The party had learned its lesson. In previous presidential primary campaigns, the various candidates had damaged each other so badly in the large number of debates that the ultimate nominee and the party had been weakened in the general election campaign. His low-budget campaign also meant that his campaigns, in the different primary and caucus states, would be built almost completely on volunteer efforts. He was simply fed up with the big money in politics and the "buying" of political offices, and he would have none of it. He intensely wanted to show that even acquiring the highest office in the land did not require it, although in his mind he was honestly doubtful. Still, *this* was the way it was going to be if he was going to do this. In the announcement of his candidacy, Stephen made the point about the contribution limit clearly.

He went back to his old friend John Frost to help get the campaign off the ground. John agreed to play the central coordinating role, but was not in the position to travel around the country. Through his party contacts, he knew of an individual in Iowa who had expressed much support for Stephen's political efforts in Pennsylvania. He had been involved in much political organizing in Iowa, mostly on a volunteer basis, for TEA party and pro-life political candidates and knew the political ropes in the party and generally in the state very well. When Frost contacted him, Jim Danielson readily signed on. Stephen and John knew that if only small donations were to be accepted it would be necessary to use Internet campaign fundraising extensively. Social media would also have to be the means of raising the veritable army of volunteers that Stephen would need in the different states to mount a serious campaign. Grass-roots organization would be the key, especially in the small states that dominated the electoral schedule during the first month and a half of the primary campaign. Again, John's contacts were crucial. He knew of a few key people right in Pennsylvania who could do the job at minimal cost.

The fundraising and organization operation went into effect six months before the Iowa caucus in January. Iowa and New Hampshire, the site of the first primary, were both states where the candidate's presence was important. The plan was for Stephen to visit each state once a month from then until Thanksgiving, speaking at carefully chosen events and to certain groups. After Thanksgiving, until two weeks before the Iowa caucus, he would spend long (four-day) weekends once a month in each state. Stephen, who disliked flying, bit the bullet so he and Marybeth could quickly get back and forth. During the two weeks before the Iowa event, he would be in the state full-time and then shift to New Hampshire for the following week before its primary. John worked out his whole schedule in each state from his base in Harrisburg. He logged long hours on the phone and at his computer using email and Skype. Jim Danielson was handling things on the ground in Iowa and gradually built up the volunteer campaign organization there. John also got a coordinator and field organizer in place in New Hampshire, Jane O'Malley, who had a lot of experience working in conservative statewide campaigns there—including for presidential candidates—and had long been involved in Catholic and pro-life activism. John astutely also turned the potential liability of Stephen's not being able to be present as much in the states as some of his rivals due to his gubernatorial duties into an advantage by making sure he sent a constant flow of information for dissemination to Jim and Jane about Stephen's ongoing initiatives in Pennsylvania for objectives that many of the party's rank-and-file would be supportive and even enthusiastic about.

The candidate field had taken clear shape by the time Stephen launched his efforts in both states. Usually, in the party there were an abundance of conservative presidential aspirants, who would proceed to split the bulk of the primary and caucus vote and damage each other politically by their rhetorical attacks, and a singular so-called "moderate" who would then slip through and win the nomination. This time, there were two prominent moderates, both senators and long-time Washington insiders (Jim Langford of Missouri and Kenneth Graham of Nevada, a one-time conservative state that California transplants and a booming Hispanic population had moved to the left) and only one other conservative, also a senator and former Congressman, Andrew Bartlett of Tennessee. Another conservative governor, one of the party's most prominent, Bob Goodrich of Florida, was all poised to make a run, but was sidetracked by a scandal that had erupted in his administration a few months before. He was not involved in it, but was tarnished by it since it involved a few high appointees of his. Stephen started out at the bottom of the polls. One of the moderates, Langford, was leading the pack with only about 23%. The moderates pretty much dismissed Stephen, who they thought was "too extreme."

Stephen's first appearance in Iowa was to a Christian Political Action conference, most of whose members were Protestants. Evangelicals were an important force in the party in Iowa. They would be receptive to his message on a range of cultural issues, but it was unclear about how they would react to his up-front Catholicism. John and Stephen thought it important to reach out to the Evangelicals right from the beginning. Stephen had decided that, while he would be prudent in the campaign, he would pull no punches about his positions and the critical questions confronting the country.

Stephen hit stride immediately as he started his talk by saying, "My fellow Christians." There was an almost thunderous response in applause and cheering. He had the rapt attention of the attendees after that. "I don't have to tell you about the challenges and threats that we face in these times in our country. The secularist-leftist juggernaut is rolling through our culture, disturbingly led by the government in Washington, which has not only incessantly tried to completely uproot our religious—and, yes, Christian—past and traditions and entirely eliminate our pubic witness and influence, but more and more has tried to restrict our freedoms, to make us and our institutions embrace their agenda on marriage, sexual morality, the value of human life, what the meaning of human dignity is. They are trying to shut us down and call us bigots because we dare to say that morally reprehensible behavior is indeed morally reprehensible, that you cannot change what marriage means so that men cannot marry men and women marry women—and for that matter that people cannot marry animals—and because we call religiously-based terrorism for what it is. We have people in the highest offices in America who, while they bend over backwards to refuse to call Islamic radicalism what it is, go out of their way to find fault with and try to marginalize Christianity. The reality, which so many of them want to bury, was written about so clearly by Tocqueville in his great book *Democracy in America*: America was distinctly a Christian culture. It was not a Christian government, a theocracy like Iran is, but a Christian *culture*. Our Founding Fathers had a Christian view of man, and knew that free government without a religious way of life was impossible. When we see the attacks on religion and religious institutions in America and the attempts to stifle any objection or dissent from serious Christians and other traditional believers to the wayward moral agenda of secular leftism—even pastors being threatened for their sermons—I say: Make no mistake about it: *the issue now in America is liberty*—it is really about whether truth will be allowed to be proclaimed."

The audience erupted again and this time the applause went on constantly for five minutes. The people had not heard a politician like this in a long time—but maybe that was because, at heart, Stephen was not a politician. That became apparent in the rest of his talk, when he again became the professor. He spoke about how liberty differs from license. He talked about the natural law background to the American Founding and (knowing that Evangelicals sometimes shy away from natural law, which they see coming from man's reason separated from God) emphasized that natural law is nothing more than God's law that He has written into man's nature even though his fallenness makes it difficult for him to uphold it. He discussed the correct and incorrect notions of diversity and tolerance, and about how men share the same nature and are bound by the same moral standards and that there can never be what he called a "moral pluralism." He also spent a few minutes talking about the nature of marriage, its centrality for society and the political order, and said that while there was not an issue about the legality of contraception he summarized how it stood at the center of the problem in many ways. Aware that Evangelicals, like most Catholics, had long-since bought into the contraceptive mind-set, he noted how increasing numbers of younger Evangelicals were questioning contraception and mentioned the Evangelical spokesman who said that the battle against same-sex "marriage" was lost when contraception was accepted. He vigorously criticized the elements in the other party who tried to characterize those who opposed the near-nationalized U.S. health care system's paying for contraceptives as "anti-women." To the contrary, he impressively and quickly summarized how contraceptives badly damaged women's health, how most were abortifacient, and how the sexual libertinism long vigorously promoted by feminism and the rest of the left undercut women's dignity. He further said that the breakdown of the family, contributed to mightily by easy divorce—"where a party can just unilaterally cancel his or her marriage vows, easier than being able to break a business contract or walk away from an apartment lease"—has been a major cause of poverty among women. "These are the things that have truly been against women."

Stephen's rhetorical and educative skills, along with his obvious sincerity and kind manner, were magnificent. He made a great impression on the conference audience. He left them open to and thinking about even the points they were not inclined to agree with. At the end of his talk, substantial numbers of them lined up to give their names to the singular political aide he had brought with him to volunteer for the campaign. His Iowa campaign was underway with a great burst of grassroots enthusiasm.

He had several other speaking engagements during that first visit to Iowa. The buzz afterward was that people in the Evangelical community were genuinely excited and his campaign's organizational efforts were proceeding very well. Some of the state party people were taking notice and by the end of the month he had gone up five points in state polls.

During his next visit to Iowa, he made a special effort to visit black neighborhoods in Davenport, home to the state's largest black population. He knew there was no political advantage to it since most of the state's blacks were in the other party, but he wanted to bring a message to them. Through intermediaries, he made a connection with a black pastor of politically conservative leanings who invited him to speak to a black religious organization and to an inter-church youth group. His appearance was reported widely in the local media and in local black publications. He began by addressing them as "my Christian brethren." His message was one of personal responsibility ("as Jesus wants of us"), turning away from government dependency, the need for marital commitment and solid family life, and the black community undertaking educational and economic initiatives. The government schools had failed inner-city communities, and the solution was a range of private educational alternatives big and small, even involving collaborative efforts by parents and churches to compensate for what the schools haven't done right. The solution to the poor economic situation of black communities lay partly in enhanced efforts at starting a range of small enterprises, individual entrepreneurship and cooperative, even neighborhood enterprises. He was painfully direct, but his honesty and concern for the people he spoke to readily came through. Many came up to him after the talks and he spoke to small groups of them for some time afterwards. He related well to the young people.

John Frost and Jim Danielson scheduled several talks for Stephen with suburban-based rank-and-file party and community groups in Iowa. He encountered various people who did not agree with some of his perspectives, but his eloquence, strong effort to explain his thinking, willingness to engage them, and his charitable attitude invariably gained him respect. At times, between scheduled talks, he pursued a mini-version of his lieutenant governor's race as he walked the busiest areas of small towns and the commercial areas of cities introducing himself to people. Occasionally, as discussion started with small groups of people on some topic he essentially became a soap-boxer and ended up giving a small public speech.

In New Hampshire, he tackled economic issues in a way that had hardly been seen in a presidential campaign. He went much deeper than dealing with the current pressing issue or two and suggested approaches, even involving structural changes, that seldom were mentioned even in academic circles to say nothing about political campaigns. When he spoke to a group of factory workers, he spoke about the need to insure job security for people and not just or primarily by government efforts. He talked about a new attitude that was necessary in the American economy that placed the needs and dignity of the worker, of all people, at the center. While market considerations were important, the market always had to be guided by sound moral principles. While profit was important, "the economy was made for man, not man for the economy." Those playing different roles in economic life had to commit themselves to that. While the state had a role in helping to shape a good and just economic life, the main means to rightly regulate economic life had to be from them—managers, owners, corporate officials, and the workers. There was no magic "invisible hand." It was moral men who made moral institutions and moral economic activity. Those in political leadership should encourage that and keep them on track, and insure that economic activity would promote the general welfare. That was the attitude present in America's Founding Era, and now needed to be recovered. He also called for workers to be involved more in decision-making in the workplace. That promoted human dignity by treating workers like the thinking, reasoned, responsible people they were. He said that government could put restraints on companies to stop them from just picking up stakes and moving plants out of their long-time locations and to other states or overseas. After all, these actions had profound effects on their communities. Mostly, though, corporate executives needed to develop a spirit of responsibility to their communities and their employees. They should not just be driven by economic forces— much less a desire for excessive profits—but by, again, a concern for people. He also criticized runaway executive salaries, particularly when they were not even carrying out a true entrepreneurial function. There needed to be a better balance in salaries, the role of corporate managers was overvalued and that of regular workers undervalued. It was not the kind of message that some in his party liked to hear, especially the self-styled moderates.

This was actually part of the same message he boldly brought to state business leaders when he talked to them. He spoke to the Chamber of Commerce in the state's largest city, Manchester. He commended entrepreneurship, which he called "a great American tradition, starting back in colonial times." He exhorted corporate leaders to "a renewed sense of duty to the communities that their businesses and plants are located in and to a patriotic spirit that makes them see the need to keep jobs in the country that gave them their opportunities in the first place, America." They always have to be concerned about being profitable, he said, but they should not seek excessive profits when that means causing job losses and hurting communities. "Remembering that workers are people with dignity, and not just factors in production" was central, and allowing workers to participate in decision-making, where appropriate, in the workplace would help promote good morale and "make people realize they are part of a team." A just wage is a moral mandate, and businesses should constantly be attuned to it. He lamented how two incomes were now sometimes insufficient to produce an adequate wage for a family, even though people were acting providently and in the past one wage-earner usually was sufficient. He lamented excessive government regulation, which especially hurt smaller enterprises, and said that the best regulation would be by morally well-formed and public-spirited businessmen, workers, and executives themselves. He also faulted companies for giving into to pressure groups like the homosexualist lobby to sign onto their agenda. He said it reflected how too many in the corporate community had bought into a morally relativist mind-set, and needed "to return to true morality"—to the natural law that had undergirded the American Founding.

The smaller businesspeople present had a good reaction to what he said. The representatives from the big corporations tended to be resistant. As was his practice, however, he engaged them in a lengthy question-and-answer period, standing firm in what he said and explaining his thinking. It became hard for some of them who challenged him to dispute what he was saying. Most who were there were impressed with how he stood for positions even when he knew they wouldn't be popular with many of his listeners. This was not what they had ever expected of a political candidate, and he earned their respect even if he didn't convince them. The sharpest exchange was with two executives, probably part of the homosexualist movement. He knocked down one after another of the homosexualist claims about the nature of homosexuality, the supposed benevolence of same-sex "marriage" and childrearing, and emphasized the increasing totalitarian ethos of the homosexualist movement, as he did with the protester in State College, Pennsylvania. He closed by saying firmly—looking ahead to what in fact was going to happen—that a Bernard administration would not allow victimized citizens to any longer be bowled over by the homosexualist juggernaut that the courts and leftist political enablers had given a green light to.

Meanwhile his organizational efforts in both states were by far the best of any candidate, even if they were overwhelmingly grassroots efforts. He was steadily climbing in the polls in both states. He was winning the bulk of the conservative vote, doing better among working-class voters than any of the candidates from either party. He was within striking distance of the top moderate, Langford, as the only candidate debate in either state—it was in New Hampshire—a week and a half before the primary and on the eve of the Iowa caucuses loomed.

Stephen resolved at the debate not to allow himself to be either set up by the journalist-questioners—as George Stephanopoulos did to the candidates with contraception in a Republican primary debate in 2012—nor to stay just on the narrow topic of questions they asked. His answers would be take-offs into other issues that were important, but which the questioners wouldn't ask about. He was also going to take the preemptive offensive against the other candidates—since he expected that they, especially Langford who was now seeing Stephen as a threat, would try to go after him. It was going to be his usual well-honed combination of confrontation and education.

Stephen performed masterfully during the debate. Langford, with the help of one of the questioners, tried to pin Stephen into the corner on a rape and incest exception for abortion. Stephen just laid out all the facts and hammered away at Langford as being oblivious to the reality of the human life involved. He kept repeating that and also put the questioner on the hot seat. He had control of the debate throughout. The *coup de grâce* came when Langford said that the "shipping of jobs overseas" was exaggerated and that companies were outsourcing tasks to foreign companies as a way of cutting costs and because they could not find enough workers here to take on unskilled jobs and that this did not hurt Americans. Stephen pounced, saying with great emphasis that it was simply untrue that there was no available domestic labor and that Americans' lives and affairs were made more and more difficult every day when they had to deal with foreign-based sales representatives on the phone who they couldn't understand and didn't know enough about American geography to be able even to track lost mail-order packages. Too many in the American business community didn't care about customers anymore, or took them for granted. "Decent service was sacrificed on the altar of cheap wages, and not just American workers but the American public was being made the sucker. The public

142

policies permitting and even encouraging easy outsourcing, Senator, have helped create this condition." The live audience roared its approval. Langford stammered for a minute, then responded vacuously. In the end, even the media commentators who were mostly opposed to Stephen had to grudgingly concede that his performance was masterful. Since there was no formal candidates debate scheduled in Iowa, the state's public television and radio carried the debate live from New Hampshire and Jim Danielson went further. Observing Stephen's great capability in public presentations and debates, he gambled that he was going to do well in this one. In order to get more people to watch it, he rented public halls around the state and used his volunteer communication network to contact people to come and watch it together. Afterwards his supporters would answer questions about the candidate and he could pick up more volunteers from the attendees. Moreover, it also served as a dry run for the "get-out-the-supporters" effort on caucus day a few days away—since the name-of-the-game in Iowa was who could get the most supporters out to the caucus sites. So, Stephen's debate success in New Hampshire resounded in Iowa.

Stephen won in Iowa and New Hampshire almost going away, by 10 percentage points each. When surveys asked voters why they supported him, the typical answers indicated that he had a populist appeal, he was a "straight-shooter" who understood the issues and the country well, and who "would do what he said."

Coming up right after New Hampshire were the Nevada caucuses and the Missouri primary. It was conceded that Graham and Langford would win easily in their respective home states. Stephen surprised everyone by making a trip to each state, heading to nearby Missouri right after the Iowa caucus and to Nevada two days after the New Hampshire primary. He was the only other candidate besides the favorite sons to visit the state. Danielson and an old political contact in Missouri helped build a volunteer organization there, which was made up heavily of Christian activists. In Nevada, a Hispanic Christian conservative state representative, Rey Badillo, undertook the same effort. They lined up as many local media appearances as possible when Stephen was in the states. The small-donation fundraising was increasingly successful and enabled Stephen to run a few media ads in local markets. He made clear that he would have nothing to do with sound bites. His few ads featured clips from his talks and the New Hampshire debate, where he briefly discussed selected issues. The focus was the educative function of politics. Stephen surprisingly won over 30% of the vote and a healthy number of delegates in each state. The Hispanic vote in Nevada was mostly in the other party, but it made up a respectable minority of the electorate in Stephen's party. Badillo's efforts attracted the majority of the Hispanic vote in the Nevada party caucuses to Stephen. Many of these Hispanics were serious Catholics or Evangelicals. The big tests were coming in the next ten days in the Carolinas, however. The South Carolina primary came first, followed by North Carolina's three days later.

The combination of Danielson's TEA Party and pro-life contacts and Badillo's contacts from the party's national Hispanic organization and national organization of state legislators enabled the campaign to quickly put together a solid and dynamic organization in the Carolinas. Further, Stephen's dramatic early electoral successes were generating excitement in the party's conservative and Christian activist wings and many volunteers were coming forward. They were further energized as more information was made available about his record in Pennsylvania and as people realized that he was doing all of this on a shoe-string budget with a small-donations only policy so as not to become beholden to monied interests. His reputation was developing more and more as, at once, a man of the people, a defender of traditional moral and American principles, and a candidate who had every intention of acting on what he said.

Stephen's success was also causing his opponents in the party and the media to bear down and hatch plans to ambush him. Langford and Graham decided to extend the olive branch to each other for awhile and discussed how they could put the pressure on him during the coming debate in South Carolina, which would be widely televised in both states and was generally thought would be the most crucial factor in both primaries. Stephen's antenna was up about such a possibility. He had developed a good sense about likely political developments, and so was usually able to stay a step ahead of his adversaries. He thought about what they might want to target him about and prepared for it. He also planned on how he would go on the offensive against them.

The scuttlebutt was also that some of the people on the party's national committee and some of its top donors, mostly from the corporate community, were agitated by the possibility that Stephen could be on his way to the nomination. Not only did they perceive him as a threat to their cozy relationships with top party officeholders, but also his spurning of big campaign contributions made them think their influence would weaken. They also squirmed when he talked about things like a moral obligation to pay a just wage and his readiness to take on the homosexualist movement. They had long since made their peace with the homosexualists, and some companies had even quietly introduced "gay affirmative action programs." Indeed, some top

144

corporate types had even become vocal supporters of the homosexualist agenda across the board. Stephen was a candidate who "talked morals," which also made them uncomfortable. They were even more unsettled by the fact that he was not the usual "yahoo" that they normally associated with this. He was a political intellectual, and was making sound, cogent—and readily understandable— intellectual arguments for his positions. They were taken off-balance about how to deal with him. They poured increased amounts of money into the Langford and Graham campaigns, but the effectiveness was in doubt since the debate was clearly going to overshadow buying more misleading sound bite ads in the media. Also, despite the two moderate senators' consultations on how to deal with Stephen they were at arm's length. Each was concerned that any move might only help the other one, since they were natural rivals appealing to the same segment of the party's electorate. Unwittingly, they were playing into Stephen's hands. He expected that they were going to claim that he was somehow unfair to business or picking up on the anti-corporate rhetoric of the left. They probably were calculating that that could even turn his conservative base against him.

Indeed, in his opening statement Langford made an oblique reference to "certain of his opponents who think they can improve the economy by stymieing the free decision-making of businesses." Then, as economic policy was the first topic for questioning by the journalist panel, Langford went in for what he thought would be the early kill. He accused Stephen of "wanting to interfere with the market by telling businesses that they had to pay wages higher than the market level in the name of 'justice.'" He said that, inevitably, this would involve more government control. It was the "anti-big corporation stuff one associates with the other party."

Stephen responded by repeating the essence of his point from his Chamber of Commerce talk in New Hampshire. He then pointedly asked Langford if he believed morality had anything to do with economics. Langford vaguely said it did, but that wasn't the point.

"What *is* the point, Senator Langford?" Stephen asked.

"This will invite more government control."

"So someone shouldn't talk about morality in public affairs at all because there's the danger that it will led to more governmental control?"

"No, I'm not saying that."

"Senator, the fact is that you have received 80% of your contributions in this campaign from big donors, mostly corporate executives and corporate PACs. You will be indebted to them, just as

145

you have been in your state. 85% of your campaign contributions in your last senatorial campaign were from large corporate sources both from within and outside your state. You have not been hesitant to introduce numerous bills that they have supported. That's right from analyses done by the GAO in Washington and the Center for Responsive Politics at one of your state universities." Stephen had done his homework. Then came the clincher: "You have taken 80% of your contributions in this presidential nomination campaign from big donors. I have a strict $500 limit on contributions. No individual has given me a contribution larger than $500." He added sternly: "You have compromised your independence."

In the course of the rest of the debate, Stephen kept finding opportunities to repeat the contrast between his and Langford's donors: 80% big donations versus his $500 limit. He didn't stop with Langford. He kept mentioning that nearly the same percentage of Graham's donations came from the big boys and that 50% of Labatt's were. He cited a report from a Washington good government organization—unlike most of them, this one didn't have a reputation of tilting left—that said that on numerous occasions Graham had introduced legislation supported by corporate PACs that had contributed to him.

He found another point later in the debate to hit at Langford and Graham. Stephen joined them and Labatt in saying that government regulations had gotten out of control. He pointed out emphatically, however, that they were part of this and raised a question about their sincerity. As an example, he mentioned how they had each voted for a transportation bill that provided federal funds to states that enacted laws making it illegal to eat in one's car when driving. He said, "This is a pointed example of how government is smothering the individual...and they have been part of it." Although he disliked "tooting his horn"—some said he had a problem with excessive modesty, which could hurt him in the campaign—he contrasted this to his successful efforts in Pennsylvania to cut down the governmental regulation of people's lives.

One of the journalists tried to throw the moderates a lifeline. Taking his cue from Stephanopoulos, he tried to characterize Stephen's opposition to federal funding for Planned Parenthood and for contraceptive family planning funding in the foreign aid program as "insensitivity" to women's needs. If he thought he was trapping Stephen, it actually gave Stephen an opening to put pressure on the journalist and also to attack his opponents' records—and at the same time to educate.

"Mr. Fleming," he said to the questioner, "Are you always so prepared to come to the defense of organizations that have been tied up with the Ku Klux Klan?" Fleming didn't reply, but his face bore an obvious look of surprise. "Mr. Fleming, you didn't answer me. Why are you so ready to defend organizations that have been tied up with the KKK?"

"What do you mean, Governor?"

Stephen proceeded to speak about Planned Parenthood founder Margaret Sanger's famous 1926 talk to the women's wing of the KKK in New Jersey. He also mentioned Sanger's "Negro Project," and her 1939 statement to one of her cohorts on the project, Dr. Clarence Gamble, that "We do not want word to go out that we want to exterminate the Negro population." In his usual deft manner of providing essential information in brief fashion and then stating clearly and emphatically the point made—so that everyone got it—he highlighted the history of Planned Parenthood up to the present time when they were aggressively trying to "market" their abortion services to increase their profits. They were now even requiring their affiliates that didn't do abortions to do them. He also recounted the mounting reports of abuses at their facilities, concluding with "if that constitutes being "sensitive" to women, maybe you have to reconsider what you mean by the word "sensitive," Mr. Fleming." He wasn't done. "All three of my opponents have voted consistently in Congress to keep the funnel of federal money flowing to Planned Parenthood. Senator Langford has even made endorsing comments about them at times. Is this "pro-woman," Senators? And what about Planned Parenthood's past with the KKK and of racial cleansing? Even now, around 80% of their facilities—and they have the largest chain of abortion clinics in the country—are in minority neighborhoods."

Labatt tried to protest that he didn't support Planned Parenthood. Stephen simply responded, "Then why do you keep voting to fund them?"

"It's part of a bigger bill, with other things in it."

"Isn't that an excuse, Senator? Is that good judgment? Is that political courage?"

Stephen clearly had put all three of his opponents, and Fleming, on the defensive. The reaction of the audience underscored that.

He was still not finished. Glaring at Fleming, he said, "Do you really think that funding so-called 'family planning'—it's really an aggressive effort at population control in the Third World, targeted mostly at women of other races, and poor women, to boot—in Africa, Asia, and Latin America is 'sensitive' to women's needs? Here's what that funding consistently results in." He launched into a brief, but expansive, catalog of outrages from women left to battle the medical complications of sterilization after the family planning/population control teams leave their villages to the devastating female health consequences of birth control pills there to how the after-effects of a procedure leads to their husbands throwing them out and their taking up with other women. "Is all this sensitive to women, Mr. Fleming?" Then, turning to Langford and Graham, he said, "This is what you, Senators, have been consistently voting for."

Stephen's performance in the debate was so devastating that it essentially neutralized the effectiveness of the pro-"family planning" issue for the rest of the election year.

While battered, the hard-nosed politician Langford tried one more gambit later in the debate. There was a question about controversial decisions of the Supreme Court, and he immediately tried to turn it against Stephen.

"Governor Bernard in his state refused to carry out decisions of his state's courts and he's said that a U.S. president should be prepared to do the same with decisions of the U.S. Supreme Court. That's dangerous. That would threaten the rule of law. It would threaten freedom. That would make the president like a monarch. A president has the obligation to follow the law. His or her role is to make good appointments to the Court to get people on it who are committed to the Constitution."

The moderator turned to Stephen for a response. He was ready. "Senator Langford, you're correct that the president has to make good appointments to the Court, but I'll tell you that presidents of our party haven't done a very good job of it. The other party does, though, at least as far as getting justices who further their political agenda. The justices their presidents have put on the Court have moved our country's law further away from the Constitution. I should point out, Senator, that you as a member of the Senate Judiciary Committee haven't done much to stop that. You have voted for all of the Supreme Court nominees those presidents have made in these last twelve years. More basically, aren't you saying that the Constitution equals what the Supreme Court says it is? No matter how outrageous its decisions, are you saying they must be accepted?" He prodded Langford and stared at him with his piercing firm look. "Is that what you're saying, Senator?"

"No, I'm not saying that. What I'm saying is that the president can't take it upon himself or herself just to refuse to accept the Court's constitutional role."

"What role is that, Senator?"

"The Court interprets the Constitution."

"Are you saying that it can never interpret it wrongly, or read the justices' own political or ideological predispositions into it? Are you saying that the Court's opinions are to be accepted and upheld no matter what—even when the opinions have no foundation in the Constitution at all and in fact are actually even against the Constitution?

"No, I'm not saying the Court can never be wrong, but we can correct that with better appointments." A slight look of satisfaction came over Langford's face, as he obviously thought he had bested Stephen on this.

"You certainly haven't done much in that respect. You just keep voting for the other party's Supreme Court nominees, who keep issuing one decision after another against our constitutional tradition and what our party says it stands for." He paused momentarily, and then posed a dilemma to Langford. "Tell me, Senator, if the Supreme Court upheld an action of a renegade state governor who had rounded up all the members of a certain ethnic group in his state and put them into a concentration camp do you think the president would have the authority to do something about it—even though the Court ruled it legal and constitutional?"

"That's a wild hypothetical situation. It could never happen."

"Don't try to avoid—to run away from—my question, Senator," Stephen replied insistently. "Could a president do anything about it or not? Answer me."

Langford hesitated. "*Answer me*," Stephen insisted again. The large assembly room was silent. Everyone's eyes were on the Missouri senator.

"Well, yes, yes, of course, he could do something about it," Langford said slowly.

Stephen instantaneously jumped in. "Then you have just made it clear, Senator, that you believe that there are circumstances when a president definitely can act to resist and, in fact, go actively against the Supreme Court—and, by implication, any lesser court—when it makes decisions that go against the basic rights, the fundamental human dignity, of the people. I'm glad to see that you don't think that the Supreme Court is incapable of acting against the Constitution. That's what I've been saying all along. I always made that clear to my law students."

Langford decided not to press the point any further. Labatt spoke up and tersely seconded Stephen's position. After that, it was time for the candidates' brief closing statements. Not one of the other candidates

149

said a thing about Stephen during them. They made some vague, broad remarks. Stephen spoke last, and with fervor, consummate intelligence, and his usual capability of saying many things briefly and understandably, mentioned freedom, restoring American constitutional principles, protecting citizens' rights including those of the most vulnerable including the unborn, and—building up to a crescendo at the end—"the coming dawn of a new age of respect for our cherished tradition of ordered liberty." After his last word, the audience exploded in applause and cheers.

Stephen won both the South Carolina and North Carolina primaries with nearly 50% of the vote, swamping the other three candidates.

Labatt withdrew the day after the North Carolina primary. The two moderates hung in to try to challenge Stephen in the Michigan primary at the end of February. There were no scheduled debates, but Langford went around the state meeting most with party regulars to get their support to head off the "extreme conservative" Bernard. More than once, he encountered party people who responded by saying that he had accused Stephen of being a leftist in the Carolina debates—a number of cable channels had broadcast them into Michigan—and now he was calling him just the opposite. They asked, "Which is it?" This made Langford look blatantly inconsistent, opportunistic, and even desperate. He was having trouble raising money from his corporate friends after the Carolina debacles, and was able to get only a limited number of his usual sound bite ads attacking Stephen on the air in the state. Stephen easily countered them with his simple ads in local media markets, using excerpts from his campaign talks and especially the Carolina debates— similar to what he had done before. Moreover, opposition by the state's governor, Lewis Gradison, blunted Langford's "party-insider" strategy. Gradison wouldn't endorse anyone, but he had gotten to know and respect Stephen by following his efforts in Pennsylvania and developing a good relationship with him in the party's governors' organization. Graham's campaign in the state was not as active, but he had some support especially in the business community in Detroit and some of its suburbs. Stephen had his usual strong volunteer organization that was built around conservative Christians, small businessmen in the towns and smaller cities, and rural areas. The two moderates drew from the same segment of the party's electorate and divided up the vote. Stephen won about 60% of the vote.

After Michigan, Langford and Graham largely suspended their campaigns. In the weeks immediately ahead, the major contests were in Ohio, Illinois, and Stephen's own Pennsylvania. After Pennsylvania, Stephen was probably best known in the neighboring state of Ohio where he had had his joint university teaching appointment. He was also a friend and collaborator of that state's governor, who was one of the few who announced his support for Stephen in the primaries. Stephen won the Ohio primary going away. Illinois and the party there were more "moderate," but Stephen still won against the moderate candidates. They did a little campaigning there—it was mostly with a last-ditch "stop Bernard" effort—but he still attracted a little over half of the vote. He won in Pennsylvania with 85%. The nomination race was over. Stephen was going to be named the party's nominee at the convention in Houston. The party had never met there before, but Texas was the largest state in its electoral coalition now. Also, the party national committee, which included many Evangelicals, wanted to show solidarity with the clergy there who had been under a quiet assault since the demand by the city's leftist leadership from the other party some years before that they had to have their sermons approved by them to be sure that they were not "crossing the line between church and state" by encouraging their congregants to oppose the city's pro-homosexualist policies and proposed ordinances.

In the meantime, Stephen undertook the effort of contacting different top officeholders and officials of the party around the country. He knew that some of them were not enthusiastic about him. They perceived that he would be a president who was prepared to "rock the boat" and go decisively in new directions. For too long the party had allowed the other side—the left—to define the terms of the national political debate and move the country in a certain direction. Stephen thought it would be valuable to let them get to know him. He knew that forging personal contacts and relationships can be reassuring to people, and he wanted to try to make the case to them—for those who would listen—for the public positions and the vision that he was putting forth. He was resolved that he was not going to change it, however. Its fundamentals were not negotiable. He also knew that there would have to be a few full-time campaign aides, but that would be all. One would be John Frost. The campaign to come would not be the usual kind.

One leading senator of his party, Marlin Gregg of Colorado, who was regarded as a conservative, more or less, but who was known for often taking "moderate" stands and trying to make common ground with the other party, took the initiative to contact Stephen. He came to Harrisburg to see him when he was back there on state business. He came to make a "hard sell" to Stephen to "just slightly"—his words—soften his stand on some issues for the sake of party unity and because he believed the party would be hurt in November otherwise.

"Governor, whenever anyone gets a major party nomination for the highest office in the land, he can't take rigid ideological positions. He has to moderate. You know that it's necessary to forge a broad enough coalition to win, and he has to be the president of all the people," Gregg said to Stephen.

"Senator, the first thing I have to ask you is who's being ideological?"

In a typical politician's way, Gregg didn't want to come right out and directly accuse or confront Stephen. He wanted to make it seem more indirect and nuanced, as if it wasn't really coming from him. "Governor, many people perceive you that way. They think that if you don't compromise, at least somewhat, on some of your positions it will hurt the party. It may not just be you who loses in the fall, but you may hurt other candidates."

"What positions or issues of mine are you talking about?"

"Governor, the abortion thing for one. Look, you know that I vote pro-life. The national organizations always rate me 85% or so, but you need to bend on the rape and incest thing. Also, can't you be more 'live and let live' with the gays? You make the business community nervous. They have accepted that. They're even into this transgender thing. People think that you're too close to the extreme religious activists. Then, there's the immigration thing. I have talked about the immigration mess, but we can't take any sharp steps on that. Our party has been trying to get the Hispanic voters. We'll lose them more than we are already. And your comments about there being a constitutional crisis—they make you sound extreme."

His characteristic firm look came over Stephen's face as he piercingly stared into Gregg's eyes. "Senator, it's disturbing that you are calling facts and truth mere matters of ideology. It's even more disturbing that you're pushing those things aside—even when it concerns the life or death of the innocent—for reasons of politics. You tell me to make exceptions about abortion. This is a human being, and you tell me I should say it's okay—or at least the law should look the other way—to snuff out his life for something someone else did. The point is that someone is killing an innocent human being. *That is the central reality.* To be impervious to that for political reasons is reprehensible. You can't even talk about life or health of the mother exceptions. For almost as long as *Roe v. Wade* and *Doe v. Bolton* have been around, with the state of medical know-how, it has not been possible to say in absolute terms that abortion is at all necessary to save or help a sick mother. You talk about a 'live and let live' attitude toward the homosexuals, but can't you see that the real issue there is

152

this movement's totalitarian orientation and outright repressive actions? What's happening is that they are expecting our First Amendment liberties to give way, *routinely*, to their claimed sexual freedoms— some of which involves pretty ugly stuff. When you talk about 'extreme religious activists' it sounds like you mean people who want to uphold sound morality—the natural law, which man's right reason can make known to him—and they see what can happen, and has happened historically, to nations that abandon it. Maybe you ought to read some of the great thinkers who wrote voluminous works about the causes of the decline of nations and civilizations. Repudiating sound morality is right up near the top. A lot of our political leaders over the years have quoted Tocqueville. Tocqueville says in one place that social turmoil has its origins in the troubles of the marriage bed. So, when we talk about morality that includes sexual morality, and it affects political life in a profound way. For some time now, the homosexualists and their allies have been trying to impose on us a radical view about marriage and the family and we have scarcely been resisting even though the implications for the country are overwhelming—and how could it be otherwise since the family is the foundation of the social order. Yes, Christianity and Judaism and most other great religions have traditionally understood that, but so did Aristotle. This is hardly religious extremism—it's national self-interest, national survival. It's not the kind of thing that you compromise on. Senator, you don't have to tell me that compromise is the lifeblood of politics. I have been prepared to compromise on many things as Governor of Pennsylvania. To believe that one can compromise on everything, however—to believe that there are no irreducible minimums, no perennial truths that have to be maintained—is not only irresponsible, but it's very, very dangerous. As far as immigration is concerned, I have made clear that the immigration laws have a lot of room for improvement, but to say that people can just snub their noses at them and violate them with impunity is destructive of the rule of law—a central principle for a republic like ours, and for avoiding arbitrary rule. The case can and often has been made that the tax laws are unfair—they are probably much more unfair than the immigration laws. On top of that, people are not even sure what they mean. They can't understand them. Even the IRS doesn't know what they mean. So, are you prepared to say that people can just ignore and violate the tax laws with impunity? The past couple of administrations have just ignored the immigration laws—and a lot of other laws—because they haven't liked them. They have ignored what Congress enacted. They have abused executive authority, when they did not have the rightful discretion to do so. You have that, plus the unremitting assaults on free speech and religious liberty by homosexualists and others, which have been so much acquiesced in by the courts—don't you call that a constitutional crisis? Oh, and about what you call 'moderating': Have we seen the other party moderating at all? They have proceeded for a dozen years to impose an unadulterated leftist agenda on the country. The best we ever seem to do in response is to slightly ameliorate the damage they have done. Mostly, we end up institutionalizing the changes they have made—which are usually bad. In the long run, we end up being a party to the mischief."

Senator Gregg saw that he was not going to convince Stephen. He saw face-first that Stephen was not the usual kind of politician. He thanked Stephen for his time, got his coat, and left. Stephen had no doubt that he would let others among the party's top officeholders who thought like him know the story about their party's presumptive nominee. It would be only a matter of time before everyone in his party would see what kind of candidate he was and decide how they would go in the general election.

Stephen knew that there would have to be a campaign manager. No one per se held that position during the primaries, though John Frost played a kind of coordinating role. Stephen asked him about becoming the campaign manager, but he quickly declined. He said he simply didn't have the knowledge or experience to handle a nationwide campaign. The same question had been on Stephen's mind, but he wanted to offer it both because of Frost's unassailable loyalty and the fact that he had done such a good job with the primary campaign. They and Marybeth, who was always Stephen's closest advisor, discussed how many full-time campaign staffers were needed. Stephen strongly preferred only a few, although Marybeth and John thought that handling a national campaign would require many more. They finally agreed on ten full-time staffers, all of whom would have to have considerable previous experience: the national campaign manager, a fund-raising coordinator, a director of communications whose role would partly involve dealing with the media along the lines that Stephen had in mind, a coordinator of volunteer efforts and campaign scheduling (the latter was going to be a more limited task than normal for a presidential campaign, however, in light of the kind of campaign that Stephen was intent on running), and regional coordinators for New England and the Middle Atlantic region, the Southeast, the near-Midwest, the Great Plains, the Rocky Mountain and Southwest region, and the Pacific Coast. There would also have to be a few secretaries. Stephen insisted that the professional staffers could not be the typical campaign "hired guns" who would be ready to change loyalties at the drop of a hat and switch from one candidate to another. They would have to be firmly committed to Stephen's principles and positions and the kind of campaign he planned to run. Stephen was also insistent—John wasn't the least surprised by this—that he and he alone would be in control of the campaign and make all the major decisions. He prevailed upon John to take the position of volunteer and scheduling coordinator. He had done a masterful job of building up the volunteer organization during the primary season. He agreed to that. Stephen knew that his small business near Lancaster had suffered in the past few months and his devoted wife and family had gone without his presence too much as he had poured himself, out of loyalty both to Stephen and his principles, into the campaign effort. Stephen needed him, but didn't want him to suffer any further economic disadvantage. He would be paid respectably. They discussed who might be good for the various campaign roles. Both from John's party connections and his experience in the primary campaign, he suggested a small number of people. Marybeth also mentioned a few possibilities. Mostly, they talked about possible campaign manager choices. It was agreed that whoever that would be should be permitted to recommend people for some of the other slots even though Stephen would have the final say on who to appoint. He also was firm about continuing the $500 per person campaign contribution limit, though since he would be the nominee of party, the national party organization would provide some funds. He made it clear that he would limit how much he would take, however.

If Stephen's lieutenant governor campaign had been iconoclastic, the presidential campaign would be even more so. He was not going to resurrect some of the campaign efforts of the early 1970s, but of a much earlier time. He did not want this to be the usual presidential media campaign, but partly a "front porch" campaign of the kind last tried by McKinley and Harding. To be sure, John and Marybeth were somewhat uneasy about this. They wondered if the usually hard-nosed realist Stephen was being realistic. As the three of them talked about it and all that Stephen had in mind, however, they softened up. They also saw how committed Stephen was to it, and they realized that when he was set on a certain course it was difficult to dissuade him. Moreover, his unusual lieutenant governor campaign had been a smashing success. Actually, as he talked to them more about it they became more convinced that it could work and be effective. He said that he had been thinking about this approach for some time, but it all firmly had come together in his mind only a few days before and that's why he hadn't previously discussed it with them. He said that whoever became campaign manager would have to accept and work within this framework.

In the days that followed, Stephen and John consulted among the people who had played a significant role in the primary campaign and several prominent state and national-level party committee members about who might fit Stephen's precise bill to be campaign manager. The man they settled on was Jeff Witherspoon, who had had considerable campaign management experience in his native Indiana and other states, had had a prominent position with the party in the state, and also had led a 501 (c) (4) policy advocacy organization in Washington, D.C. that focused on defense matters. Witherspoon traveled to Harrisburg to meet with Stephen and the two talked for an entire afternoon. Stephen laid out in detail how he wanted to conduct the campaign and what his expectations of a campaign manager were. They talked at length about their views on a broad range of issues and broad strategies to get them into public policy. They also discussed each one's basic political philosophy and beliefs about the role of government. Stephen was very pleased on most things, but had a slight, vague uneasiness about Witherspoon's noncommittal attitude on how to deal with the moderates in the party. Stephen had always trusted his gut reaction about political matters; it had served him well. Witherspoon seemed so good, however, that he was willing to push it aside. Something held him back from doing that or maybe it was just that a phone call summoning him to take care of some important gubernatorial business interrupted their meeting just as they were about to discuss Witherspoon's compensation. They stopped with a general understanding that he would be hired and it was planned that he would spend his final two days in Harrisburg talking with John Frost and a few of the other people Stephen and John had in mind for top campaign positions who they had asked to come to Harrisburg.

John had not met Witherspoon before. He had known about him mostly by reputation. For one who had been involved with the rough and tumble ways of politics and especially intra-party skirmishes for so long, John was a man of kind and gentle demeanor. People sometimes said about him that it was hard not to like him, and he bent over backwards to try to understand people. As soon as he and Witherspoon began to talk, John saw problems. John was telling him about the ins-and-outs of the primary campaign, but he seemed uninterested. He seemed to almost start lecturing John about how campaigns ought to be run. John moved the conversation back to talking about the kind of unconventional campaign that Stephen wanted. Witherspoon didn't criticize that—he evinced an attitude of why Frost was bringing this up when, after all, Stephen had talked to him about all that—but then went on to talk only about a more run-of-the-mill type of campaign. After they were done talking, they went to a prearranged luncheon with the others who were being considered for the different positions and a couple of the main volunteers at this, the national campaign headquarters. Witherspoon almost ignored a few of the people and went on talking about his experience running campaigns and how to run a national campaign, and seemed to brush aside most of the questions the other people asked him. He also mentioned different people he knew who would be good at different roles in a national campaign. The implication was that he had other people in mind for campaign spots. Finally, he talked glowingly about different leading Congressional figures of the party who he knew well, including a couple that John knew would press Stephen to downplay certain of his positions. The looks of a few of the other people and, after Witherspoon had left, the comments they made to him caused John to realize that campaign turmoil could easily be brewing.

That evening, John called Stephen and related everything that had happened. This was all that Stephen needed to hear to tip him decisively to act on his gut reaction of the day before. In the morning, he called Witherspoon to tell him simply that "plans had changed" and he would not be bringing him aboard. Stephen then called John who simply said, "I think we may have dodged a bullet." Both of them could foresee leaks left and right about campaign dissention that a hostile media would have had a field day with and that would have badly hurt Stephen. If this campaign were to succeed, pretty much everything would have to go right. At least, there was no room for self-inflicted wounds.

Then Stephen said to John, "There is only one person who can be the campaign manager." Stephen said that John could be helped if a consultant with national campaign experience, but who would be reliable and loyal, could be retained. It would also lighten the workload demands. Stephen offered to talk to John's wife, Jennifer, about how much he needed him in this role.

"Don't worry about that," John replied, "She believes in you, too."

The immediate concern was to get prepared for the party convention and to unify the party as much as possible, without compromising Stephen's basic principles and objectives, before then. The course of action Stephen and John decided immediately to pursue was to have the presumptive nominee talk to leading officeholders from the party, mainly members of Congress. He would talk to the ones receptive to him, those who were noncommittal but might be open, and even ones who were cool or actually hostile to him—except for the Senator Gregg types who seemed to be following a different drummer and were unlikely to be reconciled. Some of them might accept him in the interest of party unity, but he had a sense—correctly as it turned out—that they could not accept a nominee of the party who seriously meant to reverse the direction of the country and might just put up a left-of-center independent candidate to oppose him, like John Anderson who opposed Reagan in 1980. Stephen was also aware, however, of serious fissures within the other party and scuttlebutt that there could be a challenge to its nominee from the more extreme left. He was taking the chance that such a scenario could divide up the vote across the political left to his advantage. It would be better to take that chance than to compromise any of the crucial elements of his agenda, which he saw now as crucial for the country. Besides, the Senator Greggs who always clamored about "moderating" kept ignoring how the party's "moderate" presidential candidates over the years did not have a stellar track record of getting elected. In fact, they often lost support for the very reason that they lacked a coherent and cohesive set of principles. Stephen certainly understood the need for prudence in politics, but that was too often confused with opportunism and a lack of sound principle, even an abdication of moral direction. He knew that what it really meant was an awareness of the unlikelihood of very often achieving completely morally satisfactory results in politics, and the need of a statesman to carefully navigate the innumerable obstacles in his path in order to prod the political order as best he could in the direction of a sound moral vision.

John Frost had just put on staff a long-time campaign volunteer secretary as the chief secretarial staff member for the campaign's headquarters. She made arrangements for Stephen to take two separate trips to Washington to meet individually with many members of Congress from the party. In the meantime, Stephen enlisted his fellow governor, Jim Morrisey of Ohio, who had supported Stephen throughout the primaries and was an active figure in the party's governors association, to talk to other governors from the party who had distanced themselves from Stephen or supported one of his primary opponents. Stephen had told Morrisey that he wanted it made clear to the other governors, as it was to the people in Washington, where he stood and to convince them of the value of the approach to governance that he was going to be setting out in the campaign.

This approach called for a rollback of a runaway federal government, for charting out a definite, uncompromising path of reducing its size and scope. "Rollback" was not the term that would be used, but "gradual disengagement." Stephen realized that, except for the most troublesome ones, government programs could not just be eliminated in one fell swoop. Not only was there the matter of people depending on them and facing hardship if they were quickly cut, but there would be other repercussions as well. Other people and entities, and the economy, could be hurt in a myriad of ways that would not even all be foreseeable. Genuine alternatives had to be looked to. These would not be other programmatic ones or simply saying that the states could take over (the governors would hardly want to hear of new burdens they would have to assume). What was needed was work to stimulate civil society as Stephen had tried to do in Pennsylvania to take over wherever possible. That would involve the president doing what American presidents had hardly ever done: actively encouraging the public to financially support them. One programmatic approach he was poised to propose was called "fiscal subsidiarity," where people could forego paying a portion of their tax dollars if they contributed to different non-profit or charitable organizations or institutions. It would be different from the present tax deduction-for-charitable-contributions scheme that had become increasingly inaccessible for many people because the amounts given now had to be so high to take a deduction. This would be a one-for-one replacement: for every dollar given to a civil society organization, one's tax liability went down one dollar. The federal government certainly had a regulatory role in economic affairs, but the path of increasing micromanagement through regulation had to stop and be reversed. Two ways to restrain destructively self-serving activities especially by big corporations and other powerful economic entities was by an aggressive presidential bully pulpit and also by a resumption of efforts, such as in the ill-fated First New Deal and as championed by Catholic thinkers a century earlier, of pushing to build up internal codes of ethical conduct and self-restraint within different sectors of the economy. The different sectors would be seriously patrolling themselves with government stepping back, but overseeing them with a watchful eye and prodding them. He was less than sanguine about social regulation that was aimed to achieve various cultural ends. This had started in a big way in the 1960s and he sought to sharply scale it back. It had often been used to promote destructive cultural transformation pursuant to the ideological and morally relativist agenda of the left. Stephen also intended to exert strict control over the federal bureaucracy, having an immediate massive review of federal regulations across the board and eliminating all that were not necessary or that were not directly based on enabling statutes. Any new

159

regulations would have to be directly approved by the president. Along with gradual disengagement would be a gradual decrease in the size of the bureaucracy, of the federal civilian workforce. In line with gradual disengagement and scaling down the bureaucracy, Stephen planned on sending a legislative program to Congress that would stress simplicity and spelling out clearly what the law in question sought to do and what was expected of those it applied to. Statutes would be limited whenever possible to twenty pages of text, with very clear language. No longer would there be "legalese" that even lawyers couldn't understand. There would no longer be vague provisions or wide gaps that bureaucratic rulemaking would be expected to fill in; it would be a sharply restricted notion of delegation to executive agencies. Stephen wanted to stress persuasive governance as much as possible. The federal government, led by the President, would be more oriented to *persuading* the public and different kinds of private sector entities to pursue certain courses of action instead of always legislating and mandating. Persuasive governance also, of course, involved a strong effort to educate: marshaling the evidence, laying out the arguments, and making the case—repeatedly, insistently—for a certain course of action. Finally, Stephen was going to be aggressive in turning back assaults against human dignity and distorting and undermining American constitutional principles and the tradition behind them. This meant the uncompromising protection of innocent human life from fertilization to natural death and of the family as the cell of society and true marriage as the basis of it. It also meant restraining the power of the federal courts, which had perhaps more than any other governmental institution imposed the leftist, secularist cultural agenda on the country. Stephen's approach during the general election campaign and afterwards, if elected, was going to be what it had been up to this point in his political career: education mixed with confrontation—*repeatedly and insistently*. This would be the programmatic and governance framework for a Bernard presidency. Stephen's educative effort for the general election campaign would begin first with these top party people and then continue with the general public.

As Stephen met with one member of his party's delegation in Congress after another, it was apparent that most of them had not thought much about a political perspective such as he discussed with them. His "go on the offensive" posture was something the party had been reticent about, and Stephen sought to convince them of its necessity and how its absence had been a significant part of the cause for the party's failures. The fact that the party had been exiled from the presidency for a dozen years, however, made a number of them willing to listen in spite of their contrary proclivities. He had the distinct sense that by the conclusion of his meetings with most of them he was winning their respect and admiration and that they believed this was a man who would be a strong leader of their party in the fall election campaign.

Stephen and John simultaneously began to take the campaign to the country at large. To be sure, it would get into full gear right after the convention. In the meantime, he began to issue very well thought out and precisely worded statements about a range of public questions. The thrust of these early statements was to provide a searching critique of the general thinking and specific positions of the political left and to aggressively show how they had become increasingly intolerant and repressive. It was going to be a more broad-reaching version of that confrontation with the homosexualist activist. He coupled this with appearances by way of television and radio hook-ups in many local media outlets around the country that featured the same focus. His campaign avoided the national media who they knew were mostly hostile to him. This early strategy established the offensive posture of the campaign and put the other party and his likely other left-leaning opponents on the defensive. He did not at this stage lay out policy proposals or a program. That would follow. For the time being, his campaign wanted to shape the terms of the debate, which was something their party had usually failed miserably in doing. Meanwhile, polls—not done by the campaign, as Stephen made it clear that he would not be driven by polls—showed that the public was unsure what it thought of him, that it didn't know enough. These local media forays and certainly the convention were going to be critical in helping the public shape their early views of him before the general election campaign started.

Stephen used some of the local media appearances to educate about American constitutional principles, since part of the reason he had even decided to run was to stop their perilous erosion. Once in awhile, the local media programs featured a call-in format, and Stephen agreed to answer callers. The education-confrontation approach was played out well in such a call-in radio program in Peoria, Illinois. Stephen talked about how the American Founding presumed natural law principles and how these principles came forth directly from human nature rightly understood. The source ultimately of these principles was the Creator Himself. They sprang from the divine nature or essence of which man was made in the image and likeness of. This was pointedly recognized by the Declaration of Independence, which referred to the "Laws of Nature and of Nature's God." As part of this natural law, man had rights—natural rights—that gave him the prerogative to do certain things or have certain things (most preeminently life and the things necessary for it, liberty, and property) so that he could be able to be more fully human—that is, so his dignity could be furthered—and carry out his obligations in life. He said, "Since the laws of nature are from God, man's basic rights are ultimately from God. The state can legislate other rights, but if they are to be valid they can never go against natural law." He explained further how this provided the whole notion for the Constitution being viewed as "higher" or more fundamental than legislative enactments, so that the enactments had to conform to it to have force.

A caller angrily disputed this. "God is not the source of rights, the state is. We don't have to believe in God to have government or to have rights."

"I'm stating to you what the 'Men of '76' and our Founding Fathers who drew up the Constitution, believed. The language of the Declaration is clear. I just quoted it. That's not subject to dispute."

"Like I said, we don't need God to have government."

"You realize, don't you, that what you're saying is that man is the determiner of everything. When you say that government is the source of rights, you're saying that man is the source of rights. If he can give them, he can take them away—presumably for any and all reasons. That's the very stuff of tyranny. You're justifying tyranny."

"That's not what I said. Some rights can be protected, the important ones. People do that. They don't need God."

"Tell me what will be their basis for deciding what rights are the important ones. It will be just what the men in control will want them to be. What standard will they appeal to? If it's just their own opinion, why would one ruler's opinion be any better than another's? Why won't whoever has power just decide that on the basis of what's to his own benefit, or why won't he suppress rights he disagrees with or the exercise of which he believes to be threatening to his power? If men are the ones who set the standards without reference to any higher law or Authority, you have tyranny." He added with his characteristic firmness, "So, I ask you again: why are you promoting tyranny?"

"It won't work that way. They'll protect the rights that should be protected."

"How will they know which rights these are and how can we trust them to uphold them?"

"It will be the rights that the community has agreed to and human rights that have widely been accepted."

"What will be the grounds for saying that even those rights are correct, true, or complete? After all, you've said it's just a matter of opinion. If a few politicians can get it wrong—the leading lights of the community—couldn't the mass of people, even if it's a majority, get it wrong and be oppressive? Weren't John Stuart Mill and Alexis de Tocqueville fearful of the tyranny of the majority."

"The majority won't get it wrong. Are you against majority rule?"

"Didn't the majority have it wrong about the right to own slaves for a long time earlier in American history? Oh, and about majority rule are you saying that the majority can rule anything, even suppressing minority rights—like the most basic rights of the people brought over from Africa into slavery? Isn't this the problem if you 'make man the measure of all things?'"

The caller didn't respond, except to say quickly, "That's different."

"Why is it different? Why are you making government the source of all rights? Why are you opening the door to tyranny? Tell me, why are you supporting what easily leads to tyranny?" Stephen insistently continued, "Answer me, why do you want to promote tyranny?"

The program moderator stopped the exchange after that.

Later in the same week, Stephen was on a television call-in program in Dayton, Ohio. He had to be in Harrisburg for state business that day, but a hook-up was arranged from a station there. A female caller, who was aggressive just like the man in Peoria, challenged Stephen on not wanting to compromise on issues like abortion. "We have to reach a middle ground on these things. You can't be absolutist," she said. "Your party in Congress held up some important legislation because it didn't want to do things like fund overseas abortions, and you have said that no abortion is acceptable. Politics is about compromising, but you aren't willing to do it on this and other issues."

"It's true that compromise is the lifeblood of politics, but you don't seem to understand that not everything can be subject to compromise. There are basic moral questions, such as those involving innocent human life as here, which you can't compromise about since to do so would assault human dignity and human good. It would also pave the way for many other evils. You should know that! Do you mean to tell me that you believe that there are issues that you would not compromise on? What about slavery, or racial discrimination, or genocide? Do you think some of those things are acceptable—as compromises?"

"Those things are different. Everybody agrees that they're not right. Society rejects them."

Stephen jumped in, not letting her finish her thought. There was an abruptness, even a slight anger, in his manner that was not typical of him. "It wasn't always the case that society rejected these things and in fact they are not even now completely rejected throughout the world. Look at the sex slavery carried out by Islamist groups and others in our day. It's obvious that some people don't think that genocide is wrong. Look at the ethnic cleansing that occurred in the Balkans and elsewhere. Look at the massacres of Christians and other religious minorities in parts of the Middle East. Is it enough just to have a consensus in society, or certain societies, about something to render it not given to compromise? Isn't this a matter of right and wrong? Some things are fundamentally, utterly wrong by their very nature and should be rejected. If you concede that genocide is wrong and should never be permitted, it must be because you acknowledge that human life—innocent human life—should not be destroyed. Then, you have to be opposed to abortion too, and have to say it should not be permitted."

"It's a woman's right. It's her body. Her life will be disrupted by an unwanted pregnancy," the caller objected.

Stephen's sharp, astute mind went right to the contradictory character of her statement. "Well, what about those people who lead genocides who say that it's the right of my majority group to eliminate the minority who are a cancer on our body politic? What about the slaveholder who said that having slaves was his right? He could make a definite claim to that effect because our Constitution before the Thirteenth Amendment didn't forbid it."

"The fetus is just tissue, a part of the woman."

"Is that so?" Stephen responded quickly. He proceeded to state, with his considerable capability to summarize well substantial amounts of information, the basic facts of life before birth. After that, the host said it was time to go to a break and the call was ended.

That evening, as they sat at the table after a quiet dinner, Stephen said to Marybeth, "Darling, you have been quiet tonight. That usually is a sign that you have something important to say to me."

Marybeth looked up and said very directly but with her usual gentle tone, "Stephen, I've been listening to some of the call-in programs you have been a guest on. We've talked a lot about the need to face down the opposition, but you've always done it kindly and charitably. You seem lately to be so concerned about the confrontation part that you're not being so charitable. You have to remember that. It's not just that you could be hurt politically—since people want a leader, not a satirist—but it will make you a worse person. An uncharitable person is not what you are or have ever been."

An embarrassed look came over Stephen's face and he looked down for a few moments. "As usual, Marybeth, you're right. I guess I have been too intense. I've lost my sense of balance recently. I'm in this to further the cause of right and I'm lamenting the loss of virtue in the country, but the highest virtue is charity. In spite of how troublesome—even destructive—the views of some of these people are, I must respect and love them as persons. Thanks for bringing me back to my senses as you do so often."

They embraced and held each other lovingly. "Do you see how good I am to have around?" Marybeth teased.

"I knew that from the first night we met."

In fact, Marybeth was "around" the campaign a lot. She was no "trophy" politician's wife, even though her beauty, charm, and kindness had been a great asset to Stephen from the time he started his run for lieutenant governor of Pennsylvania. She was regularly involved with John Frost and the others in campaign discussions, planning, and advising. She was in the inner circle. How could it be otherwise, since she was always his closest adviser? Her advice on many different levels was invariably on target.

Marybeth's advice got Stephen on the right track again in his "interpersonal relations" in the campaign. He was back on stride in making sure that the educating, explaining, and where needed confronting approach was done within a constant spirit of charity. In fact, when some local media personalities started to ask average citizens their opinion of Stephen they often got such reactions as "tough but decent" and "strong but kind." People sometimes expressed the view that "he probably couldn't win because he's a decent guy." John arranged short media ads for local markets that featured a very short monologue—about a minute—of just one person or another who had gotten to know or had worked with Stephen in either his university or his public service work who related his or her experience. The people typically testified to his work ethic, honesty, integrity, considerate manner, and charitable way of dealing with everyone he worked with— even if he disagreed with them or had to strongly oppose them. Stephen agreed to the spots, so long as they did not unduly embellish him. He figured that the opposition would sooner or later falsely attack his character, so it was best to take the initiative in the image battle—so long as it was truthful.

Two weeks before the convention, Graham announced that he was running as an independent. His Senate term was coming to a conclusion at the end of the year and when he threw his hat into the presidential nomination race late the previous year had said he was not running for reelection. In his announcement, he said that he was now making the race as an independent because the party had been "taken over by extremism." When he made that comment, elements in the party strongly criticized him and even some leading party figures attacked him for leaving. Even some of the left-leaning media thought his comment was overkill, partly because Stephen's demeanor didn't quite fit the bill of an extremist and partly because it sounded a bit like sour grapes. One reporter challenged him about why he left when Langford, who wasn't beaten as badly in the primaries as him, was not bolting the party and going the same route. Graham made some vague reference to having had discussions with Langford and that he was seeking his support. This set off a flurry of media speculation and a denial from Langford, but it damaged the moderates' position in the party because suddenly they were looking disloyal. The effect was to put a damper on any last-ditch attempts to derail Stephen at the convention. There had been reports that despite his commanding lead they would try to win uncommitted delegates over to their side to make the long-shot effort to deny him the nomination, as well as to soften the party platform. The fall-out further just stilled their voices of opposition to Stephen.

A week before the convention, Graham appeared at a news conference and announced that Gregg would be joining him on his independent ticket as the vice-presidential candidate. Gregg still had two years on his senatorial term. Some in the media started to speculate that this could signal the beginning of a wave of departures from the party and that Stephen could not hold the party together behind him. As it turned out, that didn't happen and both Graham and Gregg began to face criticism from the party's national committee that they were turncoats and hurting it.

In the meantime, the divisions in the other party were increasingly evident. A favorite of the hard-left, Lana Greenleaf, the popular senator from New York, had aggressively challenged President Gavin Frederickson in the primaries. She had come up short, but still won 40% of the cumulative vote and a sizable minority of the delegates were poised to push a hard-left platform at their convention. Figuring he should try to "move toward the center" against the "arch-conservative" Stephen, Frederickson tried to keep her supporters at bay. The result ultimately was that the party's platform was somewhat more moderate than it otherwise would have been, but still decidedly leftist. If that was a kind of concession to the hard-left, it still wasn't satisfied. After their convention, Greenleaf unenthusiastically endorsed Frederickson—and didn't work much for him in New York that fall— but a fourth candidate entered the race. Former Governor John

Harlington of Connecticut became the hard-left's new darling and standard-bearer. He ran as an independent in some states and as the candidate of a green-type party.

Stephen secured the nomination at his party's convention, and far from displaying a lack of party unity there was a visible enthusiasm among the delegates. It was a "conservative" party, and the conservatives—including a substantial Evangelical and conservative Catholic element—were in control. Stephen's efforts to win over top party Congressional figures, with a small number of exceptions, had been successful. He had successfully used his educative approach even with them. It, combined with his attractive demeanor and kind, respectful manner, their awareness of how the political winds in the party were blowing, and the fact that most of them were conservatives too, even if less solid and principled, were responsible for this. Morrissey's efforts helped with the party's other governors.

Stephen had been pondering his vice presidential selection since after the Pennsylvania primary. He wanted someone who thought as he did, about the Constitution, government, and the critical issues of the time. It would also have to be someone who had a strong, personal Christian commitment. He figured that the most likely person would be a serious Evangelical Protestant, since he was a Catholic. He also thought that someone with Washington experience would be needed. Even though he had taught for years about the national government, he thought that it would be a good balance on the ticket to have someone who had actually been in the thick of things. Moreover, he thought this would be necessary to counter the claims that would surely be raised by the Frederickson campaign about his lack of national experience. Someone from the Sunbelt seemed preferable since Stephen was from the Frostbelt, Pennsylvania and with an Ohio connection, and because the party was so strong there. It was another aspect of "balance." With all these criteria, the number of potential running mates quickly was whittled down to just a few. The more Stephen read and learned from people in the know, the more it seemed to come down to Senator Michael Clarke of Texas. He was not an Evangelical, but a high church Anglican—a member of a congregation that had broken from the mainstream U.S. Episcopal Church over women's ordination—with close ties to Evangelicals in his state. He was one of the minority of Protestants in the country who never had accepted contraception and took seriously the Biblical injunction to "be fruitful and multiply." He and his wife had seven children. Even though he had been in Texas for thirty years, he hailed originally from Michigan and had gone to his adopted state to pursue business opportunities as a young man. Stephen announced Clarke as his choice two weeks before the convention. They had gotten to know each other well by then, and in fact genuinely had become friends.

Only parts of the party's convention were on NBC, the one of the "big" networks that was covering the conventions at all this election year, but as usual they all planned to cover the acceptance speeches. To counter the expected critical commentary about the speeches, John Frost and his other top campaign people worked hard to get them covered as widely as possible on cable television and social media as well. Stephen and all of them knew that the acceptance speeches were key to creating a first and perhaps defining impression with many voters.

The convention delegates were mostly party regulars, but many of the delegates were people who had been committed to Stephen from the beginning. Some came into politics because of Stephen's candidacy. They had become excited by the presence of a candidate who sought to seriously change the course—the downward spiral—that the country had been going in. They were philosophically conservative, and the majority influenced by their Christian religious beliefs. Even the "party-regular" delegates were being won over to Stephen, as he made a point of reaching out to as many of them as he could and his charitable and kind character attracted them.

Stephen wrote his acceptance speech by himself. Throughout his time in politics, he had had no use for speechwriters. He intended to use it to very directly set out the major themes of his campaign. He would be talking about the same things as he had been since his lieutenant governor campaign, but the American Founding and the culture that spawned it would be the framework. All of the themes fit well into that. As a political science and constitutional scholar, he had written often about the principles of the Founding and the culture of that time. He had never had a "my country right or wrong" attitude and had little patience for those who did. As a Catholic, he understood that God had anointed no political order as his favored one. His extensive study, however, had led him to conclude that America in its original conception was indeed "a new order for the ages" and that it was entirely correct to embrace a reasonable notion of American exceptionalism. Along with the nineteenth-century American Catholic political thinker Orestes A. Brownson, he concluded that America—in its Founding conception—had stood above other nations in history in reconciling the securing of individual liberty with the protection of the common good, and of properly balancing liberty with order. The speech would emphasize the need to protect liberty rightly understood and recover American constitutional principles. The Founding culture, he would insist, provided the basis for properly addressing the problems even of a technological age.

Amidst the cheers of so many like-minded delegates at the convention he said with his usual look of rock-hard firmness, "My fellow Americans, in this election *liberty is the issue*." He then proceeded to speak about some of the major assaults on liberty in recent times in the country: the suppression of dissent against the leftism that had gotten control in the country, including a large number of IRS audits of conservative and Christian organizations and blatantly unconstitutional "fishing expedition" raids on the homes of leaders of major conservative organizations in three states under so-called "John Doe" laws; the government-generated legal actions across the country against not just business owners who refused to provide services for same-sex "weddings" but landlords who refused to rent apartments to cohabiting couples and even people who wrote "letters to the editor" criticizing the homosexualist agenda; a wave of federal criminal prosecutions against small landowners for environmental offenses that clearly stretched the intent of the laws in question; the prosecutions and revocation of the medical licenses of physicians in a few states when they refused to withhold treatment from people who had injured themselves while unsuccessfully attempting suicide or had refused to refer patients wanting to commit suicide to physicians who would assist them; homosexualist organizations lobbying to have lawyers who filed briefs against their agenda disciplined and disbarred; the major recent push by the federal Department of Education to mandate secular, morally relativistic curricula in religious higher education institutions as a condition of continuing in the federal student loan program; and the continuing federal effort to one way or another mandate all health insurance plans to pay for contraceptives, sterilizations, abortions, physician-assisted suicide, and so-called "sex-change" operations. "The other party's and the left's agenda of promoting and foisting on us a false notion of liberty—sexual freedom and the freedom to destroy the unwanted innocent and of self-destruction at any cost, even the subversion of our *true* constitutional liberties—has created a crisis that is undermining our democratic republic. It has opened the door to tyranny." He hesitated for a moment, then insisted tersely and resolutely: "This assault on our true freedoms and our Constitution—and on human dignity—*is going to stop*." The convention delegates and the people in the galleries exploded in applause and then, suddenly, chants rose up of "Liberty!"

He then proceeded to give a brief background of major Bill of Rights provisions and succinctly but emphatically explained how these kinds of actions were a clear assault on them and how the Bill of Rights provided no basis for the rights now asserted by the left. "Perhaps worse of all is the assault on the rule of law, the very thing that distinguishes a free nation from a tyranny." He mentioned how local and state governments—"with an approving eye from Washington— were trampling on the rights of religious people, especially Christians, by requiring them to do things like take part in and thus endorse what he always referred to as "same-sex so-called marriage," even while they allowed its proponents to withhold business and other services from the religious believers who they know opposed it.

Then, he shifted gears and started talking about the different qualities of the people of America's Founding Era, the elements that made up the culture that gave rise to the Constitution. He talked about their courageous and independent spirit, their willingness to sacrifice in the present for an expected future good, their cooperative attitude and concern for the community and the general welfare, how while they "lived for liberty" they were in no way individualists "focused only on themselves" and "did not allow liberty to go to an extreme and become license." He mentioned how an attitude of friendship and civility characterized their culture. The fact that they adhered to a strict code of morality—including strong sexual morality and an ethic of family stability—which was grounded in the near ubiquitous Christianity of the culture "in no way compromised their commitment to civility. This is contrary to too many voices today who say that civility is not possible when people live in a religious culture and have a strong moral code." He paused, and then completed his thought with a statement that caused the convention to erupt in long applause: "In truth, it is the assault on morality and religion, especially Christianity, which has caused our society, our culture, to become coarse, uncivil, and nasty. Let us return to the light that follows from sound morality and an awareness that we depend on God."

This was an educator's history, political science, and sociology lesson presented at the people's level. He was not pandering to the people, however, but—in a very "unpolitician-like" manner—calling on them to renew themselves so American culture and politics could be renewed. It was another "Ask not what your country can do for you, but what you can do for your country" moment. They also must stop turning to government to solve their problems. There needed to be "a reawakening of personal responsibility." He then spoke about out-of-control bureaucracies and government trying to manage "every nook and cranny of our lives."

He also didn't seek to ingratiate himself across the board to some on the conservative side of the spectrum, who seemed to have a near-absolute view of freedom when it came to economics. He said in Founding times, "people could not have envisioned economics as somehow operating by its own laws, unaffected by ethics," and pointed out how there were also many laws—on the local level—that restrained economic freedom for the sake of the common good. "They believed in economic freedom, but *not* economic license. They valued entrepreneurial effort and self-initiative. They took for granted exchange and market activity, but they had no use for laissez faire—in economic life any more than in sexual or reproductive matters. They continued a tradition that went all the way back to Aristotle in the ancient world: private ownership of property was natural and necessary, but men were not free to use their property or their wealth in a rankly selfish manner without regard for their fellow men or their community." He contrasted that to today, where managers of large corporations seemed to dispense with ethics, not just in encouraging the likes of illegal immigration amnesties so they could more easily pay less than a just wage but also in suddenly moving factories so that people and communities economically suffered and seeming to do whatever "the anti-family homosexualist movement" asked of them. He also faulted them for their lack of patriotism in readily shipping jobs and facilities overseas. Profits were important, to be sure, but he said "it was a deformed corporate thinking that fixated on the bottom line to the exclusion of all else." Again, he hit on the theme of human dignity. "The economy is made for man, not man for the economy."

He raised the theme of "gradual disengagement" that he had talked about throughout the campaign. The welfare state, he said, was fiscally unsustainable, as well as being damaging in other ways: it caused ongoing government dependency, encouraged irresponsibility, created the basis for political manipulation as politicians kept pouring money into it to get votes, and it ended up subordinating true human needs to bureaucratic imperatives. While government had to be ready to provide a safety net and there would be circumstances when it necessarily would be called on, he stressed his theme of building up the "civil society" sector, the non-profit, charitable organizations to be the "the first line of help for people, along with their families." As he had been saying in the primary campaign, government could not suddenly pull back from its providing role, "lest people in need become dislocated and suffer." What was needed now was a firm commitment by the national government to go on a path of gradual disengagement from many of its entitlement programs—"pulling back in proportion as civil society can be better built up and pick up the slack." Where entitlements would have to continue, Stephen sounded the theme of Marvin Olasky that increasingly they should be tied to personal improvement and changed behavior—like getting a job, taking responsibility for children one has sired, and staying out of trouble with the law.

As far as the family was concerned, Stephen again brought the audience to its feet when he said with his trademark firm and resolute tone, "And it's time for the national government to once again promote and in every way possible—but not intrusively—assist the nuclear and even extended family, instead of doing what it has for decades: assaulting, redefining, and trying to destroy it!"

Near the end of his acceptance speech, Stephen caused the audience to suddenly fall silent when he announced that he would be resurrecting the notion of the front porch campaign, and that this would be the major way he would conduct his campaign. He shook them from their momentary silence by then saying, "Watch what we will do with our front porch campaign. It will be a campaign to explain, discuss, and educate, not the sound bites we have gotten so used to in political campaigns and that President Frederickson will be using, as he did four years ago!" The crowd roared. One or two party people had advised Stephen not to refer to his opponent as "President," to avoid highlighting the fact that he was the incumbent. Stephen would hear nothing of that, however. Appropriate respect was due to the man in the office and to the office itself. Stephen then concluded, "Work as hard as you ever have in this campaign. Together, we can—*we will*—bring back the America of our Founding Fathers and restore the liberty and the Constitution that they bequeathed to us. May Almighty God bless you and bless our beloved country. Constantly pray for His help in this effort."

The two nominees and their wives came together on the dais, shook hands, and waved to the delegates, but did not linger as is often the case. The commentators immediately jumped into the discussion about the front porch campaign, which took them completely by surprise. As had been the case with the media many other times, Stephen's unconventional kind of politics captured their fancy and their interest and they evinced a certain admiration for him even as most of them deeply disagreed with him.

CHAPTER 6

A Campaign Scarcely Seen

A fter the convention, in late July, Stephen began his front porch
campaign. It was actually a kind of *modified* front porch
campaign. He knew it would not be appropriate to do it from the
Capitol steps in Harrisburg and it was not feasible to do it from their
apartment close to the Capitol. The other tenants and those living in
neighboring apartments almost certainly wouldn't like the expected
crowds of media and other people who would be present for his
planned front porch sessions, and the city wouldn't like the blocking of
traffic that would go along with it. So, what Stephen arranged to do was
to conduct his front porch campaign at John Frost's house, which was
in a semi-rural area about ten miles from Harrisburg. He had five acres
of land around his house and plenty of parking space and it was easily
accessible just slightly off an exit of a major highway. When turning
off the exit in the opposite direction there were a couple of shopping
plazas and a few fast-food and eat-in chain restaurants. From there, it
was only a short distance to the main street one of the old towns nearby
that had virtually become part of the exurbs of Harrisburg. This
location would have the further advantage of attracting average
citizens, in addition to the media, to the front porch sessions. People
could even combine shopping with an excursion out to hear Stephen
and could then go nearby to eat. The campaign planned to publicize
them extensively and, especially, to make sure that its nearby
supporters would know about them and to have their volunteer
organizers arrange carpools from different places in the region to the
sessions.

Beyond that, he knew he would have to "hit the hustings" to some
extent—but not in the "jet-setting" manner of typical present-day
political campaigns. Moreover, there was an important symbolic value
to that. He did not want to convey that, if elected, he would be a

president who would simply direct the country from a distant center—Washington, D.C.—detached from the people. That was a big part of the country's problem. He would "connect" with the people where they were across the whole country, even as he would resurrect the simplicity of an older kind of politics and continue his effort to recover its educative function as he mounted and spoke from the front porch. With an approach reminiscent of his lieutenant governor campaign, but by motor vehicle and not on foot—which wouldn't have been possible—he planned to traverse the country from east to west twice in a campaign bus and mini-caravan. There would be no large entourage. It was just a few vehicles. Stephen even insisted that security be kept to a minimum. He would travel on major interstate highways, getting off to visit cities and towns along the way. Most of what he would do on these cross-country excursions would be to meet average people and listen to them. His speeches would be short and a media cohort would not travel along with them. In fact, the campaign's travel schedule would not even be released to the national media. He wanted any media interactions he had on the trips to be with local media. Still, his campaign stops would involve mostly his interacting with citizens in the places where they are. The front porch parts of the campaign would be where he would be facing the major media, although as much as possible he would do it on his own terms. He and John Frost had worked it out: After a week of "front porch campaigning," he would begin the first excursion. It would last a month. It was the time when the Pennsylvania General Assembly would be out of session and it was a slow time for state government. At the beginning of September, he would be back at the front porch campaign near Harrisburg. Then, in October, he would traverse the country the second time. He would then resume the front porch campaign for the last ten days of the campaign.

The front porch campaign actually began in Houston, where from the steps of the parsonage of a local Protestant church to which the pastor had invited him, Stephen denounced the city officials for the well-publicized case of some years before—which after national criticism and legal actions they backed off of—when they issued subpoenas to local clergymen for any sermons critical of their ordinance allowing people of one sex who claimed to identify as members of the other sex to use public restrooms of the opposite sex. He said, "one of the most egregious assaults against churches in the current crisis of religious liberty took place here in Houston. So did one of the greatest stands against oppression, as religious leaders and the faithful fought back." He then proceeded to discuss, in summary fashion, the history of religious liberty struggles in the European background, the meaning of the First Amendment religion clauses, and the central importance of religion for a democratic republic—and, for that matter, any nation—in the thinking of the Founding Fathers. His ability to produce precise quotes from the different Founding Fathers was almost breathtaking to behold. The plan for the front porch campaign was for him to speak about a certain issue, to explain the serious nature of it and its implications for the American political community, to educate, and to rebuke the actions and policies of the opposition and others in politics responsible for causing or accentuating the problem. Then he took questions from the media who were present, but with an insistence on proper decorum. He asked them to raise their hands and not call out and he wouldn't recognize anyone who didn't follow that. He was always prepared to spotlight the media for their ideological biases and lack of professionalism in how they addressed him and different topics. He made sure that he had the facts about how they had treated the different topics he planned to address in his front porch speeches. Right with the first question, by a reporter from one of the Houston area newspapers, he called them to task for the way they had glossed over the obvious religious freedom implications of the sermon affair, and how they had editorialized in support of the city officials. Stephen's debating skills and his charitable approach were seen in how, after a brief back-and-forth, he had the reporter clearly contradicting himself about the First Amendment but still set him down gently. Still, Stephen's persistence in bringing up media transgressions and willingness to confront their bias kept them honest throughout the fall campaign and helped insure that they would report about him and his positions truthfully and fairly.

Stephen came back to a hero's welcome in Harrisburg from his supporters and just average citizens. As his plane touched down at the Harrisburg International Airport, he was surprised to see a large crowd awaiting him, later estimated at 10,000. He was almost choked up as he spoke to them briefly, upon alighting from the plane with Marybeth at his side. "I can't convey how much I appreciate the many citizens of Pennsylvania who have supported me these last few years. You are now sharing me with the entire country as we try to restore the principles and the truths this nation was founded on—founded here, in Pennsylvania, in Philadelphia, in 1776 and in 1787. These truths, which shaped the American Constitution and American life, came almost from the beginning of civilization: from places like Jerusalem with our Jewish and Christian forebears, from ancient Athens with our Greek philosophical heritage, from ancient Rome from whence our early legal and political tradition and the Christianity that was the prime force in shaping American culture emerged, and London that provided the immediate basis for our whole tradition of legal rights and free government. My fellow citizens: This is what is now at stake. This includes our basic liberties. Strong forces in this country, made up of a deformed elite (which is especially strong in Washington), have mounted a sustained attack—sometimes subtle, sometimes not so subtle—on these principles and truths. I resolutely devote myself, in this campaign and if I'm elected, to do everything I can—and there is a great deal a President can do—to restoring these, to restoring the America of our Founding Fathers. With God's help, I—*we*—can be successful." He would refer to a "corrupt elite" many times in the coming campaign, but always with a proper balance, so it did not seem like a mindless, distorted populist appeal or create an us-against-them mentality. He made it clear in many of the short speeches he gave as he traveled, however, that the elite had been working for a long time to try to distort the public's thinking on many questions. That was always a lead-in to his attempt to educate. He usually found that average people responded well to what he said. They tended to have a sense—even though it had been submerged in an era when the culture, media, and popular entertainment had persistently bombarded them with a different message—that what he said was right.

Now that he was back in Harrisburg, Stephen launched into the front porch campaign at its home base. He and John had decided on a carefully drawn up plan, with Stephen talking on a designated topic each day. John and the campaign's director of communications, Mark Quigley—who brought to the campaign considerable experience in local media, with Fox News, and as a media relations staffer for a Congressman—initially gave the entire schedule to all significant media outlets around the country and then were in daily contact with them to remind them about it. The campaign developed close relations with almost all the national and local conservative and religious talk radio programs in the country and were able to interest them in even sending representatives to the "sessions." They were also sure to give them extensive clips of each day's session that they then usually freely played on air. They also were careful to monitor each day's treatment of the sessions by the various media outlets and were quick to follow up with public statements and press conferences led by John if they believed anything was misquoted. Both Stephen and John called them out on any perceived bias. Their "monitoring" of the reporting and Stephen's readiness to highlight their transgressions had its desired effect: the media were kept on their toes and became careful about how they were covering the sessions and his campaign. What happened, in fact, was that the front porch sessions were extensively covered. The big, mainstream media could not twist or distort anything he said because there were so many other media entities also covering them. The care and spadework that Stephen's campaign had done would pay off.

A couple days later, the campaign caravan went north from Harrisburg on U.S. 11/15 to I-80 and made its first stops in some of the same Pennsylvania towns along its long stretch that he had visited in his lieutenant governor walking campaign. They greeted him, like in Harrisburg, as a hero come home and launched him with much enthusiasm on his cross-country campaign.

The caravan followed I-80 across northern Ohio, where it meshed with I-90, jogged up into Michigan following a kind of semi-circle on I-94, 96, and then 69, and then back across northern Indiana and Illinois. It then veered north on I-94 through Wisconsin and Minnesota, and to Bismarck, North Dakota (a state now with oil and natural gas wealth). Then, they took U.S. 83 to Pierre, South Dakota, linked up with I-90 again to Sioux Falls, and then went south on I-29 to Omaha. They there returned to I-80 and proceeded across Nebraska to Cheyenne, Wyoming and then Ogden, Utah. Then it was I-94 through southern Idaho and northeastern Oregon, and then I-82 and 90 to Seattle, Washington. From there they proceeded down the Pacific Coast on I-5 to Sacramento. At Sacramento, they headed back east on I-80 to Salt Lake City and then south on I-15 to link up to I-70 in southern Utah. They proceeded on I-70 to Denver, across Kansas, Missouri, central Illinois, Indiana, Ohio and then to south-central Pennsylvania until it became I-76, which took them back to Harrisburg. Stephen campaigned in literally a few hundred communities off that basic route, "pressing the flesh" to be sure, but mostly listening.

The October campaign excursion followed a more southern route. At Harrisburg, the caravan picked up I-81 south through Maryland, Virginia, North Carolina, and eastern Tennessee and shifted onto I-40 at Knoxville. They proceeded on it across Tennessee, Arkansas, Oklahoma, the northern panhandle of Texas, New Mexico, Arizona, and California. At Bakersfield, it was onto I-5 to Los Angeles and San Diego. Then it was north through the mountains of southern California on I-15 to Riverside, and then I-10 to begin the trip back east. On I-10, they visited Phoenix, Mesa, and Tucson, Arizona, crossing what in the tumultuous current era had become major drug smuggling routes and increasingly lawless expanses of territory. Then, it was through southern New Mexico to El Paso and across Texas. I-10 took them to San Antonio, the first of the major cities of Texas they went to, and there they switched onto I-35 to Austin, Waco, and Dallas-Ft. Worth. From there, the caravan proceeded on I-20 to Shreveport, Louisiana and switched onto I-49 to go to Lafayette, Baton Rouge, and New Orleans, and then went onto I-55 to Jackson, Mississippi, and U.S. 80 to Montgomery, Alabama. From Montgomery, it was I-65 to Birmingham, then I-20 again to Atlanta, and then south on I-75 down the Gulf Coast of Florida to Miami and Fort Lauderdale. Then they worked themselves northward on I-95 along the Atlantic Coast to Jacksonville, Savannah, various points in South and North Carolina, Richmond, Baltimore, Delaware, Philadelphia, New Jersey, the New York City area, Connecticut, Rhode Island, eastern Massachusetts, southern New Hampshire, and finally all the way to Augusta, Maine. From there, it was U.S. 2 to I-91 along the New Hampshire-Vermont border and then I-90 across Massachusetts and northern New York to Syracuse, where they got on I-81—where they had started the trip—and headed back to Harrisburg. The result of the two trips was that Stephen had visited all forty-eight contiguous states. The media-oriented, fly-to-major-metropolitan-areas campaigns of his opponents didn't come anywhere close to that, to say nothing of not meeting anywhere near the number of people—average Americans—face to face that he did.

On his two campaign trips, Stephen especially mingled with people in the small towns and suburbs. He also went into the old working-class Caucasian neighborhoods of the big cities, which had experienced considerable decline and social pathologies over the previous half-century that had been almost ignored. He also did not hesitate to go into the black and Hispanic neighborhoods, to speak the same message as he had done during the primaries. Again, sympathetic minority clergy were his companions in this effort. He knew he was not going to win these areas, but he believed he could get some votes and, more importantly, he wanted to make clear that the deep-seated problems of these communities should not be forgotten about.

In the meantime, racial conflict reached a point in the country that surpassed even the 1960s. Riots, precipitated usually by small incidents, tore through most major cities and even some smaller ones around the country. Initially, police actions triggered them, but the leftist national administrations had substantially weakened the police as a result of a series of civil rights investigations and actions. The new norm seemed to be that the police were backing off from aggressive law enforcement efforts against certain minorities, even in very high crime and gang-infested areas. The result was that other minority groups, such as Koreans and Chinese, who owned businesses in these locales turned increasingly to organized self-defense and even vigilantism. Resulting clashes became the new forces sparking urban rioting.

Stephen made it clear that, despite security concerns, he was not going to allow these developments to deter him from entering these inner city areas. Stephen was being told the same story by his black community contacts in different cities: some in the community were getting fed up with the ongoing cycle of rioting. They were also aware that many of the rioters were kind of professional troublemakers from militant organizations who were making the rounds from one city to the next to stir up trouble. So some in the black community were willing to listen to him. In Toledo, an episode occurred that both highlighted the crime situation and brought unexpected attention to Stephen's campaign and much admiration for him. Accompanied by a minister from one of the local black churches, he was speaking to a small group that gathered in a parking lot outside a small shop run by one of the congregants. He kept an eye on two young black men, perhaps eighteen or nineteen, who had appeared and were milling on the edge of the crowd. Stephen's usually reliable instinct told him something didn't seem right. Stephen had agreed that just one Secret Service agent could accompany the campaign trip; he said he wasn't going to be "smothered" by security. The agent seemed to be looking at another part of the small crowd and didn't even seem to notice the two. Stephen was speaking, but was unobtrusively following the men's movements. Suddenly, he saw one of them quickly put his hand into a woman's shoulder bag, pull out her wallet and slip it into his side pocket. Then, almost as quickly he did the same thing to a woman standing beside and slightly to the front of her. Neither was aware of what was happening. Almost instinctively, Stephen dove into the group and confronted the man. As people stood confused by Stephen's sudden lunge forward, the man pulled a switchblade knife from inside a vest he was wearing. Before he could raise it toward Stephen, the candidate knocked it from his hand. As it hit the worn blacktop with a thud, the Secret Service agent realized what was happening and knocked the man to the ground. The other man started to run away down the block, but the agent quickly radioed the local police who were in a stand-by mode a block away and they intercepted him. When the hubbub simmered down and the men were taken into custody, Stephen calmly finished his remarks and added, "No neighborhood should have to put up with such things."

The Toledo media quickly ran stories about "The Hero Bernard," which the national media had to pick up even if they didn't support or like Stephen. The women, both black, whose wallets were pilfered were interviewed and said how grateful they were to Stephen. The interview was spread around the national media and Stephen's courage became the talk of local and national evening news shows. Even two of the late-night hosts took a minute out of their satiric routines to commend him. The critical leftist commentary appearing for the next few days about his candidacy was almost ignored as plaudits came from every direction.

Marybeth was right there with Stephen and saw the whole thing. When she finally realized what had happened, she was visibly shaken. That night, as the two of them got ready for bed in their compartment in the touring bus, they knelt down in prayer to thank God that nothing had happened to Stephen.

Average citizens began to connect some things in their minds after this episode. Stephen had shown courage and toughness in what he did. He was also showing courage in being willing to venture into the inner city areas, instead of avoiding that issue. He was forthright in presenting a message of responsibility—of "tough love"—that would not be popular with some there, and on the campaign trail he had spoken sharply about how with the rioting the incumbent administration was failing to carry out the "first purpose of government": to maintain order. Maybe, people thought, he is the one to take the decisive action needed to curtail this spiral of urban violence.

Before the first month of the Harrisburg-based front porch campaign, Stephen, Marybeth, John, and Mark Quigley sat down to discuss how to handle questioning from the national media, who would be Stephen's major interlocutors after his talks. They would be hostile and it was anticipated that they would fire "gotcha" questions at Stephen whenever they could. Stephen was going to be analyzing national questions in his talks directly and forthrightly. He was not going to hide or disguise anything or talk around questions—that wasn't him and "politics as usual" wasn't what the country needed now. He wasn't going to allow the media to get him off on tangents or trap him into saying something that could be embarrassing or get him to discuss a question in the way it—or, really, his leftist opponents, who they were often carrying water for—wanted him to. The front porch sessions would be carried out on his terms. In light of all this, everyone agreed that the routine approach would be for Stephen to say, "Why don't you ask President Frederickson that question?" or "Why don't you ask President Frederickson about such and such related thing?" or "Why don't you ask President Frederickson about such and such other problems or implications of his position, instead of just asking this kind of question of me?" If he had another person or persons there with him—like during the primaries when he had persons on the stump with him who had been conceived from rape when discussing abortion for the "hard cases"—his campaign team would brief them in advance about likely media attempts to confuse them, but would allow them to answer questions. It would be contrived and lacking in genuineness to do otherwise, but Stephen would freely step in if he saw a question going in such a direction. Stephen meant to be in control of the sessions. The media would have to show up. They couldn't ignore the front-porch sessions because they were the campaign of one of the two major-party candidates for half of the fall political season, but they would not be allowed to hijack them to use for their purposes.

Although each day's session—six days a week with no campaigning on Sundays—would generally be on a different topic, the campaign announced that the first week's sessions would all be on family and the related sexual and life issues. Stephen thought that appropriate, since these subjects—that is, the radical transformation of thinking about them—was at the center of the left's agenda.

He started by talking about the family as having the natural purpose of rearing good persons and producing good citizens. Invoking the great ancient Greek philosophers, he said that the family was the main place where personal formation—the formation of the soul—took place, and it was because the family had broken down so much that we had so much juvenile delinquency, crime, illegitimacy, and child maltreatment, and he laid out substantial historical facts and social science data to back all this up. He explained why the state could not pick up the slack—it could not love a child in the way a parent can—and how attempts to systematically displace the family, such as in Communist states, had been abject failures. He then went into a brief discourse about the nature of family affection. If families or parents were deficient, what should be done is to strengthen the family, not make it dependent upon the state—like with the welfare system—or put it under universal monitoring by state bureaucracies like the CPS. Parents by nature have responsibilities, but they also have rights. He made a justification of this from ethics, and brought it down to an easily understandable level. Moreover, his presentation was made additionally engaging by his subtle sense of humor, so the initial skeptical looks on the faces of many of the media people as he started his talk began to dissipate as he went on. He explained why these rights were natural—and emphasized that they were part of the natural rights tradition behind the American Founding—and contrasted them with ersatz rights, which had abounded in the current era with reference to the family and to the sexual and human life matters that were intimately connected to it. Just as there was a purpose or end to the family, there was one for all the human faculties, including the sexual. He also explained why sound family life requires a father and a mother, and why each had different and unique things to bring to child rearing. Then he spoke about what marriage was—how it was not just something involving an overly romanticized notion of love—and he went further and briefly discoursed on love. It sounded like something out of C.S. Lewis. He closed by saying that we could not dispense with nature whether we liked it or not. If we ignored it, there would only be the will and that got us back to the Greeks talking about the soul. If the will was in control and reason pushed aside, then power and force is all we are left with. Those who are the strongest, most adept at exerting power and using the most force can then control—and all kinds of outrages ensue.

When Stephen was done talking, the questions began. While he knew that some of the journalists pulled their proverbial knives out after hearing about mothers and fathers and the suggestion that there may be a purpose for sex other than pleasure, he saw that many of them were completely off-balance by his talk. It was so *unlike* any political talk they had heard before that they were unsure about what to make of it or how to respond. Stephen easily found himself going back into the role of professor and much of the questioning took on a kind of college seminar room back and forth. When a hostile question came, Stephen was successful in moving the exchange back to the professor-student mode.

In addition to the media being there, the campaign had offered transportation to interested citizens to come to the front porch sessions, so there was a crowd of several hundred people. Television news reports that evening and in the next morning's newspapers went something like "Governor/Professor Speaks to National Media" and "Professor-Politician Instructs Media." The campaign made sure they didn't just rely on the media to report about Stephen's front porch campaign. It was being filmed and sent out live to various Internet venues, including YouTube.

The questions and discussion went on for almost forty-five minutes before Stephen said it was time to break for lunch. At mid-afternoon, he said, they would reconvene to talk about—he phrased this in a deliberately underwhelming way—"a couple of sub-topics under the subject of the family: same-sex so-called marriage and same-sex parenting." He made sure the "so-called" was clearly stated and above the volume of the rest of the sentence.

That afternoon, Stephen's approach turned from philosophical to attacking. The adversary was the homosexualist movement. He recounted one after another example of episodes where the movement, supported by opportunistic, agenda-driven, or cowering public officials, went after hapless private citizens who would not cooperate in furthering the movement's political objectives for religious or moral reasons. He attacked the movement—as he had done since State College—as "totalitarian" and "utterly repressive." He would not stop at simply making an appeal to religious liberty. It was not an uncontrollable status or inbred condition of a person that was involved, but freely chosen conduct. It was homosexual behavior that the movement had driven the law to protect and even celebrate, nothing else. It was "immoral conduct." He briefly shifted back into a teaching mode to explain why this conduct was immoral, with bluntly stated philosophical points and an incisively stated catalogue of the health consequences of same-sex behavior. While many of the average citizens in the crowd cheered and applauded, the shock and anger on the faces of the media representatives was palpable. Stephen quickly shifted back into the confrontation mode and, looking directly at the media contingent who were in a special reserved section at the front to one side, he faulted them for their lack of professionalism in not exposing the homosexualists' abuses and, in fact, for often carrying the water for them. He gave obvious examples of this and as he spoke he looked many of them right in the eyes.

Then he turned to same-sex parenting and brought to the microphone the three people who stood directly behind him on the porch. The one middle-aged woman and a young adult man and woman had all been raised by same-sex "parents." They all told unhappy personal stories of lives of confusion, forays into sexual promiscuity, and ongoing knawing feelings of absence that only after years they realized was because none of them had a father (all had been raised by lesbian couples). While most of the media representatives had skeptical looks at the beginning, it was clear that many became absorbed by what the trio were saying as they went along. It was clear that they had never given much thought to what they were hearing. The trio handled themselves with equanimity while answering media questions, but could only partially sublimate their emotions as they talked about what were obviously painful upbringings. One young woman journalist asked if they were not allowing themselves to be "used" by Stephen. The older woman quickly fired back—the only time there was a hint of anger from any of them—that she "was happy and relieved to tell her story because there was no one who would listen for so many years." If anyone was using people like her, she said, "it was the gay and lesbian movement who think nothing about sacrificing the lives of kids just to further their agenda." The other woman jumped in to say that Stephen "was the first politician" she had come across "who was willing to take seriously what people like us have experienced."

While most of the national media tried to downplay or not cover the appearance of the three, some did and the campaign was completely prepared to use all avenues of the "alternative media" to make sure their comments were widely disseminated. Moreover, the local media in attendance covered it and sent it out on the wire. This put pressure on the rest of the major media to report it and also had the effect of making them gun shy about ignoring significant parts of Stephen's front porch sessions on family issues the rest of the week.

The next day, Stephen's session was about abortion. He talked about the biological realities of fetal development and showed slides on a large screen next to him about it. He talked in specific terms about what happens in abortion, including late-term ones, but avoided slides. He didn't want the media to make the claim that he was using "scare tactics." He talked about the all-too-typical unsanitary and unhealthful conditions of abortion clinics and the poor treatment often afforded the women who came to them. He cited numerous cases that had gotten public attention, starting with Gosnell in his home state some years before. He explained why the "hard cases" claims, such as for rape, were really a canard, as there were few such cases. He talked about how abortion hurt women in other ways, including psychological damage and lives turned upside down by regret and guilt. He didn't veer away from talking about contraception, explaining how most chemical and pharmaceutical contraceptives were actually abortifacient, at least part of the time, but this didn't stop the large drug companies—whose closeness to government he discussed—from pushing them. They acted deceptively, he said, both to the women using their products and the larger public—and what's more public officials and regulators were almost silent about it. He said, "that is the real 'war on women.'" He faulted the media—the people right in front of him—for remaining silent about all this. He said they "failed to do their professional duty because they had bought into an ideological agenda," which, again, "made not just children but also women the victims—one was literally destroyed and the other badly damaged." In the question period, some in the media tried to twist things to put him on the spot, but with his superb "quick on the spot" debate skills he turned their questions back on them as members of the public in attendance cheered.

That afternoon, he introduced four women: one, a noted speaker on the pro-life circuit, talked about how she had been conceived when her mother was brutally, forcibly raped, but that she "chose life" because she knew the young being within her was a human person. She began to sob as she said how grateful she was to her for letting her live and then raising her with love.

Another woman talked about how she had gone to a clinic for an abortion at, roughly, fifteen weeks. The next morning, she awoke with significant vaginal bleeding. It turned out that there had been an incomplete abortion—the child was dead, but fetal parts were left inside—and she was now hemorrhaging. She got to the phone and had to be rushed to a hospital. Besides the bleeding, an infection had set in and she wound up spending three weeks in the hospital.

A third woman talked about the severe side-effects of her prolonged oral contraceptive use, which had begun when she was in her late teens. She had been sexually active in college and later married, divorced, and married again. She had continued on oral contraceptives the whole time, although different ones at different periods. There was a tendency to high blood pressure in her family and she had shown signs of it, but her physicians had not thought that to be a problem. It turned out that at 33, she suffered a slight stroke that was traced to undiagnosed blood clots. After that, she was also diagnosed with pre-cancerous growths in her uterus. The physician she was now seeing said that there was little doubt that the long-term use of the Pill was the cause of all these maladies. For a moment, her anger welled up as she said that when she looks back now she believed that the medical profession "didn't care" about her.

The fourth woman, in her early forties, talked about her abortion twenty years before. She said, "not a day in my life goes by that I don't have deep regrets, wondering about that child I had killed." She talked about the aftermath: years of severe depression, prescription medicine abuse for a while, and a suicide attempt. She finally got herself on a "path to healing and forgiveness" with the help of a religiously-oriented group that worked with women who were suffering the effects of their abortions.

When they asked for questions, one prominent national media person who was there suggested, like the previous day, that Stephen's campaign was "using" the women. Almost as one, they pounced on him. One, who was from Pennsylvania, said that she had supported Stephen's work as governor because he was "so concerned about the babies and women like me who had suffered so much." She said that she came to him to offer to help him in the campaign; the campaign didn't come to her. She blurted out that the media person should "be ashamed about his unfeeling attitude." The exchange was repeated widely on talk radio the next day and even one of the other major networks—along with Fox News—ran it.

A major online leftist news and commentary site later that day talked about the "sob stories" at Stephen's afternoon front porch session. Before beginning his discussion of euthanasia and physician-assisted suicide, the next life issue, the next morning, he brought this up and said it was a further example of how so much of the major media was out of touch with people and even reality, its unprofessionalism, and its being driven by an ideological agenda instead of a search for truth. Everyone in the media there knew what outlet he was talking about and as he spoke he stared at its representative, who probably was responsible for yesterday's unsigned commentary piece.

Stephen explained—in his usual deep but relatively terse manner—about why legalizing euthanasia and physician-assisted suicide, instead of advancing and dignifying personal choice, would actually be an assault on the weak, infirm, and vulnerable. He averred that it would destroy all confidence people could have in the medical profession as healers—which was the major reason medical organizations tended to oppose it—and inevitably would bring on the "slippery slope" that would lead to the killing of more and more groups of people. He provided information—that seemed to surprise some of the media people there, even though a little digging would make it easily available—that insurance companies and government agencies in the states where physician-assisted suicide had become legal were, in effect, encouraging it for the seriously ill because it was less expensive than medical procedures and extended nursing care. People in the audience gazed intently at him as he talked about hearing of people standing in line at pharmacies for a prescription consultation hearing directions being given to the family members of persons seeking to kill themselves about how their loved one should take the lethal medicine. Then, instead of having live guests give testimonies, people spoke on a Skype hook-up on a big screen behind him. One, from Oregon, said how a physician attending his elderly mother who had Alzheimer's disease tried to talk him into letting him prescribe a lethal combination of drugs to take her life. After him, they connected with a middle-aged couple from Belgium who, speaking broken English, related how their daughter in her early twenties who had experienced chronic depression but had no other significant health problems and was in no way terminally ill was assisted by her physician to commit suicide. Then, a medical journalist from Holland spoke in clear English about the euthanasia situation in his country, which he said was "completely out of control, spreading to more and more categories of people." He talked about the Groningen protocol, which allows for the euthanasia—infanticide—of babies and children under twelve. He mentioned how euthanasia spread from killing competent, terminally ill patients to people who were not terminally ill but chronically disabled, to people who were incompetent—such as people with dementia—when their family members or the institutions they were in insisted they would have wanted it if in their right minds, and now to children. While many parents had almost an obsession with having "the "perfect" child and readily agreed to infanticide of seriously disabled newborns, others felt themselves under strong pressure from attending physicians to do so. Some physicians and medical facilities had gotten to the point of simply saying that palliative care for critically ill children was "no longer worth it." The attitude now was "just give them a lethal dose of drugs and let them die." Further, public opposition to euthanasia and infanticide was coming to be seen "almost as heresy," since it violated an increasingly deeply engrained ethic of individual autonomy in countries like Holland and Belgium.

The next day, Stephen focused on the runaway so-called child protective system that he had moved to get under control in Pennsylvania. As a law professor, he had written and consulted on the topic and so could speak to the audience with obvious authority. Still, some of the media questions evinced skepticism about there being a systemic-level problem. In the afternoon, Stephen presented several parents who gave personal testimonies of how the CPS, sometimes with the aid of law enforcement agencies, came after them after false anonymous reports of child abuse or neglect or because they disagreed with one aspect or another of their innocent childrearing practices. One case involved the increasing phenomenon of "medical kidnapping," in the manner of the Justina Pelletier case of some years before.

One Friday, Stephen's topic was family breakdown: the plague of illegitimacy, fatherlessness, one-parent homes, and the near-50% divorce rate. He talked about the consequences: high rates of juvenile delinquency; high incarceration levels, especially for minority males in adulthood who were the products of fatherless homes; the much greater incidence of "genuine child maltreatment"—as opposed, he said in reference to the previous day's topic, to "what the CPS mostly chases after"—in the absence of an intact family with a biological father and mother present; the solid studies of recent decades showing the marked short- *and* long-term psychological, personal, emotional, and educational consequences of divorce on children; the economic decline of women and families caused by divorce and family breakdown; and the burdens placed on society—and taxpayers—in so many ways to have to pick up the pieces or take on tasks that intact families would be able to handle on their own. He asserted that "the ethic of autonomy, runaway individualism," a decline of morality and religious practice— he backed this up with impressive statistics about how family religiosity was a major factor in keeping the family whole—and public policies that furthered them—such as no-fault divorce and welfare state-type programs that substituted entitlement for responsibility— were the major culprits in family breakdown. He made it clear that the federal government did not perhaps bear the prime responsibility for much public policy misdirection in this area—after all, family law was mostly a state matter—but it had contributed, especially with its innumerable welfarist schemes and could do many things "to encourage better public policies on a state level."

During the media questions, Stephen avoided—as he had through the campaign—stating an abundance of specific policy proposals. He said that there were many possible good initiatives and a new administration would have to look carefully at them. Also, the campaign knew the danger of the media's latching onto something and using it to club the candidate. One journalist asked Stephen—he somehow associated all conservative-inclined candidates with laissez faire—if his criticism of the autonomy ethic extended to economics. Stephen replied, "Wait until you listen to me next week." That was when he would talk about economics. On this afternoon, he had two people give personal testimonies. One talked, simply, about how important it had been for him to grow up with his two natural parents. The other, a young black man, lamented the sense of loss he had experienced never having known his father. He had many problems as a teenager, but the help of his pastor and people working with youth at the church his mother brought him to enabled him to get on the right path. Both were raising intact families and were successful small businessmen.

As the week progressed, the crowds of everyday citizens were getting larger at the front porch sessions. In spite of the considerable space to park on John Frost's property, it was becoming congested. The campaign wasn't spending money on national media ads, so it started to hire buses to bring supporters and other interested people in from Harrisburg, Baltimore, Philadelphia, New Jersey and other places not too far away for a day's sessions and vans were manned by volunteers to take them to and from the nearby shopping areas at lunchtime. The campaign had initially thought that the front porch campaign would be mostly directed to the media, who would then report about his talks and bring the educational campaign to the broader population via the airwaves. Even if the media deeply disagreed with him, Stephen and his people figured they couldn't avoid doing this because they were there to report on the campaign of a major party candidate and it *was* the campaign. Now, though, it was also attracting larger numbers of people who just came out to hear him. The whole idea of such a campaign—so different from what had long-since become the norm—was capturing the fancy of increasing numbers of people. The campaign also did not hesitate to make use of current technology. It started to bring the front-porch sessions to the broader public by means of You-Tube.

On Saturday, the crowd ballooned even further. It was a weekend and people were freer to come than during the week. Stephen and the campaign knew that Saturdays were slow news days, so on the first Saturday of the front porch campaign he picked a topic that he knew would get media attention: immigration. In his talk, he made the case for regulating immigration in the name of a nation's common good and made many of the same arguments that he did earlier in the campaign about how the corporate types and the other party wanted uncontrolled immigration for their own selfish, opportunistic reasons. He also scored successive presidential administrations for their unwillingness in diplomatic dealings with governments from south of the border to hold them and their economic elites responsible for developing their economies so people wouldn't be motivated to head north. "They grew wealthier," Stephen said, "but did not use that wealth to improve the lives of their countrymen."

The following week, he tackled economic issues. Recalling Steve Forbes' 1996 campaign in the primary season, but without precisely calling for it, Stephen said that consideration should be given to a national flat income tax in place of the graduated one. He laid out all the information about how revenues would not be adversely affected and spoke about the putative advantages. Stephen's caution about specific policy proposals was tied in with his aim to maintain an offensive posture, making searching critiques of what was already in place and educating about a better way. He was not going to allow himself to be put on the defensive. In no way was he going to appear vague or lacking in resolve. There was never a question about where Stephen was coming from or where he stood. He was not a chameleon "moderate." He did say that a flat tax would make possible the

189

abolition of the widely unpopular Internal Revenue Service—which had lost much of its credibility amidst ongoing issues of political and ideological favoritism, incompetence, uneven application of the tax laws, and increasing repression of the average citizen—and its replacement by a small bureau within the Treasury Department. He rattled off a long litany of specific episodes of major abuse and said it was time for a smaller unit in the Treasury Department to simply receive tax payments each year.

He talked about the ever-deepening national debt, and quoted Thomas Jefferson's famous dictum: "We must make our election between *economy* and *liberty* or *profusion* and *servitude*." Taxation follows debt and, Jefferson said, "in its train wretchedness and oppression." Then Stephen recounted ways in which that had begun to happen in the U.S. He mentioned different proposals that had been put forth to control federal spending. One that he singled out for special mention without specifically endorsing it was the long-proposed "Penny Plan," which would cut one cent out of every dollar of total federal spending (excluding interest payments) each year for five years and put a strict cap on federal spending. Gradual disengagement from different programmatic areas was the course of action that now had to be followed, though he refused to provide specific proposals. While government at different levels should always be a last resort or safety net to help people in need, he said that the problem had become that it had become the first resort. Entitlement spending had long since gotten out of control and he explained its adverse effects for both the government and the economy. He explained why Social Security was not by its nature an entitlement; people had paid into it. He discussed the principle of subsidiarity and kept repeating the role that government had to play in building up civil society, which he insisted could deal with much of what government entitlements currently deal with—and, after recounting many government boondoggles, much more effectively.

Then he launched into a critique of out-of-control federal regulatory law, giving brief but copious examples. This was something that in many areas required "outright rollback." Much spending would be cut, along with the agencies in charge of enforcing them, by a "rollback" of much federal regulatory law—"and justice for citizens and businessmen mistreated by regulators would be achieved as well." He emphatically added, "If I become President, America will no longer be a managed state." This brought cheers from the crowd of average citizens.

He called attention back to the First New Deal's notion of "a kind of enlightened self-regulation," but as part of gradual disengagement. Industries needed to lay down standards for certain kinds of internal regulations, prodded by and overseen by the federal government. "The President's and the government's bully pulpit can be used to achieve a lot, without the downside and sometimes outright counterproductive results of the regulatory state. Rigid, runaway bureaucracy was one of the consequences and it was time to seriously and decisively address it since it has become a crippler, instead of a helper, of our democratic republic." As he spoke, it was clear that the media people knew little of the First New Deal and it seemed as if they were taking it in and being educated by Stephen.

He also discussed trade policy and economic globalism. He said that "free trade" had become an ideology for some, and typically wasn't free anyhow. Nations, he said, should not erect rigid barriers; this would hurt both themselves and other nations. They could adopt reasonable policies to protect their indigenous industries and jobs. He talked about commutative justice and explained how it applied to trade practices. He said it required positions of relative equality among nations, and frequently poor nations—which previous U.S. administrations claimed they were concerned about, even as they pursued trade policies that hurt them—do not have the resources or wherewithal to attain to such equal status. He faulted too many large companies for a lack of patriotism. While the need to make a reasonable profit was necessary, they were concerned only narrowly with their bottom lines and gave little heed to the good of their country and countrymen in their decision-making. He returned to his criticism during the primaries of companies that didn't care for their local communities, either, as they so readily pulled up stakes, closed up local factories and left their employees behind, and departed to go elsewhere. He insisted that a great economic challenge of our time was for people to once again be in control to a greater degree of their economic destiny. The globalist idea had good points—which he intelligently recounted—but left people at the whim of economic forces well beyond their control. Such policies, promoted by successive administrations of both parties, were often more concerned about multi-national corporate financial considerations and the good of foreign governments and not our own people. We had to renew an emphasis on a smaller scale, more localized economy wherever it was feasible to do so and he mentioned many ways the federal government could encourage that.

As the front porch days went by, Stephen discussed one topic after another. Criminal justice reform was one. He talked about the "outrage" of such things as traditional common law protections being weakened, over-criminalization and turning tort matters and even mere issues of manners and personal conduct into crimes, prosecutors widely pursuing cases on the basis of theories instead knowledge that a crime had even been committed, the widespread manipulation of grand juries by prosecutors so that they no longer played the role of protecting the innocent, the proliferation of sting operations that were in any true sense entrapment, and how the plea-bargains and guilty pleas in over 90% of criminal cases—even when people are innocent—had long since grossly compromised the right to a trial of one's peers. He mentioned about how these things had motivated him to push reforms in Pennsylvania and told his audience about how the sting operation motivated by politics had tried to target him. Education was another topic. He deplored the control the federal government now exercised over it and the dependency of schools and colleges on federal largesse, the "foolhardy notion" that was taking hold that everyone should go to college that was decimating standards, the crisis of student indebtedness—"the next serious economic crisis"—and, especially, the loss of any sense of purpose of education and the evisceration of the liberal arts. Yet another topic was the environment. He slammed thoughtless, runaway regulation that often had almost no basis in statutory law and the disregarding of evidence about whether some things truly presented an environmental harm, and instead the substitution of "mindless ideological rigidity"—"uncritically responding to the lobbying of absolutist, environmentalist interest groups"—as a basis for proscribing activities such as shale oil and gas exploration. Another related issue was the whole range of ways in which property rights were being undermined, from environmental regulations to excessive zoning regulations to historical preservation laws. He said that even if some of this was done on a state and local level "there were various ways that the federal government could act to stop unconstitutional overreach." In an erudite—but, as usual with his talks, easily understandable—way, he showed that the roots of such developments were in the erosion of respect for property rights in Western political thinking that went back to Karl Marx ("Marx, the founder of communism, instead of *our* Founding Fathers, was influencing our view about private property"). Perhaps the hottest topic he addressed was civil rights. He said that the notion of civil rights had long since become "contorted," and was now being used to assault nature and the natural rights of other persons—as was seen with same-sex "marriage," transgenderism, and abortion—to defend "morally reprehensible behaviors that violated the natural law"—such as sodomy, which term he had no reluctance to use—and to denigrate certain groups of people and "anoint as superior" others. On this, he gave many examples of the disadvantageous position the "civil rights— or rather civil *wrongs*—mentality" had placed Caucasian males in and how it had led to the extolling of homosexuals ("*so-called* LGBT persons"). He excoriated the homosexualist movement as acting far from the spirit of civil rights and brought up repeatedly its repressive and totalitarian actions. He said that it was "folly to say that race prejudice and injustice was as bad or worse than in the Jim Crow era" and that "the claim of 'racism' was being used to cover for abhorrent and even criminal behavior and to secure certain people's wealth and position." He was unsparing in targeting the civil rights establishment, "who had blackened the legacy of a noble cause." He went deeper, however, to say that the whole notion of equality had been distorted. What equality meant in the American Founding and in the religious, moral, and political traditions that had forged it was that each person was equal as a "child of God," was held to the demands of the same natural moral law, and was entitled to equal protection and application of the laws of the state. It had been distorted for the past several decades so that equality now meant sameness, so that such things as the fundamental differences between men and women were rejected. It also had come to mean that equal results had to be aimed for, which was unrealistic and the cause of repression and *inequality* with the way it exulted favored groups. In both cases standards were decimated, with deficiency in abilities ignored and weak performance or even incompetence made acceptable just because someone was of a certain group—as in affirmative action and quotas. In some cases, it was "inviting outright disaster, as in the blatant lowering of standards for women to become military personnel or firefighters." That was even apart from other issues of how such things ignored the realities of male-female interactions and relations and the implications for a military force in combat. As one supporter put it, in all of his sessions, his offensive charge "was melded beautifully" with his educational efforts.

One week's sessions were devoted exclusively to foreign policy and international affairs. He was fundamentally in the realist school that hearkened back to the great twentieth-century international politics scholar Hans J. Morgenthau. Stephen explained why national interest had to be paramount, and that the reality of international life was that nations had to accumulate power—which, in itself is morally neutral and can be used for good or bad. Contrary to what some claimed, Morgenthau never believed in a Machiavellian approach or dismissed moral considerations from international politics. He was rather like

Abraham Lincoln: the sound statesman had to realize that the moral outcomes in international affairs were typically going to be less than completely morally satisfactory. Stephen discussed this and said that prudence was the great virtue for the statesman, especially when operating in the international arena, as he had to navigate its treacherous waters to try to surmount as best he could the many obstacles presented to achieve as morally good outcomes as possible. These results would often be morally quite deficient, but he explained how if one ignores the realities and pushes for what he believes to be a completely satisfactory moral position he often creates a much worse moral situation in the end or in the long-run. He briefly talked about Wilsonianism and the Treaty of Versailles as the quintessential example of this. In the final analysis, this was not a truly moral approach to foreign policy but *moralism*. What was needed in politics generally, and foreign policy in particular, is to aim for a gradual movement toward a better moral position, and the truly prudent statesman would have a good sense of when and how he could push further and how far at a time.

He addressed a number of specific foreign policy questions. He asserted that the U.S. had been mistaken to try to project its power and engage in military interventions in places like the Middle East and to foolishly think it could make nations that had histories only of strong-man rulers into democratic republics almost overnight. The result had been to unleash even more extremist and destructive forces like ISIS. A renewed respect for diplomacy, using especially U.S. diplomats right on the ground in countries as opposed to the incessant "globetrotting" of top officials, was needed. Persuasion, whenever and wherever it could be used, was the best tool of foreign affairs. For sure, it had to be backed by strong American military power and prestige—but these things had been allowed to badly deteriorate during twelve years of leftist administrations. To have such standing, however, did not mean one should eagerly use it—nations that truly had power did not have to throw their military and other might around, but they could promote their interests and sound principles because they were respected. By the same token, the U.S. would not shirk from meeting existing alliance and bi-lateral treaty obligations. He pledged, for example, that in the Far East the U.S. would not remove her naval vessels from international waters that Communist China suddenly claimed were hers. We would call her bluff. While we would not allow our immigration laws to be pushed aside so that anyone could just feel free to enter the country at will, we would readily accept religious and political refugees—and refugees from our supposed allies in Europe who were being imprisoned for such "'grave' offenses as homeschooling their children." We would use vigorous diplomacy and pressure to get nations—allies and adversaries—to uphold genuine human rights, not spurious ones like a "right" to same-sex "marriage." We would also vigorously oppose any attempts internationally to give special privileges to certain groups—"creating a new elite"—in the name of defending such "phony rights." We would "vigorously, insistently oppose the shenanigans" at the UN, where interest groups and bureaucrats were actively working to twist international agreements to claim that they mandated such rights and using pressure tactics to impose them on underdeveloped countries. This would include financial pressure on the UN "up to and including *cutting off* our dues." Where the U.S. would be prepared to engage in military intervention would be to stop outright cases of genocide, as in Rwanda in 1994 and as perpetrated by Islamists in different places.

Whenever Stephen talked about the different issues, he was careful to show how his opponents all, in different degrees, embraced positions mostly at odds to his. A Bernard presidency would surely go in a substantially different and sounder direction.

After his month of front-porch campaigning, many in the mainstream media and an assortment of leftist publications were saying that Stephen represented the genuine prospect of reversing, as one of the latter put it, "all the cherished progressive achievements." They recognized, however, that he was making his case effectively, had been successful at unremittingly maintaining the pressure on his opponents and keeping them off balance, and that his kind and charitable approach and deep integrity made him difficult to oppose. They were also aware, as the campaign went on, that he was gaining more and more enthusiastic support from average citizens. One issue they tried to tentatively raise against Stephen was his lack of experience. He had only three years as a governor and had never held national office. The issue didn't gain much traction even among the other "progressives," however, since many of them were unenthusiastic about Frederickson and some were openly or quietly supporting Harlington. In spite of his Washington experience, Graham didn't raise the experience issue probably because it hadn't given him any advantage over Stephen in the primaries.

In the meantime, Stephen's grassroots organizing effort, spearheaded by his regional campaign staff people but made up of an army of volunteers, was performing phenomenally. The campaign stressed the need for door-to-door canvassing, not the robocalls and email contacts that the party's recent presidential candidates had relied on so heavily with disappointing results. To be sure, the campaign used phone contacts where appropriate but never allowed them to supplant face-to-face efforts. Stephen also had a couple of long-time supporters who designed a masterful social media campaign. Besides regular contact with identified supporters, they routinely disseminated portions of his front porch talks to a larger social media audience and to carefully purchased email lists of the kinds of citizens who would likely support him. This was partly done to insure that if the mainstream media downplayed coverage of them, they would get out anyway. As it was, though, the campaign had developed so many avenues for disseminating the talks and the popular reception was so good that the media couldn't help but to cover them. The campaign knew that they had to do a superlative job of identifying Stephen's supporters and then of getting out the vote on election day for him to have a chance to win. This had been another great failing of the party's candidates in presidential elections for some time. Even though Stephen's modest-sized national staff oversaw the effort, it was the incredibly active local volunteers who made the operation a success. Almost every county in the country had a volunteer leader, chosen carefully from the lists of volunteers with their talents and reliability clearly established by Stephen's regional campaign staff people. They were the pivotal figures in making everything work.

The campaign persisted in taking only the small donations of $500 and less. It could not stop the formation of super-PACs to support the party's ticket, however. The campaign was assiduous in avoiding any contact with them in accordance with the law. Stephen thought it was necessary to avoid any possible appearance of impropriety. In fact, on occasions he even publicly denounced the super-PACs if they mischaracterized or embellished any of his positions, or tried to bring the campaign down to the level of the sound bites that he so strongly disliked, or if they unfairly attacked his opponents or sought to create an ugly kind of politics. They were the ones running the ads against his opponents and supporting his various stands. He preferred the kind of campaign he had fashioned. Still, Stephen's strong, clear, courageous stands on so many crunching, crucial issues resulted in the formation of a larger number of supporting super-PACs than usual for the party's national ticket.

Even though everyone knew that the bulk of the vote for Stephen in November would come from the so-called "non-minority" population and they had to be gotten out in very sizable numbers, he worked indefatigably to take his campaign to the black and Hispanic communities. He especially continued to work, as he had in the primary season, through clergy in those communities. Even though he took his campaign there, it did not stop him from preaching his message of personal responsibility and breaking away from government dependency. He simply would not make "feel good about yourself" appeals or pander to elements in the electorate. He kept challenging them to self-introspection and improvement. He coupled this by making clear that structures needed to be built up right within the communities themselves, often around the churches, to provide assistance to people when they genuinely needed it—"an assistance that would insure their dignity, in contrast to cold and distant government that doesn't." The mainstream media noticed his minority outreach and commented that it could result in Frederickson's vote, especially, being reduced somewhat there. The leftist political leadership in those communities made the mistake of not taking Stephen seriously enough, figuring that no presidential candidate from his party could get much support there anyway. One thing that the campaign was cautious about was voter fraud. They remembered such things as the highly improbable 100% totals for Obama in some precincts in 2012. They developed an elaborate scheme of close poll-watching and inspections, which was coordinated among the campaign staff, the local volunteers, and the party committee people in minority precincts—who were notably enthusiastic about Stephen's candidacy—where it was thought fraud could be a problem.

Stephen's second bus tour across the country showed the heightening grassroots enthusiasm for his campaign, especially in so-called Middle America: the smaller communities, the medium and small-sized metropolitan areas, and the rural communities (his call for winding down federal subsidies was counterbalanced by his trenchant criticism of the substantial take-over of American agriculture by big agribusiness). The South, Great Plains, the eastern Midwest (Ohio and Michigan), the Rocky Mountain states (except for Colorado), and his native Pennsylvania were especially the places of his strength. Even as the leftist mainstream media spoke persistently critically of him, they marveled at his grassroots support. The media was obviously shaken that there was more TEA party-like sentiment in the country than it had thought. They also were constantly taken aback by his masterful campaign organization effort and awed by its almost exclusively volunteer character.

After the bus tour, Stephen was back for the final phase of the front porch campaign. In the last ten days, he simply covered in summary fashion all the different topics he had spoken about at length in the earlier phases. He responded to major challenges and objections—and often distortions and disinformation—about some of the issues. This time he was joined by several noted authorities who backed up what he had said, such as the intense doubt he had raised about global warming in one of his earlier talks. He had gone for the jugular in saying that it had become little more than political ideology without scientific backing. Some in the media, not unexpectedly, had tried to challenge that and other positions he had taken, but he had continued to be deft throughout in avoiding being put on the defensive but taking the offensive against them. One thing that characterized his campaign was that, in many respects, he directed it as much against the left-leaning media as he did his leftist opponents. Stephen, John Frost, and Marybeth had decided at the beginning that that would be necessary because the mainstream media had routinely carried the water for the other party's candidates. In his second cross-country trip, he repeatedly criticized the national media and the popular response was clearly supportive.

Actually, it was almost astounding that Stephen had escaped much likely attack from the mainstream media during the fall campaign. While that was because he had them on the defensive, it also reflected the fact that they didn't take him seriously enough, didn't think he had a chance to win. Another reason was that the three candidates to the left spent a surprising amount of time attacking each other and a lot of the campaign news seemed to be generated by that. There was genuine dislike between Frederickson and Harlington, and almost constant sniping and attacks by each side.

Despite the increasing grassroots enthusiasm for Stephen's campaign that the media was noticing, Frederickson's private polling— Stephen didn't do any of that in his low-budget campaign—was consistently showing that he was maintaining about a 10% lead over Stephen (35-25%), with Harlington and Graham garnering a firm 15% and 8%, respectively. Throughout much of the campaign, the undecided bloc was high at about 15-17%. Frederickson's campaign, aware that the President lagged in popularity, reasoned that if they could rally their party's base (left-leaning secular suburbanites and yuppie types in gentrified parts of cities, leftist activists, and minority groups) they could win the election without a great problem. The key thing was to neutralize Harlington and reach out to the base to make them see that this rebellion against Frederickson was completely unmerited—he had really faithfully promoted the party's agenda. So, the campaign made the strategic decision to spend most of their time focusing on Harlington and not targeting Stephen anywhere near as much as would have been expected. This was especially surprising given that Stephen represented a direct, fervent challenge to the whole structure of secularist-leftist politics in America and that his campaign was consistently on the offensive against it. Despite the fact that Harlington was a shade more to the left than Frederickson, it was the President—as the embodiment of the leftist-oriented major party—who for all practical purposes was most on the defensive from Stephen's onslaught. Frederickson's strategy was understandable, however, when considering the surprisingly high percentage that Harlington was polling. He had to first pull his coalition back together, which he was confident of doing since he figured that on election day—faced with the possibility of Stephen winning—they would vote for him. Plus, he thought that Graham's breakaway and what he called Stephen's "right-wing extremism" would cripple him enough so that Stephen wouldn't be able to garner enough popular support to win. Additionally, Frederickson's campaign people thought that Stephen's economic views precluded his being able to get the support of his party's moderates and the Chamber of Commerce types who they believed were crucial to his winning. They also figured that he had never shown himself a vote-getter in Pennsylvania, since he had never actually run for the governorship itself. The President's campaign pollsters made the same mistake that the pollsters did in the Truman-Dewey election many decades before: They figured in the end that at worst the large undecided vote would just split between the two major party candidates and with Frederickson's substantial enough of a lead, he would then win comfortably. While the major independent polling organizations didn't necessarily see this the same way, like Frederickson's pollster they neglected to take account of something that had also shown up in surveys on same-sex "marriage." The survey results ended up being skewed because some people felt intimidated about saying they actually opposed it. Now, some voters felt reluctant to say that they tilted to Stephen because he represented such a resolute challenge to the *weltanschauung* of the times.

This all was a huge miscalculation for Frederickson. The *coup de grâce*, however, was his to failure agree to formal debates during the campaign. He correctly figured that there would be enormous pressure on him to include Harlington in the debates, but he didn't want to give the "turncoat" and "renegade" Harlington a platform that might advance his campaign. If he refused to allow him to be included and insisted on just the two major party candidates, however, his campaign would be hurt by the resulting bad publicity as had happened in some previous elections. He had other reasons not to debate, however. He had seen Stephen's success in "thumping" the other candidates in the primary season debates, and he didn't want to let that happen now. With Stephen's masterful debating skills and his effectiveness at running an offensive-oriented campaign, he reasoned that giving him another podium before tens of millions of viewers wasn't worth the risk. Further, Frederickson and his campaign knew that he wasn't real good in a debate-type situation. He preferred the stump speech, at which he excelled. Moreover, he and his handlers subscribed to the old adage of "you don't debate when you're ahead."

Frederickson's unwillingness had caused much frustration among the members of the Commission on Presidential Debates. Finally, they arranged a national debate for a week before election day with just Stephen, Harlington, and Graham.

The continuing ill-will between Frederickson and Harlington led Harlington's campaign to decide that their candidate's best debate strategy would be to simultaneously attack Frederickson and Stephen. Graham's campaign had all along been scrambling to try to distinguish itself from the other left-of-center candidates in the race. It was apparent in the debate that he was a bit gun-shy about targeting Stephen since Stephen had manhandled him in the primary debates. So, he decided to mostly focus on the absent Frederickson. Stephen and John Frost correctly gauged the likely strategies that Harlington and Graham might pursue. The order of the opening statements was decided by lot, and Stephen was last. Harlington and Graham spoke generally and did not address either Stephen or Frederickson. Stephen immediately assumed his trademark offensive posture in his statement and honed in on the repression that leftist government, as practiced by both Frederickson and Harlington, had brought. He talked about their "nastiness" in going after people who would not "celebrate" every aspect of the homosexualist agenda. He rattled off certain statements Harlington had made that had a distinctly anti-Christian tone to them, and he mentioned Harlington's seeming suggestion that Christians who tried to resist same-sex "marriage" should be imprisoned. "Quite the contrary to Governor Harlington's repeated claims about people who oppose sexual immorality—or shall we say, oppose *his* version of sexual morality—being bigots, this sounds like someone who's bigoted against Christians (and we should say also serious Jews and Moslems)—and President Frederickson cannot seem to see anything wrong with this, since he's never uttered a word of protest or objection. In fact, his administration has applauded the use of state power against people opposing the homosexualist movement and tried to interject federal power where they could. Oh, and let's not forget how he tried to push through the Connecticut legislature when he was governor a bill which would have required crisis pregnancy centers to tell women looking for help how and where to get an abortion, even while the abortion clinics had no obligation imposed on them to tell women about abortion alternatives. Let's not forget that the abortion clinics are in business for profit pure and simple, while the crisis pregnancy centers are all struggling non-profits." Then, with Stephen's great ability to educate profoundly in a brief, summary fashion he showed how this represented a "gross assault" on the First Amendment freedoms of religion and speech. At the end of his statement time he said, "This election, as I've said from the beginning, is about restoring liberty and the Constitution. Actually, it's about something more than that. It's about ending the ugly, extreme self-interested, hypocritical kind of politics that has taken over America. Governor Harlington shouldn't forget to tell you that two of his main contributors in his last gubernatorial election were the two biggest abortion providers in his state. The election is about one thing more—which is the most basic thing: I mentioned nastiness. For Governor Harlington to go after people who don't agree with him and his political friends in this manner is nothing other than nasty. For all their disagreements, President Frederickson has never mentioned any of this about Governor Harlington; it seems to be a non-issue for him. This election is about ending such nastiness. It's about simple charity and decency."

Stephen's comments left both Harlington and Graham off-balance. They were clearly not expecting such a direct, stinging indictment from Stephen right at the beginning. Harlington tried to talk about all his achievements in Connecticut, but in his reply to him Stephen just went right back to his initial comments and then mentioned more, similar actions by him. Then he turned to Frederickson again, and pointed to ways in which he had used federal power in a similar "repressive, nasty manner." He followed the same pattern for the whole debate. He also made sure to read Harlington's statements on a number of issues that had showed a distinct pattern of flip-flopping on different issues, such as same-sex "marriage." At one point Stephen said, "When Governor Harlington first ran for governor of Connecticut ten years before, he said that he opposed copying neighboring Massachusetts' action of establishing same-sex "marriage" as a right and a year or so after that said that allowing same-sex couples to adopt children was "something he couldn't support because it isn't fair to the children." Six years later, he was moving to shut down religious service agencies that wouldn't place children with practicing homosexuals. However, he's no different from President Frederickson in this regard. Only a few years before he went into the White House the President said—and I quote him—

marriage 'could only be what it always has been, between a man and a woman.' Now, his administration is telling Catholic and Baptist adoption agencies to get out of the business or lose their tax-exemptions. He is now supporting the sporadic initiatives within his IRS to revoke the tax exemptions of churches who teach that homosexuality is wrong and that they will not carry out same-sex 'marriages.' Governor Harlington is going around advocating the same thing. There is only one word to describe both President Frederickson and Governor Harlington: bullies of the worst kind—and because they are using the full force of government to buttress their bullying it is tyrannical. The two of you go around saying that you are doing these things because you want people to be free to 'love each other,' but you don't seem to pay any attention to 'love thy neighbor.'" Graham saw no reason to in any way try to defend Harlington or the absent Frederickson, even if he agreed with them about homosexual rights. His attempts to raise issues about Stephen seemed almost pathetic footnotes to the main focus of the debate that Stephen had set in place. He kept the pressure on Harlington and Frederickson, always coming back to the point about decency, until the proverbial final buzzer. He also didn't fail to use the debate to educate, nor did he forget about Marybeth's admonishing him about charitableness. He said that the deepening repressiveness and the lack of decency and charity in American politics ignored the most basic requirement for a good political community that had been sounded by moral leaders from Aristotle to Pope Benedict XVI: civic friendship.

Media polling after the debate showed that Stephen had "won" it hands-down. It was three or four days until the results of the debate showed up in the presidential preference polling. It seemed as if many people who had had held back from supporting Stephen because they weren't sure if they agreed with him on different public issues thought about it after the debate and decided for him. When asked why, they typically cited his honesty, simplicity (they could personally identify with him), decency, courage (not just in confronting a range of issues that so many politicians ran from, but many also remembered his handling of the knife-wielding man earlier in the campaign), and also the fact that he had convinced them to think more about some public questions that they had ignored or had gone along with the flow about. He had gained seven points, and with only a weekend and a Monday until the election he was only five points behind Frederickson. Still, 10% continued to be undecided and Frederickson's campaign still had no sense of urgency as they persisted in their Dewey-like confidence that the undecided bloc would split evenly and their man would still win by a healthy nine or ten percent.

Others on the left were becoming alarmed, however. Was it possible that this "wild conservative"—who really meant what he said and (worse) probably would act on his beliefs—could be elected President? It was a bit late for the left-leaning mainstream media to go after him in a big way. He never gave them interviews—preferring, of course, to do this mostly with local media during the campaign—so they tried to do last-minute things like get ahold of local media interview clips and find whatever they could to bring to public attention to derail him. There wasn't much that was not already known, however. He didn't hide his beliefs. Broadcast journalists at CNN thought they could nail him on his campaign trail statements about transgenderism. They did a story on their nightly news report the last week of the campaign bringing together different clips where he made it clear that there was no such thing as a "transgendered" person—no one's chromosomes could ever be changed and the reality of one's sex, present from the moment of conception, was imprinted permanently in one's mind, soul, and—despite efforts to change its appearance—body. CNN's timing couldn't have been worse, however. Besides it not stirring up people other than homosexualist activists against Stephen—who already hated him anyhow—a story then gained much popular attention around the same time from Chicago about a sexual assault on a woman in a public women's restroom by a man who was there because he "identified" as a woman.

MSNBC was certainly no friend of Stephen's, but they like others seemed to be caught by surprise by his crushing debate performance. A few days after the debate they started to criticize him at every turn. They were unprepared, however, for the way he turned the tables on them with a blistering, systematic response to their list of claims, including pointing out in detail how they twisted numerous things and simply misstated history in claims about such things as the resistance by the executive to the Supreme Court. They looked foolish going up against a law professor. They were further embarrassed when Stephen, working from information from the crack research work of his campaign staff and volunteers, brought out that the network had consulted with various leftist interest groups throughout the campaign. He accused them outright of "outrageous bias." In his usual manner, he pounded away at MSNBC repeatedly for two solid days in that last week of the campaign. It turned out that Stephen had hit a nerve with voters. Tracking polls in the last two days before the election were showing a movement of the undecided bloc to Stephen and the reason many of them were citing was that he showed toughness in standing up to the media. That reflected a deep suspicion and skepticism that had been growing within the electorate for many years about the media.

Frederickson's private polling over the two days before the election showed a movement of most of the undecided bloc to Stephen. By then, it was too late for him or his campaign to do anything about it.

On the Friday evening before Election Day, there was a dinner party at a large townhouse in Georgetown that brought together a number of Washington's leading "progressives." It was meant to be a gathering of politically active types connected with the other party and their supporters from K Street and the left-leaning think tanks and media. It was a swanky affair, not quite "white tie," in a swanky part of the Nation's Capital. The hosts were Larry and Cecile Randolph. He was a prominent fund-raiser for left-of-center causes and had close ties to the other party's national committee. His wife Cecile was a long-time activist for the other party in Georgetown. Their adult daughter was a top staffer for the Progressive Alliance, an umbrella organization for leftist public policy advocacy groups. He had worked with her recently in raising funds for a few of those groups that were developing community organizing and "Empowering the People" programs for inner city black, Hispanic, and Caucasian working class neighborhoods. These programs stressed the "political education" role of the community organizer, instead of just the more typical focus on voter mobilization. The Randolphs were known for these kinds of parties and whenever they had them the numbers of BMWs, Cadillac Escalades, and Lexuses parked along the streets in that part of Georgetown noticeably increased over even their normal substantial number. The tracking poll data was a day or two away from showing up in the media, so with the reassurances coming from the Frederickson White House—virtually no one at this particular gathering of Washington "beautiful people" was supporting Harlington—the mood at the party was quietly upbeat. The election campaign—even with their political activism for the other party—did not stop the hosts from taking their annual fall trip to the Caribbean, where they owned another home in an upscale resort area of the Dominican Republic. They had "felt good" for most of the fall about the "progressive" electoral chances this year. As the campaign wore on, however, Larry Randolph started to experience a nagging uneasiness and after the debate he became downright troubled. As the caterer's red and white-clad servers scurried about the rooms offering a large selection of hors-d'oeuvres—these dinner parties were bigger affairs than the Randolphs' regular cook and maid could handle—Larry sat down with two other "progressive" big wigs from the K Street crowd to talk about the election. He had a somber look on his face as he said, "I don't care what Frederickson's people are saying. I don't like the way this is going. This right-wing nut Bernard is coming on strong and I think it's too late now to do anything about it. He even fires back at the media and gets away with it. The people—the rabble, and not just the right-wing religious types—seem to eat it up."

"Larry," said one of the others, "I wouldn't worry about it. The President has it under control. His pollsters tell him he's in good shape. Besides, the country's not going to elect someone as way-out as Bernard. Even with that traitor Harlington in the race, it hasn't made much of a difference the whole time. Our party has the big electoral vote advantage. Besides Bernard's party is split, too."

"Frederickson made a mistake by not debating. He let himself be hit hard by Bernard before millions of people—millions that Bernard had not reached in one fell swoop like that before—and he wasn't there to defend himself," Randolph responded.

The other man spoke up. "I think he's right, Larry. If he got any advantage from that debate, it'll just be a blip. Regardless of how Bernard's responding to the media, they're going after him is going to have an effect. If people who were not already going to support Bernard are now considering it, all that the media is saying will give them second thoughts. Besides, a lot of those people who have been supporting Harlington are going to end up voting for Frederickson. Frederickson's polling people have been showing that Harlington's support is soft and after his bad debate performance a lot of them will just switch to the President."

The first man spoke up again. "Besides, Larry, you know how these politicians from their party are. They always say they're going to do this and that, these big things, and they never do. At bottom line, Bernard is a politician just like the rest of them. Besides, look at the polls. The public is on our side on almost all these issues, and they know which party's on their side. If Bernard got elected, he wouldn't be able to take a sharp turn even if he wanted to."

Randolph wasn't convinced. "I just hope you're both right. Bernard hasn't been a typical politician in Pennsylvania and he's gone after even settled things up there. The other thing is that people are attracted to him. They think he's a good guy, not like the usual maneuvering, power-grabbing politician—but *good*."

For weeks before election day, Stephen's grassroots effort had been gearing up its get-out-the-vote effort. Most of it was focused on election day, but the big canvassing push worked to also identify

Stephen's supporters who were likely "early voters" and made sure to follow up with them in plenty of time. Stephen and John knew from the beginning that turnout was the key to their success. In the past, when the party nominated their usual run-of-the-mill moderates, the people who hewed most closely to the party's principles and were most enthusiastic about them—which were the majority of its rank-and-file—didn't turn out in big enough numbers. It had become a major reason for the party's lack of electoral success for most of the last generation. Now, they had a candidate who was very direct about those principles—which increasingly came down to original American constitutional principles and sound cultural norms—and his intent to carry them out. Stephen and John also knew that the other party had drawn rings around theirs in recent presidential elections in getting their core demographic groups out to the polls. They were not willing to allow the other party to outdo them on that this year. It didn't. Stephen's get-out-the-vote "machine" turned out to be every bit as impressive as his whole organizational effort all along.

Of the 17% undecided bloc, 14% wound up going for Stephen and only 3% for Frederickson. Frederickson was able, in the end, to pry only 1% of Harlington's vote from him. The percentage vote totals were: Stephen - 40%; Frederickson - 39%; Harlington - 13%; and Graham - 7%. Graham garnered his vote mostly from "moderate" elements in the party (especially in the business community). The 1% he lost from previous polling may have gone partly to libertarian types, as their party finished at close to 1%.

The key thing, of course, was electoral votes. As the vote totals poured in on election night it became apparent that Stephen's narrow popular vote victory was going to be sharply magnified in the electoral vote totals. He won both of the states that traditionally closed their polls earliest in the evening, Indiana and Kentucky. Both states, neighbors along the Ohio River, had substantial Evangelical Protestant elements and their turnout for Stephen was extraordinarily high. It was thought that their already strong support for him was enhanced even further and their turnout overall sharply increased due to the national attention given to the shuttering of small churches (one in each state) by the IRS, with the assistance of local authorities, who had lost their tax exemptions due to their to their refusal to perform same-sex "weddings" and then their inability to pay their tax bills. A couple of homosexualist organizations had started to target especially small Evangelical churches by sending same-sex couples to them to ask them to "marry" them. They figured if they could knock off small churches first, then they could go after the Orthodox and Catholic churches.

When the anticipated refusals came, they filed complaints with the IRS seeking to get their tax exemptions revoked. These were early efforts following from the Supreme Court's same-sex "marriage" decision. A few bureaucrats—maybe because this is what they "thought they should do" in light of the changed legal situation for same-sex "marriage"—made decisions to move against the churches and their timing, from a political standpoint, was particularly bad. So were the decisions of a few local law enforcement officials to provide the routine back-up support that the IRS asks for when they appear to close down entities—almost always for-profit businesses—for delinquent taxes. The spectacle of churches being shut down by the IRS was too much even for some supporters of the Court's decision. The governors of the states criticized the local officials for their action and public opinion was so strong against the one county sheriff that he resigned. As the totals started to come in, it was projected that Stephen would win about 60% of the vote in both states, which was astounding. Not surprisingly, Stephen was not winning most of the Northeast—although there were some surprises. The left-of-center vote in New Hampshire was divided between Frederickson and Harlington. The libertarian candidate seemed to pull even more of the vote that might have gone to one of them. This enabled Stephen to win the state with 45% of the vote. A similar thing happened in another small state, Delaware. In that so-called "moderate" state, Frederickson, Harlington, and Graham divided up nearly 60% of the vote among them and Stephen slipped through to win with 41%. There was a surprising, solid core of Bernard loyalists in the state who were familiar with him and his record in neighboring Pennsylvania. Harlington won narrowly over Frederickson in his home state of Connecticut, denying him electoral votes that usually went to his party. Most importantly, Stephen won his state, Pennsylvania, with a solid 55% of the vote. Stephen almost swept the Southeast. He lost Virginia to Frederickson, though not by much. With an aggressive grassroots organizing campaign by conservative Catholic and Evangelical religious activists and Harlington pulling some of the leftist vote, he even cut into Frederickson's stronghold of northern Virginia although not enough to add to his downstate advantage and win statewide. Stephen's support from a surprising number of black ministers in Georgia was perhaps the difference there, as the black vote advantage for Frederickson—even in Atlanta—was cut, and Stephen won the state by about 49 to 47%. Neither Harlington nor Graham was much of a factor there. Florida was thought to be a toss-up, but the Evangelical vote, the Cuban-American vote (Stephen had hit hard about how the other party since Barack Obama had "coddled up" to the

Castros, giving them concession after concession with nothing in return except exchanging ambassadors and doing nothing to help "the oppressed and brutalized Cuban people"), and again the reduced margin for Frederickson among the blacks, as well as the fact that both Harlington and Graham pulled votes from Frederickson, enabled Stephen to pull out a 4-percentage-point win. The rest, from West Virginia to Louisiana, were his. The Plains (Texas to North Dakota) and the Rocky Mountain states except for Colorado, New Mexico, and Nevada were also in his column. New Mexico was astoundingly close. Although traditionally favoring the other party and despite Stephen's strong stance against illegal immigration, he lost it to Frederickson by only 1%. The reason almost certainly was his strong organizational effort and appeal to the conservative inclinations and concern about family issues among the Hispanics. The other party needed to take heed of that and his enhanced success among the blacks in the election, since from the start he had reached out to each of these groups at the grassroots level. The West Coast—the "Left Coast"—except for Alaska, went for Frederickson. Stephen made a surprisingly strong showing in California, however, as Harlington and Graham both pulled votes from Frederickson. Stephen finished only five points behind Frederickson. Graham was perhaps a bigger factor in Oregon than anywhere else. It was probably the only state where he drained a significant number of votes from Stephen, although even without that Stephen would not have won there. Stephen still finished in second place, with the Evangelical and Mormon vote solidly behind him, but it was not close and Harlington and Graham were not far behind. In the Midwest, an all-out effort by Governor Morrisey and a superb effort by the party organization—with a heavy Evangelical and conservative presence—and Stephen's own campaign, which collaborated exceptionally well with the party people—enabled Stephen to win easily in his "other" home state, Ohio. While losing in Illinois, Missouri, and Wisconsin, he scored big (even if narrow) wins on the shoulders of strong Evangelical support in Michigan and Iowa and stunned almost all prognosticators with a one-point victory in Minnesota. The combination of a conservative Catholic-Lutheran-Evangelical bloc and a strong showing by Harlington did it for him there. The overall result was to put Stephen just over three hundred electoral votes.

Post-election surveys about why people voted for Stephen showed that his "goodness" was a major reason. Another was that they believed that he would provide leadership. People decided that they wanted a leader, not another politician.

One line in Stephen's late-night acceptance speech amidst an almost previously unseen election-night combination of jubilant celebration and prayer stood out and continued to resonate in the minds of both pro- and anti-Bernard people in the weeks and months ahead: "As God is my witness, you can be sure that I will do the things I said I would in this campaign." There was no question that Stephen was going to provide leadership, as the people who voted for him wanted.

CHAPTER 7

A First Hundred Days That Throttles
The Nation

I f there was no time for an inaugural ball on January 20, there was
certainly no time to unpack and comfortably move into the White
House. Marybeth was in charge of that. Stephen huddled with John
Frost, who was now going to be his Chief-of-Staff—but not in a rigid,
H.R. Haldeman gatekeeper kind of fashion at the point of a hierarchy—
and four others who essentially had comprised his transition team, two
in domestic policy, one in constitutional issues, and the other in foreign
and military policy. Although all three were academics, people that
Stephen either knew or knew of for their expertise, they were not the
types who were lost in an ivory tower. In fact, the reason he had turned
to them was that he knew that they had their feet firmly planted in
reality—in politics and the world of affairs as it really was. During the
transition period they had consulted people, most of whom had been in
government, who could make sober-minded assessments about the
situation in each federal agency and how Stephen could exercise the
control over them in the way a President should and change them. They
had come up with a clear, precise set of recommendations—though not
in volumes that no one would ever read. Stephen had instructed that he
wanted the recommendations limited to two pages per agency, and no
more than thirty pages for the whole report. The whole transition effort
had proceeded quietly and Stephen made sure that the small number of
people involved in it understood that they were to make no public
statements and be circumspect in their private comments. These people
had proven themselves and would now be his close-in advisers. Like
when he was governor, he would have a very small White House staff.
Something closer to the four people that Lincoln had immediately
surrounding him appealed to Stephen, and he didn't buy the usual

argument that that wasn't any longer possible in an age of vast and complex government. Stephen didn't believe that government generally had to be as vast and complex as it had become. Besides, he intended to return to the practice of the Cabinet being in the role of presidential advisers instead of primarily managers of huge bureaucratic agencies. The regular White House employees would continue; he would have nothing of the Hilary Clinton-type of summary firing of the career people there to replace them with friends. His new close-in aides would be close liaisons with the Cabinet, working with, assisting, and advising them but never telling them what to do or acting in any way as their superiors.

Another utterly crucial element to his redirecting of the country was his maintenance of a grass-roots organization that he had built up during his campaign. John, in addition to serving as his chief-of-staff, was in charge of keeping intact and building up and developing this organization further. It would not be some kind of street-protesting fifth column, but an organization along the lines of the Tea Party which would be independent but would help support his efforts and more importantly educate other average citizens about what he would be doing. This network would play a key role in helping to make possible a permanent shift in the direction of the country. Stephen, from the top, could stop the erosion of constitutional rights in the short-run, but nothing could be truly sustained without the support of the average citizen.

In two hours he would have the first meeting of his Cabinet members-designate. Unlike the usual Cabinet-selection politics, he did not consult widely with his party nor did he seek to "balance" his choices according to gender, racial, ideological, factional, or geographical considerations—and he made it clear in public statements that he *wouldn't* do this. He picked highly qualified people who thought as he did and could be counted on to carry out a strikingly different agenda than usual that would decisively move the country in a sharply new direction from where it had been going for a long time. He was ready to work with his party's leadership in Congress. As the result of the election, they controlled both houses by small majorities. He was wary of them, however, since most members had been long-time Washington insiders. He made it clear to them that he would not be hesitant to challenge them and would have nothing to do with the usual slick, almost underhanded kind of politics that dominated Washington. His first dealing with them was arranging hearings after Congress convened on January 3 on his Cabinet appointees, even though of course the formal appointments couldn't be made until Inauguration

Day. Stephen appointed men of great integrity and thoroughly checked them out so no unpleasant surprises would appear at the confirmation hearings. There was grumbling from the other party and some in his own that there were no women, but he dug in his heels and insisted that "chromosomes would not be determinative as to who should get Cabinet or other federal appointments." As it turned out, the appointees were all approved, even though some in the other party would have liked to have blocked at least some of them. Stephen wanted the Cabinet in place quickly to begin to move on the part of his agenda about getting control over the bureaucracy, but was prepared to proceed even if it wasn't.

Stephen's meeting with the Cabinet secretaries-designate consisted mostly of a rehash of how they would be moving quickly to assert this control. He had selected the men for his Cabinet on the basis not just of a willingness to do this, but an enthusiasm for and deep-seated commitment to the idea. He also chose them on the basis of an assessment of their toughness and ability not be co-opted by the top career people in their agencies, which happens so often—the "capture" phenomenon that political science scholars of American bureaucracy write about. He restated another thing to them, which was part of what he would say to the nation: how he would be moving immediately on a massive rollback of bureaucratic regulations.

Stephen prepared his first post-inaugural address to the nation. It would be a shocker that would make clear that he was going to act to use executive power decisively to protect the Constitution from further attack by the powerful forces of the left and restore traditional citizen liberties that were increasingly being run roughshod over in the name of ersatz rights and the ongoing efforts to bring about a veritable cultural revolution. As usual, Stephen had no plans to allow speechwriters to compose his every talk. This was a particularly crucial one of his presidency and, along with his inaugural address, he intended it to set the tone. Moreover, so many of the people who had voted for him were expecting him to come through after he had emphasized the need for bold executive action during the campaign. He had spent the weeks before the inauguration writing his inaugural address, this planned first speech of his presidency on constitutional issues, and a quick follow-up second speech that would lay out both his leading legislative proposals and other executive initiatives to address certain national questions. The inaugural address had set out his vision and the next two would spell out his initial actions. He believed that it was necessary to strike early with his boldest actions, since new presidents tend to have an initial reservoir of good will, people want to extend them the benefit of the doubt, and organized opposition to them takes a while to gain strong force.

Stephen let only Marybeth and John read his address before he delivered it, though the other members of his team knew what he planned to do in his early presidency. As during the transition period, the rule was that everyone was to maintain silence and avoid the media so that no one would be tipped off about the content of the speeches until he delivered them. This was both to catch certain opponents off-guard and not give them a chance to mount a preemptive attack and also to not allow distortions by a left-leaning media to become implanted in the public mind before he even presented his plans and arguments.

Stephen, Marybeth, and John sat down to a private dinner in the White House before the address. They got their plates and ate by themselves on a collapsible table that had been set up in the White House Library. Stephen wanted them to be entirely alone for the dinner without servers coming through so he could be comfortable about their talking openly. There was probably more to his motivation than that. There was a side of Stephen that only the people closest to him saw: the seemingly supremely confident Stephen had moments, especially before a major initiative or decision, when his confidence could waver. Not surprisingly, since this involved a decision that would have a greater import than any he had ever made, this was one of them. In a sense, he wanted Marybeth and John there to seek reassurance in the final hour.

Even before Stephen said anything, Marybeth spoke up. She could see his tenseness on his face and both she and John knew that Stephen wanted this private, quiet dinner with them to buttress him in a difficult moment. They knew there was no question in his mind that he was making the right moves and no danger that he would at the last minute moderate or change his course, but he just needed a little confidence boost. "Stephen, darling, you're doing the right thing. This is part of what God called you—put you here—for. What's more, you'll succeed. It's the only course to go to protect all of us, to get the country back to what it was meant to be. You have known all along that it's the only way."

John didn't say anything. There was really nothing more that he could say, and it really had to come from Stephen's closest advisor and life-long companion and soulmate. Stephen just had to look at his face to get a further reassuring confirmation. It was time for him to go to the Blue Room, where his speech would be telecast from, to look over the text before the broadcast people would arrive to start to set up the cameras, sound systems, and other machinery they would need. He wanted to prepare himself to present the speech in the ambiance that he would actually be in.

When Stephen left the room, John turned to Marybeth. "If you're at all concerned, don't be. I knew from the moment I first met your husband that he had what it took to lead, no matter how difficult the time or the situation. I just could sense that. That's why I've been with him all the way from those first days in Pennsylvania."

"I'm not concerned at all, John. From the moment I met him, I knew not just that he was the man I would spend my life with and who God sent to me but also that he had an incredible strength and goodness. That has carried him all through his life and when the presidency beckoned, I had to be sure that he alone would decide if he would pursue it. I knew he was supremely capable of undertaking it, even if the challenges it would present would be even greater than what most previous men in it have had to face. I think God called him to this—not just to this office, but also to do what needs to be done to help save our Constitution, our country, and our whole way of life. When Bishop LaGrange came to see him to urge him to run I became convinced of it."

Besides wanting to go over his speech and acclimate himself to the environs, Stephen wanted to pray his rosary before the television people arrived. He remembered a priest-teacher of his from high school, who had become an enduring friend of his, saying late in 1989 as Communist regimes were collapsing with scarcely a whimper in Eastern Europe that it was the result of seventy years of old ladies saying the rosary. He also remembered the great victory of the Christian fleet over the Islamic Ottoman Turks in the 1571 Battle of Lepanto, after Pope Pius V had called for all of Europe to pray the rosary. The rosary on different occasions seemed to be tied in with helping to stave off or reverse grave political developments that posed mortal threats to Christianity and Christian civilization. It seemed to him to be the obvious thing to do with the decisive political moves he was about to make.

Two hours later, Stephen faced the cameras in the Blue Room with only his speech in front of him. This was going to be his first big effort as President to try to reverse the developments that both the morally skewed left and the timid right had allowed to unfold for some time. More importantly, it was the challenge to make the case for them—to educate—and to build up support for the course he was about to embark on. The times were crucial. With the social, cultural, moral, political, and legal deterioration that had occurred, not just the

Constitution hung in the balance—even though he believed that this was the thing he could have the most immediate effect on to stop and reverse the slide, as difficult as that in itself would be—but the entire future of the American political society.

The broadcast crew leader gave the signal for the ten-second countdown to the start of the speech. As the cameras started to roll, Stephen looked intently at them and with his usual almost instinctive slight smile his face betrayed its usual combination of determination, kindness, and firmness.

"My Fellow Americans: During the presidential election campaign, I talked about the grave threats to our Constitution, our American traditions, and even to the practices that have defined sound civilization caused by decisions and actions emanating from institutions of government, both on the federal and state levels, in the last several years. Opposing these developments and this worldview that they have resulted from, then, is not reflective of a competing ideology, but of a need to defend and restore the very principles that undergird our Republic, of the obvious meaning of certain provisions of our Constitution, of civilized norms, and indeed of common human experience and common sense itself. For example, to say that killing the innocent is not killing and that marriage can be something other than between a man—a male by conception and birth of the human species—and a woman—a female by conception and birth of the human species—is nothing less than an affront to reality. It is even worse to say—as so many of the advocates of such a false and bizarre notion do—that others must be forced by law by the heavy hand of the state to embrace, even enthusiastically, such a notion. This is the very character of tyranny, and it will no longer be tolerated in the United States where true liberty will reign once again.

"To restore our constitutional principles and end such intolerant, repressive practices—that evince a mind-set of totalitarianism—that have also affronted the necessary spirit of civility that must rule relationships within any community, I am announcing the following immediate initiatives. First, the U.S. Supreme Court decision of a few years ago which claimed—contrary to every part of the American constitutional tradition—that there was a right to same-sex 'marriage' and unleashed a torrent of repression against churches, religious universities and other religious institutions, and religiously-motivated individuals will no longer be enforced by the federal government. This means that states that oppose issuing marriage licenses to same-sex couples will not be compelled to do so. Supreme Court decisions are not self-enforcing and require the action of the executive branch to be

216

carried out. As our great Founding Father, Alexander Hamilton, wrote in Federalist Paper 78 only the executive has the sword. There is ample historical precedent for the position I am stating. Accordingly, I have ordered the U.S. Marshal Service, which normally has the responsibility of seeing that federal court orders are enforced but is actually an executive branch agency and under the direction of the President, to stand down on this.

"This action, of course, will protect the legitimate freedom of the states. Some states, however, whose judges or political leadership demonstrate the same flawed moral and constitutional thinking as the U.S. Supreme Court have engaged in a similar violation of religious and rightful individual liberty. In some cases, they have not only assaulted religious liberty, but have forced individuals to act in such a way as to be required to implicitly give their support to something which they believe—and they are right about this—to be immoral. Their right to what the Supreme Court itself has called—and in other contexts, at least, has protected—expressive association has been grossly violated. We have seen this with events planners, photographers, bakers, printers, and even newspaper editors. In one case, still underway, a state agency—ironically called a "human rights" commission—has slapped on a baker of modest means a fine of one million dollars and thousands more to pay the state's legal expenses because she refused to bake a cake for a same-sex so-called "wedding," something she as a Christian knew was immoral. Then, on top of it, the agency enjoined this woman from speaking, privately or publicly, about the matter and the agency proceedings under threat of imprisonment. Such action is outrageous and callous. The evidence shows that this agency was doing this at the behest of political interest groups. As President, I will not tolerate such a blatant flouting of the First Amendment rights of freedom of religion and speech. Speaking of the Marshal Service, I have ordered it to send a round-the-clock guard to this woman's place of business and home to block any attempt by state authorities, including its judiciary, from carrying out these unconstitutional, and hence unlawful, orders. I have dispatched federal marshals in several similar situations in other cases in a number of states around the country. This, or the dispatching of federalized National Guardsmen, will be my response to such further incidents as well. These innocent, religiously-motivated people—standing up courageously for what all of history until now has known is right—will not have to bear the crushing burden of defending themselves in front of hostile and what are often deeply biased state agencies and courts anymore.

"I have also ordered the new Secretary of the Treasury to halt the outrageous, illegal actions by the Internal Revenue Service to revoke the tax exemptions of churches that refuse to perform so-called same-sex "weddings" and to immediately restore the tax exemptions that have already been revoked. I have also ordered him to bring to an immediate end all monitoring of clergy sermons on this and other topics. Also, the federal government will no longer interpret the Johnson Amendment, as it's called, to preclude discussion or comment on public issues or the issuing of public policy statements by clergy or churches. Any IRS operative who tries to do this will face immediate disciplinary proceedings. Also, I will be working with members of Congress to repeal the Johnson Amendment, which has been part of the basis of this assault on churches and religious institutions in violation of the First Amendment. In light of the abuses of recent years of targeting organizations with a certain socio-political viewpoint— violating the free speech guarantee of the First Amendment—I have also ordered the Secretary to suspend *all* current tax exemption revocation proceedings and to make decisions on all current applications for tax exemptions within fourteen days, strictly following the provisions of the law. Again, any IRS operative who violates these orders will be subject to discipline.

"The support for something so contrary to the natural order as same-sex so-called 'marriage'—to the point now where those who will not accept it are maligned and even suppressed—has occurred because of a deeply flawed notion of equality that has been pushed by opinion-makers in American life and has now been widely, if unreflectively, ingrained into our collective psyche." Stephen then proceeded, in his usual manner in an abbreviated and easily understandable way, to educate his listeners about the true nature of equality, how it was understood in the American tradition, and why the equality of persons with same-sex attraction was in no way violated by not allowing them to "marry" someone of the same sex. This required him to tread where hardly any politician recently had had the courage to go: the nature of what marriage is. Then he talked about the understanding of liberty in the American constitutional tradition, how it is not the same thing as license and why it would be destructive to view it that way, and the nature and reach of freedom of religion and speech that were so crucial to a democratic republic.

Then he stated other steps he was taking to reverse the convoluted notion of equality that had been allowed to shape federal policy. "The most basic role of the state is to provide security, defense, and order for its people, but in the name of this false notion of equality and a

218

destructive so-called gender ideology—which effectively says not only that there is there no difference at all between men and women, but that gender is simply a social construct, a matter of opinion—the morale and thus the effectiveness of our military forces has been compromised. Many outstanding members of the military have left the ranks because of the bold, foolish, and unreasonable social experiments that have been thrust on it. These damaging policies have also consistently been enacted irrespective of the evidence showing how bad they are. No longer will ideology trump the facts and common sense. I have ordered the following changes to immediately be implemented. First, persons with same-sex attraction will no longer be allowed into the military. This will not be a question of restoring a "don't ask, don't tell" policy, but of going back to the previous policy before it: persons will be asked if they have same-sex attraction and evidence sought and they will be excluded. One has no "right" to serve in the military. Those previously admitted under the permissive policies of the last few leftist administrations will be mustered out, receiving honorable discharges and retaining eligibility for any veterans' benefits earned. Nor will anyone who has undergone so-called "sex-change surgery"—which does not really change anyone's sex—be permitted to join the military—and the military will no longer pay for any such surgery for its members. For that matter, the federal government will not pay for it under any other of its programs. Also, all previous presidential directives permitting women into combat or combat-support roles of any sort, or permitting women in combat zones at all have been reversed. Nor will military training take place in a mixed-sex manner, and the situations of mixed sex-military housing arrangements will immediately be ended. Also, the U.S. Marine Corps will again be exclusively male; women currently in it will be given the option to switch to one of the other services or receive an honorable discharge. Similarly, all special forces units such as the Army Rangers and Navy Seals will be exclusively male. If anyone challenges in court any of the changes I am hereby enunciating for the military, this administration will defend them for the sake of building up a further record in support of them but we will not accede to any judicial order to change them. This is because they are completely within the President's prerogatives as commander-in-chief and also because they go contrary to no law of Congress respecting military policy, which the Constitution gives Congress the power over." Then, Stephen again turned educator—now a professor for the masses—to discuss evidence for the statements he made and such basic things such as why the differences and dynamic between men and women indicated these changes and why there was no such thing as a "transgendered" person."

He also turned his attention to the intelligence community. He stated that he had issued an order that not only was torture of detainees—already forbidden by law, but not necessarily always upheld—but all physical assault; food, water, and sleep deprivation; and psychological and emotional pressure and manipulation—including "waterboarding"—was forbidden, and that any operative engaging in it would be immediately suspended and subject to dismissal from federal service. To insure that his order was complied with, he ordered the heads of the different intelligence agencies to video-record all interrogations. Such practices were also now prohibited in any context in the carrying out of the routine duties of these agencies. Political assassination was also forbidden; no longer would there be the phenomenon of "killing on the orders of one's government." Stephen did not exclude the possibility of covert operations, but said such activities could only be carried out with his express orders and he would have to be continually apprised of the developments. Also, there would be no more issuing of "suicide pills" and the like to operatives to take if they were on the verge of capture. Stephen said resolutely, "the federal government would not be an enabler, much less encourager, of the evil of suicide."

He announced one more jarring change respecting the distorted notion of equality he spoke of: all affirmative action requirements involving the federal workforce and federal contractors, concerning any designated group, that had been established by executive order or regulatory law by any president were immediately eliminated. *"True* equality, meeting qualifications, showing competence, and merit were now going to be the only standards.

"Recent administrations have poisoned race relations in America and obliterated the true notion of equality. This will be one of many efforts to right the conditions that their policies and actions have encouraged. Similarly, the civil rights actions filed against governmental entities and public school systems on the basis of supposed statistical disparities without even any allegations of intent to violate civil rights will no longer be permitted. As Mark Twain once said: 'There are lies, damn lies, and statistics.' Statistics misused can cause confusion and worse conditions. What's more, this has obliterated the meaning and intent of the civil rights laws. We also will no longer go on 'fishing expeditions' against local police departments to find supposed violations of civil rights. Make no mistake about it," he added firmly with his penetrating eyes gazing right into the cameras, "police respect for the Bill of Rights protections of citizens across the board will be expected, but we will no longer tolerate federally-generated pressures that make the police unwilling to be assertive enough against lawbreakers for fear of being dragged into court for civil right violations. Nor will we pursue civil rights violation prosecutions when a state court has exonerated police officers for charges stemming from some incident. This started with the senior Bush administration in the Rodney King case and has gone on. Such utilitarian legal actions—going after someone to stop a lawless reaction by others, which in that case was rioting—are outrages. It is also, functionally speaking, double jeopardy—a violation of the Bill of Rights.

"If we will no longer tolerate the disregarding of the rule of law in an area it should be most upheld in, civil rights, we will also not tolerate it in the matter of immigration law either. For years now we have heard about the flood of people entering the U.S. from our southern border, but neither political party has done anything decisive about it. We have to be frank that the reason for that has been both political and economic. Some in one party have sought the votes to be gotten when these people who have violated the law become citizens—after some expected sweeping amnesty. They have also been driven by ideological imperatives: they don't think that national borders or having a homeland should mean anything anymore—that somehow we're all citizens of the world and nothing else. Some people in both parties—probably more in mine—like the idea of having people around who have entered the country illegally because they know that all too many businesses want people who will work just for minimum wage or maybe even less. So much for concern about a just wage and so much for concern about the economic well-being of one's own countrymen. Further, people in both parties have been intimidated by advocacy groups who accuse them of race prejudice if they don't allow people—and it has been a massive number of people who have done this—from south of the border to come illegally and stay here. No demographic group has the right or prerogative to violate the law. No group—regardless of race or color or ethnicity or anything else—has the freedom to violate the law. The rule of law—at the very center of our constitutional republic and an indispensable principle if justice and civility are to exist—demands nothing less. What's more, the lack of commitment of these people to the United States and our principles has serious implications for the stability of the political community." With that, he launched into a brief explanation—bringing principles of social ethics down to the level of the masses—of why it is necessary to have people who share a common set of principles that unites them, a shared notion of the common good. He gave stark historical examples of the torments and even collapses that nations have experienced that did not have such a civic bond.

"Our immigration laws are not unjust. We allow a large number of people to emigrate here legally each year, who have followed the rules. We have one of the most liberal immigration policies in the world. A nation also has the right to protect itself. In fact, its leaders are derelict in their duty if they do not do everything possible to insure that—this is their *first* obligation, *it is government's first obligation.*" He recounted numerous examples in recent years of how uncontrolled entry into the U.S. had caused widespread crime and increasing social turmoil. "I have ordered intensive enforcement of our immigration laws. People apprehended trying to enter the country illegally will *immediately* be sent back. They have no right to be here, so are entitled to no judicial process. The same is so also of those who recently entered the country illegally and are still in areas close to the border. I have ordered an aggressive sweep to locate such persons so they can be deported immediately in accordance with current law. We will take full advantage of the expedited removal proceedings of current federal law. As far as those who have been in the country for more than a short period, I have ordered an intensive effort to locate them through multiple means to offer them the opportunity for voluntary repatriation to their home countries instead of waiting for formal judicial proceedings, as the law permits. Those who refuse to accept that offer will either be placed in detention facilities or under house arrest and will not be permitted to work in the meantime since any employment they will have gotten will have been without the proper documentation required by law. Unaccompanied minors will be turned over to the nearest police authorities across the Mexican border. If from another country, they will be taken to the police or governmental authority at the nearest port city of that country or to one of its consulates. We will offer to take them directly back to their families. Efforts will be stepped up to complete the wall that Congress funded to be built along the Mexican border. I have directed that it be completed within two years. I am also sending to Congress a series of proposals to simplify and make more reasonable the qualifications for people to become naturalized citizens. People should not have to spend a near-fortune to go through the procedures or wait years upon years for naturalization. There will also be proposals for criteria for naturalization for persons who came here illegally many years ago and have not been regularized or were brought here illegally by their parents and have spend their whole lives

222

here, or who have otherwise contributed substantially to their communities in the U.S. However, there will be strict requirements for them to meet to be regularized."

Next, Stephen turned to speaking about the respect for innocent human life—even while his most dramatic initiative about this would wait for the near future. For now, he announced that he was re-imposing the rule first instituted by the Reagan administration that federally-funded family planning clinics could no longer provide abortion counseling. The Supreme Court had actually upheld this, even while the Clinton administration pulled back on it. This effectively would now defund outfits like Planned Parenthood, which not only counseled for abortions but also performed them. Stephen said the legal issue here thus had been resolved decades ago and this cut-off would immediately go into effect irrespective of any further federal court action. He also said that he had directed the Secretary of Health and Human Services to immediately rescind the rationing provisions of the general federal health care law and Medicare end-of-life counseling requirements—"both have been appropriately labeled by some as death panels, since they clearly encourage care for the elderly and seriously infirm to be limited or stopped"—and the mandate that all employers providing the remaining non-government insurance and health plans—even if they have religious or moral objections—provide payment for abortions, sterilization procedures, and contraception. He explained the threats to life and religious liberty of these provisions. He also said that he was working with his party's leaders in Congress to immediately repeal the substantial federal takeover of health care, and if the other party filibustered, it would simply end by cutting off all funding for it. Its funding would end at the conclusion of the current fiscal year. He would include no appropriations for it in the next budget and if Congress still approved any funding he would veto it. He also directed the Secretary of the Treasury to forbid the IRS to continue to take more tax from people who have no health insurance. Contrary to what the Supreme Court had decided in upholding that, Stephen said it was not a tax. Anyone in the know got the upshot of what Stephen's statements meant. Even if Congress didn't formally repeal it, with no funding it would be dead.

"The family is the bedrock not only of civilization, but of a good political community. Its crucial role in forming good persons and thus good citizens makes it particularly crucial in sustaining a democratic republic like the United States. If people's souls are not rightly shaped within the family, the kind of self-control necessary for the responsible operation of republican institutions—where in an atmosphere of much freedom, as Tocqueville said, the only thing that can stop that freedom from becoming destructive is interior control—will not happen. There has been, however, a relentless assault on the family from many quarters for the past several decades. One part of that has been the effort to undercut parental authority and rights, even though these rights are grounded in the natural law that is the foundation of our political order (recall the Declaration of Independence mentioning 'the laws of nature and nature's God'). Parental and family rights were also upheld by the Anglo-American common law tradition from which our nation's law descended. Nowhere has the violation of parental rights been more dramatically evident than with the systemic abuses of what has wrongly been called the 'child protective system.' This is a system that was supposedly set up for the laudable goal of stopping child abuse and neglect. However, almost from the start with the federal Mondale Act of 1974 (the Child Abuse Prevention and Treatment Act, or CAPTA) it has been used to intrude—massively—into families where in no real sense has abuse or neglect occurred. Instead, we have seen bureaucratic operatives—many of whom have never even raised children—intervening into families at the drop of a pin, often because of anonymous calls made to hotlines and because the so-called 'child protective agencies' do not like parents' legitimate childrearing practices. In other words, they use the coercive power of the state to impose their mere views on hapless families, and create turmoil in good families by their unwarranted interventions. Too often, they even resort to the greatest punishment a parent can face: taking their children away from them. To be sure, the Mondale Act has itself been responsible for this since it never even defined what 'child abuse' and 'child neglect' actually are, and state laws enacted pursuant to it have not either. In an era when 'the perfidy of vague and overbroad laws'"—the terms were second nature for constitutional scholars like himself, but he knew that the average citizen readily knew what they meant also—"has swept over the country, it is especially regrettable here: where it can badly harm the most intimate of human relationships, that of parent and child, and destroy the most basic and crucial of institutions, the family. What's more, hardened criminals—murderers, rapists, and the worst kind of thieves—are given many more rights of due process than parents are when subjected to CPS investigations, which are often triggered by these anonymous, and sometimes malicious, complaints. This anti-parent, anti-family tyranny ends *now*—nationwide, as I strove mightily to end it in Pennsylvania when I was governor there. Several years ago now, Congress by law required states to screen out questionable complaints made against parents. This requirement has never been implemented by many states. I have ordered the Secretary of Health and Human Services to cut off federal grant funds from any state that does not have such a screening requirement in place within two weeks time. Further, any state that does not have in place, within one month's time, a probable cause standard before it even commences an investigation of parents, full due process guarantees for parents under any level of investigation by an agency, or that does not respect the right of a family not to have its rights protected against forceful or deceptive entry into their homes by agency or law enforcement officials in the absence of a warrant—which the courts have consistently upheld—will have funds cut off. Also, they will have to implement the traditional 'reasonable man' standard from common law to determine what child abuse and neglect are if they are to be eligible for funding. That is, what they investigate as abuse or neglect must be a kind of behavior that a reasonable man would understand to be such. No longer may the CPS target parents for childrearing practices that its operatives or someone else doesn't like. That is a misuse of the role that it was anticipated to play under CAPTA. I have also sent legislation over to Congress to amend CAPTA to eliminate its fatal flaw of not defining what abuse and neglect actually are, which perhaps caused most of the systemic CPS abuse that we have witnessed for a long time. If Congress does not do this, I will veto the reauthorization of CAPTA. One authority in this area said, 'everyone knows that child welfare in the U.S. needs to be reformed but no one wants to do anything about it.' I am doing it now.

"Then, there are the shocking and outrageous cases—which have been increasing in number around the country—of medical kidnapping, where children are literally seized from their parents because of the parents' unwillingness to consent to possibly dangerous medical treatments, sometimes only because of disagreements between medical practitioners about the right way to proceed. Then the children are actually forced by the state to undergo the treatment, regardless of the consequences for them. Such medical kidnapping henceforth will routinely be investigated as a violation of federal civil rights laws. If an assessment of the facts indicates that the authorities have so acted in a reckless and irresponsible fashion without regard to legitimate parental rights, we will immediately bring the matter to court or, if the situation dictates, I will order federal marshals to enter the facility where the child is being forcibly kept and have him removed and turned back over to the care of his parents. What's more, all medical facilities that have played an active role in a case of medical kidnapping will be subject to losing their federal funding.

225

"When talking about trampling on Bill of Rights protections, we can hardly neglect to address the disgraceful universal electronic surveillance, recording cell phone calls and the like, of millions of our innocent citizens by what's supposed to be *their* government. Their government has for too long been trampling on their Fourth Amendment rights. It has claimed that this massive surveillance program—at a level perhaps unparalleled in American history—is necessary to fight terrorism, to insure national security. In fact, however, this surveillance program did not stop major cases of terrorist bombings and other actions. There is a reason for that: when you try to monitor everyone, you wind up monitoring no one. You are so busy looking over everyone that the resourceful, conniving real terrorist slips through the cracks and engages in his destructive actions. We also see government agencies tripping over each other and jealously guarding their jurisdiction instead of cooperating with each other to track down and apprehend those who are threatening us. Indeed, this was a situation that enabled the 9/11 terrorists to stay in the U.S. illegally to carry out their calamitous attacks. It is because of this that I have ordered an immediate end to the massive, universal phone surveillance program."

Then Stephen delivered the *coup de grâce*. "During the transition period, I had experts conducting a sweeping review of federal regulations in many areas. I have decided to immediately rescind a very large number of regulations, a list of which will be released by the White House Communications Office tomorrow morning along with an explanation of why the decision was made respecting each rescinded regulation. I have made the decision to do this on the basis of three concerns: excessive and unwarranted violation of liberties of persons, businesses, and other entities affected by what has long since become a runaway regulatory state; the lack of evidence of problems that justify the often crushing regulations and excessive penalties that go well beyond any sense of fairness (in our legal tradition and according to sound social ethics punishments must fit the offense); and simply to reign in an arrogance which has come to typify the federal government that it knows better than anyone about any area it chooses to enter even when the results are almost outrageous in a consistent way. Such an oppressive and haughty government—as our Declaration of Independence says—'is hardly fitting for a free people.'

"Secondly, during the transition period I also had legal authorities examine questionable convictions of people for alleged violations of federal law. In many cases these also concerned regulatory law, but in others they concerned prosecutions for offenses that were not

226

proscribed under the pertinent laws. Many people have been convicted on the basis of extrapolations from provisions of federal criminal statutes or because of *theories* of what constitutes, say, criminal conspiracy—based on mere prosecutorial discretion and not the actual provisions of law. In some cases, prosecutions seem to have been carried out merely for political reasons. During the campaign, I said much about abuse by federal prosecutors. In light of all this, when the White House Communications Office issues the list of regulations that are being rescinded, they will also release a list of presidential pardons that I have immediately granted to people who have been victimized by such prosecutorial misconduct. What's more, during the transition period the legal authorities mentioned exhaustively studied the records of all ninety-three sitting U.S. Attorneys. Earlier today I informed eighty of them that they have immediately been terminated due to my conclusions from this study that they have engaged in at least some of these troublesome, unacceptable—or in certain cases, outrageous—practices. Contrary to what President George W. Bush's political opponents alleged when he removed U.S. Attorneys, these people are presidential appointees and can be removed by the President at will. That is what I have done, and over the next several weeks will be appointing new U.S. Attorneys.

"One of the reasons that innocent people have been caught up in the dragnet of federal law enforcement overreach has been because of the virtually uncontrolled use of sting operations, where people are enticed to commit illegal acts by federal agents. Sometimes, federal law enforcement officials even collude with known criminals—who have their own interests to further—to for all practical purposes entrap innocent people, or to stretch the law in questionable ways to ensnare them. The infamous Ruby Ridge affair of 1992 was the prime example of this, and so was the attempt inspired by my political opponents to target me when I was Governor of Pennsylvania. It was because of such compromising of law enforcement that the long-time FBI Director J. Edgar Hoover would never allow the agency to engage in sting operations. So, I have ordered the Attorney General to immediately end all ongoing sting operations by the FBI and other agencies in the Justice Department and to forthwith implement a policy forbidding them in the future. I have also ordered all other agencies that are under presidential control that have enforcement responsibilities to immediately cease any sting operations and to no longer undertake them. Any presidential appointee who does not follow this directive at any time will immediately be removed and any other federal employee will be subject to immediate disciplinary action. Violating the law to

227

supposedly uphold the law will no longer be tolerated in the federal government.

"These decisions have been made and actions undertaken after carefully gathering information and evidence and much deliberation. *They are final.* They are the first steps in restoring the Constitution and the rule of law, ending sad injustices, correcting policies and practices based upon a seriously flawed understanding of such esteemed principles as equality, protecting Americans anew from a cavalier disregard of the Bill of Rights, protecting the family (which as I said is at the foundation of any political order, and whose very integrity depends on the family's health), and most importantly securing protection for innocent human life (whose right to exist is the basis for all other rights and is the centerpiece of upholding human dignity)."

The next morning, before the expected onslaught of attacks from the left and the mainstream media could emerge and the protesters from an assortment of interest groups spring into action, the rescinded federal regulations and the pardons were made public. They additionally jarred the critics, so that they were almost out of breath and had to first try to regroup. In the meantime, right after the Office of Communications made its announcements, they completely surprised the media by announcing that President Bernard was calling a press conference that afternoon. This made them put off responses and even reports longer. At the press conference, which got almost as much live coverage as the speech, Stephen introduced the media to many people—in the manner of what he had done during the campaign—who had suffered because of the laws and policies he had moved to change, and briefly recounted each of their stories. This put faces on the problems and was much more effective in making an impression with people than any of the usual presenting of a mound of statistics would have been. Part of this was a reminder, since he had introduced such people on some of these issues during the campaign. Then, near the end of the press conference he issued the most jarring blow of the day. It was one that was sure to stir both intense support and intense anger both on the left and right of the political spectrum. He saved the announcement of the most important pardon for himself. He announced an unconditional pardon for James Robert Leverall, a former government contract employee with the CIA, who had fled the country to Kazakhstan after being charged with espionage for violating his Top Secret security clearance by going public about illegal CIA domestic spying and massive illegal eavesdropping on average U.S. citizens. The case had garnered considerable public attention. Stephen explained that the condition of his security clearance of not disclosing anything about his activities was simply inapplicable when confronted with illegal agency activities.

The attack started from the left and its media allies the next day about the actions Stephen laid out in his first speech, but it was much less intense than had been expected. Leverall's treatment had been a point of irritation for the left and now Stephen had come to his aid. Many would-be attackers from the left suddenly backed off. His second speech to the nation the next day further blunted their criticism because some of the main legislative and policy initiatives he announced were attractive to many in their ranks. Some of the same ones and others appealed to many conservatives in his party. The attacks were allayed by the facts that his positions seemed to reach into both sides of the political spectrum and the many, sweeping actions were initially too much for all the adversaries to absorb.

In the second address, Stephen announced a number of breathtaking policy initiatives some of which would be translated into legislative proposals but others that would be carried out by what he said might be called "presidential outreach" to the private business and non-profit sectors, or by use of the presidential bully pulpit to prod things in a certain direction. He aimed to end the "upheaval in health care" caused by the increasing federal takeover of it. He said that it had created a situation not only "where bureaucratic unresponsiveness, bungling, and unconcern for people's serious health needs abounded," but certain big health care providers—through slick lobbying and tight relationships with the federal government—were "profiting mightily" while many average Americans were suffering and "the taxpaying public was bearing an increasingly heavy burden." He said he was assembling a massive health care summit—involving insurance companies, medical facilities and health care providers, representatives of companies of all sizes, representatives of the small business community, unions, the non-profit sector, and the general public—and then establishing ongoing consultative arrangements to hammer out plans to both propose private sector solutions (including, especially, the non-profit sector) to adequately address people's health care needs and address the problems of excessive cost that were partly responsible for bringing about "the current near-calamitous situation in health care." He specifically called on "Big Health Care" to step back and not let protecting the financial advantages they had accrued "cause them to oppose this effort to work for the common good."

He said that the rescinding of a large number of regulations was one part of a long-term strategy to restore the federal government to its original constitutional role, to begin to reverse the centralization of power. He also issued an executive order that no new regulation at all could go into effect without his express agreement. He quoted Alexis de Tocqueville on the dangers of centralization and said that it had helped spawn injustices. One of these injustices, Stephen asserted, was that it had led to the wrongful criminal convictions of the substantial number of people that he had just pardoned. The other side of the strategy was to end the excessive social welfare functions and, in general, extravagant domestic role of the federal government. This was clearly "not the role the Founding Fathers had set out for the federal government and had caused great financial strain for the country and imposed unjust burdens on the taxpaying public—often punishing the responsible and the provident and expecting little in turn from those who receive benefits from the federal government." He said the country would begin embarking on the policy of "gradual disengagement" that he spoke about during the campaign. Many people, he said, do legitimately need help, and sometimes it has to come from government and even the federal government. However, he said, the federal government was only a last resort. The "safety net" was necessary, but it "does not mean that government is the default place to go to in order to meet needs." Then in his usual brief but insightful way he discussed the principle of subsidiarity. He explained the rationale of it by talking about the value of having people who are "right there" and familiar with a situation address it and how things are handled more efficiently in a more localized way. He used the example he often had mentioned to his students: "Can you imagine the problems you would encounter in getting your trash picked up if refuse collection for the whole country was directed from Washington?"

During the campaign, he had talked about the need for companies to pay their workers a just wage, and now reemphasized this strongly in light of his policy of gradual disengagement. If workers were paid a just wage, if an ethic of personal responsibility were widely in place (which, he said, requires good moral and religious formation), and if family breakdown and its resulting impoverishment of women and children were reversed government would not be called upon to exercise such an extravagant social welfare function ("it would not be looked to as the provider"). He said he thought that that there was a "distinct limit" to government being able to coercively make employers act rightly—to do things like provide a just wage. What he said he could do was to use the bully pulpit of the presidency to encourage them and to prod them, and promised that he was going to do this consistently. He would "call out companies publicly—bring to public notice" those whose actions in this and other ways did not show proper public responsibility." He didn't give unions a pass, however. If they acted in ways not truly respecting the well-being of their members—for example, excessive leadership salaries, which were "almost as bad as runaway business executive salaries"—he would publicly denounce them, too. He said that what government could do legislatively—this would be part of his legislative agenda to put before Congress—was to end the "false free trade" regimen that was in place. Putting up "stiff barriers" to trade had historically caused economic problems and international tensions, but governments should engage in "moderate protectionism," so that companies "don't just close down their domestic facilities, throw people out of work, have products made and services carried out overseas, and then just import these things back into the country." Such practices, at times, "bordered on the immoral, and ethics had to be at the center of economic life." Similarly, he was proposing legislation that companies beyond a certain size operating in interstate commerce could not just "pack up in the dead of night and close their facilities in a community with little notice and throw substantial numbers of people out of work." They would be required to give their workers and communities at least a year's notice.

His most significant legislative initiative was the flat tax that he had suggested in the campaign to replace the hundred-year-old graduated income tax and what he called "our current convoluted tax code that even IRS operatives cannot fathom and so often give out different answers to different citizens who inquire about what provisions mean." He spent a few minutes giving out the particulars of his proposal to "simplify the tax law," and explained how the effect would be "'revenue-neutral'—the federal government would bring in as much money as it presently does." In fact, he said, it would actually bring in more because of slightly higher tariffs tied in with his moderate protectionist trade proposal. As he had said during the campaign, the plan that he laid out would also replace the much criticized IRS—with many highly publicized scandals in recent years involving political favoritism, harassment of citizens by unmerited audits, and lavish retreats for its employees at posh resorts—with a smaller agency within the Treasury Department, as he had promised during the campaign.

Stephen also committed his administration to finally getting the federal debt under control. It had begun to cause economic shock waves, and now there seemed to be more political will in Congress to address it. He said the Penny Plan would now go into effect. After his further brief reiteration of the effect of it—he had discussed it during the election campaign—he looked straight into the cameras with his customary firm, resolute look in such situations and said: "This is what we're doing. There will be no turning back."

Perhaps most dramatic, however, was his proposing something like the NIRA of FDR's First New Deal, although without any dimension of coercion. Again, he had alluded to it during the campaign. He called on companies to work with others in their industries or sectors of the economy to set up "codes of conduct" that they would pledge to abide by on matters ranging from just wages to treatment of workers to involving workers more in workplace decision-making to product and service quality. He would use the presidential bully pulpit to help bring this about. He said he expected the most resistance from large companies, and asked small and medium-sized ones to step up first and work with him to help to bring this about and become examples for the rest of American economic life. He made it clear, however, that the cooperative spirit he was calling for could not be a cover for "cartelization" and the Department of Justice in his administration would "aggressively enforce" anti-trust laws.

He closed his address by returning to the themes of centralization of power and vague and overreaching laws. "Government can be put under control only when—in areas where it is not essential—it is sharply reduced. That cannot happen overnight, to be sure, but just like with cutting down on the programmatic role of government we must set ourselves on an unswerving path to make it happen gradually. The time to start is now: I have ordered an immediate and indefinite freeze on hiring federal civilian employees. No new government employees will be added and those who leave will not be replaced. Positions can be filled, if needed, by shifting employees not just from other agencies within departments, but from other departments. I have just issued a new executive order that will facilitate that. What's more, I have ordered that no new federal contract employees may be hired and, after an extensive review during the transition period, at my direction federal agencies under presidential supervision will terminate arrangements with numerous companies whose work is no longer truly needed after current contracts end.

"Speaking of federal contractors, I have abrogated the majority of executive orders issued by the previous two administrations. These concern mostly required wage levels and discrimination directives that did not conform to existing federal law.

"As far as vague and overbroad laws are concerned, these have resulted mostly because Washington politicians have not wanted to take the responsibility or face the political fallout for their actions. So, they have enacted vague and overbroad, but also overly long and complicated, statutes and passed on the responsibility for filling in the blanks and spelling out the meanings to the unelected and largely unaccountable federal bureaucracy. In the overly long legislation, things are often hidden that many of the members of Congress don't even know are there—but which come back to haunt and oppress our citizens. I have somewhat addressed these problems by the federal regulations that have been abrogated this week. I also intend to do another thing: unless a strong case can be make to me in individual cases, all legislation that is passed by Congress and comes to my desk that is longer than twenty pages in length—yes, that's *twenty pages*— will be automatically vetoed. All legislative proposals will be carefully scrutinized by my small White House staff—working in conjunction with members of Congress who see the problem—when the drafting is occurring to make sure that the meaning of provisions are clear and precise."

He had one more surprise in the era of a rampantly secular America: he ended the speech not just by saying "God bless you" to the viewing and listening audience, but also by reciting a prayer.

The public reaction continued to be uncertain since his initiatives went across the political spectrum. It seemed as if people were trying to assess things and as a result the ferocity that might have been expected with such an array of sweeping executive actions was muted. The media, commentators, and members of Congress and other important politicos wound up focusing on particular things that they didn't like, but even there they didn't seem to be able to bring themselves to a level of intense stridency since other things they did like balanced everything off. Certain interest groups were roused up the most. The national homosexual advocacy organizations organized a massive demonstration on the Mall in Washington. They promised the "biggest crowd in history defending gay rights." It took them two weeks after Stephen's first speech to pull it off, and even that time lag was ambitious to try to bring in people from around the country. As it happened—or rather, as Divine Providence willed—Washington was hit by the worst early February snowstorm since records were kept. The city was almost crippled for three days and the demonstration fizzled— as did the momentum they hoped to get quickly to oppose Stephen.

Stephen had spent a lot of time during the campaign trying to educate the public about many of these issues to prepare it for the initiatives he resolved to take, but he knew that the educational effort had to be ongoing. Stephen had anticipated that his stand on same-sex "marriage" would attract the most vigorous opposition and the providential bad weather gave him an extra measure of advantage. With his small staff's help, led by John Frost, he had lined up a number of speaking engagements in the weeks right after the nationally-broadcast speeches. Many were set to address this issue. They would be before receptive audiences, but he knew that the national media would trail along. There was no way they could ignore them because they were a major part of his early agenda. Remembering their successful campaign strategy, they made sure that the doors were as open to local media and to the "alternative" media as to the national media. The national media then could not so readily get away with ignoring or downplaying parts of his speeches. Also picking up from the campaign, they arranged to have people present to put forth their stories of persecution by state agencies for refusing to provide services for same-sex "weddings," who had been denied therapy to help them overcome same-sex attraction when they sought it, and who had been part of the homosexual scene before escaping it and related how sordid and violence-prone it was and how they had suffered from it. One man even told how a homosexualist advocacy group had manipulated him when he was younger and naïve to make him claim that he had been attacked by so-called "homophobes" when in fact he had experienced violent assaults by two older homosexual men. Stephen's *modus operandi* in these appearances was his usual: educate and confront (he attacked homosexualist organizations by name as he told of their deceit, intolerance, and bullying), but always in charity.

During his first hundred days, Stephen took to the road to educate, confront, and make the case on the other initiatives he had set out during those first speeches. He spoke to audiences that were not necessarily in ready agreement with him. He went to a TEA Party-type of citizens group in Indiana and then to a Chamber of Commerce gathering in the heart of corporate America, Delaware, to defend his call for a just wage and corporate responsibility to communities they had operations in. To the citizens group, he explained why support for a market economy does not mean that laissez faire is acceptable and that restraints even by government can be acceptable. They had been supportive of him in the campaign, but were not sure where they stood on these issues. After brilliantly answering their questions for an hour after his speech, they seemed virtually convinced. His intellectual acumen and equanimity garnered much respect from the Chamber audience, even if they didn't agree with him. He had showed during the campaign that, unlike most politicians, he was ready to stress the need for citizen responsibility—whether it involved personal morality, engaging in gainful employment instead of depending on government benefits, or actions by corporate decision-makers.

When he was back in Washington a week after the record-breaking snowstorm, he looked out a second story window just above the main entrance to the White House and observed a small demonstration in the distance in Lafayette Park. There was a young woman, apparently the organizer, holding a portable microphone. He walked outside onto the north lawn to get a better look. There were maybe seventy-five people there, and their picket signs addressed a range of issues from "marriage equality" to welfare funding to access to health care to corporate abuses to nuclear disarmament. Stephen could see that most of the demonstrators looked to be college-student age or twenty-somethings. Something motivated him to go out and talk to them. Maybe it was the same desire to engage people about the issues that led to his long question periods after his on-the-road speeches or maybe a subconscious yearning to be back in the classroom. He summoned the head of the White House Secret Service detail and asked him to walk over to the park with him. Stephen would permit only one agent to go with him. They were already clear about his unwillingness to have more than the minimal security necessary, so the head agent didn't even attempt to raise an objection. They walked in the least conspicuous path over to the park. Traffic now moved freely over Pennsylvania Avenue and E Street after years of security-motivated closures. Stephen had directed that they be reopened again, much to the pleasure of local civic groups who had argued that the closures disrupted the traffic flow and the connection of the White House with the surrounding federal areas.

When Stephen and the Secret Service agent came up from behind the crowd, the young woman organizer was the first to notice them since she was only one facing them. She stopped her diatribe suddenly and stared almost unbelievingly at them. Others began to turn around and a similar almost shocked look appeared on their faces. Before anyone could say anything, Stephen spoke up. "I'm here to talk with you."

He walked to the front of the crowd next to the still startled young woman and stretched out his hand.

"What's your first name," he asked. He deliberately didn't ask for her full name because he didn't want her to think that her name would go into some government database.

"Terri."

"It's nice to meet you, Terri. I think you know what my name is." Laughter went through the crowd. Stephen had broken the ice.

"I see signs with a lot of different messages on them, Terri. Which one of these issues are the most important to you all?"

Someone said "corporate greed," and another said, "Yes, Wall Street's running the country." A scruffy-looking young woman in the front of the crowd said, "Women's rights. A woman has to be able to control her own body." Terri picked up on what she had been saying to the crowd when Stephen approached: "Workers are treated poorly. They are not paid fairly."

"That's two major issues right there: economic justice and abortion," Stephen replied. "Let's talk about those."

He reminded them about what he had said on the campaign trail and in his early presidential addresses about the need for a just wage and a code of responsibility for companies and how the law should require them "to not just pick up stakes and move overseas and leave communities high and dry." What followed was both a small lesson about basic American law—"be careful not just to criticize 'corporations,' since a lot of different things are corporations," including the non-profit advocacy organization that Terri said she worked for—and a summary of the basics of Catholic social teaching (even while he didn't call it that) regarding the dignity of labor and the rights of workers. He didn't just lecture to them, however, but proceeded as he often had done in the classroom. He engaged them in an almost Socratic-like fashion, gently asking them obvious questions that would elicit answers that would help them see certain things. At one point, he asked them if they thought that government should try to force corporations by law to act a certain way. Many, almost reflexively, nodded in the affirmative. Someone farther back in the crowd said, almost sneeringly, that corporations can't be reasoned with, "like you want to"—referring to Stephen's talking about using the presidential bully pulpit to improve corporate behavior. Stephen asked who had said that. A young man with a long beard worked his way through the crowd to the front with all eyes on him, and in a self-assured manner said, "I did." Stephen proceeded to point out certain problems, such as how government bureaucracy inefficiency often stymied regulatory efforts, how once regulatory regimens were in place corporate lobbying often was able to move them in ways that would be favorable to business, and how particularly powerful companies were often able to use regulatory schemes to the detriment of their competitors. "Don't you think," Stephen asked, "that it would be better to try to motivate ethical behavior, by presidential prodding and in other ways, and to try to change attitudes of corporate types to make them want to be more responsive both to workers and the community—and even to show them that it's in their interest to do so?" The young man didn't respond, though he didn't seem convinced. The expressions on the faces of some others in the crowd seemed to show that they were at least wondering if what he was saying made some sense.

Then another bearded young man near the front of the crowd spoke up and said, "I'm for the government running the big corporations. That will solve the problem."

Stephen turned to him. "You're aware, aren't you, of the problems that has caused where it has been done?" He went on to talk about the serious economic and social difficulties that typified socialist states, and not just the most extreme (that is, Communist) ones. He explained why the very nature of socialist economies caused these problems to occur. It was clear that much of the mostly young crowd had heard nothing like this before. Most were listening to his professorial, but gentle and respectful discourse. Someone else, of course, could not have captured their attention as he did. The crowd might have just repeatedly jeered at his comments. The fact that this was the U.S. President in their midst, talking to them after coming on his own from the White House to meet with them—even if they would never have voted for him—made a difference.

Then he turned to the young woman who raised the abortion question. She started to challenge him, asking why he opposed abortion when it threatened women's rights. On this issue, Stephen could see that the young crowd was considerably more resistant from the get-go. He wasn't surprised, since probably all they had ever heard about was sexual and reproductive freedom. He returned to the Socratic approach with which he had begun the conversation on the previous topic. In the course of the back-and-forth discussion, he brought up the biological realities of unborn life, how the unborn child simply could not be seen somehow as an extension of the woman's body, whether abortion really helps a woman, the disconnect between destroying the unborn and respecting human rights and dignity otherwise, how permitting abortion had led to a lessened respect for human life in other ways, how the question was really not whether the unborn child was human but the value given to that life and the broader implications for that kind of ethic, and why the law had every bit as much reason to proscribe abortion as other criminal acts. After the discussion had gone on for nearly a half an hour the young woman spoke up and seemed more hostile than ever. She said insistently, "It's still my body. This is still my right. I can't be made to have a baby I don't want."

There was a long moment of silence, as Stephen looked into her eyes. What he saw was a tormented person. She looked away, as if to try to hide that torment from him. He could see what was really going on with her. She had had an abortion at some point and was experiencing the emotional trauma and guilt that eventually caught up with many, probably most, women in the aftermath. In the meantime, the Secret Service agent touched Stephen on the shoulder. "You asked me, sir, to let you know when it was fifteen minutes before your scheduled appointment." Stephen nodded and quietly thanked him.

He then thanked all the people in the crowd for the chance to dialogue with them. He shook the hand of the organizer. Then he turned to his young pro-abortion antagonist and said quietly, "Forgiveness can always be forthcoming."

Two days later, a much less behaved group of demonstrators assembled on the sidewalk in front of the White House. The hundred or so demonstrators staged a sit-in in front of the entrance used for White House tours. The head of the Secret Service detail summoned the Metropolitan Police to assist in arresting them. Stephen intervened. He didn't like the idea of arresting demonstrators unless they were violent, physically threatening, or had damaged property. He thought a different approach would actually be more effective in discouraging such actions. "We should tire out law-breaking demonstrators and make the personal cost to them more onerous than a few hours in jail, a flood of prosecutions that will clog up the courts, and an eventual legal slap on the wrist after which they'll be back at it again." He ordered that a couple of buses be quickly brought from Fort Lesley J. McNair in Washington, which is the site of the National Defense University, and that the demonstrators be rounded up and put on the buses. The demonstrators assumed that they were going to be taken to D.C. jails and processed. Instead, Stephen directed that groups of the demonstrators be brought to several far-out points in the Washington metropolitan area and some let off at each place. The spots at which they were let off were far enough from a Metro stop and they were so separated from each other that their sit-in activity would be over for the day. Stephen believed that if one such response wouldn't discourage them from trying this again, doing it a few times would. "We'll drop them off farther and farther out in the metropolitan area each time." His calculation was correct. Most of the demonstrators never came back. A small number did; they were the "professional protestors." After this approach was used several times the illegal protest activity ended.

Stephen was awakened in the early hours the next morning after the sit-in episode with word that a race riot had broken out in Las Vegas. This was the latest in a series of race riots that had rocked U.S. cities for the past five years. The view was increasingly being expressed that the two previous national administrations, controlled by the other party, had borne a share of the responsibility because they had fanned the flames of racial animosity by talking frequently about "African-American oppression" in the country, seemed to support racial firebrands who went from city to city stirring up discontented elements in inner city areas, and provided almost no national support to local and state authorities trying to quell the turmoil. The precipitating event in Las Vegas, as so often had been the case, was an encounter of an adult black male with the police. In this case, it began as a traffic stop. An unruly crowd began to gather and started to threaten the officer. He radioed for help and, when four additional squad cars arrived, the police soon found themselves being pelted with debris. Soon, gunshots rang out from one of the nearby buildings. One of the squad cars was hit, but no one was hurt. Soon looting was occurring and as the night went on it spread throughout that part of the city. Fires were set, and quickly a block of mostly abandoned buildings was ablaze. The police had to retreat, and the reports were saying that the rioters were virtually in control of that part of the city. The rioters also took control of a small section of Interstate 15 that went through the city, stopping traffic. They apparently had even attacked some motorists on the freeway after stopping them and overturned their cars. The mayor and governor, both from the other party, tried to downplay the seriousness of the situation in their initial public comments. They appealed for calm, but no calm was forthcoming. There were further reports of clashes between black and Hispanic gangs and some suggestions that gang activity had either triggered or inflamed the situation.

Stephen had already planned how he would deal with such an eventuality. He was firmly convinced that the continual race rioting in the country—the disgust about which was thought to have helped propel him into the presidency—was due to the tepid national response. He talked with two of his aides on his small White House staff—the old transition team people—with whom he had discussed the rioting issue before taking office. Then he issued two orders, one federalizing a portion of the Nevada National Guard and the other to the Secretary of the Army to deploy them immediately to the area of the riot in a manner that would most quickly and reliably end it. His condition was that the Guardsmen should utilize lethal force only if absolutely necessary to protect their and other people's lives. He wanted the rioters dispersed and subdued by non-lethal means. There was no question about his authority to federalize the National Guard in response to violence. That by itself was enough legal and constitutional justification. The rationale for that went all the way back to George Washington's leading of troops to put down the Whiskey Rebellion.

The interference with movement on an interstate highway further buttressed the case for federal intervention.

Stephen ordered that the deployment begin immediately, and said it was urgent. The Secretary of the Army personally directed the operation and updated Stephen hourly. By noon, a sizable National Guard contingent from units around Nevada had arrived on the scene. Within three hours, they had gained complete control of the situation, over two hundred people were in custody, and peace was restored. No lethal force had been used, there were no deaths, and only minor injuries were reported—almost all among the rioters. The Guardsmen and the local police had received information about the location of a secret headquarters in that part of the city of one of the gangs. They raided it, captured a dozen gang members, and confiscated a cache of weapons including military-grade rifles.

The national reaction to the quick suppression of the riot was a kind of stunned satisfaction. At a press conference early in the evening, the mayor started to complain about the Las Vegas police being "shunted aside" by the federalized forces. However, he was assailed by a barrage of reporters' questions that challenged his ineffectiveness in quelling the rioting before the presidential action. He quickly backed off. Similarly, the governor issued a statement expressing dissatisfaction about the federalization. That was met with much criticism in the state's media, who wondered why the governor had taken no action. He was silent after that. Even though the national media were no friends of Stephen's, they were almost in awe about how he had handled the serious matter so decisively and with virtually no bloodshed. If they would have wanted to allege something like that he was responding as quickly and forcefully as he was for racial reasons, that was blunted by the apparent gang involvement. Opinion polling confirmed the public perception of Stephen's decisiveness, alacrity, and know-how in stopping the riot, and the contrast with the half-hearted and ineffectual response of the previous administrations. If the public was unsure about the sweeping actions he announced in his first speeches, he won its support overwhelmingly with this and it would boost those other initiatives. His action here began to implant in people's minds—at least those who were not dye-in-the-wool leftist ideologues—that he was a true leader. The would-be troublemakers and firebrands also got a message that Stephen was someone who "shouldn't be fooled with." After five years of racial turmoil, there were to be no more riots.

It was not that he would be paying no attention to race relations, however. The network of black ministers and solid, supportive black local leaders that he and John Frost had started to build up during the campaign would be further developed and would begin in earnest grassroots, local efforts around the country to try to build character and responsible citizenship and solve problems in that community.

About a month after Stephen's stunning announcements of his first week, reports were circulating of high-level professional bureaucrats trying to obstruct his initiatives. They seemed to think that matters were business as usual, and they would be able to excessively influence and even dominate their Cabinet secretaries and under-secretaries and quietly sidetrack the efforts or even bury them—part of the "capture" phenomenon. They drastically underestimated the people that Stephen had put into place. He had chosen top Cabinet-level appointees who were in line with his principles and could be tough and in control of their agencies. Stephen called a Cabinet meeting, a practice that had fallen out of practice in administrations for some time. A plan was set up whereby the Cabinet secretaries would closely scrutinize top civil servants, meet with them regularly, be clear about their expectations and confront them routinely if necessary to make sure they were being accountable to the political leadership, and to arrange quick discipline if there was any hint of resistance or dilatoriness. Stephen also made it clear that while he was relying on his appointees, he would not hesitate to intervene directly if the case warranted it. He personally ordered the removal of one high career bureaucrat from a decision-making position as a bureau chief and he was put into an inconsequential position. The message was quickly gotten not only by the top bureaucrats but also down the line. Stephen meant to do what should be a central task of a president, but which they seldom attend to: get control of their own executive branch.

After Stephen's first speech, only two state governors moved to order their county clerks not to issue marriage licenses to same-sex couples. Certainly, gubernatorial and legislative opinion was strongly against same-sex "marriage" in a number of states, but it seemed as if the public officials in other states weren't sure how to proceed. They weren't familiar with a case in which a president announced flatly that he would not enforce a Supreme Court decision or precedent. The governor of Arkansas was one of the two who issued the order to the county clerks and announced that no same-sex "marriages" would any longer take place in the state. He also said that any licenses previously issued pursuant to the Supreme Court's decision would be considered invalid.

The ACLU and a homosexualist advocacy group quickly took a case into the federal district court for the Western District of Arkansas in Fayetteville. They acted on behalf of two lesbian University of

241

Arkansas professors who had "married" each other. The judge decided to take on the president and ruled that their "marriage" was valid in light of the Supreme Court's *Obergefell v. Hodges* decision that claimed that same-sex "marriage" had to be permitted under the equal protection clause of the Constitution. The judge, one Willard Pendleton, was a notorious leftist; he had been appointed five years before by one of the presidents of the other party. In his order to the governor, he stated that "the courts were supreme when it came to interpreting the Constitution."

Picking a fight with the President was one the courts were bound to lose. Stephen thought there might be some kind of pushback from the Supreme Court, but he figured they would be cautious because they would be attuned to the risk of a loss of their influence and prestige. Here was a federal trial court judge who did not seem to have the same sense of discretion. Maybe he didn't think Stephen was serious because the norm for so long had been that the courts went essentially unchallenged and unchecked. His response to the governor showed a kind of judicial arrogance and swagger—intensified by ideological fervor—that Stephen had no intention of being intimidated by. The ACLU and the advocacy group, too, had long since gotten spoiled by getting what they wanted by socially activist federal judges while the political branches sat tepidly on the sidelines.

Stephen got on the phone with Governor Ted Williston, who he had gotten to know from his party's governors association when he was still Pennsylvania's chief executive. He had supported Stephen from early on in the primary campaign. Stephen had discussed with his advisors back in the transition period how judicial resistance would be addressed. He now began to put it into action. He was quite well aware that if the judge were not faced down, the Supreme Court would be emboldened and the judicial archonocracy that had become implanted in the U.S. would not be ended. Stephen told Governor Williston that he was ordering the U.S. Marshals in Arkansas, backed up by an additional small contingent he was dispatching from Washington, to return Judge Pendleton's written order to him at his office and they were to carry with them a letter from Stephen saying, first, that the order was illegal since the court had no authority to act to uphold a Supreme Court decision that violated the Constitution, second, that the President as he previously had announced would enforce that decision nowhere in the country, third, that the Marshal Service was under Stephen's orders not to deliver any more of the judge's orders to the Governor, and, fourth, that U.S. Marshals were posted day and night outside of both Williston's office at the state capitol building and the

242

governor's official residence to intercept any other individual sent by the judge to deliver the order and would refuse it and remove the courier from those places. Stephen had ordered the people from the Marshals Service national headquarters in Washington to go there to check any foot-dragging by the local Marshals who ordinarily worked for the judge carrying out his orders, even though the Service is an executive branch agency.

If the leftist national media had been subdued in its response when he announced his numerous bold initiatives, it was fierce in its response to his action here. They called it things like "an executive usurpation" and said Stephen was "intimidating" Judge Pendleton and "threatening judicial independence." Stephen outflanked them, however. He already had his numerous speaking engagements arranged. John Frost and his staff always made sure they received as intense media coverage as possible, especially by local media as had been the *modus operandi* during the campaign. After the Judge made his gambit, Stephen had his staff carefully scrutinize his political and judicial background, which enabled him to show how the Judge had a long history of reading his leftist ideology into his decisions and letting it skew his interpretation of the Constitution. So Stephen shifted his talks exclusively to this matter, and additional talks were scheduled in Arkansas where Stephen and Governor Williston appeared together. He not only hit hard about the judge's background, but intensified and deepened his discussion from the campaign of the role of the courts under the Constitution, the justification of presidential and Congressional actions to check the courts and historical background of executive resistance to them, and explained repeatedly how the Supreme Court's same-sex "marriage" decision was an affront to the Constitution. It was his usual approach: confrontation—hitting even harder than usual—along with explanation, and always in charity. In a bold and unprecedented move, when back in Washington he even arranged brief presidential speeches on the sidewalks and public spaces right outside of the major national media companies' Washington headquarters. There was no way they could ignore these. When they sent out their reporters, he took their questions and engaged in back-and-forth dialogues with them in which he clearly bested them. There was no doubt that Stephen would not budge. He was impervious to the strong media criticisms and was effectively making his case to the public despite them. Actually, Stephen's accessibility to the media—he came before them much more frequently than the previous two administrations of the other party—earned respect from them and probably motivated them to blunt their criticism of him. The full force of the presidency was brought to bear on Judge

Pendleton. Pendleton was beaten. This was to set the stage for a much greater clash between Stephen and the judiciary later.

Some of the regulations that Stephen rescinded had been put in place by the previous two administrations because of their almost blind ideological attachment to the notion of global warming. Stephen knew that the rescission of the regulations would bring savage attacks from environmental advocacy groups and the media would try to portray him as something like a "flat-earther" for disputing this deeply held, almost blind-faith belief of the left. Stephen arranged for leading scientists who rejected the claim of global warming to come to the White House and appear with him at what wound up being a lengthy press conference. They did not mince any words, but attacked the claim directly as contrary to the evidence and based almost on conjecture. The support network that John Frost had built up during the campaign then arranged for them and other scientists who disputed global warming—some of whom had been virtually silenced by ideologically driven people within the scientific community—to go on a speaking tour. Again, the coordinators of the network arranged for heavy media coverage of the talks, pulling in especially local media outlets. This was effective at putting the environmental zealots on the defensive and by the end of the tour the national media and commentators were not talking about the rescission much anymore.

Stephen's small staff and the Secretary of Health and Human Services were working on his promised health care summit, which would take place in early summer. In the meantime, Stephen was working with the Congressional leaders of his party, which had the majority in both houses, on the formal repeal of the legislation that had enabled the federal government to essentially manage American health care. Since he had made clear that he would provide no funding for it in the budget, it was as a practical matter dead anyhow. The other party and assorted interest groups had been making noise about challenging Stephen's decision in the courts, but Stephen's blunt public response was that the courts have no authority under the Constitution to order appropriations and he would simply ignore any court decision to do so. In fact, he said, the Constitution was so "utterly clear" about this that his administration wouldn't even respond to a lawsuit or argue the matter in court. His stand against the Judge Pendleton in Arkansas made clear that he was serious about taking on the federal courts when they violated the Constitution. It left them unsure about whether it was worth trying to push the matter in court.

Stephen was not content just to change the direction of public policy and end judicial abuse. He meant to begin the effort of recovering the country's much-battered traditions and to reignite an understanding in the minds of his countrymen about what is needed to sustain a democratic republic like America's Founders had established. So, in the first hundred days he arranged three crucial "public seminars" at the White House on "Recovering America's Religious and Christian Heritage," "Recovering the Truth about American History," and "Recovering the True Meaning of the U.S. Constitution and Constitutional Tradition." He invited both key religious leaders and sound scholars and writers in history, political science, constitutional law, and American religion to the first one to discuss the central role of religion (as understood by the Founders and others) for any political order, especially a republic, and the Christian character of earlier American culture. He was careful to include in the seminar leading Jewish scholars and prominent rabbis, and even two leading moderate Moslem figures, an imam and a scholar, who emphasized that a solid Christian culture in America was good for their co-religionists, too. This seminar paved the way for his major push to bring traditional religion back into the center of American public life that began in earnest a short time later. The second seminar brought together noted historians—true scholars who were concerned about the facts, not pushing their ideology—to begin the effort of restoring in the public mind a true picture of America's past, instead of one poisoned by group grievances, claims of systemic oppression, racial and gender theory, historical revisionism and all the rest. The third "public seminar" featured leading constitutional scholars, figures from the legal community, and constitutional historians who simply brought forth all the solid evidence to show what the "original intent" was, what the different parts of the Constitution and the Bill of Rights provisions meant, how the common law and the natural law formed the framework for the document, what the correct understanding of rights was, and if and how the natural law—correctly understood—could be turned to in constitutional jurisprudence. The White House made an all-out effort to focus broad public attention on these seminars and to disseminate afterwards the results of the discussion that had taken place.

Stephen and John knew how massive efforts would be made by leftists and their media allies to discredit the figures who took part in the seminars, so they were careful about selecting well-respected figures, known for level-headed efforts and scholarship, and to keep pounding home their credentials. After the seminars ended, the network that Stephen and John had worked to build up went into action. They not only helped to publicize the seminar discussions, but went to work establishing small discussion groups in communities around the

245

country—the network was made up especially of local community-based groups, it was the principle of subsidiarity at work—to continue and broaden the discussion of these crucial topics across the country. Stephen also continued to "take to the road," using the same strategy as during the campaign of seeking out exposure on local media outlets, even though now the national media couldn't just ignore him since he was, after all, the president and he showed them by his rallies outside their offices that he would "take the fight to them." He didn't just defend his initiatives, but went on a continuous offensive against his critics to show their flawed thinking and ideological biases. He kept to his regimen of attack and explain, attack and explain, but always in charity. He often engaged in back-and-forth dialogues, and with his intelligence, knowledge, and debating skills invariably outdid his adversary—but always while demonstrating kindness. More and more people heard him and he gained more and more respect among the citizenry. He was helped by the facts that many were fed up with what the country had become and were open to sharp new directions and were captivated by someone in high public office who actually meant and did what he said.

His road trips and focus on local media further impressed rank-and-file citizens. Here was a president who went out among the people. He actually visited their local communities, even ones that were small, after he was in office.

At the end of the first hundred says, as a prominent political commentator put it, "the country's head was spinning." Another said that he could think of no presidential administration, including FDR's, where a first hundred days "had set the course for so sweeping of a change in the country's fundamental direction." Some conservative commentators seemed almost like the leftist ones. They were too ensconced in a "comfortable conservatism," in which they would be critics but seemed to almost hope that nothing would truly change. They had long-since become pampered Washington insiders. Some, who were really classical liberals, didn't like his economics. Some, however, extolled Stephen, with one saying that his confrontation with the courts meant "that someone was finally taking checks and balances seriously." A leading leftist talking head lamented that Stephen "was intent on forcibly destroying the progressive tradition." They didn't know what was yet to come.

CHAPTER 8

Constitutional Crisis And The Cause Of Life

A s the torrent of Stephen's initiatives of the first hundred days continued to sweep across the country, another development outside of politics created a small stir in the Nation's Capital. The Holy See named Stephen's old friend, Bishop George LaGrange, as Archbishop of Washington. Archbishop Scanlon, who was at Stephen's inauguration with Bishop LaGrange, had reached the mandatory retirement age of seventy-five just about a month after that. It was not clear since this was such a high profile see that the Vatican would quickly accept his routine letter of resignation, but it did. It is even more surprising when it announced his replacement only a month later, and outright stunning when the bishop of a small diocese like Greensburg was the one selected—and even more so that he had been at the helm there for only about a year and a half. Church watchers wondered about the meaning of it even further. Here was a bishop known for his unwavering defense of orthodoxy, tough discipline, restoration of Church traditions in liturgy, and an abject refusal to give an inch in accommodating to the secular times and culture—he was called "the young bishop who was bringing back the 1950s"—elevated to this high position in the Catholic Church in the U.S. The traditional and the orthodox often clashed with the neo-modernist and the accommodationist in the Washington Archdiocese, which many viewed as the center of the Church in the U.S. Some were saying that the LaGrange appointment meant that these latter elements were not going to be tolerated much longer. There was also some speculation that the Holy See had learned about Bishop LaGrange's friendship with Stephen and that this was the decisive factor in his selection.

LaGrange took the leadership of the Washington Archdiocese shortly after his appointment, although the Mass celebrating his formal installation ceremony would be in June. When Stephen heard the news of his appointment he called his old friend to congratulate him and assure him of his prayers. The Archbishop-designate told Stephen that he hoped he would attend the installation Mass and Stephen said he would not hesitate to be the first U.S. president to attend an installation of a new archbishop of Washington. He also asked LaGrange, who was going to be in Washington to meet the current archdiocesan officials the following week, if he would come to the White House for a quiet meeting before anyone in the city recognized him. The tone of Stephen's voice made his friend realize that he needed to turn to him again as a trusted confidant, like he did when he was pondering the decision to run for the nation's highest office. "I wouldn't in a hundred years miss a chance to visit the White House," joked LaGrange. "I've never been there." Then more seriously, conveying to Stephen that he understood his current need, added, "And we can talk."

Stephen asked to be summoned immediately when the archbishop-designate arrived at the White House. He met LaGrange at the entrance and the two men embraced. Stephen ushered him right into the Oval Office, with instructions that short of an emergency or sudden international crisis they not be disturbed.

As they sat down, LaGrange spoke up first. "Stephen—Mr. President—you certainly have aroused the country. You're doing exactly what I knew you would do. I also know that you'll stay the course."

"Fr. George," Stephen had always called him that even after he had ascended to the hierarchy. "With all that, I'm facing a decision that will make all that seem almost like college-boy stuff. It concerns the whole abortion mess. I can't allow the massacre to go on any longer— the wholesale killing, the selling of body parts, the ugly profiteering in the business of killing a whole group—and babies no less. I think it's time to forget about playing a judicial appointment game—if I'll even get any Supreme Court appointments. Actually, the Court seems to have a solid leftist majority now and the leftists are the younger justices. Some say it's close on abortion, but I'm not so sure. I think it's doubtful that I would get enough appointments even in eight years to change it. That's not even thinking of the full-court press that would come in the Senate to derail every nominee. That will probably happen with even lower-court nominees. The 'judicial strategy' was tried by Reagan and, frankly, was a failure—the worst failure of his presidency. Removing the Court's jurisdiction over abortion cases? It could never get through Congress. If it did, the Court would find some rationale to declare it unconstitutional despite what Article Three of the Constitution says. I also think that now that I'm in the position—the position that only one man is in—to act decisively about it, I should make the move. It may not work, however. I'm sure it's the thing that has to be done, though nothing like this has ever been attempted. It could indeed blow up in my face in a thousand different ways." Stephen's brow furled and LaGrange could see the anguish unmistakably in his face.

"I can assure you that what you tell me here is confidential—period. What is it that you want to do?"

"I want to federalize a certain portion of the National Guard in all of the states that have abortion facilities and deploy them, along with U.S. Marshals, to shut down the facilities. They will dismantle the facilities and shutter them. If the courts try to stop us and order them reopened, I'll just ignore them. I can't order the Justice Department to prosecute any abortionists because there is no federal law to that effect. Before the 1973 abortion cases, that was a matter of state criminal law. Effectively, I would be saying that the Court's interpretation of the Constitution in *Roe v. Wade* and *Doe v. Bolton* is rejected. Perhaps, I'm making a different interpretation: that the unborn child's right to life is protected under the Constitution. One finds that in the common law tradition that Blackstone discussed. It's the old departmental notion of constitutional construction—that any of the branches can authoritatively interpret the Constitution. Mostly, though, I would be using executive power to protect the most basic right of a whole class of citizens, the unborn. People would say I don't have the power to do that, they would claim it's a gross abuse of power and tyrannical. It would be something like I said in the campaign debate, however: If some renegade state governor put a whole ethnic group into a concentration camp and the courts went along, would anyone seriously say that the president lacked the inherent power to stop that?"

"Stephen, it sounds like you already know what you want to do. Why do you need to discuss it with me?"

"Fr. George, you know that such a move would be unprecedented. Beyond even something like Jackson refusing to enforce the Court's order to stop the Cherokee Indians' removal from Georgia or Lincoln refusing the Court's habeas corpus order during the Civil War. To be sure, the tussle with the judge in Arkansas anticipated something like this, but that is small potatoes compared to what I'm talking about here. I'd be attacked from many quarters—it would probably be one of the most vicious attacks on a sitting president in American history—and

249

once it's done, it must be sustained and there would be no turning back. Any turning back would essentially destroy my presidency, rendering it completely ineffectual. Still, I can't be sure if I could sustain it for the rest of my presidency; it could be like an occupation force in a conquered nation."

"Stephen, I don't have to tell you that you have to weigh that carefully. You've always done that before in all the decisions you've made. Do you have any uncertainty that this is the right action to take?"

"Fr. George, I don't see what else can be done. Maybe, maybe, with the technological advancements, more and more people will come to see that there's no doubt that the unborn child is human. That has been happening for some time. Still, it could be a generation, maybe more, before the slaughter ends. The certainty that this is a human life doesn't seem to mean much to the 'movers and shakers.' Certain lives simply don't matter to them, and now euthanasia is advancing. I don't have to tell you that. These people, so used to being in control, have dug in. I think that we'll succeed in stopping this only by an abrupt and decisive action that simply ends it or ends it as much as possible."

"What are you concerned about, then, that they'll impeach you?"

"They couldn't come close. Even though our party has been tepid in so many ways for so long and some of them will complain or head for cover, they won't let something like that happen."

"It may be easy to shut down the abortuaries, but what will you do about the hospitals that are doing abortions and the abortifacients that are now in use all over the place?"

"I can direct Jim Lewis, the HHS Secretary, to issue a new regulation that hospitals that continue to do any abortions risk having their federal funds immediately terminated. As far as abortifacient birth control pills are concerned—which seem to now be most of the oral contraceptives that are on the market—I can also direct Jim to revoke approval for their production and distribution. The FDA commissioners—the majority of whom are pro-abortion—may squeal, but when a presidential administration circumvents or goes against them they have no choice but to fall in line. Of course, I would not just throw around the weight of the national executive and think that that alone solves the problem. There will also have to be a major effort to win the hearts and minds of the public. I'll be working with our network and with the major pro-life organizations to make the case in an unprecedented way for the unborn child's humanity and to drive home the brutality of abortion. We'll not just answer the attacks from the pro-abortionists, but relentlessly argue for the cause of life—every argument on every front. My plan is to invite the leaders of not only the national but also regional pro-life groups to the White House the day after we close the clinics. I'll ask them to be as active as they can to publicly defend my action. Like I did during the campaign, I'll line up many women to publicly say how bad the abortion option was for them. I also plan to line up the legal scholars to explain to the public why such a move against a flawed judicial precedent is not outside of rightful executive power, but is a perfectly acceptable way to check a gross abuse of the Supreme Court. In the midst of all this, I won't be holing up in the White House but will be on the road confronting the anti-life people and also educating—the same as I have been doing all along. With this, it will have to be a relentless effort, but I'm prepared for it."

"Stephen, " the Archbishop-designate said, "It sounds as if you have made up your mind about this and have a clear plan. Why did you want to consult me?"

"Fr. George," Stephen replied, "You know that my Achilles' heel is my confidence. I know what has to be done, but I'm frequently wondering if I have it in me and if I can in the final analysis stand up under all the pressure."

"You've always done it up to now." Bishop LaGrange was silent for a long minute, then he said, "Stephen, the reason I encouraged you to seek this office was because I knew that this was in the hand of Providence, that you were God's instrument to do very important things at a critical time. I had a certain conviction of it, partly because I knew you were the one capable of doing it."

Any lingering uncertainty Stephen had completely dissipated after his meeting with his old friend. With a coterie of only a few very close advisers—John Frost, Jim Lewis, Attorney General Mike Larribee, and his White House staffer and chief liaison with John's network of supporters, Mary Molinski, who had been a long-time Catholic journalist and activist—things were confidentially planned over the next several days. He quietly consulted with Defense Secretary Willard Cullotte, the conservative academic military expert and one-time Marine who had come to Stephen's attention from his consistent writing about the dangers of the "social experiments" in the armed services of the previous leftist administrations and his reputation as a courageous opponent of secular leftist forces in the academy. Stephen didn't want to arrange White House meetings with him because with so many eyes on the Pentagon it would have been hard to disguise that "something big" was in the offing. Stephen needed to bring him into the loop, however, to help manage the federalization of the National Guard.

As the end of Stephen's "first hundred days" approached, he launched probably the most direct and dramatic executive challenge to the Supreme Court since Jackson—but one that would have much greater and broader effect on American life. It would without doubt be the most forceful blow delivered by the traditional/natural law side in the whole culture war. Despite the steady erosion of support for legal abortion, no one really knew what the public's reaction would be to such an initiative—even with the emphatic rhetorical and educational effort Stephen and his network would make to defend it. Stephen could expect utterly savage treatment from most of the media and the other party, and even from some in his own party. The attacks would be much more intense and consistent than had been directed even against his bold initiatives up to now. They may blunt even his own planned "go to the public" campaign, but that was the risk he had to take. If he was going to do this, he knew that it had to be at this early stage of his presidency. This was not just because the wholesale slaughter of the youngest Americans could not be allowed to continue one more day, but also because he was in the strongest position he would perhaps ever be during his time in office and the chances of a serious impeachment effort at this point and with his party controlling Congress were almost non-existent.

The plans were all set and, as usual, Stephen was able to maintain the tightest secrecy owing, no doubt, to the small circle of advisers he routinely employed. On the designated day—the ninety-ninth of Stephen's presidency—the Marshals and the National Guard were deployed as dawn broke to every abortion facility in the country. Careful research had been done, so that not a single one was missed. Stephen had issued the National Guard federalization and call-up order—which had involved only a small number of units—only twenty-four hours before. They had been given their orders only a few hours before and Larribee and Culotte were directly in charge of the operation. The commanders of the different units—who had been checked out for their trustworthiness and records of competence—were given their specific orders only right before they left for the targeted locations. They brought tools and building supplies, and they changed locks at all the facilities and boarded them all up. Then two armed guards were stationed around the clock to make sure that no one entered the buildings or the parts of the buildings where the abortion clinics had operated. It was publicly announced that the facilities would be turned over to their owners, if they were other than the clinic operators, so long as the clinics were no longer permitted to operate there.

As with Stephen's other initiatives, the media, hostile interest groups, and the other party were caught off-balance. While, in a certain sense, they now had come to expect that Stephen was prepared to take unprecedented executive actions no one expected something like this. Actually, though, the Obama presidency had laid the groundwork for such actions with his executive orders allowing millions of illegal immigrants to remain in the U.S. and get work permits, unilaterally imposing a range of environmental standards, and pressuring public high schools to let students who "identified" as a member of the opposite sex use restrooms and locker rooms of that sex under threat of yanking their federal funding if they didn't comply. Stephen moved before the media could. With John Frost leading the way, he arranged a unique Skype-type link-up with local television and radio outlets around the country—the same bypass-the-national-media strategy that he had consistently been employing—to announce and explain his action. He framed it entirely in terms of protecting a class of persons from destruction, which also gave him the opportunity to educate about the realities of unborn life. Mary Molinski arranged a conference call with all the major pro-life leaders and urged them to immediately publicly praise Stephen's action, which to a man they did. She had wondered if some who were known for favoring a more moderate approach would go along, but she talked them out of any hesitancy they might have had. She also began to encourage local pro-life activists to come to the locations of the shuttered abortion clinics to stage small rallies supporting Stephen's action. They showed up long before the pro-abortion groups could get something organized. John Frost from the White House and the network in the field focused attention, as they began to talk to the media, on the massive numbers of stories of how abortionists' practices had harmed women. They also hammered away anew at the notorious, diabolical selling of the body parts of aborted babies by Planned Parenthood to researchers that the media had mostly ignored since it had first been revealed some years before.

When Stephen asked for media time to speak to the nation about his action, all the traditional cable networks readily granted it. They did not want to be embarrassed again by his showing up outside their Washington headquarters and leading pro-Bernard rallies. He was scheduled to go on the air at 9:00 Eastern time that evening. In the meantime, the early media reports were scaring certain members of his party, including in the leadership, in Congress. It was the vintage reaction of what had for a long time been the mainstream of the party: a fearful, "don't rock the boat," "play the game" kind of reaction that many believed had cost them so many elections. What remained of this element—they were still well enough placed in both houses of Congress—could never quite grasp the civilizational crisis of the time and the deep-seated threat that had developed to the American constitutional regime. Even though Stephen's election had challenged, maybe even debunked, their conventional wisdom they still didn't get it that these were not times when politics as usual was in order. It was not a time for a tepid attitude.

The Senate Majority Leader, Hugh Bessemer of Indiana, was one of these, even while the leadership just below him, the Majority Whip and the party's Conference Chairman, were solidly in Stephen's corner and realized that the time of being political wallflowers was long since over. Bessemer and two of the majority members of the Senate Judiciary Committee, though not the chairman, hastily arranged a meeting with Stephen at the White House as soon as the word broke in the media about his action.

Bessemer spoke first at the meeting, with a look that betrayed fear and worry. "Mr. President, I'm going to speak very frankly to you about this. Nothing like this has been attempted before. You are going against decades of judicial precedent. The country will be up in arms against you. Our opponents will say that you are undermining constitutional government—actually, they will use much harsher terms. They will say that you are shutting down legal businesses and imposing something like marshal law. That may not be what you're intending, but it will be made to look that way. Your presidency could be mortally hurt, and so could your party. In fact, the cause of ending abortion could be badly set back by this."

The other senators from the Judiciary Committee, William Hill of New Hampshire and Lewis Linkletter of Minnesota chimed in. "Mr. President," Hill said, "You should simply use the appointment process. *Roe v. Wade* could eventually be overturned." Linkletter nodded vigorously, with the same half-fearful, half-worried look as Bessemer.

"Gentlemen," Stephen quickly started to respond, "I appreciate your coming to tell me your thoughts, but respectfully I must tell you that you are not correct. These cases have stood for going on half a century. The appointment avenue has proven singularly unsuccessful in changing what even many constitutional scholars who support the policy have long since conceded has no justification under constitutional law. Are you trying to suggest to me that the Supreme Court is allowed to turn the Constitution into anything it wants, and the other co-equal branches of the government can't do anything about it? Don't you remember what Lincoln said about such a notion: That if this would be accepted the people would have ceased to be their own

254

masters. Even apart from the constitutional arguments, are you trying to tell me that the president is just supposed to sit by and allow the body count of innocent people to keep increasing, slaughtered just for reasons of convenience? There's not a shred of doubt—biologically, logically, philosophically, commonsensically and in every other way—that these are human beings. Even the pro-abortionists aren't disputing this anymore. Keep in mind further that these innocent people are Americans. The only difference between them and other Americans is that they're in the womb, but for some people—including supposedly eminent scholars—even that isn't pertinent, because they think it ought to be legal to kill even newborns once they are out of the womb, or kill them because they have some kind of medical condition or physical deformity. Are you trying to tell me that the president isn't supposed to act to protect Americans when their lives are being threatened?"

"Of course not, Mr. President," Linkletter responded. "But when presidents have acted to intervene with federal power, like in the civil rights era, it was after a federal court decision, to enforce the decision."

"What are you to do when the courts are wrong? Are you telling me that you buy into some kind of a fantasy that the Supreme Court, even the lower courts, are inevitably correct about constitutional law *just because* they are courts—even when the most basic evidence is against them? Are you claiming that the political branches have no prerogative at all to make judgments about the meaning of the Constitution, even when history, logic, and all the facts are on their side?"

"But Mr. President," Hill argued, "We'll have lawlessness if public officials can just ignore the courts."

"Senator Hill, don't you honestly think that when courts can impose their own ideologically-based preferences in place of the clear constitutional background or blatantly read those preferences into the Constitution it's a form of lawlessness? All of us American public officials, including the justices themselves, take an oath to uphold the Constitution. Doesn't that give those of us in the other branches the prerogative, even the obligation, to act to stop those who are abusing the Constitution? Besides that, you should know that judicial decisions are not self-enforcing. They depend on the executive. For the executive to just go along with unconstitutional actions by the courts makes it a party to those actions."

"Judges can always be impeached and removed," interjected Linkletter.

"Senator, you know if as well as I do that such a response has been a dead letter. It just doesn't happen. As far as getting better judges is

255

concerned, presidents of our party who say they are opposed to these destructive trends have consistently fumbled judicial appointments, too often ending up making more appointments of people who go on to do the same thing. Or else they are intimidated by the left not to make or by supposed political imperatives not to fight for good appointments. Let's remember the stakes here: innocent human lives are being snuffed out in massive numbers by people who barely pass as physicians and are mostly concerned about raking in money."

Bessemer spoke up again. "Mr. President, all that you say may be true, but the public isn't going to see it that way. Our party will be badly hurt by this. Maybe you are willing to take the heat for this, but the whole party will be hurt. We may suffer losses in the mid-term elections next year that it will take us years to recoup from. Maybe we won't recoup at all. Just wait for the media attacks. They'll say you're a dictator."

"Senator Bessemer, you have served our party for a long time, and you have served it well. Is politics all that we're to be concerned about, however? Is that the bottom line here? It seems to me that that has too long been our first concern. We've listened to the political consultants and commentators and it hasn't helped us much for many years. In the election a few months ago, people said they wanted something different. I think they knew what they were going to get: solid principles—contesting what the left has forked up for the country for some time—and a willingness to undertake bold leadership to put them in place. Let's remember the purpose of politics isn't politics. It's to make life better for men, to create the conditions so that we can all achieve our eternal destiny—what it is that we're here for—so that one day our souls may rest in peace with God. The best rule is always to do the right thing, not to be driven by the calculations of politics. I've always found that to be the case in my life in politics as much as in the university—and in the university, incidentally, there's political maneuvering that sometimes seems to dwarf what we see in actual politics. Yes, prudence always has to be an uppermost consideration in politics and compromise is the lifeblood of politics, but that's not synonymous with just giving up most of the ship from the word "go" and running for cover or compromising on everything including essential moral principles. Prudence means knowing what has to be done at different times, knowing not only what you can do but what you *have* to do and knowing where things are at in the times you are in. It troubles me that you don't seem to appreciate the state that the country, and our civilization, are in now and have been for a long time—and that you don't see that if the right actions, even sweeping actions, are not taken on some things we may not only not get the chance again but the basic principles of our Republic may not even be intact any longer."

"Mr. President," said Hill, who like Stephen was also a man of a scholarly bent and known for his strong grasp of American history, "I know that you're an admirer of Lincoln, but even he knew that he couldn't abolish what he believed to be the evil of slavery. He knew the South wouldn't tolerate it and it would tear the country apart."

"That's right, Senator. Lincoln knew his limitations. He knew that with some things, maybe with many things, politics could not achieve a completely morally satisfying result, or at least not right away. The statesman needed always to keep the true moral vision intact and to precariously navigate the ship of state toward it, dealing with the obstacles as they presented themselves." Stephen sounded like the professor in the classroom again. "Again, however, one must know what one can do, must correctly read the situation. Abortion today is not slavery in 1860. The country will not be torn apart by putting what most people concede are the despicable abortionists out of business, especially with selling the baby parts, women dead or maimed from their abortions, and all that's happened in recent years. Nor is there going to be a political upheaval because for once a president genuinely moved to use checks and balances against a Court that a lot of people now recognize its just throwing its weight around to advance a political ideology. Lincoln knew he didn't have the power, constitutionally, to end slavery, but I have the power—as one in charge of a co-equal branch of government—to end the effects as much as I can of a fifty-year-old blatantly unconstitutional decision of the Court. If the Constitution implicitly, grudgingly tolerated slavery at least for a time, in no weight, shape, or form did it tolerate or embody a right to abortion or a right of abortionists to ply their unseemly trade with abandon. That was a pure concoction of the Court and one that the president has the full power to stop.

"Don't worry about the public thinking this is a despotic action. Education, in a more fervent and emphatic way than you have seen up to now, is going to be part of this. That the Court acted abusively a half-century ago, and the much greater abuses that have come out of it, will be driven home. That's beginning to happen even as we talk. Remember: politics is about education, and ultimately has to be about what all education must be concerned with, truth. You don't hammer people with the truth, but you help them to see it."

It was clear where Stephen stood, and the three senators knew that they were not going to motivate him to change course. All four of them stood almost at the same time, knowing that the discussion was at an end. The senators left pondering what Stephen had said; the professor had again had his influence. He could tell that at least some of the points he had made were churning in their minds.

When Stephen went before the country that evening, it was the most watched presidential speech in American media history. His speech was quintessential Stephen Gregory Bernard: an appeal to the masses, debunking the ruling notions of the secularist-relativist elite with an almost breathtakingly brilliant educational effort. It ranged from a graphic biology lesson about prenatal life throughout the whole course of development to a heavily referenced exposé about the typically abusive and callous treatment of women by abortionists to a recounting of the exposés of recent years of the outrageous practice of selling baby parts to an explanation of how Blackstone had talked about a right to personal security attaching as soon as life was present to an exploration of the reach of presidential power vis-á-vis the Supreme Court—"the Federalist spoke about how only the executive has the sword, only it can enforce court decisions"—and the lack of authority of the Court to make a decision like the ones of 1973 legalizing abortion. He made the unborn almost come to life with his description of them. He defended his actions as in line with his constitutional oath, since the justices in illegitimately reading a right to abortion into the Constitution had violated theirs. He explained why the Constitution was not, and could never be, merely what the Court said it was and why he had an obligation as head of a co-equal branch to confront the Court when it violated the Constitution. He deftly, but truthfully, cast the Court in very bad light in renegade decisions like *Roe v. Wade* and *Doe v. Bolton*. In his speech, he astutely confronted the pro-abortion left about the hypocritical way they applied their thinking about equality. They propagandized endlessly about equality, not just completely distorting the meaning our Founding Fathers gave to it but denying it to a whole class of Americans, the unborn. They were so written out of the left's conception of equality as to be not even allowed to live. He made the case brilliantly that unborn children were protected under the Fourteenth Amendment, making the case from Blackstone that he had discussed with Archbishop LaGrange. The Court failed to protect them, so he was going to do it. The Court in 1973 should have decided the cases in exactly the opposite way that it did: instead of stating that the Constitution somehow protects a woman's abortion decision—which he repeatedly emphasized was a chimerical liberty in light of how abortion actually harmed women, as well—it should have said that abortion cannot be legally permitted because of the unborn child's right to life under the Constitution. Stephen was hearkening back to the departmental notion of constitutional construction, which he had mentioned to LaGrange. Actually, in his scholarly writing Stephen had argued that the Supreme Court is the rightful branch to do this in the normal course of things. When, however, the Court has palpably and grossly misconstrued the Constitution and provided no solid basis for one of its decisions in the context of the meaning of the Constitution and the history and tradition behind it, the other branches can step in and cannot be viewed as bound by the Court's interpretation.

During the speech, Stephen's characteristic look of resolve was consistent from beginning to end. When he said, "This is the course of action that I have chosen. This is the end of legal abortion in America. The abortion industry is closed down. There will be no reversal of this course—no matter what. The Supreme Court nearly five decades ago exercised what one of its members called 'raw judicial power' to twist the Constitution to give us legal—which soon meant widespread—abortion. It was completely without authority to do any such thing. What I am doing now is to stop the outrage that it illicitly created." Then, he announced that new federal regulations were being put in place for hospitals. If they did or permitted to be done in their facilities elective abortions they would lose their federal funding. He also said that even the opportunity for what some believed would be the "abortion of the future"—chemical abortion—would be stopped. New regulations were going to be issued by the Department of Health and Human Services to revoke federal approval of contraceptives that functioned in an abortifacient manner.

In the days ahead, some in the Food and Drug Administration bureaucracy within HHS would try to stonewall the attempt to shut down the marketing of abortifacients and work with their media allies to oppose the initiative of their "boss," the President. Jim Lewis shut them down by making clear that stringent disciplinary action would be forthcoming if they persisted. As far as this and the much broader media campaign against Stephen's action went, his network led by John Frost already had gone into action. They had the full-court press on across the country, carrying out Stephen's customary two-pronged approach of confrontation and education—but always, as John emphasized repeatedly to his associates, with charity—in many different settings (rallies, talks to groups large and small, church functions, meetings with party officials and politicians from the party, and just informal coffee klatches among friends and neighbors in private homes) in many venues. Stephen himself led the charge, speaking day in and day out all over the country, never taking the stance of defending his action but always taking the offensive and driving home the reality of unborn human life and the moral abomination of abortion.

The quick liaisons with the pro-life groups and a simultaneous outreach to pro-family and conservative groups and also supportive religious bodies was successful in getting them to join the public chorus in support of Stephen's action. Thanks to the efforts of Mary Molinski and others in Stephen's inner circle, even the "mainstream" pro-life and conservative groups who there was concern might not support Stephen's action for fear that it was "too radical" and might somehow actually hurt the pro-life cause, as Senator Bessemer had claimed, were on board. The combination of Stephen's arguments and simply a perceptible shift in thinking in the country after the destructive path of two arch-leftist administrations for over a decade made people ready to embrace a sharp turn.

Stephen had had a strong concern that the U.S Conference of Catholic Bishops might be an obstacle, since its bureaucracy still had many "Catholic liberals" in it and the *weltanschauung* of the period of leftist dominance in the country had also been one of a renewal of post-Vatican II pastoral practices that often blurred unpopular moral teachings. Many bishops had also been consumed by an ongoing obsession with "dialogue" instead of strong public stands, even though the secular culture seldom wanted to dialogue back or concede even a trifle in its thinking. The initial inclination within the USCCB was to question how Stephen had gone about dealing with abortion. Some of the bureaucrats and a few bishops were mumbling about his "lawlessness." Thanks to the active efforts of Archbishop LaGrange, however, the Conference ended up issuing a terse statement of support for Stephen's actions. Even though LaGrange was new to Washington, the importance of that see gave him leverage. He successfully arranged for a preliminary vote of the bishops via email prior to their annual meeting, so the support for Stephen's action could come right away. At their meeting in June, two months later, he was to navigate the final vote of support.

On the other side, there were rallies in cities around the country and on some university campuses, although student absence because of summer vacation quelled campus activism. In spite of media exposure and support, the pro-abortionists could not build momentum. They were under attack consistently from Stephen's side and the country was not going to rise up in mass, especially after the building of pro-life sentiment for so many years and the revelations of the sordid practices of Gosnell and other abortionists and the selling of baby parts and all the rest. Stephen's side further undercut their adversaries by unearthing information that Planned Parenthood and other big abortion profiteers were helping to organize and fund some of the protests, and then hitting hard about that. Some of the protests were in front of the shut-down abortion clinics, but the marshals and National Guardsmen wouldn't budge. After awhile, the protests tailed off, although a few people regularly continued to show up at some of the clinic sites.

Big Abortion also went to the courts to try to stop Stephen. Stephen's response, as with the same-sex "marriage" issue, was to order the Department of Justice not even to show up in court to argue the case. He said that this was simply a matter of the executive branch refusing to any longer carry out an unconstitutional decision of the Supreme Court and no lesser court, or the Supreme Court itself, could order it to do so. He mentioned repeatedly in response to this his oath to uphold the Constitution. The pro-abortionists got federal court orders directing the Justice and Defense Departments to remove the federal forces and let the clinics reopen. Stephen ordered both of his Cabinet members to disregard these. He had early on installed a new head of the Marshal Service, who is a presidential appointee, in anticipation of his actions against the courts and he wrote to all federal judges in the country reminding them that the Marshal Service was under presidential control and would not carry out any court order either upholding the "blatantly unconstitutional" *Roe v. Wade* and *Doe v. Bolton* abortion decisions or *Obergefell v. Hodges* same-sex "marriage" decision and would not allow abortions to proceed anywhere in the country. Federal marshals found themselves suddenly no longer working for the courts, which were normally in practical terms their employer, but having to uphold the orders of the president who was actually their boss. When the court orders arrived at the Robert F. Kennedy Department of Justice Building and the Pentagon, they were refused at Stephen's direction and sent back to the courts. Stephen made it very clear that if the courts tried to hold the Attorney General or the Secretary of Defense in contempt he would not permit those contempt orders to be delivered or enforced either.

A group of hospitals and several major drug companies also filed suit to overturn the new regulations forbidding abortions by federally-funded facilities and the marketing of abortifacients. Stephen also refused to let the government respond to those cases, and he directed Jim Lewis to have his department notify all hospitals to inform it within thirty days if their policies would be forbidding the performing of abortions. If not, funding would immediately be cut off. Stephen was assiduous in making sure that all the procedural requirements to promulgate a new federal regulation were followed. He was not going to allow any legal issue to be raised about procedural irregularities.

Some of the legal correspondents in the media were beginning to talk about an unprecedented "constitutional confrontation" between the presidency and the courts. It was clear that Stephen was unmovable. The media attacks on him were having no effect. In fact, with his counter-offensive the media was itself under the gun. It was becoming increasingly clear that the abortion liberty in America was finally dethroned, and the Supreme Court's authority in a tenuous position.

The justices on the Court, as they were in last part of their annual term pushing to finish work on a flood of opinions that they would issue by its conclusion on June 30, were carefully following the events. Despite twelve years of leftist presidential administrations and the few appointments of justices that had come along with it, the Court's pro-abortion majority was only narrow, 5 to 4. In their stated opinions in different cases, four members of the Court had expressed their willingness to overturn the 1973 decisions. Four members of the Court were leftist ideologues, and it was unlikely that they would bend on their thinking about abortion or hardly any issues that were central features on the left's cultural and political agenda. The fifth member of the pro-abortion majority was a "swing" vote, but usually ended up siding with the left even though he was not viewed as one of their ideological compatriots. A couple of the leftist bloc were indignant at what Stephen was doing and would not bend an inch. The two others were genuinely frazzled by his direct challenges to the Court, on same-sex "marriage," but now dramatically on abortion. The Chief Justice, Robert M. Johnston, was in the anti-abortion minority and was deeply troubled and nervous by the Bernard challenge. Like most chief justices, he was concerned about the Court's prestige and the respect that people had for it. It was a sense of institutional stewardship that almost instinctively chief justices embodied.

Johnston had developed a close colleague relationship with the swing justice, Thomas McCubbin. Even though the Court was usually shrouded in secrecy it was well known by its watchers in the media and the legal academy that the two consulted each other more than other justices and frequently collaborated on decisions. It was known that they and their wives routinely socialized together. It was rumored that they even "ran interference" for each other, sometimes the Chief joining McCubbin in a close decision on an issue important to him even though he could have tilted the other way and McCubbin doing the same for his colleague. After several weeks had passed and it was clear that Stephen was not in the least bending or retreating, Johnston went to

McCubbin's office late on a Friday afternoon almost at the end of the Court's term. McCubbin noticed immediately the serious, almost urgent look on the Chief's face and he instinctively knew what was on his mind.

"Tom, President Bernard does not seem to be relenting a bit, no matter how much criticism he receives. He and his people just keep forking it back. I've never seen anything like this. I'm not sure the Court's ever been under siege like this. No one seems to buy the claim that he's threatening constitutional government. That's not selling. He knows the history, and is always driving home the point that he's doing what Jackson, Lincoln, and FDR did. I don't see anything good for the Court coming out of this. Things can't be allowed to go on like this. I'm really concerned that we could be irreparably harmed."

"I agree with what you're saying, Bob," Justice McCubbin replied. "Even Jack and Lou, our ever confident liberals, are rattled." He was referring to Justices John England and Louis Felsenthal, the two most senior members of the Court's leftist bloc. "Only Libby and Rachel are making fists and pounding their desks and saying that the Court should never give into what they're calling presidential abuse of power. They seem to think they're back on the barricades in college, demanding this or that administrator or president be canned for not supporting all the demands of their women's activism group, or whatever." He was speaking about Justices Elizabeth Wanner and Rachel Mendelsohn. "Still, Bob, we have to protect the integrity of the Court. We can't let ourselves be pressured."

"Tom, I don't think it's a question of our being pressured. Bernard's done what he's done. He's said that a major precedent of this Court was wrong—drastically wrong—and no longer applies. It's evident that he's not going to step back, no matter how much pressure he receives. Hardly any presidents ever do this, and his action is probably the most direct rejection of this Court in its history. There is nothing anybody can do about it. Is he going to be impeached? Hardly. The country is not up in arms that he's stopped the bloodthirsty abortionists. In fact, half of the country seems to be rallying around him. He's been deft at shaping public opinion, and he's on a determined path. Bernard's not intimidated by the media and the slew of interest groups like presidents usually are. He doesn't think like a politician, and if you look back at his time in politics that's consistently been the case. We're not in a good position. I don't think we have any cards to play. Oh, there are already cases challenging what he's doing, but the government won't even defend them in court. He's saying, 'Why should we make a case before you since I'm not going to obey a decision against me anyway?' You're right about our integrity, Tom. That's what I'm thinking about here, but maybe not in the way you're thinking about it."

"What do you mean?"

"I mean, Tom, that I'm not sure we're doing a whole lot for our integrity by standing by a couple of fifty-year-old decisions that almost no one believes had anything to do with constitutional law. Even a lot of the liberal legal scholars criticize them. It looks like we unleashed a slaughter upon the country, and we're the ones responsible for selling cut up babies and all the rest of it. I don't pay attention to the polls much, but have you noticed in the last few years how low the respect for the Court is out there in the public. And it's going even lower with Bernard's attacks on us. To stand by this, unflinchingly, doesn't look like integrity but stubbornness."

"What are you suggesting, Bob?"

"I'm not entirely sure. I just think we can't stand by and allow the Court to go down in all this. We can't go out there and make some PR campaign to ask for support for our abortion decisions, saying that we're defending the Constitution. That's hardly going to work. We might hurt ourselves even more by something like that. I'm wondering if we don't have to retreat, if we don't have to look to reverse those decisions. We're not going to find some Fourteenth Amendment right to the fetus's life as Bernard is claiming, but we can say that we were wrong about this whole right to privacy thing—that it doesn't involve abortion. We've narrowed this right in other ways. Maybe we should just go the whole way. Then it would become a state issue again, like before 1973. Then, if Bernard insists on the federal government going to the hilt to defend fetal life he can battle it out with the states."

"But Bob, our integrity *would* be involved here. It really would look like we're caving under pressure."

"Look, I think we're at the point now that we have to cut our losses. You've been hot and cold about this abortion thing. I ask you to think about whether you could bring yourself to join the other four of us in doing this. We could finesse this in our opinion. We could make arguments that don't make it look like some kind of ignoble retreat. There is a lot of basis for doing this: looking to the technological developments—ultrasounds and all that—that could make us say that we can now see that the Court was wrong in 1973 in saying that it couldn't decide if the fetus was a person or not. Even the pro-abortionists don't any longer claim it's not a person. You would be the ideal member of the Court to write the opinion."

"But we have to have a case."

"There are different cases in the lower courts, some challenging Bernard's actions but others that came from different states about abortion regulations. It's clear that some of these cases would eventually come before us."

"But the government refuses to even respond to those cases. Bernard is thumbing his nose at the courts."

"Let's be careful about putting him down as thumbing his nose at us. Let's remember he's in the driver's seat, and as I've been saying we're kidding ourselves if we think otherwise. Maybe we can convey the message in some way to Bernard that we're ready to reverse the '73 decisions if the government just pursued the cases. I don't know how we would do that—indirectly, I suppose.

"You've put a lot before me, Bob."

"Think about it, Tom. Let's talk more about it."

A few days later the two justices huddled again. This was after a number of things happened that markedly influenced McCubbin. Stephen made two masterful public speeches in which he both deconstructed the Court's arguments in its 1973 decisions and set out very clearly what its proper role in the American political order was intended to be and its relationship to the other branches, and provided an air-tight scholarly-type indictment of how it had repeatedly transgressed that role. There was no question about his continued resoluteness. He had dug in his heels in dealing with the Court in a way almost never seen in a president. There had also been a large rally in Washington, organized by numerous pro-life and religious organizations, to support the cause of the unborn. It was billed as a summer version of the March for Life. The justices had never, of course, commented about the annual January March for Life to commemorate the 1973 decisions but it didn't go unnoticed within the Court. Then, an op-ed appeared in the *Washington Post*, that gained a surprising amount of further dissemination in the general media, by a long prominent liberal legal scholar and civil liberties icon at Harvard Law School in which he pointedly expressed the same fear Johnston had of enduring damage to the Court if it didn't reconsider its 1973 decisions that—he said this despite his long-standing support for abortion rights—had no constitutional justification. He wondered if returning to the pre-1973 position of leaving it up to the states, where abortion rights would then gain a legitimacy afforded by legislative action, reflecting popular support, would be better. That might insure that they would endure. Some other lesser commentators had also been picking up on his theme. McCubbin had not been an academic, even though he hobnobbed with some of the legal professoriate when during the Court's long summer recess he had accepted offers to teach a summer course at different law schools. He had always been unduly impressed and deferential to legal academicians. Maybe he admired them because they had an intellectual acumen that he aspired to but knew he didn't have. Even though he was only a sometime liberal himself, he was especially captivated by the mainstream left-of-center legal academics who probably had the highest stature in the legal profession.

Then, international events also intervened. ISIS, the most radical of Islamist-jihadist organizations who were bent on reestablishing a mythical caliphate and spreading it throughout the world, engaged in multiple terrorist attacks throughout Europe. Suddenly, the mainstream media attacks on Stephen ceased and attention was fully absorbed in the tragic developments across the ocean.

McCubbin indicated to the Chief Justice that he might be willing to vote with him and thereby establish a 5 to 4 majority to overturn the decisions.

"'Might' may not be enough. I don't think Bernard will even take part in a case unless he has the clear sense that we're going to actually do it."

"Tom, we can't arrange with him for a decision to go the way he wants."

"It's not a question of arranging something," replied the Chief curtly. "But there may be ways to convey to him indirectly what the likely outcome will be."

McCubbin thought for a few minutes, and then slowly responded. "Okay, Bob, I'm with you. Have you thought about how this might be done?"

"Let me think some more about the specifics, but I think I have a general idea about how to proceed."

Three weeks later, the Chief Justice arranged through certain contacts to give a lecture at one of the law schools in the Washington, D.C. area. He did not want it to be specifically on the abortion decisions, but on the question of precedent in constitutional law. He also wanted to insure, without his aim being obvious, that the lecture would receive wide coverage in the Washington media and would generate substantial attention in Washington circles generally. He used various contacts to arrange that. Actually, in light of the direct, ongoing presidential challenge to the Court any major address by the Chief Justice was going to be noticed. In the talk, which his clerks helped him to draft, he discussed significant historical examples of where the Court had overturned precedents and he spoke about areas where he could see the Court doing so in the future. His clerks had examined Stephen's writings as a professor and he mentioned areas that Stephen had specifically called for the Court to change its position on, including legal immunity for sitting members of Congress for statements made outside the context of formal Congressional proceedings (the 1979 *Proxmire* decision), legal immunity from suit of a sitting president for acts done before taking office and unrelated to his official duties (the 1997 *Clinton v. Jones* decision), that the rights of parents are not viewed as "fundamental" under the Constitution that would mean they could be infringed only if there were a compelling public interest (the 2000 *Troxel v. Granville* decision), and the abortion decisions. Virtually no one picked up the fact that these were all Stephen's positions. Johnston calculated, correctly, both that the one person who would understand the unspoken message he was trying to specifically convey was Stephen and that by mixing the abortion decisions up with all these other decisions no one would conclude that the Court was, in effect, ready to surrender on abortion. In other words, it could back away from its long-standing precedent and still save face.

Johnston was correct. Stephen picked up immediately what was happening. It was clear to him that Johnston was seeking some kind of subliminal response to his "offer." Stephen would give it in a like manner. From Stephen's standpoint, there were two crucial concerns: to insure that the *rightful* authority of the Court be upheld—none of this could be permitted to undercut its position as both the main interpreter of the Constitution and chief governmental defender of citizen liberties—and at the same time to uphold his own actions in responding to one of the most outrageous abuses of judicial authority in American history. He did not, however, want his response to *look like* it was a response, anymore than Johnston wanted his statements to be seen as a message to Stephen. So, Stephen did not try anything so obvious as to issue some kind of official statement, or call a press conference to respond to what Johnston said, or even seek to also give a lecture at a law school. Instead, he let a week-and-a-half pass—so that people would not readily see the connection to Johnston's lecture—and in the course of one of his current batch of public speeches about abortion would speak not only about the Court needing to reverse the decisions, but also to give some indication—he knew that Johnston would read this to mean *dicta*, an unbinding, non-precedential part of an opinion— that this was a subject, along the lines of something like drug laws, where federal action would supersede state. He knew that Johnston was following carefully all of his speeches and public statements and would pick up the message.

267

Johnston's "response" was in the form of another lecture. He had actually arranged a series of three lectures at law schools, figuring that there might be a "colloquy" between him and Stephen. It was summer, so the other lectures would get only limited attention since the schools were not in full session. He knew that the key person, Stephen, would be following them and the fact that the remaining lectures would attract much less public attention would make less likely that the media and public would perceive anything like a surrender by the Court.

He had left the topics of the remaining two lectures open, except that they were to be on constitutional law topics. He scheduled the lectures two consecutive weeks, at two other Washington area law schools. He aimed at conveying different messages to Stephen in each and figured that with their following so close in succession the president would understand that they were both part of a package. For the second lecture, he chose the topic of preemption—when federal action precludes state. In it, he didn't mention abortion but spoke very positively about the decisions in which the Court had upheld Congress' legislating in certain subject matter areas that previously or normally had been state prerogatives, such as illicit drugs or mandating a minimum drinking age to receive federal highway funds. The latter was to convey the message that there was no problem with Stephen's administration cutting of funds for hospitals that did abortions.

The third lecture was about presidential foreign policy and war powers. Ostensibly, this had nothing to do with the current constitutional crisis but Johnston understood that the perceptible president would be able to discern a message he was seeking to convey in one part of it. The Chief Justice mentioned the 1952 decision of *Youngstown Sheet and Tube Company v. Sawyer*, which involved President Truman taking control of the country's steel mills to end a strike because it adversely affected the production of war materiel needed for the Korean conflict. Truman claimed he could constitutionally do this because of inherent presidential war-making power. A divided Court rejected his argument. Johnston suggested in the lecture that the Court's minority may have been correct, however. As he discussed the decision, he made a point of repeatedly referring to it as the "Steel Seizure Case." This was its shorthand designation in constitutional law writing and casebooks. The legal scholar Stephen, Johnston reasoned, would easily pick up the double entrendre: by indicating that Truman's "seizure" of the steel mills was a valid exercise of inherent presidential power, he was suggesting the same about Stephen's "seizure" of the abortion clinics.

Now, Johnston would wait to see what Stephen's reply would be.

As the Chief Justice expected, Stephen knew entirely all that was happening. The question went through his mind about whether Johnston was speaking for himself or if a majority of the Court was ready to reverse *Roe v. Wade* and *Doe v. Bolton*. He and his tight inner circle discussed this, but they all concluded that there would be no point in Johnston sending this consistent message—a veritable invitation to bring abortion to the Court again—unless he knew that a reversal would be in the offing. There would be no point to all this otherwise and the Court would have nothing to gain from it.

Stephen and his inner circle decided on a strategy. They would not defend a case challenging Stephen's seizure of the clinics. Four federal district courts had issued orders about that and Stephen had made a big point of ignoring them and saying the federal government would not respond. To change that stance now would be seen as an obvious capitulation to the courts. On the other hand, there had been a case from Nebraska in which an abortion clinic and a national pro-abortion group had challenged tight new abortion restrictions adopted by the state's legislature two years before Stephen's election. A federal district court judge in the state struck them down, saying they went against Supreme Court precedents. Shortly before Stephen's seizure of the abortion clinics, the 8th U.S. Circuit of Appeals upheld the lower court's decision and the state immediately appealed to the Supreme Court. The Court had not yet decided if it was going to take the case. Stephen and Attorney General Larribee decided to petition the Court to hear that case, and allow the U.S. Government to become an intervener and make the case to overturn the 1973 decisions. Not surprisingly, the Court quickly granted *certiorari* for the case to come before it. It also scheduled the case for oral argument early in its new term, almost right after it reconvened on the first Monday of October. It asked for briefs to be submitted by the summer's end, very much departing from its usual calendar. Stephen and his group didn't expect the Court to convene an extraordinary summer session because, after all, the justices were trying to save face and protect the prestige of their institution. To do that would make it look like they were just folding under presidential pressure. The Court signaled, however, that a decision would come very quickly after oral arguments.

During the summer months, the suppression of abortion around the country continued unabated and people seemed to become almost accustomed to the "new normal." The usual defenders of abortion rights could do little but raise small fusses. The universities with their concentrations of leftist young people were out of session, so there were no big rallies. There were a scattering of feminist demonstrations

269

in Washington and other big cities, but they were small and the public paid even less attention than usual as it was absorbed with summer vacations and activities. In the meantime, however, Stephen, his network, and pro-life forces kept up constant public appeals and speechmaking for the cause of life. The highlight, which even the mainstream media couldn't ignore, was a speech by Stephen at the National Right-to-Life Convention that claimed to a jubilant crowd—it was the largest such convention ever—that "one way or the other" the era of the assault on unborn life was over. The Justice Department filed one of its longest Supreme Court briefs ever—the Court waived page limits for the case—and covered, with voluminous supporting material, virtually every angle in making the case against legal abortion. Stephen was careful to mention in every abortion speech he gave that regardless of how the Court decided, he would not change course "one iota" on his actions "to protect all unborn human persons." He wanted to make sure that the Court didn't misinterpret the Government's joining the Nebraska case.

Stephen took part in drafting the Government's brief, which was maybe the first time a sitting president had done so. He made sure that he upped the ante even a bit more by having the brief assert that the federal government had the authority to both ban abortion and protect the unborn and to do such a thing as preserve one man-one woman marriage—it emphasized that this was "true marriage"—à la the Defense of Marriage Act, which the Court had previously struck down. In mentioning the latter, he was in effect sending another message to Johnston for the future.

At the early October oral arguments, Stephen's Solicitor General, a brilliant Notre Dame law graduate and long-time conservative public interest lawyer named Gerard Courtney, was all that anyone could expect a Supreme Court litigator to be. Meanwhile, the pro-abortion legal team seemed almost punchless and seemed to know that a new era in American law was upon the country.

The Court handed down its decision only three weeks later. It was one of the fastest "turnaround times" in the modern history of the Court. *Roe v. Wade* and *Doe v. Bolton* were overturned 5 to 4 (the leftist bloc on the Court held out to the bitter end, although Justices England and Felsenthal issued a separate dissenting opinion where they all but agreed with the majority but made some vague statement to the effect that this was not the time to reverse (because of perceived pressure from the executive?). The Court's opinion, written by Chief Justice Johnston, expressly acknowledged that even though the situation was back now to before 1973 when it was seen as a state matter, if the federal government chose to address this subject the preemption doctrine applied, and its actions would supersede those of states. There was also *dictum* in the opinion, which indicated that there was inherent presidential authority to act as Stephen had done because the president "could reasonably infer that the unborn were 'persons' under the Fourteenth Amendment." The opinion did not come to that conclusion itself—Stephen didn't expect that it would—but it did say that "in light of all the scientific and medical advances since 1973, no longer can the Court simply say that it's not possible to conclude when life begins." It held that "the states and the federal government can reasonably come to a conclusion about when life begins and protect the unborn accordingly, including forbidding and punishing abortion."

Another *dictum* indicated that the federal government "could legislate on matters affecting the family." That sounded like a nod to the Defense of Marriage Act.

In its next term, the following year, the Bernard administration petitioned the Court to reverse its decision on the Defense of Marriage Act. The Court did so at the end of that term. That effectively also nullified the *Obergefell* decision.

What became apparent in the years ahead was that the Court had entered a new era of constitutional restraint like after the challenges by Jackson, Lincoln, and FDR—just as Stephen had predicted.

CHAPTER 9

Struggles And The Unfolding Of A New Era

A fter the constitutional confrontation with the Supreme Court, Stephen went to work to get the legislative agenda he had announced through Congress. He could act unilaterally to change regulations and stop bureaucratic abuses and could prod even the private sector with the bully pulpit, but to actually change laws that had to be duly enacted by Congress he needed to work with its leadership, especially of his party (which was in the majority), cultivate the means of navigating the legislative process, and provide the right combination of persuasion, line-drawing, and subtle threats to go as far as he could without Congressional support. He did not include logrolling in the mix, since it mostly involved pouring more federal largesse into members' districts and states and he was committed to a path of gradual disengagement of the federal government from most domestic policy areas. His approach, instead, was to lay down the gauntlet about cutting programs—completely or to reduce them to some targeted level of funding—and then take the case to the public.

Stephen went out of his way not to antagonize the Congressional leadership of either party. He simply made known to them what his irreducible positions were. He was willing to compromise, up to a certain point. Nor would he change in the least his basic stated goal or course of action. When it came to domestic programs and spending, gradual disengagement was the goal and there would be no reversal of that or delay in starting down that road. He meant to get control of the budget, no matter what. There would be no more continuing resolutions. He sent a comprehensive budgetary proposal to Congress, fully in line with the Congressional Budget and Impoundment Control Act of 1974 that had been circumvented as a matter of course in recent years. He proceeded in implementing the Penny Plan. He explained that interest payments had to be met because promises had to be kept. The only programs that were spared the cutting were ones concerning national defense and public order. Stephen made it clear that he would veto any and all appropriations bills that did not stay within the prescribed limits. The projected year for balancing the federal budget— at lower levels than it had been at—was the end of his term. "Come hell or high water," he said that date would be upheld. In light of how Stephen had unflinchingly shaken up the executive branch and faced down the Supreme Court already, not many people either inside of Congress or in the public doubted him when he said that. This had been an unexpected and unintended side effect of his bold actions. It gave him great political clout in pushing these other crucial parts of his agenda. As with everything else he did, he bore down insistently to educate the public about the value of what he was doing. The Penny Plan had the advantage of being easily understandable to the public and, as was his frequent practice, he brought out authorities on the plan who he arranged to share podiums with him.

Coupled with the Penny Plan was the flat tax proposal. In light of gradual disengagement and his unshakable commitment to a balanced budget with considerably lower levels of spending, it had to be set at only 15% initially to go down to 13% by the end of his term when the balanced budget would be achieved, and then settle finally at 12%. There would also be an income floor so that no one below a certain income level would pay any federal tax and the exemptions for minor children were also generous. This would squarely be a pro-family tax plan. Also, with this new tax arrangement no longer would the average American taxpayer be putting out over 40% of his income in all kinds of taxes. This would strikingly help to reduce that.

As Stephen had said, putting gradual disengagement in place meant building up civil society, the non-profit service sector. Stephen took an active role in doing that throughout his presidency, using persuasion, rallying citizens to financially support such efforts and actually assisting them in fund-raising efforts, meeting regularly—using his position of presidential prestige—with people of considerable means to get them to contribute more and more of their largesse, and pushing through Congress tax changes that were increasingly favorable to civil society.

He consistently faced off with interest groups who were trying to preserve pet programs and spending levels. He went the whole gamut to put them on the defensive: calling them out by name in speeches and providing indisputable evidence about how they reaped excessive

274

advantages and vast financial benefits from programs they were defending, calling his "flash rallies" as they had come to be called outside their Washington headquarters, asking to be invited to their national meetings and conventions to confront them right in "the bellies of the beasts" where he made his case uncompromisingly and took on their top officials in head-to-head debates, having John Frost activate his network in locales around the country where on these fiscal issues they often joined forces with TEA Party groups and encouraged other supportive groups to speak up.

As the push for the flat tax was heating up, Stephen met with the two top leaders of his party in each house of Congress. Breaking with the traditional practice, they met at Stephen's insistence on Capitol Hill, instead of at the White House. Stephen wanted to show appropriate deference to the legislative branch. After all, tax policy was something that was its prerogative. He could propose, and push vigorously, but he could not legislate. He pushed executive power to its fullest—even beyond the usual historical norm for the sake of upholding or restoring constitutional principles and saving the country from a train wreck—but would not consider going around the constitutionally-mandated role of Congress.

The meeting with Speaker of the House Robert Clayburne and Representatives Don Holbrooke and Randy Stacey, the Majority Leader and Chief Majority Whip, and Senate Majority Leader Bessemer and Senate Majority Whip Glen Ferlock took place in the President's Room in the Capitol Building. Vice President Clarke, who from the beginning of Stephen's administration had been part of his inner circle and who Stephen met with frequently to get his thoughts on a whole range of things, was also there. In addition to his being one of Stephen's closest advisers, he was also his chief liaison with Congress. After a few minutes of small talk and pleasantries, Bessemer's brow curled up as he started the discussion. Even though so much had happened, he still was every bit the run-of-the-mill Washington politician that he had been when he came to talk to Stephen after his seizure of the abortion clinics.

"Mr. President, I have to be frank with you. Even though a lot of our party's rank-and-file like your budget and program cuts, I have been barraged with statements of opposition from K Street—including a lot of those outfits who usually like our party—and a lot of our contributors. These aren't the penny-ante contributors—I know you have relied a lot on them in your time in politics—but the people who in the long haul in an ongoing way keep our party strong. We can't function without them. These people like your flat tax and corporate tax rate reduction proposals, although they are concerned that you are being too rigid and unwilling to make some compromises with the other party on these things and meet them halfway. They think that with your hard line you are risking losing everything and we might lose the mid-term elections so badly that there will be a real anti-business climate in the next Congress. They're also against your plan to roll back federal programs. They think that will have the same effect, but just worse. You'll be handing over elections to the other party and then they'll tramp on business even worse, advancing some kind of socialist agenda. Look, they are very jittery already with the other controversial initiatives you've undertaken in other things."

Stephen cut him off. "Senator Bessemer, I think you're leaving out a couple of things. These corporate leaders are annoyed for another reason. They are losing their government subsidies, their corporate welfare. They also haven't liked my talking about business providing a just wage for their workers, and some of them don't like the initiatives I'm taking on immigration. That actually involves the same thing. They want porous borders so they can get more workers who will be willing to take minimum-wage jobs that Americans want to be paid more for. In other words, they don't want to pay a just wage. Some of them want to even muscle out Americans from high tech and other highly skilled and professional jobs because foreigners can be brought here who will take less money. The corporate welfare is why some of them are against our gradual budget cuts. They don't have to work on taking new initiatives or being good entrepreneurs or even doing the things that will keep them competitive as long as the federal largesse rolls in. To top it off, some of these top executives you're hearing from are concerned mostly about receiving their inflated executive compensation, not even about producing good quality products or services or serving their communities. Sometimes you even hear about them putting a company near bankruptcy and then skipping off and becoming a CEO someplace else and for all their past failures commanding a quarter-million dollar bonus to boot. I know very well that this isn't everyone in the corporate community, since I'm getting initially good reactions from some there—especially those who have taken business ethics seriously. I know about the kind of people you're talking about. I met them enough in Pennsylvania and I know that they're the ones who have filled our party's coffers and always have wanted a *quid pro quo*. They aren't the best corporate citizens and our party is not going to be beholden to them. They and the K Street crew that you're talking about are always saying, 'Compromise, compromise, don't rattle the left.' They keep profiting and our party keeps losing elections and our Republic comes progressively undone. Senator, don't you understand yet that such a thing is not going to happening anymore? *It's over.* The stakes are now too high for politics as usual. Maybe you have to finally understand that this is not a normal time."

Bessemer had a look of consternation, like he somehow thought even after their last encounter that Stephen was going to be swayed by what he said. Clayburne sat quietly, but the expression on his face made it seem like he was with Bessemer. Even though they had moved with the increasing conservatism of the party, they were both part of the "Washington Establishment." They had each been in Congress for over two decades. Holbrooke represented the recently ascendant populist · element of the party, the TEA Party and similar groups. The old guard had to permit someone like him to come into the leadership because of the way the winds were now blowing, but they didn't regard him as someone who really understood how Washington worked. He spoke up quickly to support Stephen. "Senator Bessemer"—he addressed him specifically even though he knew that the other Congressional leaders in the room also shared Bessemer's views—"The people who gave us control of Congress are not the ones you're talking about. It was the guy in the street whose support made the difference. These people would have little patience with our party if they knew that we were thinking of surrendering our principles because the high rollers were putting pressure on us. It's a new day now for our party and for the country. We just play into the hands of the other party and the media and the left generally if we do things like this. We'll be a permanent minority party."

Stephen spoke again. "Gentlemen, I plan to work with you every step of the way and you know how solicitous of genuine Congressional prerogatives I am—which is contrary to what we saw with the last two administrations. I also know that compromise is the lifeblood of politics. It is not, however, prudent to just jump from the beginning into compromise. Just become some people oppose something—even if they're 'important' people—that doesn't mean we just back off of it. We have to look at what's needed, and we have to be forthright in pursuing it even if we can't achieve all of it. The initiatives I've taken are all now crucial for the country. Some are things that should have been addressed long ago—like retracting federal programs—but they were just pushed aside. I'm always ready to make reasonable compromises when they are *truly* called for. That's to say nothing of the fact that there are some bottom-line, irreducible matters—positions on basic morality—that you simply can't compromise on, like abortion and what marriage is. These are the ground rules I operate by." With that, the meeting adjourned.

The issue wasn't closed, however. Stephen made arrangements the next week to speak to a business group and drove home the points that political pressure by well-heeled interests, which was coming forth in the wake of his gradual disengagement policy, would be resisted, and that the era of government-business coziness was coming to an end. He drove this home in a series of talks in the following months to a range of groups. He also explained—the educative function of politics at work again—why this was so necessary at this time for the country. He left no doubt that the course was set and would not be departed from.

Stephen also undertook a regular set of meetings with corporate officials in line with his NIRA-type initiative. It was the presidential bully pulpit at work. He talked to them about the need for a just wage for all employees, good working conditions, reasonable hours (he especially talked about the need to respect the family needs of younger managerial employees, who are often driven excessively), that workers were not impersonal cogs in a wheel and that their human dignity always be upheld, the promotion of an across-the-board good moral atmosphere, and told them they needed to back off of support for the homosexualist agenda (and made it clear that if any employees were in the least bit punished for opposing it, federal civil rights laws could be invoked against the companies). Some corporate officials listened to him and sincerely seemed to want to correct deficiencies and improve their small slice of the corporate world. Others resisted. Stephen kept up his discussion with them if they were receptive, but some clearly just tuned him out and wouldn't budge. In an action that was unprecedented for a U.S. president, he denounced the executives by name publicly. He was using the bully pulpit in the strongest possible way. He had for some time, in his speeches, been talking about ethical business behavior and he always prefaced his denunciations with a reiteration of that and an explanation and rationale for the ethical positions he asserted. Again, the educative function of politics combined with confrontation.

Stephen did the same thing with the interest groups that Senator Bessemer seemed to be so concerned about not rattling and even keeping satisfied with government largesse. Different interest groups were criticizing the gradual disengagement policy and were lobbying feverishly on Capitol Hill. Unlike past presidents, Stephen would not just be content with dealing with Congress to try to get half a loaf as the interest groups quietly pushed lawmakers to be sure that nothing would change. He went to the national headquarters in Washington of many of

278

the resisting groups and denounced them in press conferences or quickly organized rallies, and laid out substantial details about how they and the entities they represented were living "high on the hog" because of government benefits. He explained how government largesse for them had become almost a set of perks that kept enriching them. He explained further how the average taxpayer was disadvantaged as they benefited and showed why the claim that the corporate welfare that was involved most of the time provided considerably less of a public advantage than its promoters claimed. The media showed up in large numbers to both the press conferences and the rallies and Stephen's network was always geared up to come, too. Stephen talked about the "dirty little secrets" about how interest groups threw their weight around in Washington. He particularly put each individual interest group on the defensive by publicizing the cold facts about its particular behavior and actions. Stephen was always careful to set out the necessary and proper role for interest groups in a democratic republic, but consistently pounded home how things had long since gotten out of control and the public interest was being grievously harmed. This strategy of Stephen's had the effect of turning public attention to the actions of interest groups in an unprecedented way.

He went a step farther. When members of Congress of both parties criticized him publicly for retracting certain programs, he hammered away at the fact that they had gotten campaign contributions from some of the interest groups—which was almost always the case when they rushed to zealously defend the programs.

While the left detested Stephen because the nationwide shutdown of abortion clinics, refusal to enforce the Supreme Court's same-sex "marriage" decision, gradual disengagement policy, and a full range of other things (including just the fact that he had put it in a defensive position that it was unaccustomed to), some elements from within their ranks supported him on his initiatives to prod large corporations to act more responsibly. Most, though, were so fixated on regulation and government forcing business to do things that they viewed use of the bully pulpit as namby-pamby. Others of them responded positively to his strong push for criminal justice reform, even while some conservative elements were skeptical or outright opposed. In addition to the changes that had been implemented during the First Hundred Days, he stated that the Justice Department had a new policy of ending plea-bargaining except where "absolutely necessary." He said that practice "had exploded in recent decades and it was an utter scandal how it had subverted the constitutionally-guaranteed right to trial." He also firmly stated that any evidence of the "least bit of coercion of any kind" in securing guilty pleas by any U.S. Attorney or his staff members would result in "their immediate ouster." He decried civil forfeiture and was intent on reining it in as he had in Pennsylvania. He explained it and the extensive abuses it had generated to a mostly unaware public. He said that it had become "official thievery." He said sternly that any police department in the country that took property through forfeiture from innocent persons would have its federal funding immediately suspended and would have a civil rights action brought against it. He also announced the formation of a legal academic and professional advisory committee that was tasked with reviewing the increasingly expansive U.S. Criminal Code and reporting to him within six months about proposals to drastically cut it down, and to specifically seek the elimination of provisions that were in the least bit vague, overbroad, compromised traditional legal requirements of *actus reus* or *mens rea*, or which represented actions that had traditionally been addressed by civil law but had become criminalized. The left had a hard time scoring points in criticizing his criminal justice initiative because he deftly arranged to speak to a few of the less dogmatic left-leaning organizations and reminded them about their push for such reform and also because he appointed to the small advisory committee two prominent, but fair, leftist legal scholars from Harvard and Yale Law Schools.

To deal with the grumbling about criminal justice reform from his usual conservative allies—some of them fashioned themselves as "tough law-and-order types"—Stephen heavily used his professorial, educative approach. He made a strong, and mostly successful, effort to convince them that true constitutional liberties were what were really at stake. He enlisted the help in reaching out to them of a few prominent conservative commentators who had long since seen these problems with American criminal justice. If they were concerned about constitutional restoration they had to go the whole way and recognize that *excessive* deference to law enforcement interests was unmerited and unjust. They had to do their job and act professionally, like everyone else. He emphasized to them that a rehabilitative approach was not unrealistic. He told them, as he had emphasized in Pennsylvania, how it was strikingly seen in such a hard-nosed realistic thinker—even tilting to the pessimistic side—as the great Church Father St. Augustine of Hippo. He said that one had to avoid both the utter optimist of a Rousseau and the crassly pessimistic, cynical view of man of a Machiavelli. Trying to reform the criminal was the realistic, even necessary, course for public policy, especially in light of the crisis of recidivism.

When the advisory committee reported, Stephen made whatever executive changes he could—such as the Justice Department's ordering that U.S. Attorneys not enforce vague laws or compromise traditional common law protections—and sent a major reform package to Congress to cut down the Code to a third of its current provisions. He also conditioned federal aid for state criminal justice systems on the adoption of similar changes at that level. In line with his normal approach, he repeatedly was in discussion with state governors to bring them around to this on their own. Again, it was the bully pulpit instead of legal pressure.

The left and even some in his own party were seething over his anti-homosexualist initiatives in the military and his refusal to enforce the Supreme Court's same-sex "marriage" edict before the Court reversed its decision after his challenge. Stephen further roused their ire with his announced refusal to appoint any open homosexuals or lesbians to governmental positions. He kept up his offensive about homosexualism as he did so many other things. He kept pounding away at the fact that to engage in the "homosexual lifestyle," which involves sexual activity, is a choice and people have to be responsible for their choices—just as they are responsible for other kinds of behaviors. He kept explaining publicly—the educative part of his handling of the issue—that there was no evidence that same-sex attraction was inborn, and if it were there was no inevitability or need about one engaging in same-sex practices anymore than there was with heterosexuals giving into their sexual urges. Following the pattern that he started with his Pennsylvania lieutenant governor campaign, he repeatedly brought authorities and people with pertinent personal experiences onto the speaking trail with him to drive these points home—and he did it consistently. Stephen was not out just to end the intolerant, totalitarian-like scheming of the homosexualist organizations and their allies in government, corporations, and other private entities, but he also was aiming at helping to change the deeply convoluted and corrupted cultural outlook that they had helped to fashion in recent decades. He even faced off in a public debate with a prominent suburban Maryland businessman who was also an open homosexual and leading homosexual propagandist. It was a highly unusual thing for a sitting president to do, but Stephen was confident that it would help the cause. He always made sure he had all the facts he needed before he entered the fray, and then his sharp mind and superb debating and rhetorical skills invariably enabled him to outflank his adversary.

In the debate, at the Metropolitan University Club, Jarrol Weatherman, the businessman, alleged that Stephen and his administration had caused "gays" to be treated as "second-class citizens."

That was all that Stephen needed for an opening. As was so often the case with Stephen's rhetorical adversaries they were caught off-guard. "You are hardly the man to talk about receiving 'second-class' treatment or being a victim, Mr. Weatherman. You are listed as the twentieth wealthiest person in Maryland. You belong to several of what can only be characterized as exclusive social clubs in the state. You have an estate overlooking the Potomac River, and three other homes including one in the Bahamas. It is hard to say that you are somehow 'second-class' when you are on the state executive committee of your political party. It is hard to say that you are 'second-class' when you own yachts that are moored both on the Potomac and in the Bahamas. You have to face up to it, Mr. Weatherman: you have given into your baser instincts. You habitually engage in perverse sexual practices— yes, what no one thanks to the propaganda machines of organizations like the one you are the honorary leader of wants to admit anymore is perversion—where you use parts of your and other people's bodies is a way contrary for what their obvious purpose is. Admit it, Mr. Weatherman, you are promoting your homosexualist cause because you are trying to justify yourself and probably to cover up for your own deeply-held guilt. Break away from it, Mr. Weatherman. It's possible to restrain yourself, to change your life, to give up your self-indulgent and distorted sexual behavior."

"What do you mean? I don't have guilt."

"Look inside yourself, Mr. Weatherman. When a man has the kind of fury you're exhibiting, it's normally because something is tugging mightily at his will. You had a problem and it deeply troubled you. The organization that you have become a spokesman for and other organizations like it seemed to offer help to you, but it was really just an opportunity for self-justification, a ready excuse. In fact, though, they just wanted to use you to further their own radical sexual agenda." He paused for a second, to add effect to the next point. "Now, they have even made some statement that justifies same-sex behavior with minors, even pedophilia. You are really the one who has made yourself 'second-class' by the fact that you have allowed them to set the agenda for you. *Think for yourself,* Mr. Weatherman. Do not allow sexual libertarians to do your thinking for you."

Weatherman was stunned for a moment. Stephen looked straight into his eyes and he saw what probably few in the audience could notice. There was a slight tearing in his eyes, before he could finally recover and insist, "No, no, no. You are treating us badly." Then he tailed off, not quite sure what to say next. By the tearing, Stephen could see that he had hit the bulls-eye. This prominent businessman was shaken by what Stephen had said because it was true. Stephen did not say anything about it, but from the research that was done about him before the debate Stephen learned that accounts had long been circulated that a distant family member had sexually assaulted him when he was twelve and that had set him on the course that he had gone in.

No one remembered a president ever speaking like this before. Stephen confronted the adversary directly and personally because he thought it was needed in this case. He got right to the heart of what the homosexualist onslaught was really about. That debate, which got wide publicity, helped encourage the critics of this "alternative lifestyle" to "come out into the open" again and assert increasingly boldly the truth about homosexuality. As it turned out, Stephen's challenge to the Supreme Court signaled the near end of same-sex "marriage" in America and his debate with Weatherman was a watershed in moving the broader debate in the country against homosexualism. A president who not only opposed it but also campaigned against it and educated the public about it turned out to have a profound effect in precipitating a major cultural shift.

In line with his unwillingness, stated in his initial presidential address to the nation, to somehow stand aside in the name of federalism and ignore state and local governments suppressing legitimate liberties and rights, he confronted the states that were allowing same-sex couples to adopt children. He had defended legitimate parental rights regarding CAPTA, and now he was defending true children's rights (as opposed to the statists who had long sought to undermine the natural rights of parents in the name of a concocted notion of "children's rights" that really meant bureaucrats supplanting parents to control children). He declared that any state that permitted adoptions by same-sex couples would summarily have their federal HHS social services funding cut across the board. Again, he set the stage for this with another of his seminars in which he had authorities who the media normally ignored or scoffed at talk about the considerable detriments suffered by children raised in the households of same-sex couples and when he announced it in another of his nationwide addresses—the major media now knew better than to refuse him airtime—he turned over the microphone briefly to a half dozen of them who summarized, in a manner understandable by the average citizen, their research about it. As he had done in the campaign, he also presented three individuals

283

who poignantly told the trauma they had experienced growing up as the "children" of same-sex couples.

Stephen also proceeded aggressively against lower levels of government—it especially was happening on the local level—that were using various techniques, including noise and disorderly conduct ordinances, anti-sign ordinances, and zoning regulations to stifle the free speech of citizens and residents who were expressing views on issues that the left didn't like. Some of these concerned a new thing called "micro-aggression ordinances," which essentially prohibited any such expression that offended anyone in any way. An assortment of leftist interest groups had successfully pushed for these ordinances in several metropolitan areas, and then began to act as self-appointed monitors to register complaints with local enforcement arms so that the ordinances would be invoked against people. Stephen responded to what he called these "localized aggressions against the First Amendment"—he said that was the "real aggression going on"—and the other anti-speech ordinances with a combination of threats of filing immediate federal civil rights actions, cut-off of federal funds to the localities in question, and persistent, public criticism by him and his administration of the community. Hardly any local communities were up for a fight with him and backed off. He also repeatedly attacked the leftist groups involved in the micro-aggression ordinances as "anti-Constitution." His network also organized rallies—complying as they always did with regulations to get needed permits and the like—in a number of the communities. Stephen made clear in advance that the local governments had better not dare try to stop them from doing so. None did.

Stephen had a direct showdown with Governor Mike Swift from Oregon, who was from his own party but who had been cool to him during the election campaign. The state's Human Rights Commission was notorious for its hostility to Christian beliefs. There had just been a series of highly publicized cases in which it imposed gargantuan financial penalties on a number of churches for teaching that homosexual behavior is morally wrong and on individual Christians for publicly expressing opposition to same-sex marriage, including one where it ordered a lifetime 50% garnishment of a man's wages after two same-sex couples complained that they had suffered "mental anguish" from his comments. There was also a report that besides imposing a hefty financial penalty on a Protestant pastor for refusing to "marry" a lesbian couple, it was moving to have the Oregon Department of Revenue revoke his church's tax exemption. What's more, Swift had made statements in support of a move by the other party, which had a majority in the state legislature, to consider any kind of discrimination on the grounds of "sexual orientation" by a non-profit organization—this was understood to include the whole gamut from persons in same-sex relationships to transvestites—as disqualifying it for a state tax exemption.

Stephen called him and made it clear to him what the costs were going to be for his state. If it didn't back off, remove the penalties, and reimburse "every red cent" that it had made "these innocent people pay," all federal aid to the state would be stopped.

"Wait, Mr. President, you can't do that," Swift objected. "We're a sovereign state. This is a matter of federalism. You have made a big issue of federalism."

"Governor, federalism does not give you the right to trample on the Constitution and I will not tolerate that."

Swift seemed to be just the latest political elite to not take Stephen seriously or understand the depth of his commitment to redirect the country. He seemed almost oblivious to all that had been happening. His next comment also showed that he was one more elected official from Stephen's party who didn't quite grasp that Stephen was no typical politician.

"Mr. President, the party people here will not be too happy that the federal government is interfering in our state in this way. They will not be too enthusiastic for our candidates in the mid-term elections or three-and-a-half years from now."

"Maybe, you don't understand, Governor, that this is not a politics-as-usual time. The issues here are not politics, but the Constitution and human dignity and true human rights—not phony, made-up human rights but real ones. Oh, and by the way, Oregon didn't seem to help me much in the election. If this situation in your state isn't turned around within two weeks time, you can expect all the funds—*all of them*—to be cut off immediately."

He finally seemed to catch on that Stephen was serious, and he hesitated a bit before formulating his next response. "Mr. President, the state has legal rights. We're entitled to those funds."

"Governor, the courts aren't going to help you. Beside the fact that Congress has given the executive branch broad authority over the funds, the courts have no authority under the Constitution—even though they have sometimes tried to act otherwise—to order government to fund anything. You can be sure that I'm not going to allow the courts to act unconstitutionally anymore than I'm going to allow your state to do so."

The conversation ended. Stephen's administration was in close contact with the people whose religious rights were being flaunted and he got the word two weeks later that everything that he had demanded had been done. The story was that Swift had put strong political pressure on the Human Rights Commission.

The next thing that Stephen's administration did concerning Oregon, Washington, California, and a few other states that had permitted assisted suicide was to issue new federal regulations that disallowed participation of physicians in the Medicare and Medicaid programs if they did not commit themselves to take no part in physician-assisted suicide, cut off federal funds to hospitals that gave privileges to physicians who either did not make this commitment or had taken part in physician-assisted suicide or themselves did not have in place protocols to insure ordinary care and nutrition and hydration (regardless if proxy decision-makers wanted to cut these off). Hospitals that cut these off on their own against the wishes of family or other authorized decision-makers would face federal civil rights investigations. HHS funds for health programs to states that had legalized physician-assisted suicide would also be cut off if legislative changes were not made within six months. In the meantime, he and his network picked up on the euthanasia and physician-assisted suicide issues that he had hammered away at during the campaign, and had people join them in public speeches who had seen the outrages that this and other examples of legalized killing had brought in these states and Europe. Stephen was going to make the public realize what was wrong with euthanasia and why the corrupted opinion-makers commending it for so long were wrong.

So as Stephen was "gradually disengaging" the federal government from its excessive role in social welfare and restore its proper place as envisioned by the Constitution, he was also pressing the lower levels of government to themselves act according to the American constitutional tradition and the natural moral law that it had emerged from.

Another way Stephen contributed mightily to a cultural shift in the country—with even more far-reaching implications—concerned the role of religion in public life. He used the first national holidays that came up while he was in office, Lincoln's Birthday, Washington's Birthday (this was actually the official name of the recognized national holiday, even though it had come to be popularly called "President's Day"), Memorial Day, and Flag Day, to teach about how crucial the Founding Fathers believed religion was to sustain any government and especially a free one. He also stressed the religious and specifically Christian culture that had prevailed in America for most of her history.

At the special federal commemoration of Lincoln's Birthday, Stephen gave a speech at the Lincoln Memorial recalling his great predecessor's proclamation of a national fastday in the midst of the Civil War on March 30, 1863. Stephen quoted Lincoln as saying that it was "'the duty of nations as well as of men to own their dependence upon the overruling power of God.'" He went through Lincoln's terse proclamation and drew parallels between what the sixteenth president had said about the need for nations to follow God and the weakening of the religious hold upon the America of his time and on us today. He continued, "Lincoln had said further that 'those nations only are blessed' that follow Him and His demands. Lincoln had a strong sense that it was an ongoing reality of history—it did not stop just with the ancient Jewish nation of the Old Testament—that, as he said, 'nations like individuals, are subjected to punishments and chastisements in this world.' In the proclamation, and elsewhere, he stated that he saw the Civil War as 'a punishment inflicted upon us for our presumptuous sins' that calls us to a 'national reformation.' While Lincoln reminded the Americans of his time that God had made them, as he put it, 'the recipients of the choicest bounties of Heaven' and that America had 'grown in numbers, wealth, and power as no nation has ever grown'— he could have been talking about the America of today—at a time when religious practice, by any measure, was much more widespread than today and our Christian culture persisted that nevertheless God had been 'forgotten.' He said that, to further quote him, 'we have vainly imagined, in the deceitfulness of our hearts, that all these blessings were produced by some superior wisdom and virtue of our own' and we were 'too proud to pray to the God that made us.' Can we read our current traumas and calamities at least partly the same way, and that we need as Lincoln said to turn back to God in a serious way to seek about how to get out of them?" Stephen concluded by saying that the struggle now was like the one then—"although thankfully not a violent one"— to protect and, in fact, restore America's Founding principles. "One of these was that God and religion were essential for the maintenance of our democratic republic. As James Madison, called the 'Father of the Constitution' said, 'We have staked the future of all of our political institutions upon the capacity of mankind for self government; upon the capacity of each and all of us to govern ourselves, to control ourselves according to the Ten Commandments of God.'"

In the days after the speech, a number of clergy, especially ones who were oriented to the political left, publicly criticized Stephen for calling people back to religion. That was the job of clergy, not of politicians. The implication was that it somehow was an excessive intertwining of church and state. This was brought up at one of Stephen's press conferences. His response, given with the customary firm look in his face, was simply, "If it was good for Abraham Lincoln to do, it's good for me and any other president to do."

On Washington's Birthday—"President's Day"—Stephen gave a speech at the Washington Monument as the highlight of the federal holiday observation. He talked on the same theme of religion as the essential foundation of the American democratic republic. Stephen mentioned how in Washington's First Inaugural Address, he spoke of God as the "Great Author of every public and private good." Then he recounted the famous quote from Washington's Farewell Address: "Of all the dispositions and habits which lead to political prosperity, religion and morality are indispensable supports." Stephen explained how the Father of the Country could only be speaking of the God of Abraham, Isaac, and Jacob—the God of Christianity and of the Jews. He also emphasized that the morality he referred to was not something relativistic or something of human making—"radical human autonomy, where man thinks of himself as a kind of deity who can make his own rules, is the great bane of our age"—and explained the natural law tradition behind America and her Founding documents. He went on to quote other Founding Fathers about the importance of religion: John Adams said, "Our Constitution was made only for a moral and religious people. It is wholly inadequate to the government of any other." Benjamin Franklin, supposedly a notorious deist, famously said at a critical juncture during the Constitutional Convention of 1787: "God governs in the affairs of men…without his concurring aid we shall succeed in this political building no better than the Builders of Babel." In his writing, Thomas Jefferson asked, "Can the liberties of a nation be thought secure when we have removed their only firm basis, a conviction in the minds of the people that these liberties are a gift of God? That they are not to be violated but with his wrath?" Dr. Benjamin Rush stated that without religion, "there can be no virtue, and without virtue there can be no liberty." Stephen talked also about the fervent and active religiosity of most of the Founders. He also discussed why Tocqueville had said of the Americans that despite their clear separation of church and state religion was "the first of their political institutions."

Stephen declared Memorial Day and Independence Day in that first year of his presidency as "national days of prayer." Presidents for decades had proclaimed a National Day of Prayer, but it was almost *pro forma*. No one had any sense that with Stephen the proclamation was in any way merely *pro forma*. He meant it and called the nation not just to

288

prayer, but also reparation for personal and national misdeeds. The last part raised howls and was mocked by some in the mainstream media, but that just caused Stephen to go on the offensive, as per usual, against them and the other critics and to intensify his educational effort about the country's religious heritage. After awhile, when they saw that their criticism was getting nowhere, it tailed off.

An arch-secularist organization, Americans Against the Corruption of Religion (AACR) filed suit against Stephen for his religious proclamations in the U.S. District Court for the District of Columbia. Foolishly, the AACR's president, a one-time sociology professor now full-time anti-religious activist named Jonathan Dirken, tried to serve process on Stephen at the White House. It was mostly a publicity stunt, as they made sure the media was there when they showed up. Dirken was turned away, and Lennie McIlroy, John Frost's assistant, read a lengthy statement by Stephen to the media. It restated all that Stephen had been saying about the Founding Fathers and the religious tradition of the country, as well as educating the media about the clear precedents that a sitting president cannot be sued. It also summarized some of the AACR's outrageous conduct over the years and accused its operatives of anti-Christian bias, with numerous examples of its statements and actions to back this up. Dirken found that his publicity coup wasn't the success he had hoped for. One or two of the media people began to ask him about the anti-Christian bias. The whole episode was taking long enough that John Frost was able to contact a few of Stephen's supporters in the alternative media in Washington who quickly showed up and began to hammer Dirken with a flood of additional questions about that. As far as the supposed lawsuit went, Stephen simply sent a terse letter to the judge saying that a sitting president cannot be sued for his official actions—the precedents were crystal-clear about that—and that neither he nor the Justice Department would even defend the case. The judge, who was not ready to take Stephen on after the way he had dealt with the Supreme Court, dismissed AACR's legal filing.

Another judge in a different kind of religion case decided to dig in his heels. The council of the small town of Granger, Kansas—population around 1200—buoyed by Stephen's initiatives, decided to organize a "Religious Heritage Day" accompanied by a proclamation about how important religion is for free government. A small atheist organization based in Lawrence, which is a university town and the acknowledged most leftist community in the state, filed suit against Granger. A federal judge ruled Granger's actions unconstitutional. Attorney General Larribee immediately stepped in to assist Granger with its appeal to the 8th Circuit in St. Louis. Stephen declared that if the 8th Circuit, or even after it, the Supreme Court upheld the judge he would refuse to enforce the decision and order the U.S. Marshal Service not even to deliver the higher courts' orders. If necessary, he would also dispatch marshals and federalized National Guard troops to Granger to insure that the Religious Heritage Day celebration would be permitted to take place. The 8th Circuit reversed the judge and the Supreme Court refused to take up the atheist outfit's appeal. The higher federal courts no longer had the stomach to take on Stephen.

Stephen's effort to restore America's religious heritage, the public call for prayer and reparation and the rest, was not just words or public gestures. He lived it every day. Besides maintaining an administration that was morally above reproach, he and Marybeth went to Mass and received the Holy Eucharist daily. With all the security and publicity issues, special arrangements were made with Archbishop Scanlon and then Archbishop LaGrange to have a priest come to the White House each weekday morning to say Mass. When they were in Washington, they routinely went to Sunday Mass at the Cathedral of St. Matthew the Apostle. To avoid a ruckus, LaGrange let them and the few people accompanying them unobtrusively attend early Mass in the choir loft where usually only the organist and an assistant were present. Stephen also went to weekly confession with the priest who came for the daily White House Masses. Even though, unlike Lincoln, Stephen did not call for a national fast day, he fasted regularly for Divine assistance for his administration and for the return of strong religious faith and sound morality to the nation.

Marybeth carried out the normal social and other functions of the president's wife, but she was in no way a "typical first lady." Both Stephen and Marybeth disliked the practice of recent decades of how first ladies had become almost government officials in their own right. She had no staff. Stephen's appointments secretary handled her calendar, as well. She usually accompanied Stephen on his many speaking trips. Her other time was spent in volunteer work, something no other modern first lady had done in any significant way. Archbishop LaGrange arranged for her to do this under the auspices of the Archdiocese, like she had done through the Harrisburg Diocese when Stephen became lieutenant governor of Pennsylvania. Her efforts ranged from doing assignments for LaGrange to working in soup kitchens run by the Archdiocese. She insisted on having a minimal security detail, limited to just one Secret Service agent when she was out in the field for the Archbishop or even at the soup kitchens.

Despite the relative success of Stephen's persistent offensive posture against the leftist mainstream media, which had caused them to be more reticent about attacking him, there tended to be a renewed foray from some parts of it with each new initiative of his. Despite the certainty and deftness with which he handled each new undertaking and his astounding political success with the Supreme Court, the media and political assaults in the first year of his presidency, while completely expected, had been unsurprisingly far more trying than at anytime in his life. The media began to pick up steam and caused their greatest damage to him when a minor crisis erupted in his administration. A high permanent bureaucrat in the Department of HHS, who was even more notorious than most in the "permanent government" in Washington for his leftist sympathies, had been regularly—and blatantly—sabotaging the gradual disengagement policy in his bureau in the department and encouraging well-placed figures in other bureaus to do the same. Even though Stephen had selected cabinet members in part for their toughness, proven ability to maintain control of the institutional entities they headed, and ability to stay a course of action despite attempts by subordinates to persuade, manipulate, or pressure them in a different direction, Jim Lewis at HHS had been unaware, almost negligently, about what this bureaucrat was doing throughout the department. Stephen, of course, had made it clear that he would step in and "go around" the agency heads if he saw something serious that was not being addressed. Stephen did this here and, after compiling an extensive file that clearly documented the bureaucrat's attempts to undermine administration policy, suspended him from his job and moved to dismiss him from federal service. There was no question that such insubordination could merit dismissal under the Civil Service statutes and Stephen and Lewis were careful to follow all procedural rules. Before dismissal could take place, the law required thirty days' notice and that the federal employee be given the opportunity to respond and defend himself.

After the suspension, Stephen and Lewis sat down to discuss the episode in the Oval Office. Lewis spoke up immediately and offered to resign. He said that he believed he had let Stephen down on the very thing that Stephen had especially entrusted him to come through on. He had been a supporter of Stephen's from early in the presidential election campaign and strongly believed across the board in what he was trying to do. Stephen in no sense was unwilling to discharge people who couldn't or wouldn't do what he expected. He knew that a solid leader would have to be willing to act decisively in such matters, that sentiment had no place no matter who the person was or what his

291

personal or professional association with him was. Still, Stephen had considered this matter closely and given it much thought and believed that Lewis had learned from it. He had displayed the qualities of a very good agency head otherwise and except for this had kept a tight rein on the department. The bureaucrat in question had acted deftly and secretively.

"Jim, I know that you have been trying your hardest. We're human beings, we can't cover all the bases all the time. There's a lesson to be learned here. You'll know that you have to not leave any stones unturned in the department. I think a thing like this is not likely to happen again. The bureaucrats in HHS and in other departments have seen how if they do anything like this, they are walking on a tightrope and are going to fall off. Go back to work."

"Mr. President, you're a very rare person in public life. It's been apparent all along, even if some people—your ideological and political enemies, mostly—refuse to see it. You are tough, you know how to be on the attack when necessary and you are politically astute—but you are a man of charity, in so many ways. It's not some convoluted idea of sentimentality or false compassion, but genuine understanding and charity. If only the rest of them in public life would be like you our leadership would be an example to the rest of the country about how to get out of the moral morass that we've been in for so long."

"Jim, I'm just trying to struggle to be a good Christian, like you do."

"If more people who call themselves 'Christians' were like you, the secularists would have never gotten to the point they did."

Even though Stephen and Lewis handled this episode strictly according to the rules, it motivated the media to unleash the strongest—and perhaps most convincing—attack on Stephen yet for being a "dictator." The bureaucrat had contacts in the media and completely, self-servingly distorted the truth about it. The media was only too eager to run with it. It also gave the other party their biggest opening yet to jump on the bandwagon and carry out a veritable rhetorical barrage against him. They thought they finally had an opening, that laws were supposedly clearly being broken. Their members in both houses were demanding that a special joint committee be set up to investigate the administration and for the first time seriously, even after all his other exertions of sweeping executive power, started to call for impeachment.

Stephen, of course, went on the rhetorical offensive as usual, joined by Lewis. They repeatedly laid out the facts about what the bureaucrat did, the provisions of the law, the prerogatives of the president and the secretary, and the procedures that were followed. Stephen hammered away at the specific actions the bureaucrat had carried out "to undercut the elected leadership of the United States." No one could remember a case where a sitting president had so openly and vigorously "poured it on" a federal bureaucrat. If public opinion wavered at the start with the other party joining forces with the rebellious bureaucrat, as the days went by it shifted to Stephen. Stephen had fought doggedly but with dignity and his usual educational focus and again showed that he was a master at helping people see the truth and turning opinion around. The media had to just move on in the end, finally realizing that it had been a foolish cause to jump aboard the bandwagon for—even if they didn't like Stephen's gradual disengagement policy. They, of course, seldom paid any attention to Stephen's ongoing efforts to build up the civil society sector to pick up the slack. There was no special investigative committee and in spite of continued attacks on Stephen's executive actions—always effectively countered by him—the opposition stopped openly using the "dictator" language and calling for impeachment. In the end, after the truth had come out about the whole matter, the other party in Washington had egg all over themselves and the media had looked more foolish than usual.

Still, the whole affair had been especially trying for Stephen. As was customarily the case in those moments Marybeth was there to buttress him. One night, he curled up to her on the couch in the East Sitting Hall. Even though it was over, she noticed the deep weariness in his eyes and the continuation of the lines on his forehead and face that had become so evident while the whole thing was going on and which tended to show up when he was undergoing periods of strain. The bureaucrat episode had not been as critical or important as some of the other things he had done, but it probably hit him especially hard because it had come after so many of these other initiatives and crises.

"Marybeth, I think you know how difficult all these things have been," he said. "I know I have to persist, but I'm not sure how far I can take the effort. I don't have the least doubt that this has been the right course, but I'm still not sure that I have what it takes to see this through."

"Stephen, honey, you are having the effect that you hoped for. Things are changing in the country. I know that you can't always perceive it, but you are winning people's minds and hearts. Stay the course...and you know that I'll always be here to support you. So will the other people that have been with you and in this from the start. You'll succeed."

"Marybeth, I know that you're always there. That is the reassuring thing. That, plus the fact that I know I can one day face God and say

293

that I truly did all I could in this position He put me in, are the things that most sustain me. Even if I don't succeed, even if I'm eventually toppled from the presidency or drummed out of town I know I made the right choices and did what had to be done and I certainly will stay the course. That's not even in question."

"As I said, you will succeed." With that, they almost spontaneously broke into prayer together. They prayed together in the morning and then every night before retiring. What was different this time was the almost automatic way they began it and how the words just flowed from each of them.

Stephen was awakened the next morning to news of an embarrassing episode on a passenger airliner en route from New York City to Los Angeles. During the course of the flight four individuals, all elderly American Caucasians and none who were flying together, had each made five lavatory trips (the flight attendants were keeping count) and then the crew radioed ahead to LA International (LAX) about "suspicious activity" and believed that perhaps something was being plotted. The Transportation Security Administration (TSA) people at LAX ordered the pilot to make an emergency landing at Phoenix, where TSA and locally-based FBI agents boarded the plane, handcuffed the elderly passengers—two men and two women—and removed them from the plane. Then after strip searches, they proceeded to interrogate them, handcuffed and with leg irons, individually in small rooms at Phoenix Sky Harbor International Airport for over two hours. One of the women fainted and had to be taken to the hospital. One of the men kept asking for his medicine, but was told "it would have to wait." They were refused requests to make lavatory visits at the airport and the other woman at one point began to wet her seat. Finally, it was realized that they all had had to make their numerous in-flight lavatory trips because all were taking diuretics because of heart conditions. It was feared that the heart condition of the lady admitted to the hospital had worsened because of the interrogation.

As soon as Stephen was apprised of the episode, he arranged a conference call phone hook-up with the heads of the TSA and FBI offices in Phoenix, the head of the TSA at LAX, the national FBI Director and acting TSA Director, and the CEO of the airline. Stephen got a number of them out of bed—it was the middle of the night in the West—but that was not going to deter him. It was one of the few times in his dealings as president that Stephen showed obvious anger. He not only chewed them all out, but he informed the heads of the local TSA offices and the head of the Phoenix FBI office that they and all of their operatives who were involved, whose names he said he wanted to be told of in a return phone call within thirty minutes, were immediately, indefinitely suspended with disciplinary proceedings against the operatives to follow. He also asked for the immediate resignation of the acting TSA Director. Stephen had not appointed a regular Director because the agency was being eliminated at the end of the budget year. He would not be seeking any funds for its reauthorization and had informed Congress that he would veto any legislative provision continuing to fund the agency. He had also previously ordered sweeping changes in passenger screening procedures at airports to eliminate the grossly offensive actions that people were being subjected to. No one doubted that Stephen meant business and he got the return phone calls he wanted within thirty minutes. He told the airline CEO that he couldn't make him act against the crew for their outrageous miscue, but he was informing the country of the whole story. The CEO wound up firing all the flight attendants and suspending the pilot and co-pilot for six months. Stephen called a press conference that morning and told the whole story—"a case of governmental misconduct of the highest order, of federal agencies acting against the people"—and kept pounding away at it for days afterwards. After that, he kept bringing it up in his speeches about systemic governmental abuse. The remaining support for the TSA in Congress evaporated and there was no significant opposition to his winding down and then ending of the agency.

In that first year in office, Stephen took foreign policy initiatives that were unorthodox but an extension of the domestic direction of his presidency. The U.S. usually had cast a blind eye to the actions, no matter how outrageous, of European countries—her historic allies. American presidential administrations hardly ever had objected to any policies or legal developments or even human rights problems that presented themselves. After all, people thought, these were advanced Western countries and there were no human rights problems in them. In reality, these countries for a long time had influenced America negatively, with European secularism reaching over to here, even though we were always somewhat behind them in that. Presidential administrations hardly even seemed to notice. This was to end, emphatically, with Stephen. With a major foreign policy speech to Catholic and pro-life and pro-family non-governmental organizations at the UN—groups that no previous president would have ever even considered giving a speech to—Stephen denounced Holland and Belgium for their permitting the widespread practice of euthanasia, which had almost advanced to the point that anyone chronically ill of any age was imperiled. Stephen announced a number of actions that he was undertaking in response to the countries' euthanasia policies. These included reducing the U.S. embassy staffs, cutting out all government-to-government cooperation that was not clearly necessary, restricting investment of their companies in the U.S. and encouraging U.S. companies to go elsewhere instead of these countries, and a promise that the U.S. would repeatedly use its podiums in the international organizations (such as NATO and the Organization for Economic Cooperation and Development) that they jointly belonged to in order to denounce the countries' euthanasia practices. He also ordered the U.S. Representative to the UN to repeatedly attack the two countries for human rights abuses in the General Assembly. The U.S. also pushed to have the UN human rights bodies, which were normally completely unsympathetic to such issues, to investigate and condemn the countries. A not-so-subtle intimation of cutting back on the U.S.'s UN dues stopped the bodies from daring to shut off the American delegates' attacks. Stephen knew that some elements of the U.S. business community would vociferously object, so he had begun an "educational outreach" to executives in these companies to explain to them what was going on with euthanasia in those countries and to repeatedly try to show them what is wrong with euthanasia generally. To say the least, this part of the corporate world, like most of it, wasn't acquainted with such "moral catechizing." That didn't surprise and in no way deterred Stephen. It made him even more determined. The executives ended up at least listening. They didn't want any problems with the President of the United States.

Stephen's administration also lashed out at the western and northern European countries that were suppressing religious liberty and the educational rights of parents by doing such things as arresting and putting on trial pastors who criticized homosexual behavior and same-sex "marriage" in public statements, some of which were sermons in their churches, and seizing the children of parents who tried to homeschool them. He made it clear to them that the U.S. regarded these actions as human rights violations and that there would be consequences for them if they continued on this course and did not "satisfactorily resolve the cases" that had already gotten international attention—which meant favorably to those they were persecuting. Mutually valuable cooperative efforts with the U.S., which he knew were very important to those countries, hung in the balance. That Stephen was serious and placed a high priority on these matters was demonstrated by the fact that he was in direct contact with the prime ministers of the countries himself, instead of doing this through an intermediary or lower level functionary. He made it clear that this was coming directly from him. The respective leaders followed what he had been doing in the U.S. and so they had little doubt that he would take the actions he threatened. He was not one to blow smoke or bluster. In the weeks following, the U.S. embassies in the countries, under orders from Stephen, kept pressing their governments on these issues. Stephen wrote a personal letter to each of the prime ministers reminding them about what he had told them and he began to order small steps be taken to pull back on some of the cooperative efforts he had referred to. If there was any lingering doubt among the other nations' leaders that he was serious, he intended to eliminate it. Gradually, information was being passed along to U.S. diplomats that policy changes were in the works in those countries. They did this subtly, as they didn't want it to look like they were buckling under to the U.S. Stephen let them do their face-saving. He just wanted to see the changes made. He wasn't concerned about bravado.

Then, Stephen turned his attention to South Africa, which was a kind of darling to the American left. Indigenous, black rule had supposedly meant liberation. In fact, in many ways it had brought new oppressions with notorious domestic crime rates and an African National Congress (ANC) government that had imported some of most intolerant, even totalitarian-inclined, features of the Western left. One of the oppressive laws that it enacted was to force physicians to do abortions when requested or refer women to other physicians who would do them. Physicians who would not comply would not only lose their medical licenses, but also could go to prison. This is what caused Stephen to go into action against South Africa.

Again, Stephen did not go through diplomatic channels. He made an international call to the South African president, Frederick Naidoo. He called him out of the blue—Naidoo had no warning it was coming—and, after a few leader-to-leader type pleasantries that Stephen did not allow to go on long, put it to him directly: If the law about physicians and abortions is not repealed, American aid to South Africa would be suspended.

Naidoo was stunned by this totally unexpected peremptory demand by the leader of the most powerful country in the world and for a second he couldn't catch his breath. Then he got his wits back and responded in the feisty manner that had gotten him such admiration from among the ANC's supporters in his country and had helped bring him to the leadership of the government. Stephen knew about his background. In fact, he was a ruthless political operator who readily bowled over anyone who got in his way, even if he had been a master of projecting the image of the "caring politician" to his public. As a young man, he had been a dyed-in-the-wool Marxist, in line with the usually ignored background of the ANC. "Mr. President, this is an internal matter in our country. It is something for us to decide, it involves our laws. It is not something that even a leading country like yours can demand of us." For a split second, a smug, prideful feeling came over him. He was standing up to the President of the United States. He had followed Stephen's presidency and was aware of how he had shut down the abortion industry in the U.S., faced down the Supreme Court, and successfully challenged the powerful mainstream American media. It was not going to be the same with the leader of another sovereign country. Naidoo's momentary pride was quickly deflated, however.

"Mr. President," Stephen replied, "That didn't seem to be a consideration when the ANC was challenging white rule. You wanted all the foreign interference you could get. Well, this is as much or more of a human rights question as was involved there, and human rights concern universal issues. If you don't repeal that law, release from prison any physicians or others you have convicted for violating it and restore their professional standing, and cease any ongoing prosecutions under it within *two weeks* time"—he put a strong emphasis on the "two weeks"—"the U.S. aid funds earmarked for your country will be suspended."

"Mr. President," Naidoo quickly but nervously objected, "We can't possibly do something like this within two weeks' time."

"President Naidoo, your party controls the government and you control your party. Effectively, you have the power, so don't tell me that you can't do it. If I don't hear back from you, with full verification, that you have done what I have requested within two weeks of today the result is what I said. I won't keep you any longer. Good day—or I guess where you are I should say good evening." With that Stephen hung up the phone.

Similar to the Europeans' reaction, the South African government had lower level operatives make contact with the U.S. embassy to let them know that there were no pending prosecutions of physicians and that the National Prosecution Authority would initiate no further prosecutions. In the meantime, a minor law reform bill was being put before the South African Parliament in the coming month that would include a repeal of the abortion provision. It was apparent that Naidoo did not want to respond to the White House directly or permit any of his Cabinet to do so because it would look like they were groveling or something like that. Stephen didn't mind. He thought of a couple of the basic rules of diplomacy that he remembered from the great international affairs thinker Hans J. Morgenthau: Give up the shadow of worthless rights for the substance of real advantage and, second, don't put yourself in a position from which you can't retreat without losing face. Stephen didn't care if South Africa openly conceded for the world to hear that since the U.S. provided the funds, as a matter of principle she could influence her policies when she had a good reason. He also didn't want her government to face the international embarrassment of appearing to be retreating with its tail between its legs from a demand of a great power. He only sought that the government end this repressive policy, which it did.

The following week, Stephen was scheduled to address the UN General Assembly. He was going to take his initiative for a human rights policy grounded squarely on the natural law and not leftist conceptions—one, that is, which stressed human life concerns, true marriage and the family, and opposed the totalitarian impulse to suppress those who upheld them—that he had been carrying out in a targeted way with the Europeans and South Africa to a wholesale level. He was going to announce to the UN and the world what America was now standing for and would assert as best it could—in a politically realistic, not morally crusading or Wilsonian, fashion. In an address that was widely publicized around the world—UN developments tended to receive more notice abroad than in the U.S.—he put the leftist UN bureaucrats and NGOs on the defensive, just like he had consistently done with the domestic left. As in his domestic efforts, however, his approach was educational—again, Stephen the professor showed through. He threw down the gauntlet and let the whole world know that the U.S. was decisively lining up against the cultural revolution, built mostly around the ethic of sexual libertinism, which the left was trying to ignite worldwide.

Stephen began by talking about the true notion of human rights. Although he didn't state his source and most of the listeners in the General Assembly hall didn't know it, he recounted the famous catalogue of human rights from Pope St. John XXIII's encyclical *Pacem in Terris* (*Peace on Earth*) and he elaborated on them, explaining why they were rightfully considered human rights. Like Pope John, he emphasized how all these rights had corresponding duties. So, he said, it was impossible to talk about rights as if they were in a vacuum. He explained that even though there were rights, which were universally valid, there were various ways to effectuate them— that is, not just by governmental effort—and that how and the degree to which they would attach would depend on the conditions of the individual political community. For example, there is a right to education, but the extent to which that would extend would differ in a poor underdeveloped country and a highly developed one. He also explained that the basis for human rights could not merely be human agreement. That was a very shallow and dangerous notion because human opinion was often changeable and fleeting, so what at one point would be a grounds for freedom could in the future be the foundation for tyranny. Only the nature of man, behind which stood the God who created him and whose image he reflected, could be the basis for human rights.

He said that rights and duties concerned morality, as human rights could not be based on opinion neither could morality. It was another ringing Stephen Gregory Bernard apologia for the natural law. Freedom was a central basis for man's dignity, but freedom could not be detached from responsibility as based in true morality, and an unsound notion of freedom—license, runaway freedom, or a false conception of freedom—was inevitably destructive. It would destroy man's true dignity, the very thing that documents like the UN Universal Declaration of Human Rights aimed to guarantee.

He also said that the principles of morality were not separable. Men could not claim to be concerned, say, about ending international conflict, upholding human rights, and stopping things like genocide on the one hand and leading and, worse, promoting lives of moral dissoluteness when it come to sex and reproduction on the other. Inevitably, the one affects the other. Morality in the one area is going to be corrupted if it is in the other. For example, he said, when the unborn are seen as expendable—usually, for reasons of mere convenience—there is no way that attitudes about life and respecting others are not coarsened otherwise. He scored the defenders of abortion for an "intellectual legerdemain" in trying to talk their way around the humanity of the unborn child. He succinctly laid out the biological facts and said that the "outrageous development" was that they had gotten to the point of almost conceding this, but believed it didn't make a difference. These "members of the human family" were viewed as expendable, as abortion was "now virtually celebrated as a positive good." There had been many cases of genocide in history, he said, where a certain group's humanity was essentially ignored and eliminating them was held to be a good thing.

His defense of true marriage was one of the greatest speeches about it since the aggressive promotion of same-sex "marriage" had begun. He "educated" the representatives of the nations of the world, in his usual brief but comprehensive fashion, about the nature of marriage and argued that what was at stake was human rights, the right of children to have a father and a mother. As he did in speeches to U.S. audiences, he took aim squarely at the false claims of the homosexualist movement and the respectable professional organizations that long ago had been infiltrated by it and been giving it cover. He did not hold back about the unnatural character of same-sex attraction and why—morally, medically, biologically, and psychologically—homosexual conduct was destructive.

Then, he put in his crosshairs the UN's runaway bureaucracy, activist NGO's, and Western nations engaging in "cultural imperialism" by "aggressively promoting" the sexual libertine agenda. In doing so, nothing was allowed to stand in their way: national traditions, indigenous cultures, the most basic respect for our fellow man, human dignity, and truth itself. Their deception and manipulative actions, he said, "called to heaven for vengeance." Some of them and the United Nations Population Fund (UNFPA) were working to "thin out the populations of developing countries with population control." He said, "They needed to explain to the world how this was not a new genocide."

Then came the *coup dê grace*. With his typical firm look and clear, distinct tone when he conveyed unmistakable resolve—captured here on television newscasts that day around the world—he concluded his speech, "The UN has betrayed the noble purpose that motivated its founding. The United States of America will no longer provide any funds for any UN agency—or any international organization—that in any way or to any degree, directly or indirectly, openly or quietly works to promote the population control, pro-abortion, anti-true family, homosexualist, or sexual liberation agendas—and we will reduce our UN dues sharply until such time as major reform of the organization takes place so that it no longer supports such activities or tries, in effect, to order such countries to comply with such things or otherwise interferes with the domestic affairs of nations. The United States, by the way, is prepared to lead this reform effort, which must include a drastic reduction of the size and prerogatives of the UN bureaucracy and a recommitment to the original spirit of the organization."

It was by far the strongest chastening and challenge to the actions of the UN by an American president, in fact by the head of state of any country—and he delivered it right at a meeting of the main body of the organization itself. As he spoke, there were simultaneously smiles and nods and looks of shock and disbelief mixed with scowls from the sea of delegates in the General Assembly hall. When he ended, the division continued and became even more manifest. Delegates from the underdeveloped countries in Africa and Asia and parts of Latin

America and a few Eastern European countries erupted into a thunderous standing ovation, those from Western countries either stood silently without clapping out of respect or refused to stand at all. It was the beginning of a new, close relationship of the U.S. with much of the developing world.

The next day, Stephen ordered the immediate elimination or reduction of U.S. funding for different UN activities. Stephen followed the prescriptions of the Budget and Impoundment Control Act of 1974, which could have resulted in Congress overriding his decision not to spend appropriated monies but he knew that would not happen. The UN was not a particularly popular beneficiary of U.S. funding either with the American public or, by and large, on Capitol Hill. Stephen's small but sagacious group of advisers had long since told him about the reach of his prerogatives notwithstanding under the law and prevailing judicial precedents and he fully exploited them. Ronald Reagan's ending of U.S. funding for UNESCO was a clear precedent. Plans had already been underway to sharply trim UN spending from the budget requests that the Office of Management and Budget was preparing for the next fiscal year.

The UN Secretary General and the other UN top brass didn't say anything publicly after the speech, but as the next couple of weeks wore on news reports were coming from well-placed sources in the organization that they were huddling to determine what to do. Stephen instructed the U.S. Ambassador to the UN, Dr. Marianne O'Brian, who had been a conservative international relations scholar from a small college in Pennsylvania much like the university he had taught political science at, to keep the door open to them even while reiterating that the U.S. wouldn't budge an inch. There were additional reports that representatives of the Secretary General had been meeting with her frequently.

Even though in the first year of his presidency Stephen took all of the strong, even unprecedented initiatives he did for the cause of human life, true marriage, the family, parental rights, restoring the religious character of the country, building up civil society to meet human needs, corporate economic responsibility and the just wage, upholding subsidiarity, and respect for underdeveloped countries and thus solidarity—all of which were down the line with Catholic teaching and traditional social thought—he was still attacked strongly from Catholic quarters. The attacks didn't come just from the Catholic left and liberal Catholic journalists, but from within the U.S. bishops conference bureaucracy and even from some bishops. They called him a "conservative ideologue," said he was against the poor and needy with

302

his gradual disengagement approach, claimed he was creating a situation where the powerful would overwhelm the weak by minimizing government action, and said he was heightening international tensions by the pressure he was applying to allied countries and at the UN (never minding the fact that it was usually in the cause of uncompromisable Catholic moral teachings). This was the deeply entrenched, secular-inclined element in American Catholicism that usually got all the attention and had caused so much damage since Vatican II.

In the midst of this, Stephen's old friend Archbishop LaGrange stepped up to powerfully support him. He confronted the Church bureaucrat critics, most of whom were right there in Washington, directly took on critical fellow prelates, and besides repeatedly using his column in the Washington Archdiocese's newspaper, *The Catholic Standard*, to support and defend Stephen he fired off letter after letter to respond to irresponsible attacks made against him in the Catholic press around the country. He even pushed hard within the Conference to turn back efforts to push resolutions, which almost always originated within the bureaucracy and were put before the bishops, to criticize aspects of Stephen's policies and initiatives. They were doing this even though what Stephen was doing was Catholic to the core. Like Stephen, LaGrange was resolute, hard-charging, and confrontational when he had to be, but always explaining and educating. He had straightened out two dioceses by attacking the problems and the adversaries from the day he took over, demanding and getting orthodoxy and discipline. He was a sweeping reformer like Stephen was—one in the realm of the Church, the other the state, but each motivated at bottom by the same timeless principles. LaGrange's efforts for Stephen got results. The attacks from official Church institutions virtually stopped. Reining in liberal Catholic organs was more difficult, but even here LaGrange's efforts had their effect. The wholly unexpected responses to them by a leading American prelate caused them to back off some.

At the end of the first year of Stephen's presidency, no one—supporter or adversary—doubted that he had set out on the path of sweeping, dramatic change and that, as far as he was concerned, that path was firm and irrevocable. It was better, he said to those close to him, to call it restoration—restoring what America once was. For him, it was crucial that he succeed. He was about as lacking in vanity as one would find in almost any man, to say nothing of a politician, but he knew deep inside that if he didn't the country's time as a constitutional republic might be ended.

CHAPTER 10

A Breathtaking Stroke Of Foreign Policy

E ven though Stephen had been remarkably successful in pushing though the substantial series of changes that he had sought and keeping his opponents on the defensive, uprooting powerful, long-entrenched forces was bound to make him many enemies. Although his educational efforts had helped to forge a surprising level of public support, his adversaries were sure they could strike a serious blow and stall his momentum at the mid-term Congressional elections. The desire to oppose him brought into alliance a wide group of political forces some of which would normally be at each other's throats. Although his party was still somewhat divided in its support for him and especially his bold moves and efforts to redirect national policy, there was no doubt that things would be considerably more difficult for him if the other party gained control of Congress. In fact, it had the potential to be disastrous for his presidency and for the cause of saving the Constitution and the American democratic republic.

Despite Stephen's considerable success in his effort to educate the public about his undertakings and in the "propaganda war" with his adversaries, his almost unprecedented moves unsurprisingly came at the price of weakened popular support. When a leader does the things he had, besides making a lot of enemies he also finds that the mass of people that is unschooled even about the principles of their Constitution, increasingly morally unhinged, and subjected to extensive, unremitting twisting of the truth easily turns away. To be sure, many citizens lauded him, but many others opposed him or believed him to be an abject abuser of power. The mid-term election would be a kind of reckoning, even though Stephen would not allow its outcome to deflect him from what he knew was the reason that God had put so improbable of a person as him into the most powerful office in the world. He prayed daily for strength and direction and always insured that he would not allow his will to be substituted for the Divine by asking Him continually to let him know if He wanted him to pursue a different course.

Throughout his presidency, as Stephen pursued his domestic agenda, he had to keep constant attention to foreign affairs as every president has to do. It was particularly urgent at the current time as radical Islam—Islamism—surged almost all across the globe and every day brought the threat of terrorist acts. The greatest Islamist danger for some years, and the one that was now behind most terrorist attacks, was the utterly brutal ISIS operation. It had forged alliances with most other Islamist movements and organizations around the world and was the "hidden hand" behind them. There was no question that ISIS had to be outright defeated, although the past two administrations of the other party had been singularly ineffectual in dealing with it. Their weakness, it was now widely agreed, had helped ISIS to reach the height of its power.

Stephen had brought a halt to substantial immigration and refugee resettlement and suspended the granting of temporary work and student visas from Moslem-majority countries, except for Christians and others fleeing from Islamic persecution. He also ordered intensive scrutiny and background investigations of Moslems from other countries who sought to enter the U.S. to insure that they had no ties to or sympathy with Islamist organizations. He encountered strong criticism that these moves were "religious profiling," but he countered that by successfully putting the critics on the defensive with national security arguments. Moreover, his actions gained strong public support. His vigorous efforts to seal off the southern border also helped to minimize the possibility that terrorists could slip through from there. Besides the deportation regimen he started immediately when taking office and ordering strong, vigorous enforcement by the Border Patrol, the building of the wall was underway and he secured from Congress— after procedural maneuvers to skirt a filibuster in the Senate—the additional funds to complete the full span of the wall of over 2,000 miles. He also ordered that mosques in the U.S. where there was any suspicion of radical sentiments or activity be placed under reasonable surveillance, being careful not to impinge upon the rightful free exercise of religion. Critics claimed he was threatening religious freedom, but Stephen consistently hit home with the argument that religious freedom did not permit threats to public order or to the security of others. He had written much about religious liberty as a professor and he drew on it heavily. It was another "teachable moment" for the President.

In a novel move, Stephen also issued an executive order requiring members of all recently resettled Moslem immigrant groups—whatever their immigration status (other than the few who had become American citizens)—to swear allegiance to the U.S. Constitution and American laws and to specifically disavow any sympathy for Islamic terrorist groups, a set of spelled-out tenets of the ideology of Islamism, and a desire to see *sharia* law put in place in the U.S.—or else face immediate deportation. These communities were also placed under reasonable surveillance, mostly by local law enforcement working cooperatively with federal authorities. He also made sure, through his tough Cabinet secretaries, that all major federal law enforcement and intelligence arms continuously worked closely together in surveillance and information-sharing—guaranteeing the coordination that had often been lacking in the past with sometimes calamitous consequences— which especially was necessary to stop "lone-wolf" would-be terrorists who were inspired by Islamist ideology, currently coming mostly from ISIS. The ACLU, which had long since become an out-and-out leftist organization, and other leftist groups attacked these policies for violating civil liberties. Again, with his background Stephen worked persistently to counter their claims, which were weak not only because he had ordered the authorities to be careful about protecting legitimate rights, privacy, and human dignity, but also because such foreigners on American soil didn't share the same constitutional rights as U.S. citizens did. In the manner that had defined his presidency, he went consistently on the offensive while educating about this. His adversaries, per usual, could not measure up to him in the propaganda war.

These and other efforts had headed off any would-be Islamic terrorist attacks on U.S. soil in the first year and some months of Stephen's term, even by "lone wolves." He prayed in thanksgiving each day to God for spearing the U.S. over these months. He was constantly aware, however, that any day could end the relative tranquility and bring a small or even large terrorist attack, and during this time ISIS-sponsored terrorists had carried out three destructive attacks in central and western Europe and several others had been thwarted by authorities. Stephen knew that the only solution was that ISIS— somehow, in some way—had to be completely defeated and destroyed.

Stephen was aware of the risks of direct American military involvement in the Middle East, the epicenter for ISIS's "Islamic revolution" to spread throughout the world, even while he was ready to use it if necessary to stop genocide. Most observers believed that the 2003 Iraq war had the effect of unwittingly setting the stage for ISIS and unleashing ever more destructive forces in the Middle East. It had created a power vacuum and helped further stimulate already simmering Islamic fundamentalism and anti-Americanism there and in neighboring countries. ISIS was tailor-made for these conditions and it had kept growing in strength, crowding out and supplanting other Islamist terror organizations like al-Queda, until it became the main vehicle that Sunni radicals turned to for their long fancied aim of constructing a new caliphate and forcing Islamic domination worldwide. Stephen firmly believed that it was by indigenous forces within the Middle East—brought together by the U.S., which then would play an ongoing role in strategizing with and supporting them— that ISIS would have to be defeated. He knew, however, that to fashion the needed alliance to do this would be very difficult, and it clearly had to be an alliance that would not be doing the U.S.'s bidding but was wholly devoted for its own reasons to eliminating this most brutal of pestilences in a region that had historically seen many of them.

Stephen had the most crucial foreign policy meeting of his term with Secretary of Defense Cullotte and Secretary of State Francis Robertson to discuss the way to proceed. Stephen, along with his many other abilities, had strong diplomatic skills. This surprised some people, who had seen mostly his uncompromising stances and initiatives on so many issues. The basis of this, deeply woven into his character, was his boundless charity and inveterate respect for anyone he came in contact with, friend and foe alike. His practice, after all, was confrontation and education *always in charity*. Such an attitude opened the door to successful diplomacy, something that he had been noted for in his university days. Universities are a great training ground for politics since they are so charged with it. Unlike so many on that scene, however, Stephen had always kept his principles intact even as he had been a successful "diplomat." Still, he had never dealt with the Middle East and admitted that he was far from being an expert about that most complicated and explosive part of the world. Also, he did not know any of the principals there. He had a grand scheme in mind, but he would need the help of those who had the knowledge and connections to make it work. Neither Cullotte nor Robertson had these either, but Robertson was able to point them in the right direction.

Robertson had had no State Department experience before his appointment, but he had gotten to know some people in the diplomatic corps over the years when he was associated with a leading foreign policy think tank in Washington and since becoming Secretary had made the rounds quickly and become knowledgeable about and acquainted with many U.S. diplomats and top Foreign Service people.

"Mr. President," he said, "There's a career guy at State who not only knows the Middle East inside and out, but has had all of his assignments over twenty years in that part of the world and has contacts galore there. He has rubbed noses with almost anyone who's important there, including most of the heads of state and the leaders of minority ethnic elements who the governments see as problems for them and who they keep at arm's length or are fighting against at different times. I mean he has worked with and is trusted by, say, both the Turks and the Kurds—if you can believe that. He should be at the top of the career people at State, but unfortunately he's been beaten up by the politics of the department—which are intense. He had been so successful and such a whiz kid—but as humble of a guy as you'll find, like you Mr. President—that people got jealous of him and so stopped him from climbing the ladder as he should have. I think he can be the point man here. He can work with you directly to reach out to the people in the Middle East you need to bring on board and to build the kind of alliance you have in mind."

"That's very interesting," Stephen replied. "What's his name?"

"It's Carlton Gramsby. He's the son of an Evangelical minister from the South. He originally was studying for the ministry himself, but then he decided instead to study international affairs and enter the Foreign Service. I think his background is a further reason why people at State never took to him. The Northeast stuffed shirt career people don't feel comfortable with an Evangelical in their midst, and one who doesn't hide his religion to boot." Robertson was known for his blunt assessments of things, both privately and in his public lectures at conferences and to groups that he gave before he became Secretary.

"Where is he posted now?" Stephen asked.

"He's here in Washington, at the Bureau of Near Eastern Affairs at State. He's been here since last year. He was last posted in the UAE. He's got a desk job, writing reports for the different offices in the Bureau. They're relying on his background, but he was definitely underutilized by the previous administration. The career people kept him at arms length and the previous political appointees had no interest in him. So much for doing things that are good for the country. I found out about him just a few weeks ago, as part of our shake up of the Department. I looked extensively at his record with the department, which goes back over twenty years. He's the guy to call on for this. I don't want to convey the idea that they just yanked him out of the center of action and brought him home to pack away into a cubicle. He asked to return home because his wife was ill."

"This will involve a lot of shuttle diplomacy. If his wife's ill, would he be able to do that?"

"I don't think that will be a problem, Mr. President. She's doing well now."

Three days later Stephen, Robertson, Cullotte, Vice President Clarke, John Frost, and Gramsby met in the Oval Office. Stephen never left Frost, his closest adviser and political intimate other than Marybeth, out of any major deliberations. Stephen laid out to Gramsby what he thought had to be done. It was a grand plan—although he thought it was necessary one—and required a grand alliance, such as had not been seen in any of their lifetimes in the Middle East.

"As I see it," said Stephen, "this has to involve a whole group of countries in the region, some of whom are our friends and others who haven't been. I don't think the way to proceed would be to have an American force lead the way. I think this would just result in more resentment against us. The suspicion already runs high in the Middle East and the Islamic world generally that we're an imperialist power. I also don't think we could forge an alliance that way. Some of the countries wouldn't follow us. Even though they are on the front-line there and are the ones that ISIS will next be turning on, I think that if it's our war they will stay on the sidelines. They may even try to negotiate arrangements with ISIS, thinking that somehow ISIS might stay away from them and just try to dominate elsewhere. I think that would be a mistaken assessment because ISIS wants their caliphate. When they get powerful enough they'll turn on the countries that tried to make an accommodation with them. Without a broad-based front against ISIS, I'm not convinced we can score the decisive defeat of them that's so crucial. We have to convince most of the others in the region that it's necessary for them—for the sake of their own survival—to put their differences aside and join together to do this and show them that the U.S. has no deeper aims in the region except to defeat a brutal force. Actually, I see the U.S. role as mostly helping coordinate this, playing a military advisory role (that would not mean directing it because they know things in their backyard that we don't), and providing a lot of military hardware. Then after it's done we have to follow through and remove ourselves, so no one thinks we were dishonest about why we were doing this. If we don't do that, we'll just be inviting more ISIS-type movements in the future. Tell me what you think, honestly." Stephen said the last sentence with firmness and an obvious sense of sincerity that left no doubt that he did not want a "yes-man" response.

"Mr. President," Gramsby responded, "I think you are exactly right in everything you said."

Then, Stephen talked at length about Gramsby's role. "You understand that you would have the bear the brunt of having the face-to-face conversations. I'm sure you realize how vital complete surprise is in all this. If the U.S. president is off in the Middle East going from capital to capital the whole world would know about it and it would be clear in light of what's happening there now why he's there. ISIS would prepare themselves and the whole effort could become a disaster."

"I know that you have called upon me to use the contacts I have cultivated in the region, to negotiate and gain support, and to make this happen, and to rid the world of the worst of so many torments that have come out of that part of the world for the better part of a century. Mr. President, I am prepared to do all I can for you."

"Mr. Gramsby, if we can pull this off the United States of America and the civilized world will owe you its eternal gratitude," Stephen replied. "As I've told you, I have thought through in broad terms who would be involved in this grand alliance and what each would need to do. Now we have to see if we can make it happen."

What followed were several weeks of shuttle diplomacy by Gramsby to many of the capitals and other important locations of the Middle East. He also was in consultation with the U.S. ambassadors in the various countries. Stephen, who believed that the key figure in diplomacy should normally be the ambassador onsite, had spoken at length to all the ambassadors about the plans and told them that they should share the information with no one else. Gramsby knew them all and had good relations with them, which helped in securing their quiet support and cooperation. Gramsby's mission was one of the most difficult that could be envisioned in that region. He had to motivate national and ethnic group leaders to put aside or smooth over their differences and even long-standing, deep-seated antipathies—which too often were being resolved only over the butts of guns—long enough to come together in the common cause of defeating ISIS. He had to get it across to them that if ISIS weren't stopped now, all their struggles for power and territory would be for naught because they would all be its vassals—that is, if it weren't wiped out. It had to be something more even than "the enemy of my enemy is my friend" because they would all expect something besides just their continued survival in the aftermath. It would be hard to gain their confidence about that now, forgetting for the time being how hard it would be to actually deliver it later. More, Gramsby had only a limited amount of time to make the grand alliance happen. As things were progressing, ISIS was on the verge of winning several decisive struggles in countries across the region. There was a very real possibility that as many as four countries could fall into its hands in the coming months.

Gramsby had to journey to one Middle Eastern leader after another: President Khaled Hassen of Egypt, Prime Minister Aslan Aksoy of Turkey, Prime Minister Gideon Eisenstein of Israel, Prime Minister Nasser Al-Ajar of Kuwait, Prime Minister Ahmed Al-Majali of Jordan, President Abdulaziz al-Sarary of Yemen, the leader of the Houthis in Yemen Abdallah Hussein, and the leader of the Kurds Kewer Bashur. He had to get the Kurds and the Turks to work together, after being at each other's throats for so long, which might be the most formidable challenge. It might be less trying, but still a huge challenge, to get the Houthis to put aside their recent hostility toward the Yemeni government and its Saudi allies and cooperate with them. He even planned to see President Mohammed Jannati of Iran. The Iranians' post-revolutionary hatred toward the U.S. had cooled after the 2015 nuclear deal and end of sanctions—the U.S. had been downgraded from the status of the "Great Satan"—and they were now open to some measure of cooperation with the U.S. on regional security. This was helped along by their increasing jitteriness about the Sunni ISIS movement's anti-Shiite rhetoric and concern about its quickly turning east after these other countries fell and attacking Iran. The Iraqis were, for all practical purposes, out of it. After the Obama administration had made clear that the U.S. would not go back into Iraq any longer to assist the government it helped to install, ISIS had advanced to the point where it now controlled eighty-five percent of the country. The Iranians were getting even more nervous when they observed the vicious persecution of the Shiites there in ISIS-controlled territory. There was no expectation that the Saudis or the United Arab Emirates would send forces, in spite of their heightening concern about ISIS, but Gramsby had the additional task of convincing both of those countries to financially support the effort. The Saudis' unhappiness with the Houthis in Yemen would make that an additionally challenging task.

Even though the secrecy considerations precluded Stephen's traveling to the Middle East, he had to spend long hours on the phone with one or another of these leaders. Gramsby's prior contacts and good relations with these leaders got them to listen to Stephen's proposal and then helped some of them, like Aksoy and Beshur, to get over the hump of their mutual antipathy to seriously consider working together on at least some level. Then, it was a back-and-forth between different leaders to negotiate, cajole, nudge, and frighten them to come on board. Once Gramsby laid the groundwork and got people talking, Stephen had to convince them that the U.S. would be there every step of the way, providing weaponry, funding, military expertise and advice, and assistance in coordinating the effort, and also would not abandon them in the aftermath—while at the same time assuring them that the U.S. would not run the show or insist on taking command and had no ulterior motives. The one thing Stephen insisted on, uncompromisingly, was that even though ISIS was not a nation and so the Geneva Conventions didn't apply—and ISIS, in any event could have cared less about them—the coalition must religiously follow the rules of warfare. Even though ISIS was brutal toward their adversaries, the coalition absolutely must not be that way toward them. Some of the players resisted this—it was the "eye for an eye" mentality that so permeated the Middle East—and others agreed to it but with questionable sincerity. In the end, Stephen and Gramsby forged a genuine consensus on this, as they had on so many other things. Stephen and Gramsby committed the U.S. to a path of military nonintervention in the region, humanitarian assistance, stimulating more Western business investment to assist in economic development, and although they held back on pledges of ongoing military aid they did bring the Saudis and the UAE around to using some of their oil wealth to help the other countries with that. Collective security by countries in the region should be the direction for the future and Stephen was insistent that this effort would succeed in showing that they were capable of it. The Israelis were a big challenge. Stephen and Gramsby had to convince them to provide military assistance to these Arab countries as part of this operation. The Jordanians, who had been able to largely stay out of Middle Eastern conflicts since the 1967 Six Day War, had grown increasingly restive in the face of the ISIS threat. This especially followed from reports of an ISIS organizing effort within the country. A terrorist attack by ISIS sympathizers in Amman that had destroyed a half block of shops and killed a couple dozen people four months before had made the government ready to sign onto any kind of collective effort like this. The Palestinians weren't part of this. The *quid pro quo* for Israel was that the U.S. would insure that the weaponry would not then find its way into the arsenals of those who might use it against them and do all it could to push for some kind of resolution of that long-standing conflict with the help of these Arab states, who promised to put at least gentle pressure on the Palestinian Authority to accommodate and to put down Hamas and the other extremist elements within their borders.

313

The difficulty of getting the Turks and Kurds together looked like it was going to sink the whole endeavor. After working intensely over a period of weeks on this and continuing to run up against a brick wall, Gramsby called Stephen. As a natural and seasoned diplomat, Gramsby was not one to fret or become discouraged. His view seemed to be that with enough negotiating effort and give-and-take, even the most unbending and recalcitrant foreign official could be brought around. As they talked, however, Stephen detected a faint ring of discouragement in Gramsby's voice. "Failure" was not a word in Gramsby's lexicon, but at various points in the conversation Stephen thought that would be the next thing he would say. Stephen believed that securing the involvement of both the Turks and the Kurds was a crucial element in the entire enterprise. Next to the Israelis, the Turks had the strongest and best-equipped army in the Middle East and the Kurds were fierce, resourceful, and effective fighters who were almost uniquely equipped to take on ISIS in the expected close-quarters combat. It was clear also that the great diplomat Gramsby was looking to his boss for a suggestion of what to do now, a magnificent insight that could snatch victory from the jaws of defeat. As a combination of fatigue from this weeks' long effort, a deep singe of disappointment, a sense that his mind could simply generate no new ideas, and a range of emotions started to overwhelm him all Stephen could say was that they would talk again tomorrow and ended the call.

Stephen hardly said a word at dinner with Marybeth that evening. She could easily pick up when something troubled him, but tonight it was overwhelmingly clear and anyone could see it. She hardly had to guess what it concerned, since building the coalition had become almost all absorbing during these weeks. She was the only American other than Clarke, Frost, Gramsby, Cullotte, Robertson, and the ambassadors who knew about what was happening. She decided not to say anything until they retired to the sitting room next to the President's Bedroom.

"Stephen, I know that things must not be going well with what you're trying to do in the Middle East. Is there anything I can say or do?"

He then filled her in on the day's developments. "We seemed to be so close. Gramsby had made incredible progress." Then he fell silent for about a minute, which seemed more like five. "Marybeth, maybe to pull off building a coalition like this was all a pipe dream. For me to think that this could be done was foolish. Can someone be the president who could have such poor judgment? I think again, what am I doing here? Most of the Congress opposes me. Half of my party opposes me.

They can't stand my domestic leadership, and now when the word gets out—which, of course, it will—they'll begin talking about how I have no capability for the most important thing a president does: foreign policy. Maybe I was just more suited to being a professor." He was having another of his all too frequent brief crises of confidence.

"Stephen," she said with a firmness that matched what had become *his* trademark demeanor and the tone of very slight rebuke, "It doesn't make any difference if you think you were more suited to being a professor. You're here, and you'll not only do the best you can but you'll make this work. You simply have to think of how you should proceed next. You have to keep remembering—I remind you about this every time—that God opened the doors for you to be here. If He didn't want you here, He would not have let it happen. There were a thousand doors along the way. He could have closed any of them, but didn't. I know that you've been praying to Him intensely about this, but maybe you just have to pray more. You have to double down, reflect further, make choices about how to proceed now, and just ask Him to guide you along. You know all that. I know that this is the biggest challenge of your presidency, which has been a presidency filled with maybe unprecedented challenges. I know you can make this happen. With God's continued help, you *will* make it happen."

Stephen looked at her, with tenderness. He walked over to her and gave her a long, intense embrace. "As usual, darling, you're right. It does no good to doubt myself, to lack confidence. You're always there to give me the boost I need. I'm foolish to let this confound me. No one said that bringing together traditional enemies was going to be easy. It's not a question about whether this can be made to work out. It *has* to work out. One way or the other, we will have to make it happen."

She smiled at him. It was the reassuring and knowing smile that he had received from her so many times during their marriage—a marriage to a woman that he loved more than he could express and who he knew that God had sent right to him. That smile reflected how she seemed to be able to look into him and to know what he was made of and capable of better than he did himself.

The next morning Stephen called Gramsby, who was in Ankara, Turkey. He told him to keep trying with the negotiations, that we had to persist. In the meantime, Stephen would be on the phone repeatedly with Aksoy and Beshur to "pull out all stops until we make this happen." Stephen decided that he would have to try a different approach with Aksoy. The appeal to all the parties all along had studiously avoided the least hint of pressure. The exclusive focus had been on how forming the coalition and moving against ISIS now was not only necessary for the future of the Middle East, but would be to everyone's advantage. As he talked to Aksoy, Stephen continued to stress these things but also suggested, indirectly and without at all conveying that he was issuing an ultimatum, that U.S. military aid to its long-time NATO ally would be affected if Turkey didn't come aboard and work with the Kurds. Stephen knew that in foreign affairs the carrot often had to be combined with the stick—even, at times, with allies. When he talked to Beshur, his characteristic firmness came across that it was now essential to work with the Turkish government regardless of the past. No American President had ever talked directly to a Kurdish leader before, and the very momentousness of the event made Bashur take heed. The authority of the U.S., after all, was not something to ignore, especially when her leader was willing to talk to a domestic adversary of a longtime ally. Stephen emphasized to Beshur that if the Kurds helped to defeat ISIS—Stephen left no doubt how important he viewed the Kurds in that effort—the U.S. would be their fervent advocate with the Turkish government afterwards to grant them respect and recognition. He reiterated what Gramsby had been telling them that the U.S. would not push for a Kurdish state, but for largely self-governing autonomous regions in eastern Turkey and northern Iraq—what's often called Kurdistan. Stephen made clear to him, however, that the Kurds had the obligation to renounce violence in their dealings with the Turkish government and to commit themselves to seeking a peaceful resolution of all their problems. This was the condition for ongoing U.S. help in resolving the "Kurdish issue."

Stephen's intervention along with Gramsby's intensive diplomatic follow-up efforts broke the logjam. The Turks and the Kurds were on-board and also the initial steps had been taken toward resolving an additional, long-time troubling situation in the Middle East.

The coalition that finally emerged featured a security council made up of the top military official of each country and of the Kurds and Houthis. U.S. Army Major General Robert Kendrake, who had had extensive experience with the U.S. Central Command (CENTCOM) and knew the top uniformed military officials of a number of the countries in the region, was the U.S. military representative. Stephen and Secretary Cullotte agreed that he should not be appointed to head CENTCOM, whose top position was then vacant, because an appointment at this time would arouse suspicion that something was up and could compromise the secrecy of the whole operation. Stephen and Gramsby had driven home repeatedly to the different leaders that the element of surprise was utterly crucial to the success of the pending offensive to eliminate ISIS. They got the message and from all Stephen and Gramsby could see were holding up their end on this.

Kendrake had the same negotiating and conciliating skills as Gramsby. He would do among the military officials what Gramsby did and would continue to do with the political ones. He also was responsible for getting the American military hardware that was needed sent to the new "Mideast Freedom Force" as it was called and also to work with the Saudis, Iranians, Qataris, and Emirates to channel their funds—their agreed-on contribution to the campaign—to the purchase of additional hardware. The condition was that all the hardware purchased with the funds of each would go to them after the conflict ended. The Saudis, who had become increasingly certain that ISIS would seek to overrun them and gain the ultimate prize of controlling the worldwide centers of Islam, also agreed to crack down on their wealthy subjects who were helping to bankroll ISIS. Indeed, Gramsby made clear to them that if they did not join the effort they couldn't expect their old ally, the U.S., to come to their aid when ISIS later overran them. Stephen, Gramsby, and Kendrake had to continually drive home to them that the military hardware could never be channeled to elements that would use it against the Israelis and to continually reassure the Israelis about this. The Emirates also agreed to bankroll the efforts of the Kurds and the Houthis, but only with the understanding that they would relinquish all war materiel provided to them at the end. The Saudis did not want it used afterwards against the Yemenis who they had been supporting against the "upstart" Houthis and the Turks did not want the long-time rebellious Kurds within their borders using it against them. After a particularly strenuous negotiating effort—he said it was the most difficult of his many diplomatic struggles in the region over many years—Gramsby got the Houthis and Kurds to agree to end their internal armed struggles and to sit down at the negotiating table afterwards. For their part, the Saudis and Yemeni government on the one hand and the Turks on the other agreed to sit down to discuss autonomous regions for these groups within their borders.

The Israeli Mossad and the Jordanian Special Operation Forces put aside any lingering suspicion of each other over a half century after the Six Day War and agreed to work collaboratively in the first phase of the operation. Kendrake, who himself had an intelligence and covert operations background, constantly consulted with the two sides to make sure any rough spots would be gotten over. His main role in the overall military campaign against ISIS was to keep everyone working together, making sure the strategy was being carried out, and making everyone feel that its side was the heroic one as things unfolded. In effect, Kendrake was quietly running the show without anyone thinking he was. Stephen insisted that this was genuinely to be the Middle East partners' enterprise and Kendrake understood that and was himself personally fully committed to that course, but had to make sure it all stayed on track. While not involved in the fight, besides providing military hardware, the different branches of the U.S. military stateside were in charge of conducting all-out, aggressive cyber-warfare against ISIS. By the time the coalition's combat operation was ready to begin, ISIS's communications network had been virtually brought down.

What the Mossad and Jordan's Special Operation Forces did was to penetrate parts of Syria and Iraq where ISIS was in control to spread disinformation—making them think that the region was in fear of them and that they had a likely path to victory—and to work aggressively to gather intelligence about ISIS's plans and to organize an underground of ISIS opponents in the territories they occupied to conduct covert attacks to divert their attention and help cripple them as the Mideast Freedom Force's offensives on different fronts got underway. The different Arab governments also worked with leading anti-extremist Islamic clerics in their countries to carry out an intensive propaganda campaign against ISIS in the weeks before the attacks to soften any support they had among their populations and to insure that there would be no backlash when it became clear that they were part of the anti-ISIS effort. Stephen had understood from the beginning that this had to partly be a propaganda war and he and Gramsby convinced the Arab leaders that such a systematic effort was essential, so that their resolve wouldn't be weakened by claims by indigenous radicals and their sympathizers that a war of Moslems against other Moslems was unjustified.

The offensives began in early May, which timing met the crucial need for secrecy because ISIS would not have expected a major military operation against it to start at a time the punishing hot summer months were descending in the desert lands. ISIS's strongholds were in Syria and Iraq, and they also had gained a sizable foothold in Libya. The attacks all began on the same day. Turkish and Kurdish forces launched a massive ground attack on ISIS in northern Syria and northern Iraq from the northeast and northwest. Egyptian and Yemeni naval vessels brought Yemeni and Houthi forces to southern Iraq, where they simultaneously attacked ISIS there. Jordanian and Israeli troops invaded the ISIS-held part of Syria east of the Golan Heights and quickly moved northward into the rest of the southern part of the country. What was left of the scattered Syrian army, which was mostly near Damascus, joined up with them in a small-scale pincer-type move to try to surround the ISIS forces in the southeast of the country. Egyptian forces stormed across the border into northeast Libya (Cyrenaica), heading for the ISIS stronghold of Benghazi. The ground combat invasions were accompanied by a massive aerial and artillery bombardment effort. The Turkish air force carried out the bombing campaign in northern Syria and Iraq, the Egyptians and Yemenis in southern Iraq, and the Israelis and Jordanians in southern and central Syria. Kendrake and the U.S. Air Force Commander at Al Udeid Air Base in Qatar had worked with the commanding generals of these countries' air forces to carefully plan the air campaign in the weeks just before the invasions began. It was clear from the start that the stress on secrecy had worked. ISIS was "caught with its pants down."

The assault on ISIS on all fronts was relentless. With Gramsby and Kendrake working assiduously to keep the coalition functioning smoothly and to resolve potentially lethal differences, the campaign progressed better than anyone had predicted. Within two months, ISIS was virtually defeated in Libya and was in retreat everywhere else until finally its forces were virtually surrounded in the Syrian Desert in western Iraq and southeastern Syria. They still occupied the cities of Homs in Syria and Mosul in Iraq, where the coalition faced a difficult situation. The cities essentially became a prison for the part of the civilian population that had not been able to flee. ISIS, as feared, announced that they were using them as a bargaining chip. Its leaders said that if the forces arrayed against them did not pull out of Syria and Iraq they would systematically slaughter all the civilians. What they did not count on was the underground that the Israeli Mossad and the Jordanian Special Operations Forces, assisted from a distance by the CIA, had assembled and armed in the months leading up to the military campaigns. The underground rose up and battled the ISIS forces in those cities, sometimes in fierce hand-to-hand combat. They were backed up by precision coalition airstrikes, assisted by a communications network that the Mossad and the SPO had helped put in place among the supportive civilian population. Then, the coalition's ground forces stormed the two cities and crushed the ISIS occupiers.

By early July, the Mideast Freedom Force had overrun the last ISIS strongholds. Forces were positioned in a dragnet fashion encircling the places where the ISIS fighters had been to stop any of them who tried to flee. Perhaps some had gotten away, but it was precious few. A heavy coalition naval presence, backed up by U.S. Sixth Fleet, was in place to stop any ISIS fighters from fleeing Syria by the Mediterranean. A similar Egyptian, Yemeni, and Kuwaiti naval force, backed up by the

U.S. Fifth Fleet, was positioned to intercept any of them trying to flee into the Persian Gulf from southeastern Iraq near Basra. A number of small crafts holding ISIS fighters were seized, some after firefights. The Turks had their forces ringed along their borders with Syria and Iraq and the Iranians, who did not play a part in the fighting, agreed to do the same along their long, mostly frontier-like border with Iraq. In one case, the Iranians seized a platoon-size group of ISIS fighters who tried to cross the border north of Abadan. ISIS was crushed. There were also reports that their allies in other regions, like Boko Haram in Nigeria, Chad, and Cameroon, were demoralized by the developments. Those countries used the opportunity to join together in a major offensive against those Islamist terrorist groups.

Once the war against ISIS had begun, Western news outlets gave it massive coverage and the American and European publics were transfixed by the developments. They especially were taken aback by the almost "lightening" character of the war, where what had seemed like the increasingly powerful and threatening ISIS—which a few months before had seemed ready to overrun the entire Middle East—was routed on multiple fronts so quickly. There was constant buzz in the media about how such an effective coalition among such diverse elements in the region, including some who had been long-time adversaries, could have been forged. There was also much speculation about what the U.S.'s role had been, especially since the Bernard administration had said very little about it. It had shown itself to be the most "leak-resistant" administration that anyone could remember. The media fixation on the Middle Eastern developments was so intensive that all their grumbling about Stephen's domestic initiatives and policies seemed to cease in the meantime.

Indeed, it wasn't until a couple of weeks after the war ended that Stephen addressed the nation on prime time television to talk about the war and what the U.S. involvement had been. He wanted to wait because Gramsby had been engaged in intensive negotiations in Syria and Iraq with different political and ethnic factions to get them to agree to a new frame of government in which they would all agree to participate and work out their recent and long-term differences peaceably, through negotiation. In Iraq, the most sensitive part of this concerned Sunni-Shiite cooperation. In several phone calls to Stephen, Gramsby talked about how he had to combine intensive efforts to secure accommodations with "knocking heads." Neither Stephen nor Gramsby was interested in "nation-building" or believed that they could solve age-old suspicions and hostilities. Both were acutely aware of the U.S.'s failures not long before to construct a stable Iraqi government. All that they were aiming for in both countries was to get a functioning government going after ISIS was ousted with a framework to accommodate the different ethnic and religious groups and to keep them dialoguing with each other. Gramsby, who was not one to leave loose ends or fail to complete his primary tasks, finally reported to Stephen that he was satisfied that that much had been achieved. Probably the bitter taste of ISIS oppression and the ongoing pattern of violent conflict for some years had provided for the different elements an overwhelming incentive to come together to make this work.

In his televised address, Stephen explained all the planning and negotiating that had gone into the war that vanquished—he prayed permanently—ISIS. Then, he spoke about and commended the efforts of Cullotte, Robertson, Kendrake, and especially Gramsby. He called Gramsby an American hero for the ages, a "premier American diplomat," and "a warrior for peace." He urged that he be considered for the Nobel Peace Prize. He also spoke glowingly about the countries and leaders who made up the Mideast Freedom Force. Throughout his whole address, he was careful not to stress or often even mention his own efforts. Stephen had shown throughout his almost accidental public career that he exhibited a character trait that was certainly rare in politics: humility. He was careful, though, not to make it a kind of humility worn on one's sleeve, where one would make oneself look humble just to invite gushing and overdone accolades from others. He had seen a lot of that kind of false humility in his student days, in law, in the professoriate, and in politics and he would have none of it. Besides, he genuinely believed that the generators of success in this great campaign to eliminate this terrible scourge over the Middle East and projecting out to the Western world from there were all these others. He believed that his role had been only a minimal one.

Stephen announced that the next day he would hold a press conference with Gramsby, since he believed that the White House Press Corps would want more inside details of the often difficult negotiations both before and after the war that he had been at the center of. Stephen opened by just making a few brief comments. Mostly, his role was to introduce Gramsby. He had told the diplomat that it was really *his* press conference, and that after the introduction he would quietly slip out of the James S. Brady Press Briefing Room and leave it to him.

After the introduction, in unaccustomed fashion the Press Corps gave Gramsby a polite round of applause. When Stephen saw what was happening, he joined it. As Gramsby came to the podium, he quickly

321

turned to Stephen as the President started heading for the exit to the West Colonnade.

"Mr. President," he said, "It is not my place to impose on you, but I would most appreciate your staying for a few short minutes. I want to say something before I take the questions."

Stephen turned around a bit surprised, but his gentle smile signaled to Gramsby that he would stay.

Gramsby proceeded to thank Stephen for his "too kind comments," and to say that the President was "an exemplary humble man, always ready to give others credit." He said, though, that the success of "ridding the planet of the poison that is ISIS" occurred because of the President, "who knew what had to be done and had the plan in mind from the beginning." It was not only he, Gramsby, through his negotiations, but Stephen "who made it possible to break through to the various national leaders by his long hours on the phone with them." He concluded, "We owe a great debt of gratitude to President Bernard, who has shown what leadership in the cause of freedom and peace is truly like."

Stephen responded with a slight bow of the head and a quiet but clear response, "Thank you, Mr. Ambassador."

Most of the Press Corps were leftist-oriented and had a not-too-subdued hostility toward Stephen for his policies. Most of them, however, found Gramsby's comments touching and were impressed by Stephen's demeanor at the press conference. Many related it all in their reporting and because of the striking character of the moment it was run in the major nightly network news reports that evening. Even though they and their editors knew that it would make their political adversary look good, they felt compelled to show it. The result was that public support and respect for Stephen, already buoyed by the defeat of ISIS and the major blow that had been dealt Islamic terrorism, increased even further.

The mid-term elections were just around the corner. Election campaigns were heating up as the fall descended. Stephen's popularity had dipped because of the tough decisions he had made and his bold exercise of executive power. This was so, even while popular respect and admiration for him continued because of his obvious honesty, integrity, humility, and courage. His many opponents had not been able to hurt him as they had hoped because of his ability and consistent effort to keep them on the defensive and educate the public. Still, he had trampled on many feet and that is bound to cause one to lose support. So, before the war it had looked like the other party was going to make significant gains in the House and Senate elections. The defeat of ISIS and the revelations of the U.S. role and, even further, Gramsby's praise for Stephen changed the equation. Almost overnight, his popular support sharply increased. Within his own party, his Congressional critics, like Senator Bessemer and Speaker Clayburne, fell silent and others who had been lukewarm or fearful of too strongly defending him because of their own political concerns suddenly loudly commended him. Within a few more weeks, by mid-September, the polls were showing that a solid majority of the electorate, about 60 percent, said they planned to vote for the Congressional candidates of Stephen's party in November. That was up 15 percent from the weeks before the war. As the campaigning got underway, it became clear that the other party's attacks were falling flat and they were scurrying around for issues. The claim of abuse of executive power wasn't going far. Actually, it hadn't been taking off well even before the war because of Stephen's persistent educational efforts.

Stephen took to the stump during the campaign season to support many of his party's candidates. He especially hit the hustings for those who had stood by his efforts. As the weeks went on, however, even those who had been cool to him sought his help and he obliged, but always made sure to make the effort to educate them too—to make them see the wisdom and legitimacy of even the bold moves he had taken. He also used his campaign appearances not just to promote the candidates, but also to continue his effort of educating the citizenry. On occasion, he encountered hecklers. Recent presidents had avoided venues where this might happen, but Stephen often engaged them in his inimitable professorial way having even a back-and-forth dialogue. Inevitably, the media—both local and national—picked up on these encounters. At first, some in the media thought they could use them to embarrass Stephen, but after awhile they saw that they made engaging news. Stephen's stock with the public went up even more by his deft handling of these episodes.

The mid-term election results modestly increased the margin by which Stephen's party controlled each house of Congress. They went against the usual tendency of the "in-party" losing seats in mid-term elections, even though in recent decades the tendency had become more pronounced in the second mid-term elections at the three-quarters point in a two-term presidency. His party also increased its number of state governors and took control of several more state legislative houses. Exit polling and phone surveys conducted in the days right after the election showed that the war was not the only reason that people voted as they did, but many were attracted by his budgetary and tax policies. They strongly supported his putting the clamps on the federal

323

bureaucracy and standing up to the interest groups. As time went on—seemingly as people thought about it more—the surveys had also revealed support for his firm use of executive power in standing up to the Supreme Court. Although uncertain or tentative about his gradual disengagement and First New Deal-like business "codes of conduct" initiative, a majority said they were "open" to them. Most were tentative about the renegotiations of trade agreements that were shortly to start, but believed that the U.S. had been at a trade disadvantage and were willing to give it a try. Stephen's educational efforts and seizure of the rhetorical high ground were having their effects. Even a significant percentage of the public that identified with the other party said it was impressed by Stephen's personal character, courage, and leadership. He was extolled as a "good" or "very good" Commander-in-Chief. The public had now seen him lead effectively and decisively in foreign affairs, and any questions it had about a former governor who had never been in Congress spearheading international efforts almost instantaneously evaporated. They were especially impressed with Stephen's ability to defeat ISIS not only without another extended commitment of American troops, but without virtually any military involvement at all.

Stephen and Marybeth returned to the White House early on Election Day after two weeks on the campaign trail. They watched the returns all evening and Stephen took numerous phone calls, many from his party's candidates thanking him for his help after they gave their victory speeches. Late on election night, as Stephen and Marybeth knelt together in prayer, they thanked God for the outcome and for assisting Stephen in so many ways. They also thanked Him as they had many times each day since the war's end for the successful result. Stephen said, "God, that was the truly important outcome and we thank you mightily for it, for making it possible to stop the evil men who had taken so many lives of your children and would have taken so many more. I hope I have served You as You willed and please know that I continue to put myself before You as Your instrument." Marybeth prayed, "You have chosen my husband for a difficult task, and it hasn't been easy. Please continue to make Your will known to him and to assist him and bless him in his efforts."

As they laid down in bed, Stephen embraced his loving and devoted wife. He said, "God gave me challenges that I would have never imagined, but He has been my partner every step of the way. I have needed the wisdom and discernment that could only have come from the Holy Spirit. He also sent me another partner who has stood solidly with me and made it possible each day for me to continue."

With that, he kissed Marybeth. "He said to her, "Thank you, darling, for keeping me on track, for giving me the boost I needed when I was once more being tempted by discouragement. How could I ever thank God enough for you?" She prayed silently as she had every night of their marriage before closing her eyes, "Lord, thank you for sending me Stephen." They turned over and, after a very long day, quickly fell asleep.

CHAPTER 11

A Final Campaign, Consolidation, A New Grassroots Movement, And Renewal— "If You Can Keep It"

A fter the midterm elections, Stephen intensified his efforts on his many domestic initiatives while also continuing to keep an eye on the Middle East in the aftermath of the defeat of ISIS. Gramsby's diplomatic efforts were of necessity ongoing, especially to keep the elements in Syria and Iraq cooperating and on-target to rebuild their political institutions in a satisfactory way to them all, and also to make sure that the promises to the Kurds and Houthis were carried out.

Stephen asked Gramsby to return to Washington for a few days' consultation. Stephen, Gramsby, and Robertson huddled at the White House for two solid days, and at the end of their deliberations they all agreed that the most reliable way to make sure that the agreements that were made on the different sides were upheld would be direct presidential intervention and the best way to do that would be a "reconciliation and rebuilding" conference in Washington. Stephen was not one to let the bureaucratic machinery roll on and on until something could be set up. So, he worked through Gramsby and the conference was set up for late January.

The outcome of the conference, which was publicized but which Stephen's administration kept the media away from, was what was hoped for. There was no unrealistic expectation that it would transform Turkish-Kurdish relations or result in viable and effective governments in Syria and Iraq overnight or even completely solve the Houthi problem, but it intensified the momentum in those directions. Stephen made no sweeping public claims about the success of the conference, but nevertheless it caused the public assessment of his foreign policy effectiveness to rise still further. Another U.S. diplomat in the Middle East—a Gramsby protégé for many years, named Bill Buckner—continued discussions with Iran after their cooperation in the battle against ISIS. Stephen made clear that the U.S. sought better relations, even though he was firm about the regime being more moderate and respecting human rights. Its leadership seemed to further back away from its decades-old view of the U.S. as enemy. Moreover, Stephen's view about how to deal with Iran was the same as Ronald Reagan's was in dealing with the Soviet Union when he came into office: do what can be done to influence change within the country, as difficult as it might seem (in the end, of course, it had helped lead to the collapse of the Communist regime). Stephen set down this approach, despite some disagreement from other old Middle East hands in the State Department, because he knew that the evidence—surveys and the like—had shown that the public, in opposition to the leadership, in Iran was the most pro-American in the Islamic world. There was a new opening with the defeat of ISIS and the threat that it had represented to Shiite Islam. Buckner brought to the Iranians Stephen's proposals for cultural and educational exchanges and openings for American investment to make possible critically needed infrastructure development. These things would appeal to the leadership, but also take advantage of—and, in fact, further buttress—the Iranian public's pro-American sentiment. When these developments were announced a few months after the Washington conference, they resulted in Stephen's stock with the American public going up still more.

Still, Stephen realized that economic concerns were almost always central for much of the American electorate. He remembered a saying he had once heard during his student days: $e^3=V$, that is "economics, economics, economics is the basis for political victory and success." He thought it was unfortunate that most people didn't see well enough the crucial nature of the main focus of his presidency of protecting and restoring constitutional principles—even though his educational effort was making a difference with that—and were driven more, as usual, by what they thought government should do for them economically. Still, he was certainly aware of the importance of that—but not for reasons of politics but of principle, that it was part of what had to be corrected in a major way for the sake of national restoration. That's what such major initiatives as his flat tax, the Penny Plan, and the NIRA-type scheme in place of excessive regulation aimed to do. Stephen had been able to implement the Penny Plan with his first budget; he'd made it clear that he would veto any budget reauthorization bill that didn't adhere to it. Since his party controlled Congress and he asserted himself strongly with the chairmen of the various pertinent committees, especially the Budget Committees, he prevailed. The federal budget was on the way to being balanced within the next year or at most two, and then spending would have to be capped to insure that there would be no more deficit spending, which Stephen had made clear to Congress he was going to proceed to do in the next budget after that. Now that his party had larger majorities in each house of Congress, Stephen had been working with the Chairmen of the House Ways and Means Committee and the Senate Finance Committee, both of whom had supported the flat tax for some time, to get it passed in the new Congress. Both committees had held extensive hearings on flat tax legislation the previous year and it passed the House, but the leadership of Stephen's party did not bring it up for a vote in the Senate because of the other party's threatened filibuster. Stephen had worked closely with Vice President Clarke to get the usually difficult Senate Majority Leader Bessemer to support the flat tax, and the plan proceeded early in this session to circumvent the likely filibuster by attaching the legislation to a Social Security funding bill that no one would dare to filibuster or sidetrack. Stephen had made clear from the beginning of his presidency that he would accept no more raids on the Social Security Trust Fund and the Social Security bill was the beginning of an effort to strengthen the Trust Fund. Public support for the flat tax had grown, as Stephen had made it a major part of his public educational effort and had also sent out other leading figures in his administration, led by Secretary of the Treasury Mark Grisinger, to explain and advocate for the flat tax. This strong educational effort—actually, it was the first time a president had so strongly and consistently advocated for it—had won over a substantial "undecided" bloc in the public and had shifted the support from 42 percent against to 64 percent for. That shift in public opinion may have been the crucial factor in motivating the consummate politician Bessemer to strongly push for it in the Senate. Moreover, the other party, whose members of Congress and rank-and-file were less supportive of the flat tax, were so busy opposing other of Stephen's initiatives that they failed to give enough attention the issue until it was too late. The legislation passed about a month after the Washington Mideast conference. The flat tax would not go into effect for another year, and the phase-out of the IRS would take place over three years. After only a year of the flat tax being in place, just before the party conventions, economic commentators were already talking about how the tax change was responsible for a noticeably stimulated economy. The voters were seeing it too, and responded with approval in surveys about Stephen's "handling of the economy."

As far as the NIRA-type initiative was concerned, it was one of American history's great examples of the bully pulpit. Besides his unprecedented role as "First Educator," Stephen realized that domestically, as in foreign affairs, one had to know when and how to apply pressure. It was not the pressure of a threat, such as "if you don't do such and such, the government will use such and such a law—even twisting it to be able to it use effectively—to come after you." That was the kind of governmental action that Stephen believed had been routinely used by administrations of both parties too often—it was probably used· at historic highs while the other party ruled over the previous dozen years—and he found it morally reprehensible and an affront to a free people. His willingness, instead, to publicly denounce companies that were not acting responsibly and to have press conferences and even rallies outside their Washington headquarters to focus attention on their irresponsible and unjust behavior—to, in effect, defeat them in the court of public opinion—was effective enough. These avenues were not his first recourse, however. He first tried mightily to make the case to company executives who thought too much of their bottom line and too little of the good of their workers, their communities, and the country generally by meeting with them. In effect, he used the persuasive and bully pulpit powers of the presidency to get them to do the right things. He also went to trade association meetings and asked groups of CEOs from the same industry to come to the White House where he tried to convince them to put in place voluntary standards of conduct which all the companies would agree to follow—particularly as they pertained to just wages, personalizing the workplace, keeping their facilities in the communities they were situated in, limiting outsourcing, and treating both workers and consumers respectfully. He reminded them about how he had stripped away mounds of excessive federal regulations on business, much beyond what any president had ever done before. He also made clear to them how they were going to benefit from the corporate tax cut that was part of the flat tax legislation—the U.S.'s high corporate tax rate was long thought to be a major reason for companies to relocate abroad—and made clear to them that as a kind of *quid pro quo* they now needed to do these other kinds of things. He also was careful to warn them repeatedly that he wouldn't in the least tolerate using these industry-wide self-imposed standards as a smokescreen for companies to collude to try to corner the market and keep out competitors. He reiterated that that would quickly bring anti-trust actions. The White

House made the public aware of these meetings and their outcome and was also diligent about commending companies and industries that responded well to his requests.

Stephen also spoke frequently to union and worker groups. The national unions and labor leaders, who had long since become radicalized and were now across-the-board arch-leftists—were in the pocket of the other party. Stephen went around them and reached out to local union groups, ad hoc individual groups of workers, and professional associations that opposed white-collar unions for public sector employees on different levels. He let them know about his support for workers' dignity and interests and about the value of the NIRA-type efforts—helping to shape more responsible attitudes by corporate officials and build business-labor bonds that would redound to the benefit of workers—and the other things he was doing. He also continued his campaign approach to promote these economic and other initiatives of arranging interviews and meetings with local media since he knew the national media wanted to ignore him if they weren't criticizing him. He generally continued his practice of "going out to the people" in many ways, even going to malls and crowded business areas. He saw it as an ongoing campaign, not for election but to call the country back to a sound morality and way of life.

Stephen viewed small businesses as natural allies, and he wiped out even more regulations that were especially oppressive to them and had the effect of giving larger businesses a competitive advantage over them. Many of the regulations had not only hamstrung them, but didn't even really pertain to their activities—even though they had to meet the costs of compliance. Stephen not only regularly spoke at small business association conferences and gatherings, but also often visited small businesses and talked to their owners or heads. John Frost always worked through local media outlets to get coverage of these speeches and appearances.

As far as human life and family issues were concerned, the abortion clinics were shut down all across the country. Hospitals had virtually stopped doing them as well, since they feared imperiling their federal funding. Their appeals to the federal courts went nowhere, since the Supreme Court had backed down in the face of Stephen's challenges. The abortifacients were now almost all off the market. The national educational campaign about abortion and unborn human life was as intensive and unremitting as Stephen had promised. National and local pro-life organizations were inspired by what the administration was doing to intensify their own educational efforts. Secretary of HHS Jim Lewis and the other top political appointees of that department joined

331

him in the campaign of public speeches, talks to organizations, appearances in schools and campuses in cooperation with Department of Education officials and with no reluctance about facing off against campus demonstrators. Sometimes campus pro-life and conservative groups invited them, but at other times they approached the university administrations and prodded them if they showed reluctance or were afraid of campus turmoil erupting. It was hard to turn down a chance for a visit by the president or a Cabinet official to their campuses— even if they were concerned about demonstrations. The Bernard administration stressed the need for free speech and a true diversity—of positions and thought—on campuses when they faced university administration reluctance. It especially tended to see a quick change of heart when it let it be known that universities were expected to have a regimen of open inquiry and discussion, along with establishing firm policies to stop disruptive actions, if they were going to continue to receive federal financial support. They wanted to take advantage of the federal student loan and grant programs as long as they were around. Stephen's administration had been in extended discussions with major banks around the country about their handling student lending exclusively as it pushed a plan to gradually withdraw the federal government from this over a period of several years.

One of the things that Stephen had become nationally known for was the Lisa Allen nursing home starvation case. He was committed to stopping the slide toward euthanasia, the withholding of basic care and nutrition and hydration, and physician-assisted suicide nationally. It was not a state matter, anymore than abortion was. This involved the fundamental right to human life and there would be no states where death chambers for the innocent would be permitted. As with the pressure exerted on health care institutions about abortifacients, the Bernard administration's pledge that hospitals receiving federal funds—which was almost all of them—would have their funds cut off if they engaged in any of these practices proved effective. Also, the threat that physicians, nursing homes, hospices and other facilities would lose their eligibility to take part in Medicare and Medicaid if they were involved in any of this or if they knowingly or negligently allowed it to take place in their facilities further checked the growing culture of death. Stephen made clear that if any court tried to block such a cut-off, its orders would not be obeyed and as with abortion he carried the day. Remaining federal funding for embryonic stem-cell research was also gone.

While Stephen put down the gauntlet on health care facilities when it came to abortion, physician-assisted suicide, and euthanasia, he

332

worked vigorously to encourage their providing of more charity care. This was part of his gradual disengagement policy, which would aim at slowly scaling down Medicaid and other federal involvement in health care. Most of his efforts in this regard were exhortative. He did not wish to threaten when he didn't have to, but he made it clear to health care institution administrations that if they received federal grants— which, to be sure, the government was "gradually disengaging" from— "it was only reasonable" that they should expand charity care arrangements. The effect just of his meetings with leaders in the health care sector was to create a momentum that near the end of his first term had already resulted in marked increases in charitable care across much of the country.

Of course, the push for charitable care was just part of Stephen's use of the persuasive powers of the presidency to build up the civil society sector. He met with people from non-profit organizations routinely, even arranging for them to come to the White House for discussions and mini-conferences. He broke from the usual presidential practice of just hob-nobbing with officials from national organizations, and made sure that John Frost's staff learned about and invited local leaders and even just notably active charity workers from the non-profit sector, or else arranged for Stephen to meet them in their local areas. Stephen made sure that everyone understood—and with his track record, no one doubted him—that gradual disengagement meant that federal money was winding down over time. The civil society sector now had to step up to the plate to intensify its private fundraising efforts. What he would do—he was also trying to encourage state and local officials to proceed along the same lines—would be to get government out of their way.

At the beginning of the final year of Stephen's term, there was suddenly another different and unexpected matter involving the judiciary. Justice John England, who was a long-time member of the leftist bloc on the Supreme Court, decided to retire. He had turned eighty, had a number of health problems, and reportedly had been frustrated by the Court's no longer being able to exercise the kind of power it did before Stephen's challenge to it. He was the member of the Court who, some said, was most displeased with the kind of "understanding" that had been reached with Stephen as the Court's authority seemed to be ebbing away. His stepping down gave Stephen his first chance to nominate someone to the Court. Even though with Stephen's successful dramatic moves to restore the judiciary to its proper place in the American constitutional order, redress the imbalance among the branches, and strip away the false notion that the

Supreme Court was where ultimate sovereign power in the U.S. rested, an appointment to it did not have the usual urgency, it was naturally still one of the most crucial decisions Stephen would make.

Unlike—inexplicably, considering its importance—so many presidents who had almost no idea about who would be good Supreme Court justices and often looked to political appointees in the Department of Justice to suggest nominees, Stephen as a former constitutional law professor knew the lay of the land. He needed to do little deliberating about this, as he had known for years who he would appoint if given the chance. Dr. Michael R. Jeffrey was a noted constitutional scholar from the University of Pennsylvania Law School, who Stephen had gotten to know well early on in his professorial days. Like Stephen, he was both a J.D. and Ph.D. (in political philosophy and ethics). He had done postdoctoral work at Cambridge University in England and had published a slew of books in American constitutional law, classical and medieval political philosophy, and ethics. He had written a major treatise on the natural law. He was a leading pro-life and pro-family scholar, one of America's most eminent Catholic scholars but with close ties to traditionalist Anglicans, Evangelical Protestants, and Mormons. He was even much respected by reasonable leftists in the legal academy. He was also active and had even served in prominent positions in mainstream national legal organizations like the American Bar Association, the American Association of Law Schools, and the American Law Institute. He had never been a judge, but he regularly conducted continuing legal education programs for judges and had argued several cases before the Supreme Court.

It was difficult to raise an objection on qualifications grounds to Jeffrey. There could be an opening due to the fact that he had no prior judicial experience, even though that was not a qualification for any federal court judgeship, many Supreme Court justices historically did not have it when they were appointed, and it had only been raised as a "requirement" in recent decades. Nevertheless, Stephen anticipated that issue and got the jump on it by arranging for numerous prominent legal figures to sign a letter giving him their highest recommendation. Not surprisingly, in light of the role he had played with them and despite its frequent leftist bias, the ABA ranked him "highly qualified" to sit on the Court. Jeffrey's testimony in the nomination hearing before the Senate Judiciary Committee was masterful. Stephen had told him not to play the political game, saying that he couldn't comment on topics that might come before the Court and fudging on his views. Jeffrey explained how the natural law was at the base of the American Founding and the common law tradition and made a ringing defense

334

from a legal, historical, and philosophical standpoint of the unborn child's right to life and of the way marriage had always been thought of. He even explained how homosexuality and its many expressions, such as transgenderism, were not innate characteristics and could never be equated to, say, race or ethnicity in the civil rights laws. He even defended Stephen's executive actions, explaining at length the background of Articles Two and Three of the Constitution and the Founders' intent about executive power and the history of presidential-judicial relations. His scholarly honesty just aggravated the opposing party in the Senate more. They had already decided that they were going to oppose whomever Stephen nominated, and were threatening a filibuster. Senate rules had gone back and forth about whether the filibuster could be used on presidential appointments, and currently they permitted it. Jeffrey's obvious qualifications and brilliance made no difference to the other party. They didn't much raise the usual objection to late-term appointments that "we should wait for the results of the coming presidential election." Their stance was payback, pure and simple, for Stephen's bold executive actions regarding the Court and otherwise, grounded in the fact that their ideology was in a decisive retreat in the face of Stephen's multi-pronged onslaught. With the senators from the other party apparently to a man opposing him and the support of a few members of Stephen's party uncertain—and in light of Jeffrey's frankness on so many things and Stephen's frontal challenges to the Court—it was not clear that he would be confirmed.

Stephen made two deft and uncommon—though not unprecedented—presidential moves, both of which he had thought about in advance and had in reserve. The first one was to ask the Chairman of the Judiciary Committee, Senator Carl Andrews, who was from his party if he could appear before the Committee. Andrews was taken aback and told Stephen that he wondered if it could actually hurt the nomination and harm the presidency if he did this. It could make it look like the president saw himself as subordinate to Congress by appearing, and would also give the members from the other party an opportunity to embarrass him during questioning. He thought of President Gerald Ford's appearance before the Criminal Justice Subcommittee of the House Judiciary Committee to talk about the Nixon pardon after Watergate. Stephen explained to him how he thought the effect would be different. First, the hearing was being nationally televised—the leading networks, even apart from the usual C-Span coverage, decided to do this in light of Stephen's dealings with the Supreme Court—so he could use this as a further educational moment, to explain better both presidential power and the Supreme

Court's role and power under the Constitution. Second, his doing this would be symbolic of how he—following the Founding Fathers—believed that Congress was the first among coequal branches. Even though the other party didn't score as many points as it had hoped with their attacks on him for abusing presidential power by resisting the courts, this would be another part of the "positive side" of the educational effort and would show that he was truly "putting his actions where his mouth was." His positive push had been consistently seen with his relentless effort to drive home the historical precedents and constitutional basis for his actions and he had coupled it with a "negative defense" by driving home the abuses of executive power of the other party's recent presidential administrations with such moves as their unilaterally altering the federal civil rights statutes and changing immigration law by means of executive orders. Finally, he believed that he could put the other party on the spot for their attempt to block the Supreme Court nomination of one of the most widely respected legal scholars in the country. He also told Andrews that he could hold his own in the questioning and, in fact, was confident that he could turn the tables on the other party.

That is what happened. His adversaries on the Committee were no match for his constitutional erudition, the dignity with which he conducted himself, and his usual ability to put his opponents on the defensive when needed but still be supremely charitable. The other side appeared to be little more than chirping sectaries, to use the term of the late great conservative scholar Russell Kirk. In fact, it became so clear to the Ranking Minority Member that his party was beginning to embarrass itself that he wound down their questioning time.

During the questioning, there was a particularly notable back-and-forth between Stephen and Senator George McIver of the other party. "Mr. President, don't you think you have dishonored the Supreme Court and dealt a destructive blow to our system of three independent branches of government and to separation of powers by your disobedience—no, your repudiation—of its decisions? I have to say that I'm fearful for our democracy."

"Senator McIver, you should know that a public official does not promise obedience to the Supreme Court, but to the Constitution. You took such an oath as I did. Are you trying to substitute the Court for the Constitution as the focus of our allegiance?"

"But, Mr. President, the Court interprets the Constitution."

"Are you saying, Senator McIver, that the Court equals the Constitution? If that's what you're saying, I find your lamenting about the 'loss of democracy' to be curious because that Court is by far the least democratic branch of the U.S. Government. If you're saying that the Court is sovereign, that whatever it says is the Constitution even if there is nothing in the Constitution to back it up, then it in effect *is* the Constitution. That is rule by a small elite, what could be called an archonocracy. Is that what you're advocating?"

"No, of course not, but when it has issued a decision we're bound by it."

"So, you *do* mean then that the Court equals the Constitution."

"No, it's not the Constitution, but when it says something is unconstitutional, we're bound by it."

"Do you mean, Senator, that we should accept it?"

"Yes, it should be accepted."

"If that's the case, Senator, why did you so sharply criticize—it's fair to say, attack—the Court when it said in the *Mercantile Exchange* case three years ago that corporations had free speech rights in many respects the same as individuals do. You said the Court didn't understand the Constitution. You clearly didn't accept what it did. I seem to remember that you did the same thing in the *Graham v. Illinois* case, which disallowed most gun control legislation."

"Mr. President, that's different. You disobeyed the Court. That causes disrespect for the institution."

"Senator McIver, you were quite unremitting in your attacks on the Court after those two decisions. Even the media thought you were, as one correspondent called it, "pounding" the Court. Some legal scholars said that the Court's decisions were not novel or without precedent. Are you trying to tell me that you might not also be causing disrespect for an institution by relentless criticism whose basis is questionable?"

McIver just responded by quickly repeating that it's not the same thing as disobeying.

"If you're so concerned about a President challenging the Court, why have you not been critical of Andrew Jackson, or Abraham Lincoln, or Franklin Delano Roosevelt with his 'Court-packing plan'? They were all examples of resisting the Court—of 'disobeying' or taking steps to override the Court. Do you find fault with what they did? Do you find fault with Alexander Hamilton in Federalist 78 saying that only the executive, not the judiciary, had the sword—that is, the power to enforce? So what is your objection? In fact, during your public criticism of those two cases you referred to the Court-packing plan in an approving way, as an example of what you called 'public rejection of the Court.'"

McIver didn't respond right away, and Stephen proceeded to close the ring on his argument. "Or Senator, might your inconsistency simply

337

come down to ideology? You'll resist the Court when it makes decisions contrary to your ideology, but when it agrees with it you are laudatory about them—even if the Court can't find any real constitutional basis for the decisions you approve of. Isn't that just making up a new Constitution? Isn't that what you have said here you are opposed to: The notion that the Court equals the Constitution?"

McIver's tone softened. "Mr. President, I will just say that I'm concerned that your actions have dishonored the Court, that they have dishonored a coordinate branch of government."

"Senator, how is it dishonoring the Court to hold it to the Constitution, which is our fundamental law and which is supposed to bind all the branches of the Government?" His next statement completely took the wind out of McIver's sails and rhetorically undercut the opposition's gambit to brand him as an abuser of executive power. "By the way, it was my concern about respecting and honoring a coequal branch, the Congress—in fact, maybe the *first* among coequal branches—that made me want to come before you today."

That ended Stephen's appearance before the Committee. He was the last "witness" to appear before the Committee. The next day the Committee voted. All the members of his party voted for Jeffrey. One member of the other party, surprisingly, defected and also voted for him.

Stephen huddled with Bessemer and Ferlock and wanted to bring the nomination to a floor vote quickly. They agreed. Bessemer, for his frequent coolness to Stephen, had been almost as enthusiastic about Jeffrey as he was, having gotten to know him and respect his work from various Washington conferences over the years and his efforts as Chairman of the U.S. Commission on Civil Rights over a decade before. Bessemer told Stephen, however, that despite their being put on the defensive during the hearing the other party was still going to filibuster. Stephen's party had only 55 seats in the Senate—and a couple of those were "soft" in their support of Jeffrey—and even with possibly two likely votes from the other party supporting them, they were going to fall a couple of votes short of invoking cloture. They could employ the "nuclear option" to change the Senate rules to once again prevent filibusters of nominations, but Bessemer was concerned that it might not be supported. Not only would every senator of the other party oppose it, but also a number of senators from their own party might not support it because they had become "fed up" by the back-and-forth change of this rule "for obvious opportunistic reasons." So, what Stephen, Bessemer, and Ferlock agreed to do from both ends of Pennsylvania Avenue was to work hard to try to try to corral—even from the other party—the votes needed to break the filibuster.

The three of them met with senators opposed to Jeffrey. Bessemer and Ferlock focused on those they judged the most likely to come over, whereas Stephen cast the net more widely hoping that the force of argument and the driving home of the evidence of Jeffrey's supreme qualifications would carry the day with at least a few of them. They could bring around only one additional opposition senator, so they were still two votes short. The other party had become so driven by leftist ideology and was dominated so much by its fiery, activist interest groups and they had such a desire to "punish" Stephen for his unprecedented, successful use of executive power in reversing their previously entrenched "progressive achievements" especially on marriage, family, and human life issues that hardly any of its senators would budge. The Whip Ferlock was virtually certain of the vote count; the filibuster couldn't be shut down. Often, in situations such as this presidents wouldn't even want to have the cloture vote taken because losing it would look like a sharp rebuke and damage them publicly. It would be almost as bad as losing an up-and-down vote on the nominee. They would often prefer just to quietly withdraw the nomination. Stephen calculated this differently, however. The opposition had already taken a hit with the public from the hearing, and he believed that they would end up hurting themselves even more by stopping such an eminently qualified Supreme Court nominee. He would drive home this reality to the public even more than he already had and then move onto his next step. So, the cloture vote was taken and mustered only the expected 58 votes. Then Stephen proceeded to his next unprecedented move.

Two days after the cloture vote, Stephen was able to secure airtime from the major television and radio networks for a nationwide address about the Supreme Court nomination. They were quite willing to grant him the time because the whole matter had been a national story that had attracted the public's attention—and maybe they saw that this would be the final page in it. Maybe, too, they thought it couldn't hurt their ratings. They hardly suspected just how dramatic it would be and how it wasn't really going to be the climax, but something like the continuation of an ongoing saga. Stephen had told Jeffrey when he had initially offered the appointment to him not only that because of the things that had happened confirmation could be difficult, but also that he expected that there would be a filibuster attempt and, if his party in the Senate couldn't succeed with a cloture motion Stephen wanted to give him to a recess appointment. Jeffrey was initially hesitant, but they

339

talked at length about it and finally he agreed. Stephen had confidentially told Bessemer and that he planned to proceed in this manner and was able to convince him and Senator Andrews to schedule the hearings so they would finish shortly before Congress's President's Day recess. So, in case the filibuster couldn't be broken he would proceed with a recess appointment. That's what he announced to the country in his address. In his address, he explained to the public—most of whose citizenship education for decades had been almost non-existent—what the nature of a recess appointment was and how it was provided for in the Constitution. He also told them how recess appointments to the Supreme Court had started with George Washington and that President Eisenhower had made three. He also recounted the large number of recess appointments generally that recent presidents had made to various offices. This, obviously, was aimed to blunt the claim that almost certainly would be forthcoming from the other party that his action further proved that he was some kind of "dictator." He recounted the whole situation of the Jeffrey appointment, starting with his supreme qualifications that he had driven home from the start. He simply laid out the facts about the opposition's actions all along the way and repeatedly referred to its digging in its heels for ideological reasons (especially because of its rabid support for abortion rights and its anti-family mentality). That gave him another opportunity to educate—as he, of course, had consistently done so energetically—not just about the president's recess-appointment authority, but also about the true connection between abortion and family issues and the Constitution and how crucial solid families were to sustaining a free government and citizenry. Stephen with his trademark resolute tone and look also asserted that, if he were reelected, once Jeffrey's one-year recess appointment ran out he would nominate him again for the seat. In case his party couldn't hold the Senate in the fall election, he decided not to tip off the opposition about his further intention—which the nominee was agreeable to—to keep giving Jeffrey recess appointments throughout the remainder of his presidency to keep him on the Court.

Stephen's political calculation was correct. After his speech, the public support for Jeffrey on the Court and its disagreement with the other party's blocking his confirmation increased.

With the appointment solved for now and things like the Middle East negotiations continuing to progress positively, Stephen turned his attention to the reelection campaign. Since the mid-term elections, the resistance to Stephen within his own party, especially in Congress, had almost disappeared. There was no challenge to his re-nomination taking shape. He nevertheless traveled to primary and caucus states to combine speaking at party functions with other public appearances before more general audiences. In dealing with his party compatriots, Stephen spurned the usual approach of rousing the troops and saying little of substance and instead sought to educate even there. He wanted the regulars and activists in his own party, who were themselves often poorly formed in terms of ideas and political philosophy, to understand why the party needed to stand for certain principles and why those principles were sound. Despite a lot of murmuring and quiet dissatisfaction, especially among the long-time party people and the movers-and-shakers, he progressed inexorably with this effort. His "instruction" had a sufficient depth, but in his usual way he made it understandable. He was trying to convince them more fully of the thinking and positions that he asserted—positions that had long since become closely identified with his presidency. He also didn't hesitate to combine the educative approach with the confrontational one even within his party. The difference was that he mostly confronted individually and face-to-face people whom he thought were either obstructionists in political philosophy or policy or who were driven by ego more than the party's common good or whose predominant concern was self-advancement. He got people to thinking that one could truly be driven by sound principles and an unselfish sense of service *and* still be successful in politics. So, he sought to have his party populated not only by people who had the right political philosophy formation but the right attitudinal and moral formation.

Errol Eichelberger, a noted left-of-center political commentator—he was one of the seeming few "reasonable liberals" around anymore—who did a regular segment on one of the traditional networks' evening national news programs presented a thoughtful, perceptive analysis of Stephen's presidency at the end of the primary and caucus season. For all practical purposes, it summed it up. He said that Stephen had "redefined the presidency." Unlike previous presidents, "Bernard did not remove himself from the day-to-day life of the country and stay behind White House walls and a retinue of advisers and security whenever venturing out into the country to give speeches before carefully selected audiences in favorable venues." He actually "mixes with average citizens and discourses even with those who disagree with him." Further, "he doesn't use his political operatives to make the decisions or seem to make the decisions so he can hide from negative popular reaction. He makes them, and it's clear he makes them. As everyone knows, it's been a presidency marked by an almost unprecedented use of executive power to right what it has seen as the erroneous or excessive use of executive power in past administrations and to directly take on what it has seen as the excesses of power in the other branches—especially the heretofore virtually untouchable courts." He said further that it "has also been a presidency that, with a sweep and in a fashion probably never before seen, has not only sought to challenge and seek to mitigate the prevailing political direction and ethos—as, say, Reagan did—but to outright defeat it and dislodge it, institutionally and in terms of its hold on people's minds. It seems as if we have never seen such a confrontation of a set of ideas as thoroughly and as forcefully by any previous president—it's an all-out assault. And a confrontation it has been, but a confrontation not to embarrass and not *primarily* to politically defeat but to change the minds of the citizenry about the ruling perspective and to urge and prod those espousing it to rethink it—effectively to convert them, with a combination of persuasion and tough love. With Bernard, we have seen in breathtaking fashion the recovery of the long lost educative function of politics. It is likely that it will become the new standard for American presidents, but I suspect there will be few who will be able to do it as effectively as Bernard has.

"Bernard hasn't even stopped with matters in the political or public policy realm or with efforts to restore what he sees as the real meaning of the Constitution. He has used the persuasive and educative power of the presidency to perhaps not *ignite* a social and cultural revolution—one that will put back in place what he and some others see as a more sane way of life and that he believes is needed to sustain the American constitutional regime—but to assist it in whatever way he can from the position of the highest political office in the land. He seems to know that a president cannot himself change a culture, but that he's not irrelevant to the effort."

He concluded, "Perhaps the reason that Bernard has been so effective at doing this is that he's not a career politician. He came to politics and rose in it, it seems, somewhat accidentally and maybe thinks and acts like the educator he was before. What educators do is mold minds and ultimately help change cultures, and that's what he's continued to do but with a classroom as large as the country. But Bernard also was a lawyer, and so unlike some professors he has his feet planted in the world of rough-and-tumble realities, and knows that you have to be resourceful, persuasive, confrontational when needed, tenacious, and astute—which doesn't necessarily mean manipulative—to succeed. This combination of talents and skills—along with an integrity and decency that is readily discernible to people even if he doesn't wear it on his sleeve—has enabled him to achieve a success

342

and a level of popular support in what he's undertaken to do that hardly anyone could have expected. And no matter whether or not you agree with what he's done, you have to concede his success."

Stephen, for his part, knew that it wasn't just him. He may have the kind of personal capabilities and make-up that Eichelberger described, but he also was aware that he was only God's instrument—or one of them. He knew that God had given America another chance, in spite of all the moral corruption that tore through the culture, because so many of her people—and there were still many, many decent God-fearing people—had prayed so hard for it. He also knew that so many things simply had had to break his way. Some people would call that luck or fate, but he knew it was actually Divine Providence. He had once heard it said, "there is no such thing as luck in the course of Divine Providence."

The party convention and the election campaign loomed ahead. Stephen had seriously contemplated stepping out after his term and not running for reelection. Maybe his work was done. He and Marybeth had talked about it quite a bit. They had prayed about it, together and individually. For her part, Marybeth had thought from the beginning that he needed more time to further advance his initiatives. In the end, they both agreed that God seemed to be leaving the door open to Stephen's continuing for the second term. The increasing popular support he was receiving, coupled with the sense of peace that each had about their shared inclination to continue, ultimately put them over the hump and convinced them that running again was His will. True, Stephen knew that with the popularity he had achieved he could leave and history would reward him with a kind of legacy. No one could know what the second term would bring. It could end in an unraveling, in a disaster. Things could quickly go in just the opposite direction of how he had been trying to move them. He had no doubt that the deeply entrenched, unbending leftist opposition would do everything they could to damage him and bring him down. After all, their whole worldview—what drove them—had kept rupturing under his fire, like how a small fissure on a car windshield keeps expanding and cracking. They would jump on anything they could to destroy his presidency. Even though he had been supremely circumspect about the subordinates he had appointed and deliberately sharply limited the number of political appointees in the executive branch and kept the White House and Executive Office of the President staffs smaller than at any time since the New Deal and kept them under close presidential oversight, if one single person made even a well-intentioned bungle that could be the only opening they would need to pounce. He remembered things like the Iran-Contra affair under Reagan. Still, Stephen decided that he had to take the chance and face the unknown of the next four years. The bold initiatives had to be furthered, the successes—even when they were so far modest—had to be consolidated if they were to endure.

Stephen's reelection campaign was going to be very much like his on-the-road efforts to make the case for his initiatives and to get people to understand why he was undertaking them. He would be making many personal appearances and getting out extensively to be among the people, as well as speaking before many different organized groups. He planned something like a cross between a Trumanesque whistle-stop train tour and a bus tour by an entertainment troupe on the county and state fair circuit. The approach would be the same, as well: go on the offensive, continue to educate about the problems and explain why his solutions were the correct ones, and put consistent pressure on his opponents for their views but never to personally attack them or assault their dignity.

As far as his party was concerned, this time they were definitely with him. He had helped to, in some sense, redefine the party. The views he represented were strong enough in it beforehand, but the movers-and-shakers were usually the least enthusiastic for them and the elected officials among them often didn't do enough to advance them— or at least they certainly weren't a priority for them. Stephen's time in office so far had had the effect of firmly identifying certain positions with his party: protection of the Constitution, innocent human life, and true marriage and the family; the centrality of traditional religion to sustain a free political order and renewed respect for America's Christian heritage; sharply scaling down the size of government and gradually transferring as much as possible the addressing of human needs to a rejuvenated civil society; and restoring sound economic morality—and then actually *doing something* about these things. He also had refashioned it into a party that repudiated Washington privilege and had a renewed sense of service.

It wouldn't be just a personal or a party campaign, however. The citizen network that John Frost had initially helped to form, but that Stephen was careful to insure was independent even if the White House often consulted with it and went to it for help, got into full gear. Stephen firmly believed that well organized and trained grassroots citizen organizations that were committed to restoring a sound culture and American Founding principles were essential. The network would be crucial to continue what his presidency had started. He got the ball rolling, getting the country over the constitutional crises and protecting

344

traditional American liberties in the short run, but the main effort at restoration had to come from the bottom up—as Solzhenitsyn had said about Russia in the post-Communist era.

John had worked with the conservative citizen activists early on to help them organize groups or strengthen existing ones. The TEA Party, which while still around had for awhile become almost invisible, was a paradigm, but he wanted to make sure that the activists would know the issues well, understand the opposition and not get outflanked by them (leftist activist groups had probably been the main force in advancing their ideology and opposing them and working to build up sound grassroots opinion would have to be in an ongoing way the network's major tasks), and use rhetoric to their advantage and not make serious verbal slips that the leftist groups and their media allies would easily jump on to discredit them. John had relied on many seasoned conservative and religious activists—always experienced, skilled, and level-headed people—to train those who would be part of the network. They had helped carry out Stephen's effort of confront but also educate. The Tea Party had had great promise, but he and Stephen believed that its weaknesses were insufficient organization or coordination, a lack of political astuteness, and an insufficient awareness of what the adversaries were like. The left had initially made them look like fanatics, when in truth the left were the fanatics. Many of the organizations that had gotten involved in the "network" to support Stephen's efforts were already extant and John had approached them to help with his effort on the local level in different communities. He and Stephen firmly believed that that was where success could be best achieved, especially since the left's most influential organizations were national ones and they were insufficiently organized locally. He also encouraged individual activists to organize, even when there were no local groups. He had driven home the point that organization is key. He and Stephen were convinced that one of the reasons the left seemed to win so much was that it was organized and its opposition, even if much more numerous, was just scattered. His activist "trainers" emphasized to people that while they needed to be tightly organized and meeting regularly, sometimes it was actually advantageous not a have a readily identifiable organization, especially when operating at the local level. That helped stymie the opposition and made it difficult for them to attack them. Following Stephen's *modus operandi* they drove home to them that at all costs they had to keep the opposition on the defensive—again, educate but also confront. *How* to do something, then, was crucial, but they also made clear to them that they always had to have a good handle on the public issues and, as importantly, history,

345

the background of the Founding, and the reasons for the principles they were defending. Stephen and John consistently emphasized that, "You can't educate if you don't first know or understand something." Rhetorical skill and "style," while important, can't—more importantly, it *shouldn't*—be a substitute for substance. It was not short-term success or winning the coming election that was the main concern. This was a larger, deeper struggle—with much higher stakes. The point the new "activist educators" could never forget was that the main objective was to save the American constitutional tradition and Western civilization. Stephen had stepped into the breach at a critical time to start to turn the tide. There might be other good leaders in the future to continue to carry the flame, but mostly it would come down to an enlightened and assertive citizenry that they were an important part of the vanguard of.

Still, the network had a crucial short-term task: to help with Stephen's reelection. It was not a formal responsibility because that might cause them to be viewed as super-pacs, but without the big money. Whether or not they fell into the category of organizations that Stephen's campaign could not legally coordinate their efforts with, both he and John firmly believed they had to be unquestionably independent during the campaign. They should not be directed or coordinated by Stephen's staff during the campaign anymore than they were in promoting his ideas or gaining support for his policies during his first term. To become a true, enduring force in American political and social life they had to be expressions of the grassroots and run by the grassroots. Still, it was understood by everyone that Stephen needed their efforts to be reelected and they were ready to rise to the occasion.

Actually, some genuine super-pacs supporting Stephen emerged at the start of the campaign. They seemed to be ready to spend big money on television ads and the like. Stephen's "go to the people" campaign was going to be the same low-budget, locally-oriented, volunteer and grassroots organizing effort that his campaign four years before was. That was the way American politicking was for a long time in the pre-big media age, and Stephen had already shown—and was intent to show further—that it could still be that way to a significant degree. If the super-pacs supporting him wanted to play the role of blunting with national advertising the national ads against him, that was up to them.

Part of Stephen's campaigning would feature a continuation of the regular public seminars, featuring accomplished authorities or just regular people whose experience enabled them to speak well about some question, which of course he had been doing since his first political campaign. Stephen believed that promoting himself for

346

reelection was not the truly important thing, but rather persuading people of the rightness of his principles and actions. They, of course, were right not because of him but because of their very nature. He would be helped in the campaign by the fact that people were convinced of that rightness.

To be sure, he expected the other party to descend to even deeper levels of viciousness during the campaign and they did. They started off, however, very much on the defensive and Stephen made sure that they stayed on it. Now they were also getting regularly pounded from other quarters. In addition, the public sentiment had shifted for Stephen but, more significantly, his educational effort showed signs of people questioning leftist thinking not only on various policy questions but also at a deeper level. Further, Stephen's efforts had not just been scattershot, only on particular issues, but he had begun to provide for people a sense of an integrated whole—of how the particulars fit into a big picture. The left was starting to be on the defensive in terms of its basic worldview. Nor could they successfully play the card of making him somehow look like a right-wing extremist. Not only had his "confrontation-education-in a spirit of charity" stance been so effective, but so many of his actions—like his stress on ethics in economics, corporate responsibility, and a just wage—were just too much counter to the popular notion of what "right-wing" meant. Also, he had given hope to those who had long been dissatisfied with the country's generations-old drift to the left even as it became more and more extreme and irrational. Now, they saw that not only would a national leader seriously take them on more than any previous one had, but that what they had long since put in place could be reversed.

The other party's response was to gyrate ever more to the left. They nominated Senator Louis Berkholz of Wisconsin as their presidential nominee, who had on various occasions called himself a socialist of some sort. Shortly after Berkholz was nominated, Stephen honed in on this. He quoted his opponent's statements about this very precisely; he wanted to avoid misrepresenting him or stretching the truth. He said that if Berkholz meant socialism, according to its actual definition, then he should be aware of its problems, injustices, and failures. Stephen discussed these and the unfortunate situations caused by it, even in its moderate—say, Western European—version, with his usual capability of making readily understandable more complex matters. It was another confrontational-educational moment. He helped people understand more clearly what many knew instinctively: that socialism was problematical. He forced Berkholz to have to defend why he was willing to support something like it. Anticipating that Berkholz would attack repeatedly Stephen's gradual disengagement policy as causing struggling people to suffer, Stephen started hammering at the troubles overwhelming welfare states everywhere, talked about the advantages of building up civil society and showed how historically it had taken care of human needs without destroying incentive and the human spirit. He also repeatedly highlighted the successes already being achieved with his efforts to build it up. Unlike most politicians, Stephen emphasized frequently the need for responsibility and explained for those who needed to hear it why that *dignified* people instead of hurting them. Stephen was also not an easy target for the anti-corporate Berkholz because of his fervent corporate responsibility initiatives. In his nomination acceptance speech, Berkholz went on about Stephen weakening federal regulation of corporate practices. It was not difficult for Stephen to anticipate that this would be coming, too. Even before Berkholz started firing away, he gave a particular emphasis to the problems of the regulatory state in his speeches (even though it had already been a frequent theme in his first term): bureaucratic bungling and overreach, loss of legitimate freedom, how it disadvantaged small business and gave more advantages and economic power to the very big corporations that Berkholz railed against, and how it consistently resulted in cozy corporate-government relations that the big enterprises often used to squeeze their competitors.

Berkholz seemed eager to avoid debating Stephen, which was odd for a challenger. Usually, challengers figured they could use debates to get themselves more before the public and try to call attention to the shortcomings in their opponents' administrations and put them somewhat on the defensive. Berkholz apparently knew how effective Stephen was as a debater, and he knew it was not his strong suit. So, he made the same mistake as Frederickson in ducking debates. He agreed to only one debate with Stephen, about two weeks before the election. Since there was only one debate, it was agreed that multiple television networks would cover it. Berkholz thought that despite his weak debating skills, with just one debate late in the campaign he could bring himself to the peak of how he could perform and plan to go on an all-out offensive and maximize the damage to Stephen. While not a good debater, he was known for his ability to charge up a crowd. He figured he could put this skill to work at the debate to create late-campaign momentum for himself. He couldn't have miscalculated more. He had not taken off much in the campaign up to then and Stephen had him on the ropes from the beginning of the debate. At the end, no one was questioning who had "won."

One other annoyance during the campaign, which could have caused Stephen considerable embarrassment, came from the U.S. Conference of Catholic Bishops. It seemed to be ready to pick up on its earlier attack on him, which was blunted by Archbishop LaGrange. While the Conference said it "appreciated" Stephen's strong pro-life and pro-family policies, various bishops continued to be somewhat critical about his action of shutting down the abortion clinics. They kept going on about how he "had not upheld the rule of law"—as if the Supreme Court had acted within the rule of law with its long history of arbitrary abortion decisions. Now, there was a rumor circulating in Washington that they were going to issue some kind of statement that, while expressing concerns about Berkholz's stand on human life and family issues, they believed that Stephen's gradual disengagement policy could hurt the poor. This was in spite of the fact that Stephen's efforts to build up civil society was down the line with Catholic social teaching and the principle of subsidiarity. Stephen contacted LaGrange, who already was aware that a small group of so-called "social justice" bishops working with left-leaning staffers in the Conference's bureaucracy were pushing hard to have its Committee on Domestic Justice and Human Development release a statement to the press in the weeks before the election along these lines.

LaGrange had already sprung into action. He again used the substantial clout within the Conference and its bureaucracy he had by virtue of being Archbishop of Washington. He was on the phone with Archbishop Frederick Bergenstein of Cincinnati, the USCCB's chairman, and Bishop Michael Aguilar of Albuquerque, the Committee's chairman and forcefully objected. Aguilar was one of the social justice bishops and while Bergenstein was known for doctrinal soundness he was often not willing to lean on his brother bishops, even when they used the Conference to promote their problematical theology. When it was clear that LaGrange was getting nowhere trying the convince them about how bad such a move would be, he told Bergenstein that if he did not squelch it he would publicly denounce the statement and would line up other bishops to oppose the statement and the Committee at the November USCCB meeting just before the election. More, he wanted the Conference to issue a statement affirming that Stephen's economic and social welfare policy positions were in agreement with—and, in fact, commendable from the standpoint of—Catholic social teaching. Open division within the Conference was something its members, especially Bergenstein, avoided as much as possible. He knew that numerous bishops would share LaGrange's thinking on this—and he also knew that LaGrange meant it when he said he would organize them to be a bloc at the meeting. Bergenstein did not relish the November meeting putting disagreements among the bishops on display for the media and the whole country to see. That led him to prevail on Aguilar to call off the Committee staff and to agree that the Committee would issue no statements. He also worked with LaGrange to put on the Conference meeting agenda a statement objectively assessing the two candidates on the main issues, which included language on Stephen's policies like the Washington prelate wanted. The whole episode was probably the beginning of the end of the excessive sway that the social justice bishops had on these kinds of public policy questions within the Conference. In time, the Conference's long-standing bias in favor of government and especially national government solutions to social problems would come to an end.

Stephen won the election with 56 percent of the vote. As political scientists viewed presidential elections, 55 percent or more was a landslide. Stephen's party also increased its margins in both houses of Congress.

LaGrange was at Stephen and Clarke's second inauguration to deliver the invocation, this time as Archbishop of Washington. It was a long, deeply thoughtful prayer, which expressed gratitude to God for the renewal under Stephen of the principles of the Constitution, the beliefs that had brought it forth, and the awareness that they require strong and sound religion. Stephen and his old friend warmly embraced after the invocation.

When the new Congress was sworn in on January 3, he had made arrangements with Ferlock, who had always been strongly with Stephen and now had become Majority Leader after Bessemer's retirement, to make a vote on Jeffrey's nomination one of the first orders of business. The hearings had been held. The majority of the Judiciary Committee had voted to recommend the nomination in the previous Congress. Stephen's party still did not have a filibuster-proof super-majority, but the combination of the other party's humbling in the election, Stephen's strong effort to mold public opinion in support of Jeffrey and to expose the other party's opposition as unmerited, moving quickly after the new session began and catching the other party by surprise, and Stephen's now making his threat openly to keep him on the Court by recess appointments caused them to back off. The other party knew, from his previous term, that Stephen meant what he said and was not reluctant to take bold moves, even if virtually unprecedented. They also knew that if he kept Jeffrey on the Court for multiple years by recess appointments, he would come to be recognized as one of its sitting justices and over time there would develop much reluctance about not letting him remain. They didn't renew the filibuster and a handful of the other party's senators even voted for his nomination. Jeffrey now had what the Constitution called tenure on good behavior on the Court, essentially a lifetime appointment.

A year later, another member of the leftist bloc on the Court, Justice Rachel Mendelsohn, died after a brief illness. When the media began to raise the cry about appointing another woman, Stephen made it clear that there were no seats reserved for one sex or particular demographic groups and he absolutely would not make appointments on that basis. It was like what he had said about chromosomes not dictating his Cabinet choices. His nominee was Robert Balcerak, a prominent lawyer in Wheeling, West Virginia who had three times been named West Virginia Lawyer of the Year. Even though he was a practicing lawyer his whole career and never had been in the academic world, he had long had strong scholarly interests. He had published several substantial law review articles over the years. Stephen had gotten to know him from conferences he had organized on constitutional law topics at his law school. Balcerak was a regular attendee, and Stephen started to ask him to be a presenter. He had become nationally renowned for his religious liberty cases. Stephen resolved that he was going to break the monopoly hold of Ivy League law school graduates on the Supreme Court, even though Jeffrey had been Harvard all the way (college, law school, and graduate school) before going to Cambridge in England. Balcerak had been a *summa cum laude* graduate of Notre Dame Law School, where he had studied under an eminent Catholic natural law and constitutional scholar. Again, with his significant legal accomplishments and broad contacts in the profession he was rated "highly qualified" by the American Bar Association. Even though Stephen refused to make demographics a consideration in his appointments, he made mention at different times that Balcerak was from a Polish-American, working-class background. These were two groups the other party had historically included in its electoral coalition. Balcerak's grandfather had come to Wheeling to work in the steel mills and his father had also been a steelworker. His mother and father had strongly stressed education for their children and it was a source of overwhelming pride for them when he graduated from Notre Dame Law School. Like so many Catholics at a certain time they had thought of Notre Dame as *the* Catholic university.

The other party wasn't too happy about Balcerak's nomination and the usual leftist interest groups issued statements against it, but there was no big effort to oppose him and no filibuster. The left was in an unaccustomed condition of disarray. He was easily confirmed, with even a half dozen opposition senators voting for him. The hold of the secular left on the Supreme Court was decisively broken.

Stephen's second term was almost miraculously without crisis, domestic or foreign. It wasn't like there were no conflicts in the world, but nothing exploded so that the U.S. got drawn into it in a substantial way. In the aftermath of the war, the Middle East experienced the greatest stability it had had in almost anyone's memory. The American diplomatic efforts continued, to be sure, but Gramsby was no longer there. He was now Deputy Secretary of State, the second-ranking official in the Department under Robertson. The Senate approved his nomination on a voice vote, just two days after his confirmation hearing that had lasted only two hours and mostly featured comments of praise and adulation. Even more significant, for him, was the announcement that he was the recipient of the Nobel Peace Prize for that year. That came after Stephen strongly promoted him for it in numerous speeches in the U.S. and on his first trip to Europe in his presidency. On that European trip, he was again an iconoclastic figure. Besides making clear that national interest linked with the *realistic* promotion of critical moral concerns would continue as the standard for U.S. foreign policy, he said that it was time for soul-searching by the Europeans. Instead of hostility to Christianity, they needed to reflect on how it had given them most of what shaped the humane tradition they were proud of. He carried his "confront but also educate" approach across the ocean. He repeatedly made the case about this in his usual deeply scholarly but easily understandable manner, speaking to political leaders and—unlike most American presidents traveling abroad—groups of average citizens alike.

Domestically, from serious natural disasters to political scandals to terrorist attacks, there were no crises. Stephen averted the possibility of scandal by keeping his administration small, paying intense attention to the character of the people he appointed, and always maintaining tight oversight. His realistic domestic security arrangements played no small role in averting terrorist attacks, including by homegrown types. The insistence on better inter-agency cooperation and coordination and pulling back on the foolish policy of viewing everyone as potential terrorists and casting a wide net with the result of spreading resources too thin and letting the real culprits slip through had proven to be wise. He also instructed security agencies to "profile, profile, profile," irrespective of the other party's and the leftist media's howling. He knew that this could be done without trampling on the innocent or really being unfair to people. No longer would eighty-five-year-old great-grandmothers hobbling with walking canes be run through the ringer as much as the twenty-two-year-old Arab male who couldn't say why he wanted to come to the country. Now the standard for, say, airport security—which he put mostly in private hands—was "use your common sense." There was also now tight security along the southern border and despite intense opposition from the other party—mostly, as usual, emotional and unable to respond to Stephen's continually made reasonable case for it—the wall was close to completion.

With Stephen's party in firm control of Congress—it had even made virtually unprecedented slight gains in the second mid-terms— and with his and Ferlock's spearheading of the effort, the recommendations of the advisory committee about scaling back the U.S. Criminal Code were being adopted. Actually, it was proving to be one of the few initiatives during Stephen's presidency that received quite a bit of support from the other party. By the end of his second term, about two-fifths of its provisions had been eliminated and the Judiciary Committees of both houses were continuing their efforts to overhaul it further.

The lack of any crises, which ultimately Stephen attributed to Divine Providence—it was a response to incessant prayer—enabled Stephen to advance and consolidate all those bold initiatives that had taken away the country's breath. Abortion was mostly stopped and most states now had once more enacted laws punishing abortionists, which cemented this. Not only had same-sex "marriage" been overthrown, therapists trying to help persons with same-sex attraction protected, and the momentum to obliterate gender as a naturally-determined reality been reversed by the fierce opposition of national policy, but the homosexualist movement was utterly on the fence. Stephen had successfully not only redirected policy, but led the way to changed attitudes that increasingly now rejected homosexualism. Where a few years before two-thirds of the public, deceived by the media, entertainment industry, and unchallenged leftist politicians supported same-sex "marriage" and a majority didn't even see a problem with letting people use the public restrooms for the gender they "identified with" irrespective of what they were, the numbers were now almost reversed. The combination of Stephen's federal hiring freeze from the beginning of his presidency and the reduction of federal employees by ongoing attrition had begun to noticeably reduce the size of the federal bureaucracy. What would come later in his second term was the fulfillment of conservatives' aim since the 1970s: the abolition of the Department of Education. That followed from the progress of the policy of gradual disengagement. There was a contracting of federal education funding at all levels. This did not ignite the firestorm of opposition that the other party had expected and hoped for. The teachers unions fiercely opposed it, but everyone knew that they were essentially an appendage of the other party. The combination of the dissatisfaction of the public with the increasingly outrageous and even destructive demands made by leftist administrations as a condition of the funding, the sense of an almost complete loss of local control, and Stephen's personal discussions with parents and school board members around the country—another part of his educational effort—had altered their attitudes about what they wanted from Washington. Stephen's intensive efforts to work with so many people and institutions around the country to build up civil society had begun to bear fruit and had shown that gradual disengagement of the welfare state could work. People saw more and more right before them in their communities how meeting human needs did not require a heavy governmental role. Bill Clinton had once heralded—without believing it or really wanting it—that "the era of big government" was over. Now, it seemed to be true. People were also happier that the federal government was not seizing so much of their income. They saw that the flat tax was indeed a fair tax. Moreover, they saw a more steady national economic situation as the Penny Plan had brought the federal government back from the brink of outright deficit turmoil. They also had begun to see the effects of Stephen's use of the bully pulpit with big business, the public denunciations of transgressors, and the NIRA type of enlightened self-regulation with the federal government as the backstop. Stephen's constant prodding about a just wage, narrowing the gap between the salaries of CEOs and other employees, and respecting the dignity of employees had begun to have an effect in the corporate community. Many business leaders were beginning to develop more of a sense about ethical behavior and corporate responsibility. Small business ventures were noticeably increasing as hurtful federal regulations had been pulled back and the built-in favoritism of many federal policies for big business disappeared. Stephen's hard-nosed trade negotiators had secured what looked like an improved outcome for the U.S., both in trade dealings with our Western Hemisphere neighbors and East and South Asian countries. Congress had agreed to mild increases in tariffs, and so far the result was nothing like the calamity that some commentators and pro-"free trade" economists had predicted. American companies started to create more jobs and the surveys showed that most people were happy with the outcome. It would be up to the next president to have to deal with renewed negotiations about the Marrakesh Agreement that had established the often-criticized

354

World Trade Organization. Not only had the threats to the Constitution—the main thing that Stephen sought to address when coming into office—been ended, but the public opinion surveys were showing that religious liberty and free speech were now given a lot of thought by people and they knew more about and had more respect for the Bill of Rights than had been the case almost since the surveys began. The hypothetical questions that used to elicit answers showing a majority believing that a certain right could readily be violated now began to show the opposite. There was also a striking increase in demands by parents and community leaders for better civics education in schools that was faithful to what the Founding Fathers intended.

Stephen and John Frost's "network" around the country had borne much fruit. Its efforts in so many communities were a sight to behold, not only in opposing every step of the way the previously unchallenged leftist groups but engaging in citizen education. They were having not just an effect on politics and public policy, but also on the culture. Stephen, John, and the others encouraging them made clear to them that they had to instruct their fellow citizens not just about Founding principles and how different policies and practices either upheld them or collided with them, but also about the culture needed to sustain them. Further, they exhorted these grassroots activists to also *serve* their fellow citizens, to be good neighbors and helpers when they had need, either through the civil society organizations Stephen stressed so much or just person-to-person. Stephen frequently talked about how important this was. Aristotelian scholar he was, he knew that a good, harmonious political society came forth from a community of friendship.

Stephen's stress on the religious and Christian roots of the country and his uncompromising defense of religious liberty seemed to have an effect in another way. Christians no longer felt intimidated and public opinion surveys showed a reversal of decades-old trends as more people were saying that religion was important to them. Following from Stephen's "public education campaign" in his second term about the true understanding of the Establishment Clause and the erroneous direction of the Supreme Court since World War II, many public schools stopped trying to sweep clean any even remote vestige of religion. A few districts reintroduced voluntary prayer at the beginning of the school day. Stephen heartily commended them and the rabid secularist organizations quickly challenged them in the federal courts. The Bernard administration emphatically supported the schools. Near the end of his second term, the newly reconstructed Supreme Court upheld the schools. The 1960s school prayer decisions were overturned, which signaled a new kind of Establishment Clause, church-state jurisprudence. Another pillar of leftist constitutional distortion had fallen.

When it came to the presidential election season in Stephen's eighth year in office, there were only a few people from his party who were looking to put their hats in the ring. One was a respected governor who had had close relations with Stephen and picked up on the gradual disengagement and building up of civil society approach as far as state-level social welfare efforts were concerned and made considerable strides in implementing sound civics education in the state's schools. Two senators also tentatively jumped in. The odds-on choice, however, was Vice President Clarke. He had believed fully in what Stephen was doing and Stephen daily consulted with him and involved him throughout his administration in his efforts. He was out usually speaking around the country as Stephen was. He didn't have the scholarly background that Stephen came into office with, but he had for years read about the American Founding as a hobby and was a quick study. He also was almost as adept as Stephen was at "confrontation plus education, in charity." Stephen selected him as his running mate because he had similar abilities as him and they had personal and philosophical rapport and so could become partners in the cause. Ultimately he knew—and eight years in office confirmed—that this was more important than any geographical or demographic diversity or balance. Clarke was easily nominated and during the campaign went before the country showing that he had been fully with Stephen in what he had done and would enthusiastically continue the "new direction." As far as the other party was concerned, they were still trying to figure what direction they should go in and what liberalism should be about. There was talk about a "new liberalism," as there had been in the 1990s. Bill Clinton had claimed to be a "new liberal," but it went nowhere. The other party ended up nominating just another leftist, who put on more moderate airs but Clarke's campaign and the policy commitments their candidate made exposed what he really was. Clarke won handily, only a couple percentage points off Stephen's pace in the last election.

Two days before Clarke's inauguration, Stephen requested national airtime and gave his final address to the nation as President. He talked about the last eight years as a time of renewal, but in a variation of Benjamin Franklin's answer at the conclusion of the 1787 Constitutional Convention when a fellow citizen of Philadelphia asked him whether the U.S. would have a republic or a monarchy—"a republic, if you can keep it"—Stephen said that what had occurred was

356

"renewal, if you can keep it." To do this, he emphasized, in line with his extensive effort to activate the grassroots, that while leadership was important the real crucial thing was "an enlightened, responsible, and ever vigilant citizenry." Further, he said that there has to be even a deeper, more basic kind of renewal, which requires a more personal, individual kind of responsibility: that people have to practice self-restraint, not surrender to their passions and immediate wants. There must be a return to true religion—the stirrings of which had seemed to begin—and sound morality, which is not fashioned by individuals themselves but ultimately comes from God and is rooted in our very nature. This, he said, is "a renewal of the spirit" and is necessary "if there is to be a true, lasting national renewal in other ways."

Stephen would be returning to his university teaching, although because of security concerns that would make his teaching in a normal classroom setting difficult, he would be doing it mostly online along with a few, occasional small graduate and law school seminars for selected students. In spite of this, he and Marybeth would accept only a very minimal amount of Secret Service protection when they left Washington. They would not allow themselves to be cut off from their fellow citizens or from a normal life. Stephen was happy when he thought that, like Harry Truman, he would be leaving office no richer monetarily, and in fact probably poorer, than when he entered it. That was what public service was all about. On Stephen's last full day in office—the day before Clarke's inaugural—Stephen, Marybeth, John Frost, and John's wife Jennifer had dinner together in the State Dining Room of the White House. While it was normally used only for larger dinners and dinners and receptions for visiting heads of state and such, Stephen thought that it might be a good way to say "thank you" to someone who had been indispensable for whatever he had accomplished. Indeed, it was only because of John that he had entered politics back in Pennsylvania in the first place.

Stephen said a long grace when the meal was served in which he thanked God for His unbounded guidance and help over the years of his presidency and also for "using him as His unworthy servant to enable His will to be done."

After dinner, they sat down and recalled all the happenings over the past eight years in Washington and talked about where the country was at now. John, who had been a voracious reader of history since high school, compared current America to previous political orders that were brought back from trying or even desperate situations by great leaders. Stephen fell silent and humbly tried to discourage John from going further, but he persisted. John had started to talk about the ancient

357

Roman Republic and, as Marybeth was beaming in pride for her husband, he said, "You're the American Cincinnatus."

"No," Stephen said. "George Washington was the American Cincinnatus."

"Then you're the new American Cincinnatus."

CPSIA information can be obtained
at www.ICGtesting.com
Printed in the USA
LVHW111253160120
643721LV00001BB/101

9 781621 379841